FATAL TRUTH

SHADOW FORCE INTERNATIONAL

MISTY EVANS

ROMANTIC SUSPENSE AND MYSTERIES BY MISTY EVANS

The Super Agent Series
Operation Sheba
Operation Paris
Operation Proof of Life
The Blood Code
The Perfect Hostage, A Super Agent Novella

The Deadly Series
Deadly Pursuit
Deadly Deception
Deadly Force
Deadly Intent
Deadly Attraction (coming 2016)
Deadly Affair, A SCVC Taskforce novella (coming 2016)

The Justice Team Series (with Adrienne Giordano)
Stealing Justice
Cheating Justice
Holiday Justice
Exposing Justice
Undercover Justice
Protecting Justice (coming 2016)

Shadow Force International Series
Fatal Truth
Fatal Honor (coming 2016)
Fatal Courage (coming 2016)

The Secret Ingredient Culinary Mystery Series
The Secret Ingredient, A Culinary Romantic Mystery with Bonus Recipes
The Secret Life of Cranberry Sauce, A Secret Ingredient Holiday Novella

ACKNOWLEDGEMENTS

Readers of my Deadly-SCVC Taskforce Series keep asking about a spin-off series with Emit, Cal, and Bianca from DEADLY FORCE. Several years ago, I outlined a protection service series with the help of fabulously talented Lori Wilde. Combining the two seemed like a great idea, and that's how the SFI series was born.

I hope readers who enjoy my other romantic suspense series will also enjoy this one, and I can't thank those loyal readers, and Ms. Wilde, enough for giving me the inspiration to launch into a new world of intriguing heroes and the heroines who love them.

With most of my books, I ask fans who follow my Facebook page to pick the name of the heroine when I start the story. The same holds true for this series. Thank you to my FB fans for picking the name Savanna...it fit this heroine perfectly.

To Mark

*and to all the men and women
who fight for
truth, honor, and justice.*

A group of former SEALs, abandoned by the United States and labeled as rogue operatives, who now work as a black ops team performing private intelligence, security, and paramilitary missions for those who have nowhere else to turn.

"Search for the truth is the noblest occupation of man; its publication is a duty."

~Anne Louise de Stael

CHAPTER ONE

Navy SEAL Lieutenant Trace Hunter stood outside the Witcher prison walls in nothing but his underwear and stared at the gray Virginia skyline.

You wore the same clothes leaving prison that you wore coming in; hence his lack of street clothes.

Eighteen months since he'd been a free man. Since his world crashed down like a Black Hawk hit by a surface-to-air missile.

He drew a deep breath, the cold November air searing a line straight down his throat and into his lungs. Yes sir, the guard hadn't been lying.

"Brisk out there," he'd told Trace as he'd handed him a pair of sweatpants and a jacket and ushered him out a rear service door not far from solitary.

The normal guards had been missing, the numerous doors and gates opening for the two of them as if by magic. But Trace was a lifer. He didn't understand why he was getting out, or why he wasn't going out the front gate.

Leaving Witcher had never crossed his mind when he'd entered, so he didn't argue as the guard directed him through the last gate. He did, however, ignore the kindness of the clothes and bugged out as fast as his feet could carry him.

Thanks to his stubbornness, his skin was now pebbling in the frosty air.

He'd briefly considered there would be a car waiting for him, or more likely, there would be a sniper on the hill and a bullet with Trace's name on it.

1

Neither materialized.

Forty yards from the prison, he came to a fork in the road. According to the sign, north lay Rileyville, Population 899. South lay Murder Creek, unincorporated. Either way was a long walk in his skivvies.

Rocks and debris on the road bit into the soles of his feet as he put his head down and headed south. He'd taken off the cheap flip-flops Witcher had provided upon entry and thrown them as far as his arm allowed. He'd survived tougher conditions in hellholes like Afghanistan, Pakistan, and Peru. North Korea had been a ball of laughs, too.

At least those places had been warm.

Who got me out?

Leaving the prison, he'd kept wondering if it was a joke, and that once he finally got to the last gate where the laundry trucks came and went, the normal guards would arrive back at their posts, laugh and tell him to turn the fuck around and go back to solitary.

He'd spent a lot of time there. No way in hell he'd been released early for good behavior.

When he'd asked why he was free to go, the guard with the clothes wouldn't answer him.

Fucking government.

He loved his country. Had done a lot of shit to keep her safe, but there was one thing he'd refused to do and it had cost him his freedom and his reputation. He knew a secret that could destroy the sitting president. Linc Norman's enemies would give Trace anything he wanted for this tidbit of info.

He wouldn't give it to them. None of them.

He also wouldn't follow the last order his commander-in-chief had issued.

So he'd been branded a rogue operative, a traitor. His story—a false one—had been plastered all over the highly-rated *The Bunk Stops Here* and then been picked up by news stations around the world. He'd become the face on dozens of cheap tabloids, usurping the Royals' latest baby and stealing the limelight from the current Disney star-turned-porn princess, all thanks to Savanna Bunkett, the host of TBSH who'd broken the story on him.

The all-American, girl-next-door Savanna did a three-show segment on his fall from war hero to traitor, crucifying him and calling into question every mission he'd been on, every SEAL who'd worked with him.

Not a lawyer in the country would touch him, and even if one had stepped forward to take on the U.S. Attorney General, they wouldn't have won. He was a dead man walking. Thanks to some back-door dealing, he didn't even get a trial; he was sent straight to Witcher, the hidden government installment built especially for high-risk prisoners like him. Prisoners who'd been the best at what they did. Highly-trained operatives and military personal who knew every trick their government had up its sleeve and how to get around all of them.

Behind him, the sound of tires on pavement broke him out of his reverie.

SUV, four-wheel drive, twenty-five miles an hour tops.

Trace didn't turn or acknowledge the vehicle's presence. It was traveling too slowly to be a casual traveler on his way to Murder Creek unless the driver was a blue-hair. Of course, a man his size walking on the side of the road in nothing but his underwear could cause any normal driver to slow so he or she could gawk.

Trace knew the driver wasn't an old lady or a curious traveler. The person or persons approaching carried danger. Probably someone working for the president or Command & Control. Maybe the person who'd gotten him cut loose from Witcher so they could gun him down on the side of the road.

Hell, the president had already had him in the perfect spot to end him. People inside had tried, but he was better, faster, more deadly than his fellow inmates. He'd sent more than a few of them to the infirmary, knowing they had only come after him because the president had offered them early release if they took him out.

He'd been well-trained for evasive maneuvers. The tree line next to him would make for good cover if he needed it. He could disappear before the driver blinked. Disappear forever and reinvent himself. Go to the Caribbean, meet some sweet native gal and start a new life. Or maybe Italy. He'd always wanted to visit Italy.

Bonus, Italy was one of the few countries where he'd never killed anyone.

The SUV cruised by him, accelerating ten yards out. Cadillac Escalade. Not official government unless the mayor of Virginia was paying a visit.

Maybe it is a blue-hair gawker.

Tinted windows. All-season, heavy duty tires. If he had to guess, he'd say by the sound of those tires on the cold highway, the vehicle was carrying some reinforced side panels.

His gawker was either incredibly rich and paranoid, or Beyoncé had heard he was out and had come to pick him up.

Doesn't matter who's in the car. Only matters what I'm going to do about it.

Escape scenarios were limited. There was one road, the road he was walking on, and the trees.

Simple.

He liked things simple.

Sure enough, the Escalade made a U-y in the valley and stopped, pointed back toward him.

Fight or flight?

While he'd kept himself in good condition inside Witcher, he was tired of fighting.

Flight it is.

He glanced over at the tree line. The shadows beckoned. The anonymity. A fresh start.

Nah. Running wasn't his style. Instead of bailing from his very exposed line of sight, he stood stock-still and eyed the SUV, still idling a quarter mile away.

He'd pushed through pain, through war, through prison. Had gotten back up every time someone knocked him down.

Even the goddamn president of the United States.

That's what soldiers did.

There was no point in running. The prez would come for him again and again and again.

It was time to make a stand, even if it was his last.

WASHINGTON, D.C.

Savanna Jeffries Bunkett looked up from the notes on her lead story when a knock sounded on her dressing room door. She scowled at her reflection in the large mirror over her table. She needed her roots touched up.

Scribbling a reminder on the top sheet, she called out, "Yes?"

Lindsey Fey, the assistant to the assistant director at *The Bunk Stops Here* and Savanna's studio-assigned assistant, poked her head in. The headphones she used to bark orders to the cameramen and crew lay around her neck. "You have a visitor."

The word "visitor" held emphasis. Lindsey's eyes danced and she was smiling.

Lindsey was always smiling. She ran her butt off, organizing everything from the scriptwriters to the coffee machine and her energy and aggressiveness had helped make TBSH an Emmy winner. She had Executive Producer in her sights and Savanna didn't have the heart to tell her she was too young and lacked specific equipment between her legs to go that far with the news channel. She was related to one of the producers, however, and in the world of cable news, that would be Lindsey's ticket to success.

Lindsey never took off her headphones while on set. Maybe not even when she was *off* set; Savanna couldn't be sure, since she didn't hang out with the staff and crew, was never invited out for drinks after filming or to the DC parties the rest of them always seemed to rush off to.

Lindsey's smile, along with the word emphasis, made Savanna's pulse speed up. "Is it Parker?" she asked.

Blonde eyebrows drew together and the smile flattened. "Your sister? No." As Savanna's hope died, Lindsey's smile returned. She leaned in, stage-whispering, "Someone big."

Big in television news or something else? From the excited countenance Lindsey was sporting, it could be Hollywood's latest action star or the Dalai Lama. Hard to know. The girl was wowed by everyone.

When a recent spike in watchers made TBSH the largest cable investigative news show since Nancy Grace, Savanna's popularity also skyrocketed. To her embarrassment, she'd become a regular face on *E! News* and grocery store tabloids as Americans criticized her hair and weight and wondered who she was dating since her breakup with Junior Senator Brady Garrison. Few seemed to appreciate her investigative skills and hard-hitting stories about corporate and political corruption.

Savanna looked back down at her notes. "Unless it's the Pope"— *or Parker. God, where are you?* —"I don't have time for a meeting. Whoever it is can wait until after the show."

She heard a scuffle and, assuming Lindsey was ducking out,

continued to review her notes on the latest political scandal she was about to blow the whistle on.

A moment later, however, the room behind her filled with an unmistakable presence and the scent of the man's designer cologne. Sharp, musky, reminding her of old leather and fresh betrayal. "Not many people say no to me."

Savanna's stomach dropped. She clenched her fingers around the pen she'd been using, the typed words on the script in front of her blurring.

"What are you doing here?" she said without lifting her gaze. Her voice sounded steady even though she was shaking from head to toe.

A crystal vase plunked down on the dressing table next to her, overflowing with a lush mix of summer flowers. Roses, hydrangeas, sunflowers. He'd figured out all her favorites.

Damn him. She'd never be able to enjoy her favorite flowers again.

Linc Norman leaned over her shoulder, ran a finger along her hairline, and pushed a coiffured lock out of the way. "What is this I hear about you doing an exposé on Westmeyer?" His breath landed on the top of her ear and revulsion snaked through her. His Alabama drawl thickened. "Tread lightly, sweetheart. I need them come next November."

Tread lightly?

Was he seriously throwing down a gauntlet?

Anger replaced her revulsion. He was drawing a line and daring her not to step over it.

We'll see about that.

Savanna bit the inside of her cheek and stared holes into the paper in front of her. She'd never taken kindly to threats, and wasn't about to now, even if the man threatening her was the president of the United States. "I told you, I won't be your lackey. If one of your supporters is committing criminal acts or fleecing the American people in any way, I'm going after them."

"Like you did your boyfriend?"

Low blow, but then, what did she expect?

"You've always been too focused on principles, Van." Norman let his fingers travel under her chin, forcing it up. "Look at me."

Savanna glued her eyes on the flowers, not willing to meet his eyes in the mirror.

He pinched her chin between his finger and thumb, forcing

her to raise her gaze. "You don't give me orders or deny me anything. Loosen up your journalistic ethics or I'll burn you at the stake."

Finally, Savanna locked eyes with him in the mirror. "I won't abandon my principles. Ever. So let me get you a match."

His eyes were several shades lighter than her deep blue ones, with gray streaks that mimicked the ones in his hair. He smiled, the corners of his eyes crinkling as if he were teasing her instead of threatening her.

But the threat was real, coming from the most powerful man in the world. "Where is my sister?" she whispered. "What have you done with her?"

The president's smile turned tolerant, the smooth Southern charm now mixing with the perfect touch of pity. If he'd been a television emcee or talk show host, he would have been her toughest competition. "Parker works for National Intelligence. Who knows where she is or what she's working on."

Perhaps Parker *was* on assignment, but she was a cognitive scientist who'd found a niche studying the brains and behaviors of terrorists. Her work for NI was more analyst and profiler than anything else. Occasionally, she traveled out of the country, but she always texted or called Savanna beforehand to let her know she'd be quiet for a few days or weeks.

They were close; normally they talked every day. They made time for weekly lunches, and once a month, they met their parents for Sunday dinner.

Parker was dedicated and loved her job. While she never shared intelligence or sensitive information, she had been more secretive than usual for the past year and a half.

And now, she was gone.

"If you've hurt her..." Savanna let the threat hang in the air. Was she really doing this? Threatening the president of the United States? "If you made her disappear, I will find out, and when I do, I will let everyone know exactly who and what you are."

A monster.

Releasing her chin, Linc Norman put his face next to hers, their reflections in the mirror looking like the Greek theatre faces of comedy and tragedy. He thought this was a joke—her fierce love and loyalty to her sister.

But the president wasn't one to take a threat sitting down. He ran his hands over Savanna's arms, his attention dropping to her cleavage. Holding the gaze a moment longer, purposely trying to make her uncomfortable. "You've pissed off a lot of high-powered people in your time at the news desk. Ruined a lot of lives and brought whole companies to their knees. Wouldn't want any of them to retaliate, now, would you, Van?"

A master at intimidation, he closed his eyes and breathed deeply, as if soaking in her scent before he leaned his forehead against her temple. "You and I both have a role to play in leading the American people and making them feel secure. Parker had one job and she blew it. Don't follow in her footsteps, Van. Do what I tell you and everyone will be happy."

Her hand now shook so hard, she had to lay down the pen. It was either that, or she'd stick the pen in his eye socket. "I want my sister back."

"We don't always get what we want." He chuckled and rose to his full height, checking himself out in her mirror. He straightened his tie, brushed a lock of hair off his forehead. "Except me. I am, after all, the leader of the free world."

Savanna held his gaze, refusing to kowtow regardless of the fact that he could ruin her career, her very life, with the snap of his fingers. She mentally cursed herself that she didn't have a way to make the bastard come clean.

But that *was* her forte. Digging in and unearthing dirt that could bring anyone, no matter how much power they had, to their knees. She'd known this confrontation was a strong possibility and had already taken measures to start fighting back.

He didn't see the fire in her eyes, or, knowing him, took it as compliance rather than defiance. Everyone gave him what he wanted when he turned on the charm.

"Remember, lay off Westmeyer." He winked and patted her back. "And enjoy the flowers."

Two Secret Service agents closed in around him as he left. At least, she thought they were SS. They could have been his thugs. Parker had once told her Norman used various tunnels under the White House to come and go covertly on a regular basis. Often his own chief of staff had no idea where he was or what he was doing.

"The White House bad boy," the press had nicknamed him. Savanna knew his antics hid a much deeper, much more sinister side.

Trembling, she took the vase of flowers and smashed it against the wall.

Light reflected off something among the shattered heads of the hydrangeas. Savanna stepped gingerly though the broken glass in the designer heels the audience wouldn't see behind her news desk. Bending down, she picked up a tiny, flexible, opaque disc.

Listening device? Camera?

Throwing it down, she ground her heel into it. Small satisfaction, but she imagined it was Norman's face.

Back at her dressing table, she withdrew her cell phone from the top drawer. No calls or texts from Parker, but there was a text from a blocked caller.

ON16?

A long time ago, Parker had given Savanna a number to text, a person who went by the moniker ON16. A person—man or a woman, she didn't know—who could help Savanna if she couldn't get hold of her sister. Extreme emergencies only, Parker had said.

Savanna had never needed it before.

ON16's text was two lines: a name and a phone number.

Savanna stared at the name, bells going off in her head. *Emit Petit.* Where had she heard that name before?

Lindsey popped in without knocking. "What did the president say? Are you going to interview him? Please say he wants to do an interview at the White House!"

She was giddy until her attention dropped to the shards of glass and limp flowers on the floor. "Oh, my God. What happened? Are you okay?"

Savanna stood, dropping the cell phone back into her drawer. She smoothed the front of her jacket and grabbed her notes. "Let's go," she said, hustling Lindsey out of the room. "We have a show to do."

And then I'm going to find my sister.

Chapter Two

Virginia

"You sure this is the guy?" Cal Reese asked.

Emit drummed his thumb against the steering wheel. The Escalade purred under him, waiting for instructions. Cal's misgivings seemed understandable as they sat on the road watching the man staring them down from the top of the hill.

"Your wife picked him. Said he was the ideal candidate."

Cal glanced down at the file in his lap. "He looks better on paper."

"Ever known Beatrice to be wrong?"

An exasperated sigh parted Cal's lips. Beatrice was classified as a genius with a photographic memory and had worked for a secret group called Command & Control inside the NSA until they'd sent an assassin after her. Now she worked for Emit, screening potential employees for Rock Star Security and analyzing cases for his secret covert ops group, Shadow Force International. Rock Star Security provided bodyguards and a solid, law-abiding front. Shadow Force International stayed in the background, performing private intelligence, security, and paramilitary missions for those who had nowhere else to turn.

"Unfortunately, no," Cal said. "I've known her since we were kids and it's been like living with God. She's omnipotent."

She was definitely all knowing. Emit took his foot off the brake and urged Rihanna, the name he'd given his favorite vehicle, forward. She was kitted out with all the latest security stuff, enabling her to withstand bullets, grenades, and even gas attacks. He and Cal had even given her her own private cache of weapons hidden under the back seat.

With her black body, tinted windows, and miles and miles of chrome, she probably looked like a demon from hell to Trace Hunter. Could be why the man braced even more as they crawled back up the hill.

Cal glanced at the display on the dash. "Bet Hunter's balls are the size of marbles right now. Forty-two degrees and he's wearing nothing but his ink and his Underroos."

Afraid the former SEAL would flee into the woods, Emit kept Rihanna at a slow ten mph pace. "Asshat refused the clothes I bribed the guard to give him. Our introduction and instructions on where to find us were sewn inside."

"And you brought me along on this venture because...?"

"You're former Teams. I'm not. Thought he might be more cooperative if you made the offer to come work for us."

They were fifty yards away now. Hunter stood straight as an arrow, showing off his muscled chest and tree-trunk legs, a definite snarl on his face as if daring them to take a strike at him.

Cal yawned, stretching as he continued to read Hunter's file. As head of Emit's new Shadow Force team, Cal had been back in the States from a tactical engagement in Costa Rica for less than an hour. "Doesn't seem like the cooperative type. Says here Hunter was in solitary confinement fifty-one times in sixteen months." Cal shook his head. "Fifty-one? Jesus. He also sent a handful of guards and over a dozen inmates—highly trained former Special Forces and Spec Ops, just like him—to the west block for medical treatment."

Emit shrugged. "I don't argue with Beatrice. She said the guy is perfect for SFI and we need men, even plain old bodyguards, since our client intake for Rock Star skyrocketed after you went *Die Hard* on us and saved the president in front of a packed house a few months ago."

Cal got busy putting the file away, seemingly uncomfortable about being reminded of his heroics. "I saved the president before I joined your team. Besides, no one knows I work for you now. I've become yesterday's news and that's the way I want it. You built the security side of the business into a multi-million dollar company all on your own, and it doesn't hurt that you're providing bodyguards to all those young, pretentious actors on the West Coast who get their mugs on the front of *People* magazine every week. You should be happy with the notoriety."

Emit *was* happy. Business wasn't just good, it was booming. Protection services were the rage for Hollywood starlets, rock 'n' roll bands, government officials, and the growing population of billionaires. Shit, at this rate, he was going to need his *own* protection detail.

But Shadow Force International—that was his dream. Ever since he'd watched *The A-Team* reruns on TV with his old man, he'd wanted to take guys like Cal and send them to hotspots around the world to help people.

Cal stared out the windshield. "Do I want to know why the government sent Hunter to Witcher?"

Men like Cal and the others—all previous Special Forces—had a unique set of job skills and the mental focus for the work, whether they were guarding rich actors or doing secret paramilitary missions in foreign countries.

If the government got pissy with them, however, the former SEALs ended up silenced and abandoned by their country. "He worked for Command & Control, just like Beatrice."

Cal let go a soft whistle. "They turned on him like they did her?"

Emit shrugged. "Hunter knows something. Something big. They stuffed him in Witcher to keep him quiet. Beatrice has been trying to find out, but her sources won't say. Or don't know."

"Why not kill him?"

"Might be why he's ended up in solitary so many times. He was fighting for his life."

A tight silence descended. Beatrice, who'd worked for the top secret Command & Control, had been in the same situation. Luckily for all of them, she and Cal had outwitted the assassin sent to kill her, but Cal still held a grudge. She was pregnant with his kid now and Emit had never seen a man more protective of his wife and future family. He knew the feeling. No one better touch his family either.

"Do I want to know how you got him out?" Cal said.

Emit shook his head. "Nope. Let's just say Beatrice has contacts and talents you and I can only dream of."

Cal looked indignant. "I have talents."

"We all do. That's what makes our team strong. You and Hunter should have no trouble bonding."

Cal and Trace Hunter had a lot in common—they were both SEALs the government had turned its back on and labeled rogue agents. Emit only had one Shadow Force team of five men; Cal was the leader. Requests for private intelligence and rescue missions were backlogged and some of the people in need were running out of time. Emit needed a second team and fast. As he eased Rihanna closer to the spot where Hunter was making his stand, he hoped he was looking at his next team leader.

Braking, he slapped Cal on the shoulder and said, "You're up."

Cal blew out a breath and rolled his shoulders. "I have the feeling this is going to get bloody before it's all over."

"We need him, and if he stays out here alone, whoever stuck him in Witcher is going to catch up with him."

Reaching behind the seat, Cal grabbed his overnight bag and a white sack filled with fast food. Emit had figured Cal needed some good ol' American fat and grease on his return from Costa Rica. Cal hadn't eaten any of it, complaining he'd picked up a bug down south.

"What's your plan?" Emit asked.

"Food, clothes, the essentials." Cal opened the door and winked at him. "Just simple kindness, bro."

Trace stiffened a fraction more when a man emerged from the Escalade. Two inches over six feet, probably one-ninety under his jacket. Moved like a soldier, his buzz cut military issue.

One hand was buried in the top of a soft-sided duffel, the other held a white paper sack with a red logo.

Trace distrusted him on sight.

There was no obvious weapon, so unless the guy planned to beat him to death with the bags, Trace decided it was safe to satisfy his curiosity. "What do you want?"

"Name's Cal Reese. Just got back from an overnight op out of the country and didn't use my change of clothes." He tossed the duffel on the ground between them. "Thought you might like some pants and a shirt since it's forty fucking degrees out here and you're"—he motioned at Trace's body—"slightly underdressed."

"I didn't ask who you were, I asked what you wanted."

Reese held out the paper sack. "Lunch?"

A whiff of hamburger and greasy fries wafted from the bag, and damn if Trace's nose didn't flare. Fast food from his favorite chain—a place he hadn't seen in eighteen months. He'd dreamed about that bacon double-cheeseburger, and each time he was about to bite into it, he'd wake up. How did this guy know?

Had to be a trick. Trace forced his starved senses to shut down so he could get back on track. "Who do you work for?"

The paper sack landed on top of the guy's go-bag. "Not who you think."

"You don't know what I think."

Reese nodded and he looked off in the distance. "I feel you, man. The government turned on you. You saw or heard something you weren't supposed to, and now you've been branded a traitor and sent to a hellhole in the middle of Nowhere, Virginia."

Something pinged in Trace's brain. Cal Reese. Callan Reese, the SEAL who'd saved the president a few months ago. The story had been all over the news and, even inside Witcher, the inmates had been buzzing about it.

Now Trace really hated him. *Fucking bastard should have let Norman die.*

But heroes, real heroes, always put their life on the line for their commander-in-chief.

"My boss and a few others pulled some major strings to get you out," Reese continued. "But listen up, you'll never truly be free. Someone will be gunning for you, more so now that you've slipped through the system. We can help you disappear for good without you actually ending up on a deserted island or dead."

The smell of the food teased Trace's nose again, making it hard to concentrate. He'd been surviving on little more than bread and water in solitary.

Walk away.

He knew he should, but he was rooted to the spot.

One more minute. He really did want to know what this guy was up to. "And in return?"

"We have a job for you. Best job around, if you ask me."

A job. Of course. There was the rub. They thought they knew everything about him, that's why they were here.

"I don't kill people anymore." He shot Reese and the guy in the Escalade a scalding look. "Unless they get in my personal space."

Point taken, Reese held up a hand and took a subtle step backward. "We're not here to force you into anything, and we don't expect you to kill people. Not many people anyway, and certainly not innocents. If you work for Shadow Force International, every operation is off the books but we take matters of life and death seriously. We don't believe in collateral damage."

Shadow Force International? Trace had heard rumors inside Witcher, but then he'd heard rumors about mysterious paramilitary groups in there on a daily basis. Everyone wanted to believe that some Hollywood-inspired black ops team was going to crash through the concrete walls and rescue them from their dismal existence, giving them a new life.

"We're looking for a team leader for a second Shadow team." Reese rubbed his hands together, blew on them. "You don't have to commit to anything right now. My card's in the bag, along with some money, a couple of burn phones, and an unregistered, untraceable gun. It's yours, the whole thing, whether you join us or not."

Fuck, and all he wanted was that goddamn cheeseburger.

And maybe the clothes.

Reese held out a hand. "Good luck, man."

Trace stared at the outstretched hand. For some stupid reason, his own hand seemed to have a brain of its own and reached out to shake it.

Reese walked toward the vehicle, but stopped after a couple of feet and turned back. "I know about Command & Control. They tried to kill my wife. She's the one who found you and picked you to join our team…and she's never wrong. About anyone or anything. Give it some thought."

At the mention of C&C, Trace's insides went as cold as his nose and his fingers. Few people in the world knew about the group, and those handpicked for it rarely knew each other.

But Trace was fairly certain he knew the woman in question. "What did you say your wife's name is?"

Reese smiled. "I didn't."

Trace watched as Reese climbed into the Escalade. Watched the vehicle drive away. Snatching up the bag of food, he found the burger and ripped off the foil wrapper. It had cooled but was still the most delicious thing he'd had in his mouth since his last night as a free man.

Once he finished the burger, he opened the duffle and dressed. There were even shoes. Half a size too small, but he didn't care.

As Trace fingered the white business card inside with nothing but a phone number on it, he realized that Callan Reese had given him more than a survival kit.

He might have given him a lifeline too.

WITCHER PRISON

The woman moved through the prison with purpose, ignoring the guards accompanying her and the catcalls of the prisoners as she passed the cells in the north wing—the most dangerous and violent housed inside these walls—on her way to see the one man ON16 had assured her could help.

A flash of her credentials and she was buzzed through the gate to the next section where the man was waiting in an interrogation room. Immediately, the cement floors gave way to carpet. The walls were painted. The carpet was a dark industrial blue and the walls were dull yellow, hardly an improvement, but anything was better than the depressing gray that covered everything in the prison section.

Her badge was scanned before she was led to an interrogation room. As she waited for the guard to open the door, she took a breath and steeled her mind. The clock was running. She had twenty minutes, tops, before her boss would know she was here and come after her.

After *him.*

She tugged at the hem of her suit jacket, a nervous habit. One she'd long ago lost through endless training. Yet, on the brink of her impending death, her training seemed a moot point. She'd foolishly believed she could outrun and outsmart the government who'd created her.

Maybe she *could* run and stay alive, but she didn't want to. She wanted to stay in America, doing her job, and able to see her family and friends like normal. She didn't run from threats.

Wouldn't run from this one if she could find another way.

Blackmail was the only option unless she wanted to conspire to kill the president. She couldn't do it herself and, even with all the nefarious and downright crazy assassins she knew, none would touch that particular operation.

She had to find a way to stop her own assassination and the man inside held the key.

The door opened and she stepped across the threshold, unsure of exactly how she was going to get Trace Hunter to cooperate.

And then she pulled up short.

The man behind the table wasn't the man she'd come for.

"I heard you were looking for one of my inmates," the prison warden said, whirling to face her with his hands in the pockets of his camouflage pants.

"Commander Polonsky." She nodded in respect although she felt none. "I'm here to see Lt. Trace Hunter."

"Hunter's in solitary confinement." His hard stare held no emotion. "No visitors."

"I'm not a visitor. This a matter of national security."

"These prisoners are all a matter of national security. They're Americans who turned against their own country. Violent, dangerous men who'd just as soon kill you as talk to you."

A pissing match? This was taking too much time. "Take me to solitary. I'll question him there."

"On whose orders are you here?"

"Whose do you think? You know who I report to."

He was silent for a moment, assessing. "Take her to Hunter's cell," he told the nearby guard. "I need to make a phone call."

He brushed past her on his way to call her boss.

She was quickly down to a few minutes. Good thing she had an exit strategy if things went to hell. They were about to. "Lead the way," she said to the guard.

Solitary was off by itself, a long walk down more halls that once more lost the yellow paint and carpeting. The pungent smell of sweat and excrement filled her nostrils, making bile rise in her throat.

They arrived at the end of the building. A row of concrete-enclosed cells formed the wall. Each cell was no more than six by four. There was no sound here, little light. She doubted a man could even lie flat and fully stretch out.

The guard pointed at the last cell. "That one."

A slit in the concrete for food trays was the only way to communicate. She leaned down, tried to peer inside.

Dark, dank, horrible. She could see nothing past the slender beam of light falling on the floor. She listened for movement, breathing, anything. Heard nothing. Her senses went on high alert.

The man was a SEAL. A SEAL with enhanced abilities. He could make himself invisible, stay completely immobile for hours waiting for his prey.

But she knew without a doubt that Hunter wasn't inside.

"He's not in there," she said.

The guard, who had moseyed away, gave a snort. "He's in there. Trust me."

"Open the door."

"I can't do that."

She whirled on him. "On orders of the president, open this door. Now."

"Lady, this guy put two of my coworkers in the emergency room last week."

"It's doctor, not lady." Feeling all of her pent-up nerves come crashing down, she fought the urge to send the guard to the ER with his friends. Trace Hunter had been her only hope, and now...

Overhead, an alarm went off, causing the guard to look up. His walkie-talkie crackled to life.

Time for her to go.

"He's escaped," she said, blowing past the guard and kicking her exit strategy into high gear. "You have nothing to worry about from him."

CHAPTER THREE

Savanna sat in an office inside Rock Star Security that made her dressing room on *The Bunk Stops Here* look like a rathole. Hardwood floor, marble fireplace, a sleek, black desk and matching zebra-stripe upholstered chairs. The woman in charge of Rock Star Security even had a window seat looking out over a beautiful English garden below.

Who had a formal garden in DC?

Taking her feet out of her three-inch Louboutins, Savanna sank her toes into the plush rug under her. The coffee provided by the male office manager, Connor, —a James Franco look-alike—was the best tasting stuff she'd ever had.

The bodyguard business must be profitable. Rock Star Security Services consisted of an East Coast and a West Coast division. A brochure on the desk stated they were expanding soon to Chicago. All run by the reclusive Emit Petit.

Savanna had done her due diligence and researched him. Even with his success—he was in the top ten multi-millionaires under 30—he led a low-key, private life. Had done a stint in the Navy, never achieving pilot like he'd planned. Entered the SEAL program and rang out after a couple of days. But he'd finished his enlistment, then gone into private security.

He was a good guy from all reports. He provided jobs to veterans, retraining them to provide security and protection services to the rich and famous. He was married and had a son.

After seeing the office manager, Savanna toyed with the idea of hiring a bodyguard of her own. Connor could check under her bed anytime.

But she wasn't here for herself. She was here for Parker.

The door opened and a beautiful blonde in a red skirt and a white blouse swept in, carrying a file folder and a pink drink that looked like a fruit smoothie. The woman wore dark framed glasses and had piled her hair on top of her head in a smooth bun. A black Lab with a pink studded collar padded along at her side.

Setting the drink on the desk, she said, "Maggie, lay." The dog took up a spot next to the desk, her dark brown eyes steady on Savanna.

Then the woman offered a hand. "Hello, Ms. Bunkett. I'm Beatrice Reese." Pointing to the brochure Connor had given Savanna, she asked, "Have you had a chance to look at our protection packages?"

As Beatrice moved to sit at the desk, Savanna noted a baby bump under the skirt. A pang of longing hit her. She'd always wanted a big family, a husband. Her career had taken off—and she loved it—but she had no one, outside of Parker, to share her success with. She'd dumped her last boyfriend—the rat—and her parents saw her as nothing more than a "common news anchor," as her mother loved to describe her.

Now, she didn't even have Parker. "As I mentioned on the phone, I'm here to speak to Mr. Petit."

Beatrice opened the file folder and took out a Mont Blanc pen. "Mr. Petit is overseeing a training exercise with our latest recruit. I'm afraid he can't make it to our meeting."

Savanna's heart sank. "I have to speak to him. It's important."

Beatrice finished a note she was making and looked up. "I assure you, I'm fully qualified to set you up with the appropriate services."

ON16 had specifically stated Emit Petit. "I don't need a bodyguard. I need to speak to Mr. Petit about a different matter."

"I assumed as much." Beatrice sat back in her chair and tapped the pen on the blotter. "Are you looking for a story? A scoop?"

"What?" The woman thought Savanna was there to interview her boss. Normally, that might be a valid question, but it offended Savanna anyway. "I have no intention of doing an exposé on Rock Star Security or Emit Petit, unless, of course, you're hiding something."

A faint smile touched her lips. "I've offended you, but I'm not sure why. That *is* your job, correct? Investigative reporting? Exposing corruption and destroying people's lives in order to improve your ratings?"

Savanna gripped the chair arms and pushed herself to a standing position. This obviously wasn't going to work out. "It's not about ratings. I blow the whistle on corruption and make sure the American public is safe."

The dog whined softly. Beatrice cocked her head. "Are you one hundred percent sure that every story you've run is fair and accurate? That you've never blackballed someone who is actually innocent?"

Savanna had always been good at reading people. Even with the best actors, the most charming sociopaths, she could see past the outer layers to what lay hidden underneath.

That was the place where she struck during an interview. Where she kept digging.

The look on Beatrice's face was unguarded, open. She wasn't purposely trying to piss Savanna off; she was simply seeking the truth.

Trace Hunter. The name pinged around in her brain. The info on Hunter had come from what Savanna had believed was a reliable source—Parker. But Parker had gotten the file from Linc Norman. She'd passed it to Savanna with instructions to run with the story.

Savanna had wanted to verify the information inside that file, but Parker had warned her not to. Hunter was in deep shit and if Savanna went digging, she could end up in the muck with him.

It had gone against every one of her rules and principles. She always did her own research.

Time is of the essence, Parker had said. *The president is counting on you.*

Just run it.

So she had. And now her sister was missing and the president was blackmailing her.

Had she screwed up? Had she ruined a man's life simply on orders of the president?

Savanna let out a sigh. She wanted to storm out of the office, but if she did, what then? She had no leads on her sister and no one else to turn to.

"I'm not here to discuss my job or old cases." Reluctantly, she resumed her seat. "I'm looking for help regarding my sister and I was told to speak to Mr. Petit and Mr. Petit only."

Beatrice made a note. "Who told you to speak to Emit?"

"I can't say."

The woman cocked her head. "Is she missing...your sister?"

Goose flesh rose on Savanna's arms. *Lucky guess, that's all.* "When will Mr. Petit be done with his training exercise?"

The pen tapped on the paper and Beatrice stared at Savanna for a long moment. "Your sister works for National Intelligence, correct?"

The realization that Beatrice Reese had run a background check on her didn't sit well. When Savanna didn't immediately answer, the woman went on, never glancing at her notes. "Parker, your sister, hasn't been seen or heard from in nearly a month, not uncommon for an intelligence operative, but her title is that of scientific analyst, not spy. She reports to the president along with, or in place of, the director of National Intelligence for the daily briefing. Her record is devoid of field assignments, but then, if she *were* an operative for NI, Langley, or even the NSA, they wouldn't list her missions, now would they?"

Savanna opened her mouth but no words came out.

Beatrice went on. "From phone records, it appears the two of you are close, communicating nearly every day, and yet, you haven't heard from her in all this time."

"You accessed my phone records?" Savanna stood once more, outrage shooting pins and needles down her arms. Insinuating her sister was a spy? "I don't know who you think you are or what game you're playing, but if you're—"

"I don't play games, Ms. Bunkett." Beatrice remained calm, her gaze as steady as Maggie's beside her. "Your sister is missing and you strongly suspect foul play by the government. You contacted an agent inside the NSA—one I happen to know—who goes by ON16 and he sent you here, to us, and for good reason."

"You know ON16?"

"We can find your sister, whether she's alive or dead, and keep you safe in the meantime."

Dead. Savanna's chest pinched, breath catching in her throat. "I told you, I don't need a bodyguard."

"The president visited you three days ago at your newsroom studio and brought you a bouquet of flowers."

"How did you...?" Savanna stopped. Beatrice apparently knew everything. She even knew who ON 16 was. "You're CIA, aren't you?"

The faint smile she'd seen before returned. Beatrice removed her glasses and set them on the desk. "Was there something going on between your sister and the president?"

Beatrice didn't mince words and she had the uncanny ability to state Savanna's greatest fears. She also refused to answer Savanna's questions. Which irritated her to no end. "Do you have a sister?"

The woman seemed unfazed by the personal question. "No."

A gold wedding band circled her left ring finger. "But you're married and, from the looks of it, expecting a child. If one of your family went missing, what would you do?"

"Exactly what you're doing now; find an expert to locate him or her." Beatrice leaned forward and opened the brochure. "Do you prefer your bodyguard to be seen or to stay in the shadows?"

"Does it matter?" Savanna considered banging her head on the desk. "You're going to assign one to me regardless."

"The president is keeping tabs on you, Ms. Bunkett. I suspect the flowers he brought you contained surveillance equipment. He's been listening to your conversations, probably has had the Agency plant bugs in your apartment and a tracking device on your car."

The plastic disc she'd smashed was in her handbag. She'd intended to show it to Emit for his opinion.

Beatrice went on. "President Norman probably knows your here, in fact, and therefore, he'll expect you've hired a bodyguard."

She used her pen to point to a highlighted section of the brochure. "I recommend this package. The service provider assigned to you will be your bodyguard and assist us with tracking down your sister."

Good God. The price tag was astronomical. A year of her salary. Fortunately, she had few expenses outside of rent and clothes to spend her money on, and a fat balance sat in the bank. Her early retirement fund.

Wait, what was she doing? Trusting this woman and this organization? Parker had told her many times never to trust anyone.

But Parker had given her the contact for ON16 who had led her here.

Her sister could be anywhere and the world was a big place. She could be a prisoner, tortured, abused, starved. Raped.

Savanna shuddered. Add the fact that the president was stalking and blackmailing her...she had very few options.

She couldn't continue alone and she certainly couldn't go to her parents for help. She'd already asked if they had any idea where Parker was and her father had laughed off Savanna's concerns. *Don't rock the boat,* he'd told her. *Parker can take care of herself.*

Unless the most powerful man in the world was after her.

Reaching into her bag, Savanna withdrew the smashed plastic disc. "This was in the flowers."

Beatrice put her glasses back on and examined the disc. "Hmm."

"That's it?"

The woman tossed the disc on the desk. "You definitely want the platinum package." She produced a paper from the file and turned it around for Savanna to read. "Please fill out this intake form and sign the contract and nondisclosure forms attached."

Savanna stared at the papers. This was all surreal. A month ago, she and Parker were planning a weekend retreat in Maine. Now she was delving into the world of bugs and spies and bodyguards who tracked missing sisters.

Beatrice picked up the phone and spoke to someone on the other end. "When will Coldplay be ready? I have a client."

Robotically, Savanna signed her full name to the contract, barely scanning the details. She flipped over to the nondisclosure. Even if she had wanted to, she'd be bound by this agreement not to discuss or report on anything related to this deal:

> *You are entering into a professional agreement. Because of our employees' backgrounds in government intelligence, we take the privacy of our employees as seriously as we take our clients' personal security. You agree to address them only by their codename, in pubic and in private. Do not share details of their job assignment with others. You will not ask your security agent personal questions or engage in any type of personal relationship. Doing so will result in immediate termination of services.*

Codenames. Add that to the list of her new surreal world.

"I understand," Beatrice said into the phone, "but this is a unique situation calling for his specific skill set."

Another pause as Savanna scratched her name on the agreement. *What am I getting myself into?*

What had she *already* gotten herself into?

"Agreed. I will brief him personally on the client's needs." Beatrice hung up and took the signed papers from Savanna, tapping their edges on the desk to align them. "Are you in imminent danger?"

"Imminent?"

"From the president or anyone else?"

"You mean, like someone wants to kill me?"

Beatrice simply looked at her.

She pulled out her checkbook and started filling in the blanks. "Well, I hope not."

"But?"

The skin between her shoulders felt so rigid, it might crack if she drew a deep breath. Her voice came out hesitant for the first time. "Honestly? I don't know."

Beatrice nodded. "Coldplay, your bodyguard, will meet you at your apartment at 1600 hours—4 o'clock—today, at which time he will be your companion 24-7. Until then, I can assign a temporary security specialist to accompany you to your home or to work, whichever you prefer."

Will he look like James Franco?

Savanna shut down the silly thought, and the nervous laughter bubbling in the back of her throat. The surreal situation, mixed with the fact she hadn't slept well in days, left her an anxious mess.

She handed over the check she'd written, proud that her fingers didn't shake. "That's really not necessary. Martin, my driver, is waiting for me downstairs and he'll take me to the studio. I have two interviews to shoot today for a primetime special next week." She started to add that she didn't believe the president or anyone else would harm her, but instead, she said, "I'll be safe."

"You're sure?"

"I'm sure."

"Good." Beatrice stood and motioned her toward the door. Maggie stood too and gave Savanna a slight tail wag. "Be at your apartment at four o'clock. Coldplay will meet you there and we'll begin the investigation into your sister's disappearance."

"You really think you can find her?"

The woman put her hand on the doorknob. "Coldplay's assignment is two-fold; keep you safe and track down your sister's whereabouts. He'll have access to all of our resources, and our resources are wide and deep. He's an expert tracker. His reach into the intelligence community, combined with his military training and Special Forces experience, make him an efficient as well as a deadly tool."

Savanna had the sudden feeling the Rock Star Security specialists were more than your average bodyguards.

"You couldn't be in better hands," Beatrice added. "Keep an open mind, do exactly as Coldplay says, even when you don't want to, and I guarantee, you'll see your sister again."

Yes, but will she be alive?

Savanna couldn't voice that fear. All she could do was nod as she went out the door. "I'll see Mr. Coldplay at four o'clock."

<hr />

1800 HOURS

Trace climbed the stairs two at a time, the stairwell of the fancy apartment building empty at the dinner hour. Or maybe the rich snobs who lived here were too good to take the stairs.

He was two hours late. Not the best way to start his first assignment for Shadow Force International. Then again, he hadn't planned to be working for Rock Star Security and shoved out the door and into the world of protection services so fast it had made his head spin.

The past couple of days had been a whirlwind. He'd struck out on his own, surviving the first Virginia night in an empty fishing shack with no heat or running water. Reese's cheeseburger didn't last long, and while the lake wasn't frozen over and the owner had left some gear behind, Trace hadn't been able to catch a damn thing.

The next morning, he'd stumbled through a snowstorm into Murder Creek, found the lone greasy spoon in town and ordered breakfast. The coffee was mud and the eggs were runny. He didn't care. It was better than prison food any day.

The small 1980s TV in the corner was turned up, a weatherman dressed in a fancy suit waving at various colored blobs on the map and declaring the storm would intensify throughout the day and continue overnight. By the next morning, they were expected to have six feet of snow.

As Trace had finished his toast, a sheriff's car had driven up. The two men who got out walked like military men, not cops. Before the bell over the door rang, he'd left the waitress a generous tip and disappeared out the back and into the woods.

His mother had always said he was as stubborn as the day was long, but he wasn't an idiot. While there'd been nothing on the news about his escape from Witcher, he'd known the men in that car were looking for him. A storm was moving in that would lock down the area. He had no vehicle to get out and no supplies to hunker down and ride it out.

He needed help.

Admitting that fact had taken every last ounce of his common sense, but now he was here. Beatrice had cleaned him up, made him shave his beard and cut his hair.

Because of his specialized work for Command & Control, the agency had scrubbed his past years ago. Few pictures existed of him before his time in Iraq with SEAL Team 3, when he'd first grown his hair long and sported a thick beard to blend in with the locals. SEALs often needed out-of-the-Navy-box appearances on their assignments, and that was the picture Ms. Bunkett had spread all over America.

He was a squeaky-clean Boy Scout now, with colored contacts and new clothes—nice threads, not the usual camo gear he was used to. The only thing he hated was the fancy dress shoes.

Petit and Reese had put him through their version of basic protection service training, and Reese's wife had explained all the ins and outs of his new job.

Beatrice. He was pretty sure that hadn't been her name when she was in Command & Control, but it didn't matter. She'd confirmed that she had played a part in getting him out of Witcher and that there were men looking for him. Nothing official on the news yet, the government wanting to keep his "escape" a secret and hoping they could find him and put him back before the public caught wind of the situation.

Petit and Reese hadn't been happy when Beatrice insisted

Trace take this assignment. They'd wanted more time to work on him, and they'd planned to send him out of the country on a Shadow Force assignment. Beatrice had other ideas, and neither man seemed eager to argue with her.

So here he was, playing bodyguard. A test run, Beatrice had called it. He'd kept himself in good shape inside Witcher, had kept his skills sharp. His enhancements from Project 24 had never faded.

Still, with a secret manhunt on for him, he had to stay in the shadows as much as possible. Beatrice had given him a set of rules to follow, briefed him on the client. Single female, twenty-eight, with a potential stalker. He was to keep an eye on her but not be obvious about it.

The stalker is high-profile, Beatrice had said. *Has possibly harmed the client's sister, but there's no proof and the client can't make public claims without evidence. We'd like you to investigate, see if you can incapacitate the stalker and discover the sister's whereabouts.*

The woman lived in the penthouse on the top floor. He climbed the last set of stairs and went through the fire door.

It was Beatrice's fault he was late and she'd supposedly called ahead to let the client know. Still, Trace felt a shot of nervous adrenaline firing below his breastbone as he rang the doorbell. There was a marble-topped table near the elevator with an elaborate floral arrangement. A ficus tree sat in the corner under a skylight, and a large painting of the sun rising over a mountain range hung on the wall left of the door.

Seconds ticked by. He straightened his tie, smoothed the lapels of his suit coat, fiddled with the brim of his baseball hat.

The hat didn't go with his outfit. He'd picked it up on his way over, feeling too exposed otherwise. Even with his change in appearance, he feared being recognized after Savanna Bunkett had done such a fine job of splashing his face all over the news a year and a half ago.

On the other side of the door, he heard a muffled voice, "Coming!"

A second later, the door swung open. The woman was out of breath, her hair swept up in a high ponytail. She was dressed in workout attire and a fine coating of sweat glistened on her ample cleavage as she wiped her face with a towel. The rhythmic beat of a drum, tambourine, and finger cymbals of Middle Eastern music echoed in the background.

From behind the towel, she said, "You must be..."

And then she moved the towel to her neck and met his gaze.
Oh, shit.
The towel stilled and the woman studied his face.
"Coldplay?"
Trace felt frozen in place. In the briefing with Beatrice, she'd referred to the client only as Ms. Jeffries.
Ms. Jeffries, my ass.
His heart stuttered in his chest for a second. Even without makeup and her signature red power suit, she stood out like a diamond among glass. She was striking, her dark hair offsetting her pale skin, all of it softened by a delicate nose and high cheekbones. Workout clothes did nothing to dampen her natural, elegant demeanor.
Before him stood the woman who had ruined his life.
Trace took a step back. Waited...
She didn't seem to recognize him.
One hand went to her hip. "Are you the strong, silent type or is this one of the rules, that you can't speak to me? I must have missed that one in the contract."
Why would she recognize me? She had one grainy photograph of me from six years ago, and I was nothing but a story to her.
Trace forced his mouth to work, struggled to get sound out. He tipped the brim of his hat down a little farther. "Sorry, I'm late."
"Randy didn't buzz me. How did you get in?"
Randy, the doorman. What a joke.
Trace shifted gears, forcing the anger boiling in his gut aside. As soon as he could get hold of Beatrice, all bets were off. "Security check of the building showed me some weak spots. I got in through a service door entrance on the first floor. I'll speak to the manager tomorrow about beefing things up."
She stepped back, using the towel on her arms. Long, slender arms with small wrists and finely-boned hands. "Come in. I'll grab a shower and then we can talk about...my problem."
Talk. Right. "I'll stay out here at the door until you're ready."
"Um, okay. Sure." She gave him another once over. "Have we met? You seem familiar."
Met? Jesus God. "No, we've never met." *Not in person. If we had, I would have wrung your neck.*
She gave him a small smile. "Even if we had, we have to pretend otherwise, right? Sorry, this is all new to me."

He nodded and stepped back, grinding his teeth. She closed the door, leaving him alone in the penthouse hallway.

Counting to a hundred to give her time to get in the shower, he paced to the elevator doors, locked the thing down, then locked the door to the stairwell. He withdrew the cell phone Beatrice had provided and punched in her number.

She picked up on the first ring. "Yes?"

"Are you fucking kidding me?"

"Sorry?"

He forced himself to lower his voice. "Ms. *Jeffries*? Her name isn't Jeffries and you know exactly who she is and what she did to me. If this is some kind of joke, I swear I'll...I'll..."

"Yes?"

What *would* he do? The woman was smarter than smart and she was, well, a pregnant female.

A man, he would beat the shit out of for tricking him like this. But he would never hit a woman. "...I'll beat up your husband."

"You can try," Beatrice said without concern. "What's the problem?"

Trace nearly crushed the phone. "You know exactly what the problem is. You lied and set me up with the woman who crucified me."

"I didn't lie. Her real name is Savanna Jeffries-Bunkett, but she only goes by Savanna Bunkett for her show. Her mother, Doris Jeffries, is from the New Hampshire Jeffries, a Daughter of the Revolution, and a top-notch lawyer. Her father, Shawn Bunkett, is the president of a private Catholic college. Her sister Parker works for National Intelligence as a glorified profiler, you might say. Her job is rather vague and ill-defined. She has a degree in cognitive therapy and a knack for understanding how criminals work, which National Intelligence has found helpful. For reasons I haven't quite figured out yet, she pulls together the president's daily briefing and presents it to him. I doubt that has anything to do with her brain research, other than to profile a terrorist here and there. A month ago, she went missing. All I can get out of my sources is that she's on assignment." Her voice emphasized assignment. "Odds are there was something...personal...going on between her and the president, or he gave her a black op job and she got caught."

Linc Norman. The president sure liked to spread himself around.

The sound of a fridge door opening came from Beatrice's end. "Who do you think passed your file—the bogus one—to Savanna?"

Trace took off his hat and scratched his hairline. "The sister?"

"If my guess is accurate, and I am correct ninety-nine percent of the time, Parker received the file outlining your rogue activities from the president."

A patient silence descended, as if she were waiting for him to connect the dots. A possible scenario spilled out without too much brainpower. "Linc Norman told Parker to make sure Savanna broke the story."

"Parker is missing. The president is stalking Savanna. It adds up, only we don't know exactly why. Norman is now keeping tabs on Savanna, no doubt fearing she'll reveal her suspicions to the world that he's made Parker disappear. She doesn't have any facts—yet—and President Norman hopes to keep it that way."

"What am I supposed to do about it?"

"I don't suppose you want to tell me why the president had you branded a traitor on national television?"

When he didn't respond, she went on. "Well, consider this your chance to prove to Savanna that you're not a traitor and that her intel from President Norman was bogus."

"How am I supposed to do that?"

"Find her sister. And if the president *is* the one who threw your ass in prison, who better to have on your side than an investigative reporter with a fan base of six million viewers? She can clear your name, Coldplay. Think about it."

He was thinking all right. Thinking his former job as a cleaner for the president might put Savanna Jeffries Bunkett in more danger than she was already in.

"She can also help you dig up dirt to blackmail Linc Norman," Beatrice went on. He heard the clink of silverware against a bowl. "So he stops trying to kill you."

Trace returned the hat to his head and pinched the bridge of his nose. "You set me up."

"I did," Beatrice admitted freely. "In so doing, I also gave you a way out of the mess you're in. I don't care about your past and the things you've done, but it would solidify your job with Shadow Force International if you're not a hunted felon."

His past was not something to be proud of, Navy SEAL or not. He'd killed for his country, sure, but his job as a cleaner went beyond that. While once he'd believed he was doing the morally right thing, helping the president wipe out threats to America, he was no longer sure there was such a thing as morally right. "Savanna is already suspicious. Even with the change in my appearance, she suspects we've met."

"So come clean. Tell her the truth. She needs you and you need her. Besides, she signed a contract."

So did I. Every employee of Shadow Force International, whether they worked as bodyguards for Rock Star Security, performed search and rescue missions, or assisted on kidnapping cases, were required to sign one. If he breached his agreement, he was out in the cold again.

Petit planned to put Trace in charge of a team. *If* things worked out. Even if they didn't hold him to his contract, bailing on his first assignment would hardly help his cause. He'd never make team leader if they couldn't depend on him.

Did he even care? He wasn't a team player anymore. Couldn't endanger anyone else.

"Follow the procedure I gave you and think about it overnight," Beatrice said. "If you wish to terminate the assignment in the morning, I'll find someone else to guard Ms. Bunkett."

A growl formed in his throat. Beatrice's logic was so...so...logical. *Be the hero again. Keep someone safe. Solve all your problems.*

If only it were that easy.

Didn't matter. He couldn't complete this assignment without risking his freedom. Morning was nearly twelve hours away. Could he keep Savanna Bunkett from figuring out who he was in the meantime?

The woman was a bloodhound when she picked up the scent of a story. Sure, it had been eighteen months since she'd run his, and she'd had plenty of stories since then, but she wasn't one to forget a name or a face for long, he bet. "She'll terminate the assignment before morning."

"You can't hide forever," Beatrice said. "And there's only so much I can do to keep you off the grid. This is your chance to clear your name. Don't blow it."

The line went dead.

Trace braced one hand against the wall and sighed. Twelve hours. He had twelve fucking hours to keep up this charade, and then what? Bail?

He'd never quit a job in his life—except the last order from the president—and he wasn't about to do so now. If Savanna figured out who he was and called the police, he'd have to, but until then, he'd lay low and plan for the worst case scenario.

...*clear your name.*

Pocketing the phone, he shook the ridiculous idea from his brain and walked back down the hall to wait.

He'd follow procedure, like Beatrice had instructed him to when she gave him the assignment. Scan Savanna's apartment for bugs, make sure her windows and doors were all secure. Check her personal security system. Then he'd stand guard for the night.

By morning—if he made it that long—he'd have a plan of escape.

Or one that would take down the president of the United States.

Chapter Four

Savanna couldn't enjoy her shower. There was a man outside her door—a sexy, but very dangerous looking man with a big, black gun in a holster under his left arm—whose features were familiar but whom she couldn't place.

She hated it when she knew she knew somebody but couldn't remember their name or from where she'd met them.

And she was damn sure she'd met Coldplay.

Coldplay. A good codename for the guy. All that sexiness wrapped up in cold eyes and an icy demeanor. He didn't like her, waves of annoyance rolling off him like the DC sleet storm headed their way.

She picked up her razor and began shaving her legs, the gold bracelet sliding down her arm. She'd skipped her last wax appointment and things were getting out of control. It didn't matter much since she hadn't had a man in her life for over six months, but still. She had to get back on her salon schedule ASAP. She'd text Lindsey and have her make an appointment first thing in the morning.

Maybe Coldplay had seen her show and didn't like it. There were plenty of people out there who didn't like her revelations about their employers screwing them out of their pensions and their favorite box store selling them goods from China filled with lead in order to keep prices low. Coldplay didn't strike her as a guy who shopped at discount stores or expected to live long enough to need a pension. He'd tried to hide his dislike under his hard, unexpressive bearing, but her internal people reader had picked up on it right away. At first, she'd believed he was acting so frosty because she hadn't followed protocol, but from the moment she'd opened the door, she'd felt as if she'd done something wrong. How could that be if they'd never met?

Had to be her show. She was Oprah Winfrey meets Snopes, blowing popular urban myths out of the water and empowering Americans to feel good about themselves. The guy didn't like her, or one of the episodes of TBSH had upset his mother or something. Savanna was used to it. Not everyone was going to like her and that was okay. She wasn't doing the show to be popular. She wanted to protect Americans from being fleeced by popular culture, big business, and the politicians they voted for.

More and more, it seemed like a losing battle.

Her fellow countrymen wanted life to be easy. Many didn't want to know the truth if it upset their little world. She couldn't blame them, but she also couldn't stand by and not inform them of the truth. What they did with that truth was up to them.

Stepping out of the shower, she reached for her towel. As she dried off, she reminded herself that she *was* making a difference. Her audience was growing everyday. People looked to her for guidance and information. Some of them—a lot of them, actually—*did* want the truth. They wanted to believe they could change the world into a better place by supporting brands, companies, and people who did the right thing, and she was giving them the means to do so.

Now if only she could find her sister.

Ironic that only a year ago, she'd partnered with the Missing Veterans Advocacy Network, a missing persons organization for veterans. A vet suffering from PTSD had contacted the organization after his ten-year-old daughter had gone missing and the police had come up with nothing for clues. Savanna had vetted the MVAN organization already, and when asked if she would bring a spotlight to their search for the girl, she'd eagerly agreed to help. After she ran a brief aside at the end of *The Bunk Stops Here*, MVAN had a dozen solid leads. Within hours, the FBI tracked her down at the house of a convicted sex offender with three other missing girls. The girls were now in therapy and would be for years, but they were back home with their families.

She had a public platform and a reach into the American population that far surpassed any police department or government entity. All she had to do was slap up her sister's picture and send out a plea for information, and she'd have the station's phones ringing off the hook, their Facebook page exploding with comments.

Dressing hastily and pulling her wet hair up into a ponytail, she suspended that thought. She couldn't. Not yet. It could backfire and cause Parker more problems. Once all her avenues were exhausted, then Savanna would consider it.

Coldplay was going to have to get over whatever hang-up he had about her and her show. She needed his help and her bank account was taking a big hit in order to pay for his services.

Defrosting him would be a challenge, but she liked challenges.

In the kitchen, she surveyed the contents of her refrigerator. She needed to eat and it wouldn't hurt to offer him something too, the three-page brochure of protocols from Beatrice be damned. Men liked home-cooked meals, and while her schedule often didn't allow time for it, Savanna loved to break out a recipe book and try a new dish.

Tonight was not a night to experiment though. Her nerves were on edge and she had to be at work early to record promo spots for the primetime show next week.

Beef tips and chopped veggies went into her skillet and she popped some flour tortillas into the microwave to warm them. While the food cooked, she went to the door to invite Mr. Coldplay in.

The first thing in her Rock Star brochure was a list of items the security specialist would complete. One was a sweep of her apartment for listening devices and cameras. The thought that President Norman had people listening to her, watching her, creeped her out. Yet, she'd found the plastic disc in her flowers delivered personally by Linc Norman. He *was* spying on her.

After educating herself with YouTube videos on where and how listening devices were oftentimes hidden, she'd already checked her smoke detectors and light fixtures and found nothing. It wouldn't hurt, however, to let Coldplay do a more thorough check.

Opening the door, she looked left, then right.

The hallway was empty.

Trace stood stock still behind the ficus tree and studied Savanna Jeffries. Her high ponytail swung, the tips of her long hair brushing her shoulders as she looked back and forth.

"Coldplay?"

She was dressed in fresh attire, but still looked ready for the gym in purple yoga pants that hugged her lean legs and a matching tank top that put her sizable rack on full display.

He stepped out from behind the plant, his hat low over his brow. "Yes?"

She startled and frowned at him. "What are you doing back there?"

"Searching for bugs."

He saw her throat work as she swallowed. "Did you find any?"

He shook his head. "Hallway's clear. Let's check your apartment."

She moved back, letting him in. As he passed by her in the doorway, he noticed she had a smattering of freckles across her petite nose and the softest brown eyes he'd ever seen.

A sweet, light scent rose from her body reminding him of his grandmother's gardenias. In her bare feet, she was probably six inches shorter than he was—five-eight or nine, since he was six-three. Without her hair, makeup, and fancy clothes for her show, she looked like a ballet dancer or a long-distance swimmer.

"Where do you want to start?" Savanna asked, shutting the door and motioning to the apartment beyond the marble-tiled foyer.

The apartment was a mix of modern and traditional. Grays, whites, blacks with a pop of color on the walls and in the fabric pillows. Plants and bookshelves warmed things up a bit.

"In here," he told her, eyeing the electronic equipment on the far wall.

"Just so you know, I've already checked the light fixtures and smoke detectors and they were clean."

He raised a brow. "You checked for bugs and cameras?"

Her hands went to her hips, posture going defensive. "Is that a problem? Does that break one of the Rock Star policies?"

"No." But it certainly made him look at her differently. He liked a woman who took security seriously and wasn't afraid to get her hands dirty.

The living room, kitchen, and dining area were all open to

each other. From the kitchen came the sounds and smells of frying meat, onions, and peppers. "Great," she said, although her tone was tight. "I'm making fajitas. When you're done, you're welcome to join me for dinner."

She didn't wait for a response, marching off toward the kitchen, ponytail swinging once more.

He watched her go, hating himself for enjoying the way her butt moved under the knit yoga pants. Whatever exercise routine she was using, it certainly did a good job of keeping her toned.

Catching himself, he forced his gaze back to the electronics. It had been one long damn dry spell since he'd been around a woman, but he wasn't insane. He hated Savanna Bunkett, or Jeffries, or whatever the hell her name was. His raging libido needed to crawl back into its hole so he could scan her house and get back out into the hallway for his overnight babysitting job.

Compartmentalization had been necessary in his life. Shutting off unwanted thoughts, focusing only at the task at hand, never getting distracted. Even as an assassin for C&C, he'd had to check his own moral compass and just do the job, no matter what it was. He was a soldier for his country. He followed orders.

Until he hadn't.

And now, here he was.

Removing a small set of screwdrivers and a digital scanner from his pockets, he made efficient work of the living room. He found a few dust bunnies and an impressive flat screen with all the bells and whistles while he shut down thoughts of pretty women, homemade food, and the fact there was a high price on his head because of his insubordination.

Soft music played in the kitchen. Savanna hummed along as she banged pots and pans and set the dining room table for dinner. His stomach growled, even though he'd eaten enough for six men in the past couple of days at the training center. After eighteen months in prison on rations made for rats, he wasn't sure if he'd ever get enough real food.

Leaving Savanna to eat alone, he headed to the bathroom. The humid air was still ripe with the scent of her shampoo and body wash, steam clouding the mirror. Why didn't she use the fan?

The smell of her bath products filled his nose and did

something to his brain cells, triggering him to breathe deeper and close his eyes. Memories of his grandmother's big backyard with clothes on the clothesline blowing in the breeze and the gardenias in full bloom assaulted him. He hadn't thought about her in a long time, the memories too sweet and too sad to think about in prison. It had been a long time ago, an innocent time, and it hadn't lasted long enough.

A sharp pain hit his solar plexus and he opened his eyes. He missed her—her bright blue eyes, her kind smile, her amazing cooking, and her ability to calm the raging monster he'd had inside him after the deaths of his parents and little sister in a house fire. That one brief summer he'd had with her had been the best time of his life, but at some point, those memories had become too painful, too bittersweet. He couldn't afford sentimentality. Couldn't stomach wondering what she would think of him and the killer he'd become.

Savanna's bathroom was as impressive as the main living area. Double sinks with a marble counter, a jetted spa tub, a shower big enough to fit four people in. A linen closet held towels, bottles of fancy lotions, a host of multi-colored nail polish and miscellaneous toiletries. He absently noted there was only one toothbrush in the vanity drawer where she kept her toothpaste and floss.

Grabbing the chair that sat at a dressing table, he checked the ceiling lights and fan, just as he'd double checked all the fixtures in the living room, regardless of what she'd said. Things changed; she could have checked the lights and smoke detectors two days ago for all he knew and the bastard stalking her had paid her a visit since.

Her bedroom was more like a small house in and of itself. A king size bed, a fireplace, a chair and ottoman, and another flat screen. The bedside table was stacked with books. The floor next to the chair also piled high. On the bed was an open laptop, colored folders, and a helter-skelter of papers. Reading glasses lay off to the side. On the fireplace mantel was a picture of two girls—Savanna and her sister?

He didn't want to invade her privacy, but he still did a thorough check of everything. He needn't have worried. He didn't find anything even remotely scandalous. No porn, no sex toys, not even a romance in her stacks of reading materials. For someone who made a living sensationalizing the sordid lives of others, she was quite boring in comparison.

And yet, even her simple bikini underwear gave him a hard on. He blamed it on the lack of sex in almost two years, but still found himself having a very specific image of stripping Savanna's yoga pants off and seeing what color of silk her bikinis were today.

What was wrong with him that he was thinking of her that way? She'd helped Linc Norman ruin his life.

A closed door opened to a walk-in closet. A closet big enough to be a bedroom, but containing enough shirts, pants, sweaters, and dresses to clothe a small village. An entire wall was lined with shelves of shoes, from ceiling to floor. The shelves were lighted as if the shoes were works of art. A second wall held purses.

He laid his set of screwdrivers on the center dresser. So Savanna was a fashion whore. What did he care?

"Impressive, huh?" the woman in question said from the bedroom doorway.

Tearing his eyes away from the display of shoes, he went to work checking the wall sconces. She'd snuck up on him. How had that happened?

"The shoes aren't all mine," she said. "My sister and I share the collection. We wear the same size, and I keep them here since her apartment is the size of a gnat. Same with the handbags."

He didn't respond, replacing the fancy metal cover on the first sconce and moving on to the next one.

"Your fajita's getting cold."

Pushy. But then he knew that from watching her show.

Push back. "Not hungry."

"You sure about that? Your stomach's been growling since you walked in."

Her tone held a trace of mocking humor. He glanced over his shoulder. She was leaning against the doorjamb, arms crossed under her breasts, one bare foot hiked up on the inside of her opposite calf, her bright pink toenails reflecting light they were so shiny.

"Look," she said, turning serious. "I understand the policies and procedures. I'm not flirting with you or asking you to divulge your life story, but if you're going to help me with my problem, we need to talk. I've had a long day and I could use some company over my dinner before I turn in. It's just a fajita and a beer. It's not marriage."

He didn't want to talk. Didn't want to sit across from her and have her figure out who he really was.

Yet, for some bizarre reason, he couldn't resist her openness, her genuine kindness. The smell of the fajitas was killing him too. "I'll be there in a minute," he found himself saying. "Let me finish here."

She smiled and it did a strange thing to his pulse rate. "Cool."

And then she disappeared.

He pocketed his screwdriver and digital scanner and blew out a nervous breath. *It's dinner and conversation.*

How hard could it be?

CHAPTER FIVE

Coldplay's demeanor at her table made the invisible Gulf Stream in the Atlantic look like a gentle breeze.

He stood behind the chair where Savanna had set a plate for him, looking at it like it was a death sentence.

She sipped her glass of chardonnay. She liked chilled white wine with her fajitas, regardless of the fact that wine experts recommended pairing a dry red with beef. In fact, she liked chardonnay with pretty much everything. "The chair doesn't bite."

His dark blue eyes jumped to hers, then he grabbed the chair by the back, jerked it away from the table, and plopped into it. "Your apartment is clean. I do recommend upgrading your security system."

A smidgen of relief fluttered in her chest. She'd been so paranoid about the possibility Linc Norman had had cameras installed, she'd taken to dressing in her closet with the lights out and letting the shower steam the bathroom in hopes it would cover the lens if there were cameras in there. Another reason to hurry through her showers and not shave her legs. "Good to know. Thank you for doing such an in-depth job."

He nodded. "That's why you hired Rock Star Security. We're the best."

Savanna liked the sound of his voice. She wanted to hear more of it. The niggling idea that she'd met him before seemed silly. No way she would have forgotten that gravelly, sexy voice or those steely blue eyes.

Her fingers tingled, her pulse seemed to be skipping to a different rhythm. She was no longer in this quest alone and her bodyguard was more than easy on the eyes.

The urge to jump right in to discussing Parker's disappearance caught in her throat. *Give the man a moment.* Coldplay was sitting at her table and speaking in complete sentences. *Progress.*

Ignoring her tingling fingers and erratic pulse, she picked up her fajita instead. "Let's eat. Then we'll get down to business."

Coldplay tensed. It wasn't that she saw the muscles pushing against the seams of his suit jacket brace or his square jaw clench or the taut cords in his neck flex. She simply sensed that he was suddenly ready to bolt, once again uncomfortable in her presence.

Ignore it. The men she met fell into two categories: those who felt intimidated by her fame and success and those who hated her for it. Her ex had been both, even though on the surface he'd seemed like just the opposite. Brady Garrison Jr. had been the perfect man. Educated, out-going, wise beyond his twenty-nine years. For two years and seven months, they'd made the perfect Washington power couple and Savanna had been sure marriage was in their future. Brady had been sure the White House was.

Until Savanna discovered that Brady was using campaign funds to redecorate his office and take trips to Monaco for weekend parties. Parties he was attending without her.

She couldn't exactly out him on her show to his constituents, although she'd thought long and hard about doing exactly that, but she couldn't turn a blind eye to his infidelities to her or his voters either.

Coldplay studied the silverware on the table, running a long, calloused finger along the edge of the knife. His hands were big and strong-looking. Savanna swallowed the food in her mouth and thought of all the things those hands could do to her.

A shiver ran down her spine. Where had *that* thought come from?

Shaving her legs, making dinner for two, thinking about sex... *Too many months without a man.*

"I'm sorry. Are you a vegetarian?" she asked. "I can open a can of refried beans and you can pick out the beef tips."

The eyes under the edge of the baseball cap rose to stare at the tablecloth. Coldplay picked up the knife and then the fork. "The meat is fine."

"You're just not comfortable eating with me."

He began to cut his fajita into pieces. "It's against protocol."

"And you never break the rules?"

Head down, he ate slowly, meticulously, ignoring her jab. Satisfied that he was at least eating the food she'd prepared, she went back to eating her own fajita, now nearly cold.

The silence was edgy. Coldplay wasn't nervous or antsy but definitely…controlled. He didn't like his assignment, didn't like bending the protocol rules to eat with her, but he wasn't dramatic about it or overtly obvious.

Military, she thought. She'd met a few military men and women through her show and seen many amongst the citizens of DC. She'd even had a Marine or two hit on her. Some were certainly friendly and outgoing, but behind their eyes they always seemed to be hiding some secret. As if they were better than you or at least more dangerous.

Juice dripped from the end of her tortilla, running down her fingers. She set down the food and licked her pinky. "What's wrong with my security system?"

Coldplay's gaze locked on her mouth as she licked another finger, his fork stopping in midair. Maybe it was that damn baseball cap throwing weird shadows, but his pupils seemed to widen.

"Coldplay?"

His gaze snapped to hers. He sat up taller. "What?"

She almost grinned, a new thought dawning. He wasn't trying to avoid her because he hated her. He was avoiding her because…

He was attracted to her?

No. That couldn't be. His initial reaction when she'd opened the door had *not* been attraction. And here she sat now with no makeup, her hair in a ponytail, and dressed in spandex that had seen better days.

"My security system?" Maybe the food had wooed him over, and she hadn't even made anything impressive. "You said I needed an upgrade?"

The knife and fork crisscrossed on top of his plate. He'd downed the fajita in four bites. "The system is old and the code is easy to override with a simple smart phone app. I'll call the office tonight and get a new one installed first thing tomorrow."

Efficient. She liked that. The producers of her show should take notes. "Anything else I need to upgrade?"

Standing, he shook his head and reached for his plate. "No, ma'am."

As she watched him take his plate to the kitchen, she finished off her fajita, mind spinning. One minute he was cool and aloof, the next, he was looking at her like she was on the dinner menu. Now, he was back to justifying his code name.

What she wouldn't give to dig under that layer of ice and find out what made him tick.

He rinsed his plate in the sink and stuck it in the dishwasher, then came back for hers.

"Thank you," she said as he whisked the plate away.

Efficient *and* well-mannered. She took a sip of wine trying to remember Brady ever clearing the table after a meal.

Nope, not once.

Good manners were never outdated, her mother always said. Brady had owned the shiniest set of manners this side of the Mason-Dixon line, but he'd never washed off his dinner plate and stuck it in the dishwasher. Of course, he never visited Savanna's place or let her cook for him either. He ate out or had his personal chef prepare dinners for him.

Coldplay seemed to like keeping his hands busy. He fussed with a towel, wiping down the sink. Taking her wine with her, Savanna went to her desk and found the file she wanted, then returned and tossed the file on the breakfast bar. "Can we talk about Parker now?"

Coldplay folded the towel and set it on the countertop. He glanced at the folder and his face went totally neutral. She almost heard his mental sigh.

But in the next instant, and without a word, he took a seat at the bar and opened the red cover.

Afraid she might spook him, Savanna carefully slid onto the bar stool next to him and held her breath.

SEALS lived by the motto "The more you sweat in peace, the less you bleed in war."

Savanna Jeffries had done a lot of sweating.

Trace read through the file she had compiled on her sister, one Parker Emery Annabelle Jeffries. In the photo headshot clipped to the front, Parker was a dead ringer for Savanna, except for the eyes. The sisters both wore their hair long, shared the same petite nose and striking bone structure.

But where Savanna's eyes were the deep blue of a peacock feather, Parker's were green. In the picture she was smiling, but the smile didn't reach her eyes.

Savanna still hadn't recognized him. He'd been sure that the moment he sat across from her for dinner, she'd figure out why he seemed familiar.

She hadn't. Maybe because she'd been waiting to get to this part.

Physical description and a curriculum vitae of Parker followed, tracking her from Vassar to a private R&D group to the National Intelligence division, then a log of sorts. Dates, times, snippets of conversations Savanna had noted and highlighted. The day Savanna last heard from her; a list of possible reasons Parker had ceased communication. Previous times when Parker had been on assignment or out of town and the history of their texts, emails, and phone calls. Parker was an analyst, not an operative. She'd left her cubicle on occasion to accompany her boss on a few overseas trips, but had never done time as an operative.

At least not on paper.

She didn't seem like the typical counterterrorism expert with her background in science and cognitive brain therapy, but apparently her skills were spot on when evaluating what made people commit acts of terror.

Another page detailed phone calls Savanna had made to Parker's friends and coworkers and the responses she'd gotten. No one knew anything.

Which meant someone was lying.

Most likely, Parker.

An analyst with no field experience was the president's pick to bring him his daily briefing? It didn't make sense.

Except that Linc Norman had a thing for pretty women, especially those willing to serve him in more ways than one.

One thing for sure was that Savanna Jeffries was good at investigative reporting. She'd explored every option, spoken to everyone she could, including people high up in National Intelligence. According to her notes, she'd met a dead end at every turn.

From the energy vibrating off her body seated next to him,

and the hope shining in her eyes, she was hoping he would find a way to bust through those dead ends.

Too bad all he could do was tell her the truth. The one thing she'd ignored.

"Well?" she said a few minutes later.

One word, but it held the same desperate hope he saw reflected in her eyes.

For a second, she wasn't the reporter who'd splashed his bearded SEAL face all over TV and caused his downfall. She was just a woman worried about her sister.

Worried? She was scared to death.

He tore his gaze away from hers. The intensity of those blue eyes was too much. He couldn't tell her what he suspected without crushing her hopes. Without hope, what did a person have?

Another lesson he was intimately familiar with.

Reviewing Parker's resume once more, he pointed to her start date with the CIA. "Are you sure this is when she started with the Agency?"

"Yes, why?"

"The president relies heavily on the Director of National Intelligence to present an accurate threat matrix to him every morning. The director relies on his top analyst to pull that threat matrix together from each of the intelligence agencies. But I've never heard of the NI's top analyst being someone without field experience. An analyst can be crafty and outthink most terrorists, but a superior analyst is one who's had boots on the ground experience with those terrorists."

A thread of uncertainty crept into her voice. "What are you saying?"

Trace didn't answer. Savanna could figure it out on her own.

"My sister is a spy?"

"*Was* a spy is my guess."

"I don't understand. How is that possible?"

"Most CIA employees never even tell you where they work, much less what they actually do, especially if they're operatives."

"I'm her sister. We share everything." She held up a hand. "Well, you know what I mean. She never shared details of her work, but she would have told me if she was an undercover operative. I would have known. She would have been out of the country on missions, gone for long periods of time."

Trace wasn't there to argue. "Was she sleeping with Linc Norman?"

The hand Savanna had been holding up fell, knocking into her wine glass. As the glass tipped, Trace snatched it up before it hit the granite counter.

Wine still went everywhere.

"Oh, jeez." Savanna jumped up and ran for a towel. She handed it to him across the bar, exchanging it for the glass, and went back for a second towel to mop up the wine running down the other side.

"You don't pull any punches, do you?" she said bending down behind the backside of the breakfast bar. "Ms. Reese didn't either."

He wiped off his hand and dabbed up the droplets that had landed on the file folder. "From all evidence, she either was a field-experienced intelligence operative or she and the president had a relationship."

Savanna stood and huffed out a breath. "Those are my only two options?"

Trace handed back the towel. "The only two I can logically see."

Her body trembled as if revolted. "There's no way Parker would sleep with Linc Norman." But her voice was soft, hesitant, for the first time since he'd met her. "Is it possible she was doing some type of work for him—something top secret—that he didn't want anyone to know about? Not even the National Intelligence director, the CIA, Homeland, or anyone?"

Command & Control. They'd been dismantled. Or so he was told. Was Parker Jeffries one of them? Had she—like Trace—been under the president's command and went against his orders?

The loud ringing of a phone made both of them turn their heads. Savanna nearly hurdled the breakfast bar in a dash to retrieve the cell phone from her desk. Trace noticed that she didn't even bother looking at the readout as she tapped the screen and put the phone to her ear.

"Hello?"

As the person on the other end spoke, her tense shoulders deflated. "Zeb, how are you?...I'm sorry, I can't really talk right now. I have company."

She was hoping it was her sister.

How many phone calls had Savanna received in the past few

weeks since Parker had gone missing? Every one of them a let down because it wasn't her?

A long pause ensued, but brought a sad smile to her lips. "I appreciate the offer, just like the last dozen times you've made it, but I don't plan on returning to public access television any time soon...no, no, I'm fine." Another pause. "No, I haven't heard from her...okay, I'll talk to you soon. We should do lunch at Geezy's."

She'd no sooner disconnected when the phone rang again. "Sorry," she said. "This one is important."

He returned his attention to the file, pretending not to eavesdrop.

"Hello, Dr. Hopland. Yes, I'm still interested in the interview... No, it's not too late. Let me get to my computer."

Savanna stuck the phone between her ear and her shoulder as she shuffled files off her laptop on the desk. "You received my email with the outline of the documentary I'm planning concerning your research?"

Trace sent a text to Beatrice, requesting some background on the entire Jeffries family. Was Parker actually missing or simply undercover and unable to make her usual contact? It took a skilled operative to lead a double life so efficiently that even her sister—a woman she had daily contact with—didn't realize she was a spy.

But if Parker was indeed part of Command & Control, why had she told Savanna she reported to the president with his daily briefing? Wouldn't she have kept that secret too?

Those working for C&C were the best of the best. Like Beatrice Reese who'd hidden her real name and identity so well Trace wasn't sure he'd ever figure out the truth, and he probably didn't want to. From what he'd seen in the couple days he'd been at the training facility, she had a photographic memory and the IQ of Einstein. Maybe higher. He'd worked with a lot of operatives over the years and each had their tics. If he had to guess, he'd say she was former NSA. He, on the other hand, had been the best of assassins. So while he'd trained and went on missions as a SEAL, some days, he was called on to work alone.

Savanna turned to him and covered the phone's speaker. "This might take a while," she whispered. "Help yourself to more wine."

She whirled back around and sat at her desk, putting the doctor on speaker as she opened her laptop.

Trace closed the folder. There were people he and Beatrice could contact, see if they could pick up a trail on Parker, but being this close to Savanna 24/7 would only come back on him. Eventually, her keen eyes and memory would connect the dots. Something would click and she'd figure out who he was.

Quietly, he left the apartment. In the hallway, he checked the lock on the private elevator and shut down thoughts about Parker Jeffries. First thing tomorrow morning, he'd get a new assignment.

Tonight, all he had to do was guard the door and the sexy body behind it.

Chapter Six

When Savanna stuck her head out the door two hours later, she felt like an idiot. She'd made a fool of herself in front of Coldplay and was pretty sure she'd been bamboozled by her own sister. On top of that, she'd been so distracted by thoughts of Parker sleeping with the president and working as a spy—but mostly sleeping with the president—she'd completely blown the interview with Dr. Hopland.

She'd follow up with Hopland tomorrow. Now, she really needed sleep; her day started with hair and makeup at six a.m., and with the morning drive, she had to be up and out the door by five.

With all the crazy thoughts swirling in her head, though, sleep was out of the question. Her nerves were buzzing, her neck tight with tension. And although it pained her to consider Coldplay's theories, she wanted to know more.

He stood beside the door, arms crossed. A statute, not even turning to look at her. "Everything okay?" he said, his voice low and controlled.

No. She was not okay. Her world was turning upside down. "Not in the least. I acted like an inexperienced dweeb with Dr. Hopland on the phone just now because I couldn't focus on her work with posttraumatic stress growth. I kept seeing images of Parker in bed with Linc Norman." She shuddered. "Yuck."

She thought she saw the hint of a smile cross Coldplay's face, but it was there and gone so fast, she might have been dreaming. "Thank you for dinner. I apologize for my bluntness during our discussion."

"Don't apologize." Coldplay had manners. She was slightly surprised. Especially since he hadn't removed his hat at the dinner table.

She moved into the hallway and stared at the night sky just beyond the window at the far end. "Usually I'm the one putting people on the spot with tough questions and unattractive theories. Now I know how it feels."

"I locked down the elevator and stairwell. You're safe."

Back to business. "Thank you."

She stood there, not knowing what to do. He didn't seem interested in small talk. *Business it is then.* "Do you think you can find Parker?"

The pause that ensued made her shift her weight and wrap her arms around herself. Why did she have the feeling that he could find Parker in his sleep; he didn't *want* to find her.

Or rather, he doesn't want to help me.

"When we were little," Savanna said, putting her back against the wall and leaning on it. "I wanted to be just like her. She took ballet, I took ballet. When she tried gymnastics, I did too. She was always more of a tomboy than I was, and as we got older, she wanted to do tougher sports. She quit ballet and gymnastics and joined a soccer team. Next it was volleyball and basketball. I wasn't cut out for those things, and I was really good at gymnastics, but when I was seven, I gave it up for a time because I loved her so much and thought she'd think I was cooler if I did everything she did. A few months later, we had a big argument and she told me I sucked at sports and embarrassed her. It gutted me. I couldn't verbalize it, but I realized then that I had to stop living my life through Parker and do what I loved instead. I went back to gymnastics the next day."

He didn't respond, didn't even blink. Just stared at the wall.

"Do you have any brothers or sisters..." She stopped herself. "Sorry, forgot again. No personal questions."

Pacing down the hall, her eyes skipped over the floral arrangement on the table. The hotel provided a new one every few days. She had a beautiful penthouse apartment, all the clothes and shoes she would ever need, a challenging but rewarding job, and she would give it all away to have Parker back.

"It's just that, she's my best friend as well as my big sister. There are days when I come home from work and I'm sure I can feel her in my apartment, as if she just left. I check my phone constantly for messages that aren't there. There's this big, gaping hole in my life right now. I don't know if she was a spy or sleeping with the president. All I know for sure is that I have to find her. She's always been there for me and now it's my turn to be there for her. If you have siblings, I'm sure you understand."

A muscle in his jaw moved.

She was getting to him. Making Parker a real person, not just a list of facts in a file folder.

"I've done dozens of stories on families. Stories about twins and other siblings who are extremely close. I tried once to debunk a theory my sister had on how *not* being your mother's favorite could make you a more successful person. Ended up becoming a believer. Parker did a lot of that, studying people and how their brains work. I do it, too, just on a different platform. By the way, I was never our mother's favorite. Parker was just trying to make me feel better about it."

His nostrils flared a tiny bit. His gaze flicked to her and then away.

Yep, definitely getting to the tough guy.

Desperation ate at her, yet she knew when it was time to ease up on the direct, in-your-face investigator body language and just be a person in need of help.

Not easy for her. She didn't like needing anyone's help.

"If you don't like me or my show, I understand." She went to stand against the wall on the other side of him, keeping some distance as she mimicked his stance in what she hoped was a non-confrontational posture. "But I hope those feelings won't predispose you to disliking Parker or refusing to help me. And I do need help, Coldplay. I hate admitting that—I'm very independent and have been that way since I was eight years old and returned to gymnastics—but it's true. I can't do this alone. I need an expert like you to find my sister."

His chest rose almost imperceptibly, but she caught the movement out of the corner of her eye. "It's possible Parker wasn't sleeping with Norman," he said brusquely.

She snorted, looking at his profile and finding she liked it. A lot. The square jaw and the smooth skin of his cheek made her fingers itch to touch him. "Well, that's good news."

"She may have been on a black op—something he ordered her to do, and that no one knows about except him—and got caught or..."

Savanna's mouth went dry. "Or what?"

He didn't answer.

"Or killed. Just say it. I know I freaked a little earlier when you started laying out your theories, and I apologize, but you have to be straight with me on all of this. I may not like it, but I *will* handle it better from now on. I promise."

Her admission didn't seem to phase him, garnering nothing more than a nod.

"What kind of black op do you think Parker might have been working?" she asked.

His eyes slewed to her, that dangerous panther surfacing. "Be warned, Ms. Jeffries. You have no idea what we might uncover."

She swallowed hard. "I'm aware it could get messy."

"*Messy?*" His hard gaze turned on her full force. His eyes burned with intensity. "You pursue this and things will get more than messy. It could be deadly. You're dealing with the most powerful man in America. Possibly in the world. Are you willing to die for this information?"

A lump formed in her throat, as if she'd tried to swallow a peach pit. "You think he'd have me killed?"

"If he's hiding something that he knows could get him impeached and/or imprisoned and he believes you could blow the whistle on him, definitely. He'll silence you without hesitation. So I'll ask you again, are you willing to die over this?"

Conviction was an emotion that got a lot of people in trouble. She'd seen it time and time again on her show. People threw out logic, made false assumptions, and filled themselves with bravado when all else failed.

She never thought she'd be in their shoes. "Yes. I'm willing to die for my sister."

His lips firmed into a straight line and he stared at her with a new annoyance lighting up his face. "She's lied to you and potentially put you in danger."

"If she lied, it was to protect me and do her job. I understand that. She would never purposely put me in danger."

He went back to staring at the wall. Tense silence descended once more.

Savanna's frustration wouldn't let her stand immobile any longer. She jerked away from the wall, feeling the urge to throw another vase of flowers. "Are you going to help me or not? Because if not, I need to find someone who will."

His Adam's apple bobbed. "I..." He hesitated for a second. "I've already asked Beatrice Reese for some follow-up information. I'm looking into it."

A new surge of hope lit up her veins, crackled along her spine. "Yes! Thank you."

"No promises."

"But this *is* part of your job."

"My primary focus is to keep you safe. Tomorrow, I'll put out some feelers, see what comes back. I can't guarantee anything beyond that."

"I understand." She put a hand on the door handle. "I have an extra bedroom. You're welcome to take it."

"No thanks."

"You're going to stand out here in the hallway all night? You don't sleep?"

"I'll be fine."

She needed another drink just to handle his attitude. "You've locked down all the entrances. At least come inside. Take the couch, watch some TV, whatever. You don't have to sleep, but I won't relax if I know you're standing out here in the hall all night. What if you need to pee?"

Under the brim of the cap, she noticed his brows bang together. "Will you leave me alone if I come inside?"

A smile broke over her face. *Score one for me.* "I promise to quit talking to you and not ask another question. Seriously, I need to go to bed and get some sleep. Four a.m. comes early."

Once again, she sensed his mental sigh as he caved and ushered her into the apartment. He would learn. When she wanted something, Savanna always found a way to get it.

Trace heard Savanna's alarm go off at precisely four a.m. as anticipated. Some old Britney Spears song filled the penthouse. She must have tapped the snooze button because all went quiet again ten minutes later, another blast of Britney finally rousing her. He heard shuffling and the bathroom door closing.

He'd spent the night thinking and pacing and thinking some more. Her open living room, dining room, and kitchen made the perfect circle for him to walk. She'd told him to help himself to food and drink and handed him the complicated remote to her entertainment system. Once an hour, he'd checked the doors and windows, wishing she had surveillance cameras. He didn't have trouble staying awake, but his mind wanted to wander. The past was always happy to resurface and flood him with memories best left forgotten.

He'd found a drawer of DVDs and come across some family movies. Savanna hadn't just been good at gymnastics, she'd reached the Olympics where an apparent injury to her wrist shut her down.

Watching those videos of her with her parents and sister cheering for her, seeing her waving from the top platform at the Olympics at the ripe age of fourteen, and then seeing her in the hospital with a brace on her wrist, had done something to his cold, hard heart.

She was a fighter. A champion. She'd known deep disappointment at a young age, her dream of the Olympics ending abruptly. Yet, she'd pulled herself out and had grown up to succeed at championing for others.

The videos kept his mind occupied for a couple of hours. He'd felt a twinge of guilt at watching something so personal, but it had kept his own memories at bay.

There was no forgetting what he'd done and, not for the first time, he wondered if Savanna had done him a favor by exposing him as a traitor, even though it was a lie. At least she'd taken him out of play and put him in a place where he probably belonged after all of the lives he'd taken in the name of national security. In service to the president.

Although he still held a severe grudge, her appeal the previous evening had softened him. His parents and only sister had been killed in a house fire when he was ten. He'd been staying overnight at a friend's house. The only living relative he'd had left was his grandfather, who couldn't seem to ever look Trace in the eye after the accident.

Trace couldn't blame him. He'd survived by not being home. To this day, he still wondered if he could have saved his family if he'd been home that night. Or if it would have been better if he had died too.

While he couldn't clear his own name, he could help Savanna

with hers. If Ginger, his little sister, had never died in that fire, if she had gone missing... Well, Trace would have crushed the gates of Hell to get her back. Even now, he wished he could take her place.

During the early morning hours, he texted Beatrice telling her Savanna needed an upgrade to her security system first thing. Next, he'd shot photos of the file on Parker and sent the info to Beatrice as well. *Copy that*, was her only reply. No questioning him about changing his mind.

He liked that.

The faint burn of being manipulated prickled under his skin, but the woman was good at her job. Reluctant respect set up shop in his skull.

Sounds of running water and Savanna humming filtered through the walls. He still had to play it cool. The second she figured out who he was, all bets were off. He couldn't— wouldn't—go back to Witcher. They'd have to kill him first.

The bathroom door opened and she padded past him with a yawn and went into the kitchen. She was wearing another set of yoga pants and a tank top. These pants had a beach scene imprinted on the ass that flowed down both legs.

He heard the sound of a grinder, then a motor noise as she stood in front of a black espresso machine. A minute later, she shuffled into the living room where he stood and handed him a travel mug. Her hair was down and combed straight and her eyes were tired. Either she wasn't a morning person or she hadn't slept despite the fact he had agreed not to stand in the hall all night.

Without a word, she returned to the kitchen. He sniffed deep, the smell of freshly ground coffee beans making his nose happy. The espresso was steaming so he watched the sweet beach scene back at the machine for a minute while he blew on the liquid to cool it.

Another round and Savanna had a second travel cup in hand. The doorman downstairs rang her and announced her car was here.

Still not speaking, she grabbed a coat and motioned him to follow.

Definitely not a morning person.

She locked up the apartment and he unlocked the elevator. On the way down, she took a big sip of coffee, sighed as if in heaven, and leaned back against the elevator wall.

He liked this quiet side of her. It fit with the early morning and his thoughts. He should have called Beatrice while Savanna was in the bathroom to tell her time was up and he wanted a new assignment. Instead, here he was, drinking her damn good espresso and following her to work.

Once he landed her safely at the studio, he'd call Beatrice, get Savanna a new bodyguard. Didn't mean he couldn't make some calls like he'd promised her last night. He could help from behind the scenes.

Yeah, that was it. Keep his distance but still help her find her sister. He was good at keeping his distance and still getting a job done.

He chanced a glance at her. Her eyes were closed, her full lips forming a sexy pout. For half a second, his libido gave a lurch and his mind went sideways before he could stop it, wondering what it would be like to touch those lips. Taste the coffee on them.

He put his head down and took a drink. A big drink that scalded the back of his tongue and his throat. He nearly choked, his windpipe seizing up.

"Are you okay?" Savanna said.

Her eyes were now open, the big blue orbs wide.

"Fine," he spluttered. "Swallowed wrong."

"It's micro-roasted Guatemalan. Organic, fair-trade. Not everyone likes the intensity, but I need high-octane fuel this early in the morning."

The elevator hit the first floor and dinged. Trace stepped in front of Savanna and hit the hold button to keep the doors from opening. "Wait here until I clear the area."

Her lips formed a condescending smile. "It's four-forty-five. No one's up except Cori at the front desk and Randy the doorman."

He gave her a look, long and patient. She sighed and leaned back against the elevator wall. "Wait here. Yes, sir. Got it."

A minute later, Trace had her secured in the backseat of the limo that the studio apparently sent every morning to pick her up. Savanna's assistant was already in the backseat, looking at him like he was Santa Claus and she had a long list of wishes.

He pegged her to be early twenties. The dark rimmed glasses and ponytail made her look even younger, like a kid playing grown up. She grinned like the Cheshire cat and fiddled with her phone. "So you're the new bodyguard."

"Coldplay," Savanna said, staring out the window as the driver pulled away from the curb. "This is Lindsey, my studio-assigned personal assistant who is also the assistant to the assistant director. She keeps me on schedule. Lindsey, this is Coldplay."

Savanna didn't sound too pleased. Trace simply nodded at the girl.

"Coldplay," she said, tapping the edge of her smart phone against her chin. "I love that group. I've been telling Savanna for months she needs to take those death threats seriously, so when she told me she'd hired you yesterday, I was so relieved."

Trace looked at Savanna. "Death threats?"

She waved a hand in the air. "Nothing more than the usual whackos who threaten every person on TV. I piss off a few people. Some more than others. It's no big deal. I've been getting them for years. Lindsey, he'll need a badge."

Trace disagreed about the potential importance of the threats but he sensed he wouldn't get anywhere on this topic with her. He turned back to Lindsey who interrupted him before he could even speak. "Got it right here." She handed him a lanyard with a studio access visitor pass.

"I'd like a complete list of the threats against Ms. Bunkett," he said, taking the lanyard. "Where they initiated from and from whom. Who deals with this kind of stuff at the studio? I'll need to speak with him or her."

Lindsey sat back, her smile fading. "Human resources probably has a file of them, you know..." She lowered her voice and shot a glance at Savanna. "Just in case."

A file? That was it? "Is anyone investigating the threats? Have they been turned over to the police? The FBI?"

Shadows played across the interior of the limo as they passed under streetlights. The girl shrugged. "I don't know."

"Coldplay." Savanna had zoned in on him, a frown tugging at her lips. *Ease up*, her eyes seemed to say. "We'll get you the list. Lindsey, put that on today's schedule."

"Right." The girl made a note on her smart phone. "I'll schedule that after the morning meeting."

"Read me the schedule," Savanna said, closing her eyes and leaning her head back against the leather headrest.

Lindsey scrolled through her phone. "Hair and makeup like usual. Then wardrobe—you're going to love the sweater Tessy picked for you—"

"No sweaters," Savanna interjected. "They make me look pudgy on camera."

She could never look pudgy, Trace thought. In fact, while he enjoyed her beautifully buff and lean physique, she could stand to put on a few pounds.

He caught himself staring at her tranquil face, highlighted here and there under the passing streetlights. Her flawless skin, her full lips...

As if she felt his gaze on her, her lids fluttered open, her dark blue eyes nearly black in the shadows.

He jerked his eyes away, staring out the window and mentally cursing himself for getting caught by her. Too many months without female contact made him suddenly feel like a starving man in front of a juicy prime rib dinner.

Needing to keep his hands busy so he didn't reach across the backseat and touch Savanna, Trace retrieved his phone out of his pocket and texted Beatrice.

How soon will F3 be installed?

F3 Home was the Rock Stars' top of the line home security system that included multi-directional cameras. When they returned to the penthouse later today, he would speak to the building manager about the lack of security around the service door entrance in the basement.

Beatrice's reply was short. *Crew and I are there now. I'll oversee the install. Ninety minutes to completion.*

B and crew must have been waiting on them to leave. Fast. Efficient. Yep, Beatrice Reese was like her husband. No wasted effort. No wasted anything.

Need a list of Parker Jeffries' aliases and if any of them have recently been used, he typed.

Copy that. Give me two hours.

Emit Petit had deep resources but Beatrice had the contacts.

Lindsey was much more at home talking work than death threats. She continued listing the day's schedule. "Nine-fifteen is your five minute lead-in on the morning show about Friday night's Westmeyer investigation. Are you sure you still want to move forward with that one?"

Savanna didn't hesitate. "Yes."

"Two days ago you said to scrap it, then yesterday, you said to put it back on the schedule. Just checking to make sure you haven't changed your mind again. Production has whiplash and Mariah isn't too happy about the flip-flopping."

Her voice was low, determined. "We're running it."

"Okay then." Lindsey rolled her eyes at Trace. Superstars. What was an assistant to do? "Morning meeting is at ten. Then you're scheduled to do the primetime special commercials at one o'clock. Where are we on the Hopland interview? Did you speak to her?"

Savanna opened her eyes and took a sip of coffee. "I have the research data from her study and a couple of examples of supersurvivors, as she terms them, but I need more specific details on the parameters of the study itself and how she determined successful outcomes."

"I thought you were getting that information last night. We're presenting the idea to Scott at the morning meeting."

"Yeah, well..." Savanna looked out the window and bit her bottom lip. "I got distracted and had to cut the call with Dr. Hopland short. I'll get the info before the meeting and help you flesh out the script. If Scott gives us any heat, I'll take it."

Lindsey's gaze cut over to Trace as if accusing him of being the distraction. A dramatic sigh left her lips.

It *was* his fault in some ways. "What's a supersurvivor?"

Both women looked at him. Savanna shifted, crossing one of her long legs over the other. "You've heard of people who've experienced a traumatic event in their life, but instead of ending up with debilitating depression and anxiety, they've found a way to turn the experience around and find good out of it? Like the mother who sets up a 5k race to raise money for cancer research after she loses her young child to leukemia. Or the army vet who comes home with PTSD and missing a couple limbs from an IED but sets up a support group for other vets, giving the men back a sense of belonging. These people suffer greatly but they turn it around. They're not just resilient, they grow from experiencing tragedy. They take the worst thing that's happened to them and turn it into the best. It's called post-traumatic growth or PTG. Dr. Hopland has a PhD in psychology and is running scientific experiments to prove PTG's validity."

"But there are naysayers," Lindsey said. "Other psychologists say PTG is bunk. That you can't simply overcome a traumatic event or PTSD by trying to find a bright side. So we're investigating."

Trace knew a thing or two about PTSD. Dr. Hopland's study sounded like bunk to him.

Yet, here he was, trying to turn his life around in a similar way to what Savanna had described. Finding a new way to live with the past.

Or was he? If he left Savanna alone, pawned her off on another bodyguard who didn't have his personal experience with the man stalking her, wasn't he simply running away again? All that bullshit about helping her from a distance was just that. Bullshit. She needed someone like him, with his insider information on Linc Norman and his special skills to keep her alive.

He put his phone away as the car pulled into the studio lot. If he could take the worst thing that had happened to him and use it to save a life this time, instead of take one, he could stop a monster from killing more innocent people. He might still have a future.

Sure he could have run away once Petit broke him out of Witcher, gone to ground never to be heard from again. Instead he'd joined Shadow Force International, working as a bodyguard, and helping keep someone safe while he searched for her missing sister.

He almost laughed at how pathetic his argument sounded as he helped Savanna from the car. Post-traumatic growth sounded like a nice bedtime story, but in reality, what he was doing was not some deep psychological bullshit.

It was simply survival. With a little revenge thrown in for good measure.

CHAPTER SEVEN

Trace had seen chaos in war, but nothing prepared him for the chaos of a TV studio in full production mode.

Few people took notice of him as he followed on Savanna's heels to her dressing room. Her name was on the door, and the moment he opened it to do his security check, his nose was greeted with the smells of fresh coffee, eggs, toast, and bacon.

A mini-buffet sat on a table against the far wall, silver domes of covered food being kept warm for the star. The room was done in soft ocean blues and held a couch, chair, coffee table, and large flat screen. On one wall hung photographs of Savanna with famous men and women she'd interviewed or done celebrity fundraisers with.

"You don't have to worry about Savanna's safety here," Lindsey quipped from the doorway. "Everyone loves her."

There had to be at least a hundred people milling around the studio. Yeah, they all had lanyards but it wasn't difficult to forge an ID badge and sneak onto the lot, especially for trained operatives working for the president.

But would they take a chance and go after her in front of so many witnesses?

"Just let him do his thing," Savanna told her assistant, even as she gave Trace a weighted stare. "I'm paying big bucks for this. I should get my money's worth."

There was something bold in the way she looked at him. Something he couldn't put his finger on.

He stepped into the small bathroom and cleared it, came back out. Bug check was next.

Overhead, a speaker crackled to life. Lindsey was paged. "Be back shortly," she said to Savanna and gave Trace one last once-over before hustling off.

Savanna moved inside, removing the covers on the silver trays and snagging a piece of toast. "Help yourself to breakfast."

He pulled out his scanning equipment and started checking for listening devices.

Sitting on the couch, she watched as she munched on her toast. "So what's our plan for today?"

"You do your thing like usual. I'll do mine."

"And what exactly is your thing?"

"Keeping you safe. Investigating Parker's disappearance."

"I need details."

Jesus, the woman was a ballbuster. "Afraid you're not getting your money's worth?"

When she didn't reply, he looked up. She was staring at him with that same look again in her eyes.

The one that made him a little nervous and a lot turned on.

"A new security system is being installed in your apartment right now," he told her, refusing to break eye contact. "I'm running a check on Parker's aliases to see if any of them have been used recently and where."

"There are strangers in my apartment right now? How did they get in?"

Seriously? "By breaking through the crappy security you currently have."

Her face fell. She massaged the back of her neck. "Are you planning to follow me around all day? Sit with me on air? Don't you need to shower or take a leak once in awhile?"

Normal bodyguards needed to switch out every few hours to keep fresh and relieve boredom. He wasn't a normal bodyguard. "Do I smell?"

"No."

"Then don't worry about it."

His detection tool flashed red as he passed it over her dressing table. He put a finger to his lips to keep her quiet for a moment, passing the wand over it again. The flashing sped up, and like a game of hot and cold, he zeroed in on one spot. Leaning down, he ran a hand underneath and in back of the mirror.

His fingers caught on a slight bump. Metal, round. Tracing the outline, he determined it wasn't part of the mirror. Digging his fingers in around the edges, he gave a yank and...

Bingo. A round metal disc fell into his hand.

Savanna was up and by his side in an instant. One hand fell on his back, sending a shock of electricity straight up his spine, as she looked over his shoulder.

He stilled his automatic reflex to jump away, instead staying half crouched and opening his hand to show her what he'd found. The bug, high-tech and effective, sat in his palm.

"Is that what I think it is?" she whispered next to his ear.

Another electrical charge zinged through his entire body. She was so close he could smell her—the shampoo she'd used on her hair, the light floral perfume of her body lotion. If he turned his head even slightly, he'd be nose to nose with her. Close enough to lose himself in those dark blue eyes. Close enough to touch her beautiful lips.

Back away.

Her hand moved to his shoulder, her breath tickling his cheek. "A listening device?"

"Yeah, it is," he murmured.

Before he could examine it further, Savanna snatched it from his hand, tossed it on the floor and stomped on it.

"Damn bastard," she said through clenched teeth, grinding the heel of her shoe into the metal.

Trace grabbed her, one arm around her waist, and swung her around, away from the destroyed listening device. "What are you doing?"

"Put me down!" she said, smacking his arm.

He let her flail for a brief second, enjoying the feel of her body against his before he set her down on her feet. "I needed to look at that to see if I could identify where it came from."

She whirled to face him, hands fisted at her sides, her eyes scared and angry at the same time. "How did he get a bug in my dressing room? He never touched the mirror when he was here on Monday."

Trace didn't need to ask who *he* was. "The president has plenty of people working for him, Savanna. Could be someone on staff or someone who slipped in pretending to be a janitor."

She digested that for a second. "So now I can't trust anyone here at the studio?"

At that moment, Lindsey burst back into the room. The

tension, thick in the air, made her pull up short and ping-pong her gaze between Trace and Savanna before landing for good on her star investigative reporter. "Why aren't you in makeup?"

Savanna took a deep breath and regrouped, smoothing down her shirt still rumpled from Trace's arm and running a hand over her hair. "I'll be right there."

Lindsey backed out, shooting Trace a *help me* look as she pulled the door closed.

Savanna stared at the smashed metal disk, snagging her bottom lip between her teeth and looking like he'd just stolen her security blanket.

Work was her life. He understood that. She felt safe here and in control. *Had* felt safe here. When the one thing you counted on to keep you sane shifted under your feet, it was hard to regain your footing.

Picking up the bug, he pocketed it. He put a hand on her shoulder, drawing her gaze to his face. "Nothing's going to happen to you on my watch."

"He's the president." Her voice was quiet, strained. "How am I going to fight him?"

Good question. Trace had fought him and look where he'd ended up.

"I'll handle it, Savanna."

And he would, one way or another.

At 0500 hours, Savanna had left her apartment on schedule, but with a man—military bearing, hypervigilant—and entered her studio limo.

At 0505, a team of three men and one woman arrived in a dark, unmarked van, and secretly entered the empty penthouse apartment with a host of black bags.

At 0530, the listening device in Savanna's dressing room at the news studio went dead.

At 0555, the team in the apartment packed up and left as quickly and quietly as they'd arrived. The black bags appeared lighter.

The woman on the building roof across the street continued to watch the upstairs penthouse windows through her binoculars as the sun rose. The air carried a sharp chill, her breath mingling with it and turning it white. Pigeons hovered and pecked at the asphalt around her feet.

Lowering the binoculars, she tugged her knit cap down over the tops of her cold ears. Her normal daytime hangout, so familiar and convenient, was no longer a safe house. She had been able to feel close to Savanna, and keep an eye on her, without anyone knowing.

The man with Savanna had to have been a bodyguard. *Good for you, Van.* But that meant the president must have escalated his threats to the point Savanna no longer felt safe. With Trace Hunter on the loose as well, Van could be in serious danger. Since she'd broken the story on him, he might be looking for revenge.

If so, Savanna would already be dead.

Not Hunter.

Had to be the president causing her problems.

A cold, hard knot that had nothing to do with the brisk morning air hardened just under the woman's breastbone.

Someone has to stop him.

But who?

The team in the van either worked for Linc Norman or was part of the bodyguard's backup unit.

Command & Control didn't use teams. Individuals only. She'd already encountered one—the goofy, old doorman who was neither an idiot nor as old as he portrayed. She had a secret way into the apartment, however, that even he knew nothing about, so she'd had no problem avoiding him.

No doubt the bodyguard had found the penthouse security to be lacking, which had been beneficial to her, and had called in the team to increase certain measures. Her secret entrance might no longer work or might be booby-trapped.

She couldn't take the chance.

Shit. She had nowhere else to go.

Except out of the country. Plenty of places lacked extradition laws and international crime took a backseat to the problems and issues the local police were forced to deal with.

Not an option. She wouldn't leave Savanna alone. She had no choice but to complete the assignment the president had given her, or stay on the run until she could dispose of him.

Like that was going to happen. Without Trace Hunter's help, shutting down the president would be a suicide mission.

So be it. If it meant saving Savanna and the others, she'd do whatever she had to.

Pulling up her hood and putting on her sunglasses, the woman scattered the pigeons at her feet and went to find a new safe house.

CHAPTER EIGHT

The mystery of women never failed to amaze him.

Friday morning, Trace watched from the shadows, keeping an eye on every person coming within a hundred feet of Savanna as the woman herself was transformed step by step into the on-air star he and millions of others had watched on *The Bunk Stops Here.*

Her thin, straight hair became thick and wavy. Her deep blue eyes grew even larger with the layers of shadow and liner. Her lips, though…the makeup artist left them mostly alone, only dabbing them with a pale peachy color that emphasized their natural beauty.

Three days in a row, he'd watched the metamorphosis and still found it hard to look away as Savanna went from pretty to show-stopping in under twenty minutes.

Back in her dressing room, she picked up a comb and redid her bangs. Then she used a tissue to remove some of the blush on her cheeks. The suit jacket Tiffany had picked today had the same blue of Savanna's eyes. She slid the jacket up and over her shoulders, buttoned the top button and checked herself in the mirror. "What do you think?"

He hadn't been asked his opinion about a woman's appearance in so long, he nearly stumbled over his response. That, and the fact he hadn't been so infatuated with a woman in just as long, and he was cooked. "Nice. You look nice."

Nice? Seriously? She looked like a cover model pretending to be a news anchor.

She seemed as unimpressed with his evaluation as he was. "Your kindness is underwhelming, but I appreciate your manners. I look like a bimbo." She picked up another tissue and began removing some of the eyeliner. "It's impossible to be taken seriously as a news anchor when you have to convey overt sexuality in order to please viewers. Men don't have to deal with this shit. They can be old, fat, bald, and wrinkly and it only adds to their air of trustworthiness."

Trace nodded. Truth be told, he'd much rather get his news delivered by Savanna, all dolled up or not, than by an old, bald guy. Best to keep his opinion to himself. He had the feeling no matter what he said, it would come out wrong.

Lindsey arrived to whisk Savanna to the news desk for her nine-fifteen on-air appearance. Trace followed.

Like the past few days, the rest of the morning and early afternoon was nonstop meetings and performances. A few people had initially given him questioning looks and Savanna had introduced him to her bosses, but otherwise, the hustle and bustle of the studio seemed to be every man for himself. No one seemed at all concerned about who he was or why he was there as long as he had his badge on display. Once, as he stood by watching Savanna do her seventeenth take of a commercial spot, one of the other anchors had asked him to get him a green smoothie from the food truck out front. Trace had given the guy the stink eye and the anchor moved on until he found another lackey to do his bidding.

Savanna nailed every direction given to her during dry runs and camera takes, the directors and producers demanding she do them over and over again. Her smile never faltered, her demeanor remaining the consummate professional through everything.

At three o'clock, she was ready to leave. She had to be back by six-forty that evening to prep for the live episode of her show at nine.

The limo was waiting for them at the front of the studio lot. Trace motioned the driver away and held the door for her.

She'd changed back into her yoga pants and wool coat. Her face was still made up and her hair blew stiffly in the wind. One hand tucked the collar of her coat around her neck and she hustled inside the warm car. "You don't have to do that, you know," she said over the wind.

Sliding in across from her, he shut them in and the winter weather out. "What, open the door for you?"

"I tell Martin, the driver, not to do it either. I can open my own door."

"No one said you can't. It's a courtesy. Like you making dinner for me last several nights."

Her chin dipped in a nod. She thumbed at the studio as the limo pulled away. "Fridays are even crazier than the rest of the week, but you should see the weekends. Thank goodness I don't work then."

Crazy was an understatement. War was chaos and death. A news studio was chaos and drama that escalated every simple story into life and death extremes. "It's an interesting place."

"Interesting being a catchall term for weird." She smiled and undid the top button of her coat. "Don't worry. I know. They live and breathe negativity. That's the news. Anything for ratings."

"Do you do anything for ratings?"

Her chest lifted on an inhale. "I inform people, educate them, and unfortunately, the people and companies I investigate are usually hiding some pretty nasty stuff. I don't need to exaggerate or walk the line of creative nonfiction. And I always do a monthly spotlight on someone or something positive. Like that Hopland PTG story. There are psychologists who dispute her findings, but my show will focus on the positive side and possibilities that post-traumatic growth is indeed a real thing." Her gaze shot to the closed partition between them and the driver. "Anything on Parker?"

The limo took a right. They might beat rush hour and make it back to Savanna's place in time for him to give her another lesson on her new state-of-the-art security system before dinner. "Still looking into aliases. If we can get our hands on those aliases, we can check to see if any of them have been in use recently and where."

"You can find that out?"

"We don't want to alert anyone that we're looking into her official career, so it's a delicate fishing expedition. Could take a few days."

"Is there anything you and I can do in the meantime?"

His answer was interrupted by her phone ringing. She looked at the caller ID and frowned. He reached for the phone, but she'd already hit the talk button. "Hello?"

The caller spoke and Savanna's gaze jerked up to meet

Trace's. She tapped the speakerphone and the instant rush of knowledge at the sound of the familiar voice made him grit his teeth.

"I told you to drop the Westmeyer investigation, Savanna." The president *tsked.* "You really should have followed directions."

"No one tells me what—"

The line went dead before she could finish.

"What the hell?" she said and then grinned. "I think someone's unhappy I smashed his listening devices."

Sounded like more than that to Trace. "Tell your driver to get off this route."

"What? Why?"

"Just do—"

Crash!

The incoming car T-boned them, the impact sending the car spinning sideways. Glass rained down on them, the squeal of brakes and metal grinding on metal filled the air.

Savanna screamed and everything went into slow motion for Trace. The sound of her scream ripped down his spine. She threw her hands up to cover her head, the car spinning, spinning, spinning, a wild, out-of-control merry-go-round, slamming both him and Savanna around like rag dolls.

Bogota. Just like Bogota. In a split-second, Trace's instincts took over. He pressed the emergency button on his arm watch, then threw his body across the divide, grabbing Savanna and taking her to the floor.

Everything happened so fast, Savanna wasn't sure how she ended up on the floor of the limo with Coldplay on top of her. What she was sure of? She couldn't breathe.

Not because he was smashing the air out of her. No, he seemed to be holding himself up off of her ever so slightly, forming a cage with his body around hers.

She was out of breath because she was looking at him eye-to-eye.

Those eyes were mesmerizing. Potent.

Powerful.

She was sure the car had stopped spinning, but her head still seemed off balance. Coldplay's nearness and the feel of his large body pinning her to the floor, made her lightheaded.

"What just happened?" she said.

His hat had come off and she could finally see his hair. Short, dark, thick. Cold air rushed inside from the broken window.

The sharp stab of memory assaulted her out of the blue. *I know him.*

She must have hit her head during the fall. Yet, there was no way she'd even tapped her head—one of Coldplay's hands cradled her skull, protecting it.

But he seems so familiar.

Coldplay gently removed his hand and rose up on his arms, shards of glass sliding off his back and shoulders as he peered out the still-intact window above them. Then he glanced over his shoulder at the broken window.

"Someone rammed your car." His voice held pure malice. "Are you hurt? Anything broken? Did you hit your head?"

Her head had been completely cushioned by his big hands. Her fingers and toes all moved: nothing hurt except for a slight sting under her ear. But shit, she was shaking. "All systems go," she said, giving him the best smile she could work up.

He squeezed her arm, not smiling back. "Stay here. Keep your head down."

The privacy divider was still up, although the far side was half crumpled from the impact. "Is Martin okay?"

"I'll check on the driver in a minute."

A man his size should have difficulty crouching in the tight space between the seats, yet he pulled it off, staying half-bent over her as he swiveled to scan the exterior of the car. "The other driver is gone."

"Gone?" Outside, people were shouting, car horns honking. She started to sit up, felt dizzy, and laid back down. "Are you sure their car didn't just spin out of your line of sight?"

He moved slowly like a cat ready to pounce, sliding up to sit on the seat and angling his head to get a better view. "Nope. We landed on the other side of the intersection. The trunk is up against the traffic pole. Lots of cars around, none of them damaged."

"They hit us with the force of a tank and then just drove away? Flippin' DC drivers." She made a disgusting noise, feeling the ooze of warm blood on her neck. "We should report it. Can you find my cell phone?"

"Already called it in."

"What?" Had she blacked out when she hit her head? *I didn't hit my head.* There was no way he'd called anyone. "When?"

"Before I hauled you to the floor."

She chocked out a half-laugh that sounded harsh in her ears. "*During* the accident? You made a call while we were flying around in the backseat with shards of glass keeping us company."

"Miss Bunkett!" It was Martin, peering in through the broken window. His dark skinned glistened with sweat even though was thirty degrees outside. He held his right arm close to his body. "Are you okay?"

"I'm fine." Sitting up was easier this round, but Coldplay put a hand on her shoulder when she tried to move into the opposite seat, keeping her sitting on the floor. "Are *you* okay? Did you hurt your arm?"

"It's nothing," he assured her and she hoped that was true.

Coldplay retrieved his ball cap from the opposite seat and snugged it down on his head. Reaching over her head, he grabbed the handle of the door. The one that still opened. "You sure you're okay?" he asked, his steely eyes sizing her up.

In the distance she heard the muffled sound of sirens. "Just a little shook up."

The sound grew sharper when he opened the door, nodding as he stepped out, those intense eyes now scanning the area. The sirens muffled again as he closed the door behind him.

"I don't know what happened," Martin was saying, no longer looking in the window at her. He seemed to be talking to Coldplay over the roof of the limo. "The light was green, I swear. That truck came out of nowhere and ran the light."

"Did you get a look at the truck?"

"Um, not really. I think it was a white cargo van."

Savanna hauled herself up into the seat Coldplay had vacated, the lightheadedness fading. She brushed glass off the seat and touched the spot on her neck that burned. Blood was coming from a cut under her earlobe.

"Call it in to your company," Coldplay told Martin, continuing to scan the area. His voice sounded clear even through the window. "Our only concern at this point is to keep Miss Bunkett safe and in the car."

Bystanders gathered. One—an older man in a suit and long,

wool coat—pushed through the crowd on the sidewalk. "Is anyone hurt? I'm a doctor."

Coldplay moved so fast, Savanna did a double-take. His coat outlined his broad backside that tapered down to a narrow waist. He filled her line of view, completely shielding her from the gawkers and the doctor. "Everyone's fine. Please step back. Help is on the way."

"But I'm a doctor," the man said as if that should give him instant access to her.

Her fingers were sticky with blood. She had nothing to wipe it off with. Leaning over, she used her shoe to clear a patch of broken glass and cleaned off her fingers on the carpet.

"Your services are not required," Coldplay said, his deep voice clear as a bell. "Move on, sir."

From the corner of her eye, she saw the glint of metal. *My phone.*

Martin said something about letting the doctor have a look at her and Coldplay shut him down, telling him to get back in the driver's seat and report the accident to the studio.

Accidents brought out the best and the worst in people. Coldplay's manners had gone right out the door.

The passenger side of the car was smashed in right where she'd been sitting. The edge of the phone stuck out under the crumpled-in plastic. She grabbed the corner of the case and gave a tug. Outside, the sirens were still blocks away. She heard the squeal of brakes and the slamming of doors close by though.

"Jesus," a man's voice said. "She okay?"

"Yeah," Coldplay answered. "You got here fast."

"Smoothie run. I was only three blocks away."

The phone wouldn't budge so Savanna adjusted her grip, putting both hands on it and tugging hard.

Pop. The phone came out with a little crunch, the glass front cracked beyond repair.

And that's when she remembered. The phone call right before they were hit. *I told you to drop the Westmeyer investigation, Savanna. You really should have followed directions.*

Her stomach clenched and her jaw clamped. Her fingers shook and not from the cold air rushing in through the broken window. At the same time, hot, disgusting bile rose in her throat. Blindly, she reached for the door handle, but the damn thing wouldn't budge, of course, because the door was jammed.

Get out! She had to get out of the car. Now.

Sliding across the seat, she fumbled with the other door, finally finding the handle and throwing it open. The door whacked Coldplay in the ass and Savanna just missed his shoes as she vomited all over the sidewalk in front of a live audience.

CHAPTER NINE

Trace evacuated Savanna with the help of Callan Reese, leaving Martin and the witnesses on the street to deal with the cops. He and Savanna would give their reports later.

He didn't buy the smoothie run as the reason for Reese's proximity to them when the accident occurred, but he was grateful for the help anyway. Together, they got Savanna to a safe location—Shadow Force International's headquarters—where Trace could examine her wounds properly and protect her at the same time.

He'd get to the bottom of Reese tailing them as soon as he had Savanna comfortable.

Which he hoped would be soon.

"This is going to sting," he told her.

They were sitting in the window seat of Beatrice's office on the top floor. Better light for Trace to see the cut on Savanna's neck. She didn't jerk away as he touched the alcohol-soaked cotton ball to the wound. She sat stoic, the only sign it hurt was the way she bit her bottom lip.

Tough woman. The pain would fade, the cut would heal. He respected her show of bravery, the discipline she was employing to stay stationary.

His own discipline was shaky. He was too close to her lovely skin—too pale after the accident and the cold—and those luscious lips that called to him to be kissed. The lips she was biting.

"You don't believe it was a hit and run, do you?" she asked, her fingers fiddled with the gold bracelet on her wrist.

He wiped off the blood where it had stained her neck, his fingers itching to trail the gentle slope down to her shoulder. "It was a warning."

"From the president."

It was a statement, not a question. "Yes."

"He tried to kill me. Over a story. We could have both died."

"He doesn't want you dead. If he did, the driver of the truck—the assassin—would have gotten out and put a bullet in both of us. Like, I said, it was a warning."

She shivered under his hand. "In broad daylight with witnesses. Crazy or stupid?"

"Neither. None of those witnesses were paying attention until the truck hit us and they were busy watching our car, not the truck. Everyone will believe it was a hit and run, and all of the testimonies will be convoluted. Traffic cams in the area will have no good shot of the driver. The truck will show up at some point abandoned, probably set on fire to destroy any possible DNA evidence."

"You seem to know a lot about this sort of thing."

"I know that the men and women who do assassination work for the president of the United States are ghosts. They don't get caught unless…"

"Unless what?"

He fiddled with the first aid kit Beatrice had given him even though the antibiotic cream and gauze were right in front of him. "Nothing."

"Assassins for the president. Who are these people? CIA? NSA?"

Me. "Neither. They are their own group."

"But the president isn't allowed to have a private group of assassins."

Trace didn't respond, wiping her wound with a fresh dose of alcohol.

She grit her teeth, but sat quietly while he finished cleaning her neck. Her wound would heal for sure, but she was still in a heap of trouble. That wasn't going away.

Unless he disposed of the trouble.

"What's up with this Westmeyer investigation?" he asked.

She unclenched her teeth, rubbed the back of her neck. "Westmeyer is a pharmaceutical company in California run by Harold Lee, who is also head of PelCon, a super PAC. Westmeyer's subsidiaries have spent over half a million this year alone lobbying the Senate and the House. I learned through a source that Lee and his wife are about to be investigated by the Justice Department and Security Exchange Commission for various activities, all leading back to campaign contributions."

Unscrewing the lid, Trace put antibiotic cream on a square of gauze and swabbed Savanna's cut. "Linc Norman doesn't want you to expose such a huge campaign contributor."

"He told me Monday when he came to the studio to leave the Westmeyer investigation alone."

"Maybe you should."

She held perfectly still under his ministrations, yet, he could feel a wild adrenaline coursing through her body, making her tremble. An accident could do that. An attempt on your life, even if it wasn't fatal, could rock you to your core.

"Thing is, I smell a bigger story behind all of this," she said. "During my investigation, I came across an email suggesting Westmeyer supplies certain test drugs to the military. I think this story goes a lot deeper than campaign contributions."

Trace forced himself not to tense. "Test drugs? To soldiers?"

"Yeah, but I have nothing solid about that at this point. It's just a theory. I don't know what kind of drugs or who's receiving them. That angle is a dead end at the moment."

He relaxed again. The military had done some experimenting on him and the test drugs were still in his veins even after all of this time. But that program had been shut down.

Or at least that's what he'd been told. Like Command & Control, you never really knew what was the truth and what was a lie.

"Do all the Rock Star bodyguards have first aid training?" Savanna asked, reaching for a safer topic.

"Yes, but mine isn't from the Rock Stars. Got mine courtesy of the Navy."

His admission seemed to shock her. She pulled away from his hand and turned her face toward his. "A sailor, huh? Are you allowed to tell me that?"

The admission shocked him too. "I'll probably have to kill you now."

She grinned and his lower half tightened at the sight of those lips parting over her straight, white teeth.

"No killing allowed." Beatrice swept in, a blueberry smoothie in hand. Maggie, her dog, wagged her tail at Trace. "At least not at the office."

Trace eyed the smoothie. Maybe Reese had been telling the truth about why he was in the vicinity of the accident.

"My cleaner is already at work on your coat," Beatrice told Savanna. "They can get anything out, including blood and vomit."

Savanna flinched and turned to Trace, "I'm so sorry about your shoes."

He glanced down at his sock-clad feet. She'd tried to miss the expensive loafers he'd been wearing, but her violent retching had known no bounds.

"I didn't like them anyway." He looked up at Beatrice. "They pinched my toes. I want boots."

"Fine. We'll get you some boots. You've earned them." She handed him a file. "The information you requested."

Trace led Savanna to the desk as Beatrice took a seat. The two of them plunked down in the chairs across from her. Trace set the file on the desktop and flipped it open.

"It's probably not a complete list," Beatrice said, "but it's the best I can do. By the way, Lieutenant Franklin from DC Metro will be here shortly to take your statements about the accident. I also contacted your producer at the studio, Ms. Jeffries, to let her know you're here. She'd like to speak to you as soon as you're up for it about tonight's show."

"You spoke to Mariah?" Savanna asked.

"I thought it prudent to let her know where you were and that you were being taken care of medically. She was relieved."

"Let me guess, she was worried about my face."

Beatrice graced her with a quick smile. "You're a TV star. Your face is an asset."

Boy, was it. Everything about her was an asset.

Not that he cared. Trace shuffled the papers in front of him. Nine identities on record. Probably more, like Beatrice had mentioned, that no one knew about.

He handed the top sheet to Savanna. "You wanted proof your sister is a spy?"

Accepting the paper, her eyes skimmed the contents. "Megan Spencer, Anna Spence, Michelle Carter, Anna Carter…" She looked up. "These were her undercover names?"

Beatrice nodded. "The ones I could get hold of."

Savanna sat back and chuckled. "Funny."

"What is?" Trace asked.

"Those names, Megan, Spencer, Anna, Michelle, Carter. They're names of her favorite handbags."

Handbags?

At his look of confusion, she handed back the paper. "Her favorite handbag designer is Macabie. They give each design a woman's name. Those names are the names of Parker's favorite Macabie bags."

Trace knew the names of every type of handgun, automatic weapon, and knife in use by the armed forces, but names of purses? No clue. "Were any of these used recently?"

Beatrice wiped the moisture from her smoothie cup. "Not that I've been able to track."

Damn. That would have been too easy but sure would have made his world better. "Who's her handler?"

"I'm working on that," Beatrice said. From the steady look she gave him, he assumed she had an idea but wasn't ready to share it with Savanna.

"What's our next step?" Savanna asked.

Trace closed the file. "Is there anywhere Parker would go to if she were in trouble? Any place from your past? A person she might contact for help?"

"You believe a highly-trained operative like Parker would contact a person from her past or go back to a childhood home?" Beatrice asked, her voice slightly incredulous.

Trace had done his homework on her, Reese, and Petit. She wasn't the only one with sources. "Who did you turn to when Rory Tephra came after you? Who did your husband ask for help in protecting you?"

'Nuff said. She'd gone straight to her husband, estranged at that time, and together they'd gone to Petit. Family and friends.

Beatrice fell silent but a hardness slipped into her eyes before she switched her gaze to Savanna. "Can you think of anyone Parker might turn to? Old friends from high school? University?"

Savanna thought for a moment. "She had lots of friends in high school and college. She was in sports, on the debate team, in the science club, you name it. I couldn't keep up with all of her extra-curriculars, and I never figured out how she did all of that and still graduated valedictorian of her class."

"She wasn't actually involved in all of those activities," Beatrice said, snagging the corner of a paper inside the file and teasing it out to lay it on top of the folder. "They were cover for her internship with the CIA."

"What?" Savanna leaned forward to examine the paper. Her gaze scanned quickly and her mouth hung open. "I don't believe this. How did she keep all of this from me? *Why* did she?"

"She had to," Trace said, feeling slightly sorry for her. It had to suck to know your closest friend and confident, a person who shared your very DNA, had deceived you so expertly. "The CIA requires spies to keep their true job a secret."

"I know that, but..." She closed her eyes and sighed. "She was living a whole separate life none of us knew about."

"It's normal to feel betrayed," Beatrice said and Savanna opened her eyes again.

"Betrayed? I'm amazed. Yeah, I wish she would have at least told me she was working for the CIA back then, but I'm pretty damned impressed she could keep that from me. I knew she was a hell of a sister, but now I know she's one hell of a woman, period."

Trace felt the corner of his mouth lift. Parker wasn't the only one. "The men and women who work for intelligence, no matter what agency, are remarkable individuals."

The phone on Beatrice's desk buzzed. She hit the speaker button. "Yes, Connor?"

"Lieutenant Franklin is here to see Ms. Jeffries."

"Ah, good. Send him in." Beatrice rose. "Coldplay and I will step out and let you speak to Franklin."

Dark blue eyes snapped to his. "Doesn't the officer need to speak to him too?"

"Yes, he'll interview Coldplay separately. For privacy reasons."

The door opened and the receptionist, Connor, motioned a man in a uniform to step through.

"Lieutenant," Beatrice said, crossing the room to shake his hand. "Thank you for agreeing to do the interview here."

Trace started to stand. Savanna grabbed his hand. *Don't leave me*, her eyes said.

Savanna didn't want him to leave. Beatrice, now introducing the cop to both of them, was grabbing Trace's sleeve and pulling him away. "Ms. Jeffries' bodyguard and I will step out for a moment."

Trace, hating himself, gave Savanna's hand a squeeze before withdrawing his. He saw the fear in her eyes. Fear that even a cop couldn't be trusted. "I'll be right outside the door. You need anything, yell."

Savanna's throat contracted and then she nodded.

Beatrice grabbed the folder and her smoothie, leading the way to the still-open door. Maggie followed. Trace did as well, glancing back over his shoulder at Savanna whose eyes were on him instead of the officer asking her questions.

She was right to be paranoid after what had happened. He didn't trust anyone either, even though he knew that Beatrice had no doubt handpicked the cop now sitting in the chair Trace had just vacated.

Beatrice wouldn't allow just anyone into SFI headquarters. Still, Trace stepped into the hallway but left the door cracked open so he could hear what was going on inside.

"I need to speak to you in private," Beatrice said, tilting her head to a conference room across the way.

"I'm staying here."

One brow raised but she didn't argue. From her pants pocket she withdrew her cell phone, punched in a code. "This came across my desk earlier this afternoon."

The screen showed a grainy black and white photograph of a woman, her face turned away from the camera and her whole body slightly out of focus as if she were walking fast when the photo was snapped. "Who is it?"

"Look closely at her surroundings."

Trace felt his insides grow cold. Even though the photo was shitty, he knew those bars, that concrete floor. "Shit."

Beatrice lowered her voice and motioned for him to move a couple steps farther away from the open door. "Facial recognition says it's Parker Jeffries. There is no record of her signing in, yet, as you can make out in the picture, she's wearing an official prison visitor's badge."

"When was that picture taken?"

"The day you escaped."

"So she was still alive. What the hell was she doing there?"

"You tell me."

"I have no idea."

Beatrice tucked the phone away. "Obviously, she went to visit someone."

Trace hated feeling like he was one step behind Beatrice all the time, but damn it, either he was missing something or she was thinking something completely ludicrous. "You think she came to see me."

The brow climbed again. "You sound surprised."

"I don't know her and never met her. Why would she come see me? To apologize for giving Savanna a bullshit story to run that sent me to prison?"

"She's been screwed over by the president and she's most likely figured out you were too."

"And what could I possibly do for her while I was incarcerated?"

"Share your secret? Maybe it's the same one she's keeping."

Trace rocked back on his heels. "Not possible."

"Well, she's looking for you and you're looking for her. I've put out a feeler to the contact Savanna used to find us. He's been off the books for a long, long time. If I hear anything back, you'll be the first to know, but don't hold your breath. Your best bet is to get in touch with Parker. Make it easy for her to find you. Then the two of you can wrap this up—whatever *this* is—with Linc Norman."

He couldn't believe she thought it would be so easy. "Parker and I are both in hiding. It's not like I can call her up and invite her out for coffee."

At that moment, Savanna emerged from the room, the cop on her heels. "We're done," Savanna said, a smile of relief on her face. "Your turn."

"Connor," Beatrice called.

The kid who posed as Beatrice's assistant scrambled from his desk near the lobby. Trace suspected he was more of a bodyguard than he let on. One Callan Reese recruited to act like the slightly incompetent youth who was better at making coffee and working a laptop than he was at security. "Yes, ma'am?"

"Accompany Ms. Jeffries to the dining room so she can get something to eat." To Savanna, Beatrice said, "Coldplay and I will only be a minute with the lieutenant."

Savanna's eyes darted back and forth between all of them, then she nodded. "I could stand to use the ladies room."

"Of course," Connor said. "Right this way. There should be fresh cookies ready in the dining room. The chef makes some every day for our three o'clock break."

"You have your own chef?"

"He was one of Atlanta's most sought after restaurateurs for years. When he retired, we snagged him."

Savanna shot a look at Trace over her shoulder. "Want me to bring you a cookie?"

He didn't want a cookie, but this woman was offering to bring him one.

Kindness. He hadn't experienced much of it, except from the people here in this organization.

Suddenly he wanted a cookie more than anything in the world.

Beatrice nudged him, making him realize everyone was waiting for him to answer. "Um, sure." he said.

As Beatrice and the cop filed into the office, Trace stood for a moment watching Savanna walk away with the kid.

After all the years of kill or be killed, a simple kindness from a beautiful, intelligent woman might be the one thing to do him in.

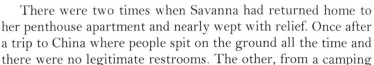

There were two times when Savanna had returned home to her penthouse apartment and nearly wept with relief. Once after a trip to China where people spit on the ground all the time and there were no legitimate restrooms. The other, from a camping trip in Minnesota with Brady where mosquitos as big as cars feasted on her for days.

Today marked the third time.

"Thank you for what you did today," she said to Coldplay as they entered her place.

The ball cap was back on his head, his eyes scanning the living room area and landing on her entertainment center. "Let you end up in a car accident?"

She shrugged off her coat. Beatrice's cleaner had indeed removed all of the bloodstains. "You couldn't have prevented that."

He helped her with the coat, gently sliding it down her arms and off, before hanging it on the nearby hook. She was getting used to his good manners and liked how gentle he was with her even though she was fine. A little tired after the day's events, and unsettled about what they meant, but overall, she felt...

Safe.

That was the purpose of a bodyguard, right? To give you the illusion of safety even if there were certain things they couldn't protect you from.

"Stay here," he said and took that weird gadget he'd used before from his pack of tools.

"You're checking for bugs again?"

"Can't be too careful."

"Even with the new security system?"

He paused and came back to her. "Can I get you something? A glass of water? Maybe wine?"

He had a smudge of chocolate on the corner of his mouth from the cookie she'd brought him at the Rock Star office. She became her mother for a moment and instinctively reached out and wiped it off with her finger. "I can't start drinking this early. I have a show to do tonight."

He tensed at her touch and she realized she'd done something wrong. "You had chocolate..." she pointed at the spot she'd just touched, "in the corner of your mouth."

His hand grabbed her wrist. Not tightly. No, his grip was firm, steadying, but she could break away if necessary. His jaw worked as though he wanted to say something, his intense eyes darkening.

So he didn't like being touched unexpectedly. Another thing to remember.

His gaze dropped to her lips and a shiver of anticipation ran down her spine. The memory of him on top of her in the car, protecting her from the flying glass surfaced. The past few days of him invading her home, her space, sharing in her world while keeping his a secret.

A dangerous warmth started low in her stomach and spread down her legs.

Dangerous. Yep, that was him in a nutshell. Yet, she stood there, staring right back at him, challenging him, because some small, very female part of her wanted to break through his gruff exterior.

He'd showered and changed at the Rock Star offices and the scent of his soap drifted to her. Something lemony with a hint of musk. He simmered with unspent frustration and restrained danger. Who and what was he underneath that chiseled, tough armor? What was the mystery behind the baseball cap and the good manners?

"I won't touch you again," she said softly and his hand started to release her wrist, "unless you want me to."

His grip stilled. She saw the slightest quirk in his left cheekbone as if he were willing himself not to smile. "I don't suppose I can talk you out of doing your show tonight, can I?"

That sexy, low voice of his, the way he was looking at her,

touching her…damn, she'd been without a man far too long. If he kept this up, she'd let him talk her out of anything. Maybe even her clothes.

Cripes, Savanna. You're a walking cliché. The famous personality who falls for her bodyguard.

But she wasn't some flighty Hollywood actress or pop star. "If anything, Coldplay, I'm more determined than ever to break that story tonight."

The quirk of his cheek broke free this time. A tiny smirk touched his lips. "You're not scared of much, are you?"

She was scared of plenty. Didn't mean she gave into it. "The president can threaten me all he wants. I'm going to do my job."

"Just so you know, Rory, our computer genius, was able to get me the HR files on the people who've threatened you publicly or by email. A couple of clear threats, but I doubt any of them have the means to track your movements or do what happened today."

"Wait. This Rory hacked into the studio's files? Why not wait for HR to hand them over?"

"They claimed the files were confidential. I'd need a warrant."

"Seriously? You'd think my okay would be enough."

"We're not done discussing you doing the show tonight," he said, releasing her wrist. His fingers trailed to her hand and he tugged her over to her couch. "This will only take a minute."

His meter came to life as he started scanning her apartment. First the living room, then the kitchen and dining areas. Watching him was rude but she couldn't help herself. He moved with the grace of a dancer, all long limbs and fluidity, but there was always that underlying sense that he could turn deadly in a second. He reminded her of a panther. Sleek, fluid, skilled.

And deadly. Don't forget that.

He'd admitted being in the military. Maybe that was it. *He must have been one hell of a sailor.*

So what was he doing working security details?

With a brief glance at her, he disappeared into her bedroom.

She sat for a moment, debating, then followed.

Her bed was still a crumpled mess from that morning. Her cleaning lady came once a month and the rest of the time, Savanna didn't worry about appearances. No one was ever there, except Parker, to see it anyway.

Now, the unmade bed seemed wrong. Exposed. She had the sudden urge to make it up.

Her gaze followed Coldplay and his device around the room, and she felt heat in her cheeks as he ran it over and under that unmade bed. Then she caught sight of a small monitor on her nightstand. "What's that?" she asked.

"Part of the new system." He picked up a remote lying next to it and tossed it at her. "I thought you might feel safer sleeping if you could see the security camera footage from bed. Check it out."

He headed for the bathroom and she sat on the edge of the bed and hit the power button.

The screen came to life, four pictures blinking onto it. The elevator doors, the fire door, her front door, and the sliding glass doors to her patio.

"The feed is connected to your TV as well, like the living room one I've been watching at night," Coldplay said, returning to the bedroom. He sat next to her, dipping the mattress with his weight. "So if you're watching something in the living room, or in here, you can at any time, switch over to the surveillance cameras to check on things."

He tapped her television remote and her news channel came up. Taking the security remote from her hand, he hit a blue button on it and the TV screen changed to the same one she saw on her monitor.

"The bedroom is your most private and vulnerable space. If you're watching TV and you want to keep an eye on your doors as well," he pointed to the monitor on her nightstand, "you have that option."

"Wow," she managed to say. It was impressive. So was his massive body sitting so close to hers on her messy bed.

He faced her. "When you get your phone back from the store tomorrow, I'll show you the app for accessing this system from anywhere you are."

The cracked screen of her cell phone wasn't its only issue. It had refused to come on at all and Beatrice had said she'd take care of it. Get her a new one.

She'd been wrong about Beatrice in the beginning. Coldplay, Beatrice—all of the staff at Rock Star Security—treated her with respect and as if she were valuable, not for her fame, but as a human being. Coldplay's act of throwing himself across her during the accident was probably just a natural response as her bodyguard, but it seemed like more. The way he'd followed her around on set and looked gobsmacked every time she was made into Savanna Bunkett had made her pulse speed up.

But her favorite moments so far were at night when they'd get home from the studio and make dinner. He was helping her now. He made an awesome Alfredo sauce.

The revelation that she might mean more to him than just a job made her happy. Rock Star Security and Coldplay weren't taking away her independence. Just the opposite. They were empowering her to fight back against the most powerful man in the world. "There's an app I can use to access the system when I'm not home?"

His gaze did that unnerving dip to her lips. "We aim to make our systems effective and efficient for you any place, any time."

Why did that sound faintly like a come on? *Because you want it to be.*

God, what was wrong with her?

Too much stress.

Most people, most businesses, would have run the other way from her problem, but not Coldplay and the RSS team. They'd taken her on without blinking an eye.

She rubbed the tight tendons in her neck. "I take it you didn't find any listening devices?"

"Place is clean." He hit another button on the security remote. "The whole system is tied into the Rock Star Security offices. If anything happens, hit this red button and it will activate staff there. They'll be able to tap into the feed and speak directly to you. They'll contact emergency services if necessary."

They'd gone over the new security system a couple of days ago, and it wasn't all that complicated, but she didn't like the feeling of being spied on. "Are they seeing this live feed?" she asked.

"No, nothing like that. Your privacy is guaranteed. Only by hitting the red button will you allow them to view the feed and see what's going on."

Security. She'd never given it much thought beyond the basics until this past week. The studio sometimes provided a bodyguard or two when she went to live public events, but those security people were nothing like Coldplay. They were more like a showpiece to keep the paparazzi at bay. "Thank you again for all of this."

"Is your neck still bothering you? I can make a call, get a physician to look at it."

"It's just stiff and tight." She didn't mention that that was a common problem with her constant sitting and computer work. "I don't suppose you're a chiropractor?"

Something sizzled between them and she hesitated. She'd never been good at flirting.

Flirting? What the hell was she doing? She wasn't allowed to flirt, and Coldplay didn't seem the flirting type. He was more of the alpha male type who took what he wanted when he wanted it.

Which only stirred her up more.

And didn't that annoy her? She'd never been into gruff, domineering men, so why did this one turn her on?

The mystery, she told herself. She never could resist a good mystery, a little danger, good manners.

Damn. She was a fool.

"I recommend you call the studio," he said, his voice taking on a slightly huskier edge. "Postpone tonight's story. Can they run a previously recorded episode?"

"We can't change the schedule this late. Besides, news is only news for a short window. If I don't go live with the Westmeyer investigation reveal tonight, someone else will jump on it and scoop me."

His eyes were serious, concerned. "It's too dangerous, Savanna."

Her lips curved into a smile. Right now, dangerous seemed pretty damn sexy. "But I have you to protect me."

"The studio lacks proper security and there are too many people milling around."

He liked to control things. People. She learned his looks, his slight nods, the almost invisible shake of his head when he was communicating with her. He was controlling her, that was for sure, and she didn't give a care.

A shiver skittered over her skin. "I'm not letting Linc Norman intimidate me."

Whenever Coldplay didn't like what she said, that telltale tick in his jaw would start up. "There's a time to back down and there's a time to retreat temporarily so you can regroup and live to fight another day."

She was about to respond when her house phone rang, the handset on her nightstand flashing and vibrating. She reached back to grab it. "I can't disappoint my viewers, and the studio will have a fit if I change the schedule this late in the day."

Her hand missed, knocking the phone off its base and sending it skidding across the wooden top. "Oh, shoot."

The handset hit the floor and spun in circles, a high-pitched voice coming from it. "Savanna? Is that you? Are you all right?"

Before she could move to pick up the phone, Coldplay was bending down. He retrieved it and handed it to her, their fingers brushing as Savanna accepted it.

At least it isn't the president, she thought as the voice continued to call her name. But it wasn't far from being the second to the last person Savanna felt like speaking to. "Hi, Mom. What's up?"

Coldplay's eyes stayed on hers as he rose and towered over her.

"Are you all right?" her mother said. "Why didn't you call us?"

From the look on her bodyguard's face, her mother's voice was as loud and grating as Savanna imagined. Coldplay could hear every word.

"I'm fine," she said into the phone, massaging her neck once more with her free hand. No surprise her mother had interrupted the closest thing to fun in her bed in forever. "How did you find out about the accident?"

"I had to hear the news from my television set."

The frigid tone told Savanna what she already knew. She was in deep shit with Mommy Dearest. "I just got home and was about to call you."

Coldplay snatched up the TV remote and hit the power button. Her screen flickered to life with the station's news desk. Her picture was in the corner above nightly news anchor Courtney Collins' shoulder as she rattled off information that was muted.

"We were worried sick," Gloria Jeffries went on. "The phone's been ringing off the hook with people calling to find out if you're okay. Who was that man with you? I saw the video."

As if on cue, Courtney's face was overplayed with a grainy video shot at the scene of the accident. Coldplay and Martin were speaking over the top of the limo.

Savanna's gaze shot to Coldplay's face. *Uh oh.*

The muscle in his jaw was going crazy, his eyes half lidded. The grip on the remote tightened.

"He's my bodyguard," Savanna told her mother. "Have you heard from Parker?"

"Bodyguard? What do you need a bodyguard for? It's not like you're a real celebrity, Savanna. This narcissistic streak of yours is really out of control."

Coldplay turned toward her, his face once again filled with concern.

Great, just what I needed. Not only was her mother calling her a narcissist and condescending to her about her job, Coldplay had overheard her. "Have you heard from Parker?" Savanna repeated.

"What? No. Parker's fine. I know her as well as I know myself. That girl never got in trouble. Never gave me a minute's grief. Stop worrying about her, Savanna, and worry about yourself."

The line went dead.

Savanna hung up and gave Coldplay a *what are you going to do* shrug. "My mother. She has a low opinion of my show." *As well as me.*

He shut off the TV. "Why don't you get some rest? I need to call Beatrice and set up extra security at the studio if you insist on doing tonight's show, but I'll be right outside if you need me. Later, you can fill me in on Westmeyer."

She hadn't noticed her legs were shaking until she'd stood. Her arms suddenly felt like boat anchors. A rest might not be a bad idea. "Sure. Help yourself to the contents of the fridge if you get hungry. There are leftovers from last night."

One corner of his mouth quirked and he gave her a nod that in her Coldplay Dictionary, she thought meant "thanks."

He closed the door softly behind him and Savanna sank back down on her bed. She'd disappointed her parents, lost her sister, and nearly embarrassed herself to death by jumping her bodyguard. A man whom she was forbidden from even knowing his real name.

For someone who seemed to have it all, she felt like quite a loser.

CHAPTER TEN

"I'm on TV," Trace said into his cell phone. "Shit."

Beatrice was, as always, the model of calm. "No one will recognize you. You look totally different than the last time you made the evening news."

He wanted to believe her but didn't. "Facial recognition software can identify me. There are people who've seen me without a beard and Einstein hair."

"Rory is tracking down the digital videos shot from people's phones and has erased most of them via TapShot. He's also erased the stoplight camera footage—there was nothing helpful about the cargo van—and any of the downloaded videos on people's YouTube channels. The single video that remains is the one the news channels possess. It was shot from a distance and the footage is grainy. You have your hat on. I don't believe anyone would recognize you."

"Linc Norman will."

"President Norman already knows you've escaped Witcher and that Savanna has hired a bodyguard. Knowing your skill set and the fact she's not backing down, if I were him, I'd be concerned. I'd want confirmation that the two of you weren't working together."

There was a suggestion in her voice. An idea she was patiently leading him too. "You think the assassin was after me?"

"I think he or she was sent to confirm whether you are now working as Savanna's bodyguard."

"And I played right into their hands."

"Your job was to protect her, and that's exactly what you did."

"If what you're suggesting is true, being with me puts her in more danger. The exact opposite of what I was supposed to do."

"She hasn't figured out who you are yet, has she?"

He didn't respond.

"You need to come clean, Trace. For her sake and for yours. The two of you together make a powerful weapon against the president."

"She insists on doing the show tonight."

"That surprises you?"

Not really. "The studio is too open with too many unknowns. I need backup."

"Of course. How many men do you need?"

They discussed the logistics and Trace hung up. He propped his hands on the table in the hall and ground his teeth. He should have left this assignment when he had the chance. Instead, he'd let misguided feelings of honor and his instant attraction to Savanna cloud his judgment. She could have been really hurt in the accident because of *him*, not because Norman was trying to scare her.

"Coldplay?" Savanna stood in the doorway to her apartment, dressed in her usual workout attire. A little black number with shocking pink stripes molded to her knockout body like a second skin. "I can't sit still. I need to blow off some steam."

A dozen different scenarios ran through his mind, every one of them involving her naked. "What do you suggest?"

Her eyes darted around and she looked flustered. Her fingers toyed with the towel she carried and she almost smiled. "This complex has a nice exercise room. I go there to use the bikes and treadmill when the weather is bad."

He didn't like crowds and an equipment room could be crowded. Outside in the open was worse, regardless of the cold. But the accident had shaken her up even if she was pretending it hadn't. He understood her need to release some of that anxiety. "Let me check the security first."

"This time of day, the residents are all at work. No one's in there. I'll have the place to myself."

Seeing her running in that outfit was going to be quite a distraction, but if the place was empty of other people…

He punched the elevator button. "We'll check it out. If I

don't like it, we come back here. I'll put you through some paces."

Savanna closed the door behind her and this time her smile totally broke free. "Deal," she said as she walked past him and entered the elevator.

In the enclosed space, he leaned against the railing and discreetly looked down on the top of her head. Her hair was pulled up in a ponytail again and smelled nice. The bandage on her neck reminded him to not get distracted before she even got on a treadmill. "How's the neck?"

The ponytail swung as she looked up at him. "No big deal. I'm sure you've had much worse injuries in your line of work."

He'd been shot multiple times and stabbed as well, but that wasn't the job she was talking about. He normally didn't guard a life; he took them.

"You never explained how you called for help *during* the accident," she said.

He caught their reflections in the shiny door, her so much shorter than him and at least sixty pounds lighter. Another floor went by, the light over their heads blinking from one number to the next.

"I have a button on my watch." He held up his wrist for her to inspect the high-tech gadget. "It sends out my coordinates to headquarters and an SOS signal. I was thinking about pushing it right before we were hit."

"Because of the president's phone call. You took it as a threat."

"He *is* a threat."

"But how did you know someone was going to run into us?"

"I didn't." How could he explain? "Not specifically. I had a gut feeling you were in imminent danger."

"That's the second time I've heard that term this week." The elevator dinged softly upon their arrival to the first floor. "I know my situation is serious, but this all seems so...surreal."

Trace punched the button to hold the doors closed. "You know the drill. Stay here and let me check things out."

She gave a single head bob to acknowledge her agreement. He stood in front of her, opened the doors, and saw nothing to make him suspicious. The grand entrance was devoid of people except for the clerk behind the curved marble check-in desk and the middle-aged doorman at the revolving doors up front.

Trace did a full scan anyway, noting every entrance and exit, every light, window, and piece of furniture. Years had passed since doing a mental inventory of every space had been ingrained in his system, but it had never failed to help him down the road. There were many places and situations where you couldn't take a gun or a knife. An assassin wasn't limited to standard weapons. Trace could kill with a stick of furniture or a shoestring. A sharpened pencil worked just as well as a bullet in some circumstances.

"Clear," he said. There were no signs designating the direction of the gym, but he'd studied the blueprints of the building. He motioned her toward the west hallway. "Stay behind me and be ready to move on my command."

"Wow," she said. "I feel like I'm in a Bourne movie."

Trace lost his step for half a second. If only she knew where Robert Ludlum had come up with the idea for Operation Treadstone. The real operation had been called Deadline, but it had spawned Command & Control's ultimate group of assassin warriors, of which he was the third generation.

"The movies are good," he said, stopping outside the door to the gym. "The books are better."

"You've read them?"

"Does that surprise you?"

"I guess it shouldn't. It's just you don't look like a guy who spends much time at home with a book."

The gym was as upscale as the rest of the building, a separate one-story wing with skylights, plenty of space between machines, and high-end equipment in pristine condition. Mirrors ran along the walls, interspersed with windows that overlooked a covered pool and, beyond that, a garden area. Even in the grip of early winter, the garden was peaceful and tranquil.

"See?" Savanna said, walking past him. "Empty."

She was right. It appeared not many of the residents took advantage of the treadmills, bikes, and weight machines. Large screen TVs hanging in every corner were turned off and a shelf unit stood against the wall between the men's and women's changing rooms full of undisturbed, fluffy white towels.

His mental scan revealed nothing out of the ordinary, although there were plenty of places for hidden cameras. He locked the door behind them. "I'm going to check out the locker rooms. Be right back."

"Knock before you enter the women's. I don't need old lady Zukaski yelling at me over you invading her privacy."

Trace gave her an inquisitive look.

Savanna headed for a stationary bike and started hitting buttons on the computer panel between the handlebars. "First floor, apartment 3," she said. "She's in her seventies and is hard of hearing, but likes to swim before lunchtime. She should be out of here by now, but just in case."

He definitely didn't need to surprise an elderly woman in the shower or scar his own retinas with that image. "Thanks for the heads-up."

As instructed, he made sure to warn anyone inside the women's locker room before he entered. Both it and the men's were empty.

The security check was quick, but by the time he returned, Savanna had already worked up a sweat on the bike. She was spinning like a mad woman, total focus on the screen in front of her as she climbed some digitalized version of a hilly landscape.

Trace hung back in one corner where he could watch. The door was locked, the entire wing empty. Beatrice had already contacted the building manager about upgrading security at the service doors, and she was lining up a couple of Rock Star guards to help him out tonight at the studio. He'd showered and changed before they'd left the office, popping in new contacts, and shaving. He was ready for the next twenty-four hours, and for a minute, he could drop his hypervigilence and breathe.

The spinning of the bike's wheels was hypnotic. The movement of Savanna's long, sculpted legs mesmerizing. Her ass stood out like a neon sign with the bright pink spandex stretched over it, her back leaning forward as she gripped the handlebars. Once again, Trace's mind went to fantasyland where she was naked, leaning over her bed for him.

Or maybe the back of her couch, or hell, maybe braced against the wall of the elevator while he took her right there.

God, he hadn't fucked anyone in so long, his mind was on overload. A bulge the size of Kansas appeared down below.

All she had to do was look up and catch him gawking at her in the mirrors and…

He started to force his gaze away but too late. She lifted her head, her gaze zeroing right in on him.

Jerking his focus away, he discreetly crossed his hands in

front of the bulge and acted like he was inspecting the stair master machine next to him.

"So we're at a dead end with Parker?" she said over the whir of the bike.

"Not yet. Her aliases haven't been used recently, but that means she's using a different one we don't know about. Smart, if you think about it. We're probably not the only ones looking for her and she doesn't know who she can trust."

"Or she's been kidnapped by the president and is being held somewhere."

"Think about it," Trace told her. "The president wants you to drop the Westmeyer investigation and he's willing to go to extremes to do it, but he's never once threatened you with Parker."

"What do mean?"

He wanted to tell her that Parker was running around free, but he couldn't. Not without divulging too much about himself. Still, he couldn't stand the idea of Savanna continuing to worry that her sister was dead or, at the very least, held captive. "If he had Parker, why wouldn't he use her to blackmail you into canceling the show tonight?"

He saw the light dawn behind her eyes. "So maybe he doesn't have her. But then, where is she?"

That he couldn't say. Parker had been on his trail at Witcher, but hopefully, his trail was still cold and she would have as difficult a time discovering his whereabouts as Norman.

If Parker had seen the news about Savanna's car accident, surely she'd make contact soon if she could to make sure Savanna was okay. Unless… "I think a more likely scenario is that President Norman is threatening to harm you if she doesn't do what he wants and that's why she's disappeared. She's on a mission for him and that entails staying away from you."

"Me? Why?"

"You're a dangerous person who could do a lot of damage to his future, Savanna, and you're fearless. Parker knows something the president doesn't want you to know, so he's keeping her away from you."

Her expression hardened. "He can't keep her away from me forever."

"Do you and Parker have any secret code words or nicknames for each other? Or a secret hand gesture you do when you're on air that only she understands?"

"You mean like that Carol Burnett thing where she would tug on her earlobe at the end of every show as a secret 'I love you' to her family?"

"Yeah. Like that."

"No, but…"

"But what?"

She slowed the spinning. "When we were growing up and my parents threw parties, we had a secret code to help each other out. If I was stuck with one of my father's cronies who was talking philosophy or something else equally boring, I would tap the top of my head or play with my necklace. Parker would intercede and say she needed me for something. If she was stuck in a group of my mother's friends and needed a break, she would do something with her hair. If it was up, she'd let it down, or if it was down for the party, she'd pull it up in a ponytail. I'd pretend to feel sick or say the dog ran away or whatever, and we'd take off. It was our own little SOS system that only broke down if we were both caught in a group we couldn't break away from."

"Tonight on your show, try it. Tap your head at the end or play with your necklace. See if it gets her to break her silence."

"You think she's watching me?"

"Worth a try."

Brow furrowed, Savanna didn't speak or break pace for the next twenty minutes. After the bike ride, she grabbed a yoga mat and a towel and made a space in front of one of the mirrors.

He couldn't help it, her slow, graceful moves as she went through a sun salutation drew his attention and kept it. Gone was the TV reporter and in its place was simply a beautiful woman stretching her body.

She was fluidity in motion, arms and legs moving to their own inner rhythm, her body folding and stretching and balancing in a dance that left his pants even more constricted. Several times, her gaze flowed to his and away as if she expected his voyeurism and it didn't bother her in the least. She wanted him to watch.

Such a fucking turn-on.

It probably didn't bother her for him to watch. At one time, she'd been on stage, performing as an athlete in front of thousands of spectators. A world stage. While he'd always hung in the shadows performing his job, she'd been on display for the whole world to see. Still was. A part of him envied her confidence, her willingness to be seen.

"Would you like to join me?" she said, catching him off guard as she flowed through a warrior pose sequence.

Join her? He'd like to take her to the floor and strip off that spandex. Explore every inch of her with his mouth and his tongue. "No, thank you."

"Yoga isn't a real sport, is that it? You're such a buff guy, you don't need yoga?"

For him, yoga *wasn't* a sport. It was more. A means to keep his body in shape and his mind from dark thoughts while inside Witcher. "I'm afraid doing asanas in a suit would be difficult."

Her eyes cut to his as she performed a side bend. "You get points for using the term but I doubt the clothes are what's holding you back. I bet your hamstrings are so tight, you can't touch your toes."

She was throwing down a challenge.

And damn if he didn't want to accept it.

Pinching his lips together to keep from smiling, he shrugged out of his jacket and tossed it on the nearby machine. Loosening his tie, he undid the top button of his shirt and untucked the tails.

Savanna slowed her routine, watching him with wide eyes. It appeared that although he wouldn't be surprising old lady Zukaski today, he might be surprising someone entirely more important.

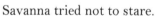

Savanna tried not to stare.

And failed miserably.

With his suit coat on, Coldplay appeared broad and beefy. Without it, she saw, he was pure muscle.

The tailored white shirt was strained to capacity as he tugged off his tie and rolled the sleeves. A corded neck showed from the V at the top of the shirt where he'd unbuttoned one button.

She licked her lips, checking the side of her mouth for drool. The action caught Coldplay's attention and he stopped mid-roll, his eyes locking on her mouth.

"Who are you going to invite for coffee?" she asked, trying to sound nonchalant while heat bloomed low in her belly. She wanted him. She couldn't deny it.

Sick. She was sick. The man was trying to protect her from danger and all she could think about were his eyes, so guarded and scared. Not scared he couldn't keep her safe. Scared he might actually like her.

He was an expert at his job, but he sucked at hiding his desire for her. She could use that to her advantage.

He'd been watching her nonstop and it had become a game to her to see how far she could push him. The bike ride had done its job to reduce her anxiety over the accident and warm her muscles for a good yoga stretch. The bonus had been watching him watch her.

Now she wanted more. She wanted him close, wanted him to tell her something, anything about himself.

She wanted more than his eyes on her.

He could make her forget, if only for a little while, this mess she was in.

"Coffee?" he said. "You lost me."

"Back at the office. You were talking to Beatrice about inviting someone for coffee. I was going to suggest The Steam. It's a new cafe a few blocks from here. Everything they do is organic, fair-trade, etcetera, and the place has a sophisticated Parisian flair. Excellent chocolates and cakes. Nice, quaint. Perfect for a first date or whatever."

He'd finished rolling his sleeves and ducked his head, one corner of his mouth quirking as he kicked off his shoes. "I'm not inviting anyone out for coffee, or on a first date, but thanks for the suggestion."

"Oh, sorry. You're probably already in a relationship."

His face came up, the quirk now a full smile. "Are we doing this or what?"

Real smooth, Savanna. Her fishing expedition into his relationship status had failed. He truly wasn't giving anything away.

Except the bulge in his pants was still there, and, oh my, what a nice bulge it was. Yoga was all about living in the moment, and it was time she did just that.

She stood in mountain pose, trying not to stare at his body in the mirror, and started to direct him how to breathe when he stopped her.

"If you're going to challenge me to a showdown," he said, "you better put your money where your mouth is."

A bet? "You're already costing me my future beach house in the Bahamas, but since I'm sure I'm going to win this 'showdown' as you call it, fine. You do all the poses I show you and I'll buy you coffee at The Steam. If you don't, I get to ask one personal question and you have to answer truthfully. And not tell Beatrice."

He chuckled. "If you win, I'll answer your question and keep it a secret from Beatrice. If I win, you'll cancel tonight's show."

"What? No way. I already told you I can't, and won't, back down from Linc Norman's demands."

"What are you worried about?" The grin on his face was pure smirk. His tone, teasing. "You just stated you were going to win this showdown."

The cocky confidence sent up a warning flag. Did he seriously know yoga? She'd soon find out. "I'm doing tonight's show. That's not on the table."

The smirk turned into a genuine smile that about knocked her off her feet. "I admire your determination, and I accept your original bet. You win and I'll tell you anything you want to know. I win, you buy me a coffee."

It was said softly but with such conviction, she knew he wasn't lying. She had to win the bet. One question wasn't nearly enough—she had so many—but she had to win so she could at least find out his name.

"We'll start with a sun salutation to get you warmed up. I wouldn't want you to pull a muscle or anything."

He faced the mirror so they were side by side. "Let's do it."

Ten minutes later, she had taken him through multiple salutations, downward facing dogs, planks, warrior one, two, and three, and even crow pose. His muscular arms held his body with no problem. His big leg muscles handled tree pose and crane without issue.

Who is this guy?

She was winded and sweating, searching her brain for a pose he couldn't do. He looked like he'd stepped out of a Men's Health fashion shoot and was ready for anything she could throw at him.

"Where did you learn to do this?" she huffed as she took him into wheel pose.

He met her upside down gaze in the mirror. "I don't believe you've won the bet yet, Ms. Jeffries."

Smart ass.

"Besides," he continued, not out of breath at all. "You wouldn't believe me if I told you."

She breathed through her nose and tried to relax into the backbend. He was a competitive guy, if secretive, but she was an expert at her job. "I've heard about every unbelievable story you can imagine. You can't shock or surprise me."

He let himself down from his backbend and leaned across the mat to place his hand on her mid-back, supporting her spine so her stomach could rise higher. "My last residence, I had a neighbor who was raised in India. His mother had studied under some of the most well-known yogis and he went along. Picked up a lot of stuff that made him a strong, centered guy. In turn, he taught me a few things."

Her arms were shaking, her knees starting to protest. Yet, she couldn't move. His hand on her back sent a shock of warmth straight to that spot in her low belly, and from there down between her legs.

"You're very supple," he said, and his eyes held the promise of something inviting.

She lowered herself to the mat, his hand moving out of the way. "You're not so bad yourself."

He started unbuttoning his shirt. "Shall we take it up a notch?"

Heat flooded her cheeks. She nearly panted. "What do you have in mind?"

Damn, her voice sounded husky, seductive. He took her hand, pulling her to her feet. "I like inversions. They get the blood and circulation flowing back to the brain."

He stripped off the shirt and tossed it aside. Savanna's jaw dropped. His body was a sculpted masterpiece from shoulders to the narrow sides of his waist. Several tattoos adorned his upper arms and back. A few scars too.

With unbridled ease, Coldplay went into a handstand. "I can hold this pose for an hour. How about you?"

Showoff. There was no way she could hold a handstand for an hour, but hell if she wasn't going to try. She flipped up onto her hands, using her core to keep her from going over. "I've never timed myself, but I meditate this way. Guess we'll see who can hold it the longest."

He chuckled again, the sound sending shivers up and down her damp skin. She'd known him less a week and he was already the most fascinating person she'd ever met.

And the awful truth was, he knew just about everything worth knowing about her and she knew nothing about him. Yet, here she was, letting him into her world, trusting him with her deepest fears. That thought should have scared her, but it didn't.

Instead, she felt safe, secure, and happy for the first time since Parker had disappeared. As she adjusted her weight on her hands, she actually laughed out loud.

"What?" he said, completely still. His control was amazing.

Sneaking a peek at him and his amazing body, she admitted the truth. "I haven't been this happy, this carefree, in a long time."

And that was no bunk.

CHAPTER ELEVEN

Savanna owed him coffee. Trace hoped he would get to take her up on the offer.

Of course, the way his life usually went, that was a pipe dream. A relationship wasn't in the cards for him. His past was too much to share with anyone, even if he wasn't sworn to secrecy. And the moment Savanna figured out who he really was, she'd most likely try to kill him.

But the image of the two of them as nice, normal people going out for coffee wouldn't leave him alone. Another fantasy to add to his growing pile.

A new limo with a different driver arrived to take Savanna to the studio at six, with Lindsey once again inside. The assistant had called earlier and told Savanna the station manager had suggested she take the night off. Savanna had refused.

The woman had balls.

He helped Savanna into the car, taking the seat across from her and the assistant. Once they went two blocks and rounded a corner, he signaled the new driver to pull over.

"What's going on?" Lindsey said.

Savanna echoed her question. "Is something wrong?"

Trace exited the car, saw Petit's big, black Escalade pull in behind them. He leaned down and reached for Savanna's hand. "New security measure."

She took his hand and slid out without question, while Lindsey protested. "I don't understand," she said. "What are we doing?"

Emit Petit, dressed all in black and wearing black shades jumped out of the Escalade and opened the door to the backseat. Trace stopped Lindsey. "You go on in the limo. We'll escort Ms. Bunkett to the studio."

He shut the door on her next question and knocked on the roof of the car. The limo pulled away.

Trace hustled Savanna into the Escalade, climbing into the backseat with her. A second later, Emit resumed his seat up front and they pulled away from the curb, heading for the studio by means of a different route.

"Smooth," Savanna said. "Why didn't you tell me you were planning this?"

Trace shrugged. "I like to keep you on your toes."

She laughed. "You really think someone might try to ram the limo again?"

"We're not taking chances."

Her face went serious, as if she were remembering the accident that had taken place only a few hours ago. "Are Lindsey and the driver in danger?"

Emit spoke up. "I've got a security detail following them to head off any suspicious activity. They'll be safe."

Savanna leaned forward and stuck out her hand. "Savanna Jeffries, otherwise known as Savanna Bunkett."

Emit crossed an arm over his shoulder and did a pseudo-shake. "Emit Petit."

"*You're* Emit Petit? Nice to finally meet you."

"Sorry I couldn't get away the other day to speak to you in person."

"I guess it all worked out," she said, flashing those blue eyes at Trace.

"The stuff you wanted is in here." Emit handed Trace a black briefcase. "Including the GPS tracker and the background checks you requested. I ran my TracMap system on all of the players, like you asked, including the sister. Nothing in particular stands out to me, but she runs in some interesting circles. Circles you're more familiar with. Maybe you'll pick up on something I missed."

TracMap was Petit's people-mapping program that showed relationships between people and groups they belonged to. It was similar to the NSA's Net Map, which was used to track everything from human trafficking networks to targeted digital attacks on government and financial websites. "Thanks, man."

Trace took the briefcase and opened it on his lap. Savanna stared at the thing as if it were a bomb.

First, he handed her a new phone, designed by Rory and field-tested by Cal Reese. It looked like her old phone, but had a couple more apps that would keep her safe. He pointed them out. "This app looks like a game, but it's actually an enhanced tracking system so that even if the phone is turned off, or the device is broken, submerged in water, or exposed to extreme temperatures, I'll still be able to track it." He pointed to the second icon. "And this one is the security app that works with your home system."

"Does it have the same number?"

"Absolutely."

She checked her call log and messages. There were several of each, but she seemed disappointed and ignored them.

Still hoping for her sister to contact her.

Trace withdrew a small velvet box and cracked the lid to reveal a set of diamond studs. "I want to make sure I can find you at all times. In case you lose the phone or it's stolen, these earrings contain tiny GPS chips. Put them in your ears."

"Afraid I'll get lost?"

The joke landed flat. Her fingers trembled as she switched out her silver hoops for the diamond studs.

Taking her hand, he held it and stroked the skin between her thumb and first finger. "Savanna, I won't let anything happen to you. These are precautions. I always take precautions, always think ahead. That's why I'm an expert at my job."

The trembling eased. She smiled and gave his hand a squeeze. "I trust you."

"Good." He didn't want to turn loose of her so he used his other hand to take out a tiny plastic bag of more trackers. "We're going to put one of these in your bra, your shoes, and your watch."

"My bra? Seems like overkill."

"Clothes and accessories can be removed or damaged. The more trackers I have on you, the more likely I am to find you. If I had my way, I'd inject a GPS tracker under your skin."

One of her pretty arched eyebrows quirked and she released his hand. "Give me those. How do I attach them?"

The spunk was back in her voice. He liked that. For the next several minutes as Emit wove his way through DC traffic,

Trace hid the tracking devices in her left shoe and inside her expensive watch.

And then it was time for the bra. He handed her the tracker.

"Here?" she asked as she touched her left bra cup.

"Not near your heart. It's highly unlikely, but the electric pulses the device gives off could interfere with your normal heartbeat."

"Great." She made an exasperated sound and moved it to the right side, sliding it under the bra's fabric. "So here? It sort of cuts into my skin."

She was holding open her shirt and bearing her cleavage. The tops of her luscious breasts peeked out over her pink sports bra. He tried not to look—or rather, to look only where she was pointing—but that was impossible. There was nothing remotely sexy about the bra, but damn if it didn't support those heavy mounds perfectly and make him ogle.

His fingers itched to touch her, even if it was only to direct where the tracker should go. "I, um, why don't you put it…" he touched the fabric in between her breasts, "here."

"Oh, okay." She fiddled with it and dropped the tracker into her lap. "Crap."

Retrieving it, she handed it to him. "Maybe you better do it. I can't seem to get it to attach to the material."

Trace felt eyes on him and glanced up to see Emit copping a peek. Annoyed, he leaned over and blocked the man's view as he took the tracker and zeroed in on the tiny area of bra between her tantalizing breasts.

Her skin was warm, a tiny gasp escaping her lips as he touched her.

"How's that?" he said. "Too invasive?"

She didn't say anything and he glanced up to meet her eyes. They were round in her face, a seductive curve to her lips that were only a few inches from his. The brim of his ball cap was nearly touching her forehead. "It's…uh…" She shifted ever so slightly under his fingers. "Can you move it a little to the right?"

Swallowing the sudden wedge in his throat and ignoring the tightness in his pants, he did what she asked without taking his eyes off her face.

His voice came out low and rough. "Better?"

Her hand came up to cover his, her fingers moving between the fabric and his fingers, guiding him. "I think maybe…here."

"Whatever feels good," he said, and the curve of her lips grew.

Emit cleared his throat from the front seat. "Everything okay back there?"

"Yes," Savanna said, her voice sexy and rough. She cleared her throat. "We're good."

As Trace started to draw away, she clenched his hand again, leaned forward, and kissed the corner of his mouth. "Thank you," she murmured. "For everything."

It took every fiber of his being not to kiss her back. Hard. To resist taking those full lips between his teeth and sucking on them. To not let his hands touch and squeeze and tweak those beautiful breasts of hers.

He licked his lips at the thought and saw her gaze drop to his mouth. "Just doing my job," he said.

And then he forced himself back upright, shifting the briefcase to cover his raging hard-on as he started pulling out files.

Savanna's phone rang and she glanced at the screen. "It's Lindsey."

She finished buttoning her shirt as she cupped the phone between her ear and shoulder. "I know," she said to Lindsey. "I'm sorry...yes, I'm fine."

Trace could hear Lindsey's voice through the phone, upset about Savanna's abrupt departure and rattling off a change of plans.

"What?" Savanna said. "I can't do that. I *won't* do that. The Hopland segment isn't ready."

"*I spoke to Hopland and I have a script for you. I was going to go over it in the car with you and then your bodyguard screwed it all up,*" Trace heard Lindsey say. "*What's his deal, anyway?*"

"He's protecting me. That's what I hired him to do. It's his job."

"*Protecting you from who? Me?*"

"He believes the accident today wasn't an accident. That someone tried to hurt me."

"*Oh, jeez! Who would do that?*"

"I don't know," Savanna lied, "but like I said, he's doing his job. And my job is to follow through on the Westmeyer investigation. So while I appreciate your work on getting a decent Hopland script up and running, I won't be needing it tonight."

Savanna disconnected the phone. Trace pretended to be engrossed in his files. Which he sort of was.

"You ran background checks?" Savanna said, fiddling with her phone.

"Those who interact with you everyday."

"Why?" She lowered her voice a notch. "We know who's after me."

"He has minions. And not the cute cartoon kind."

"And you think one of these minions is watching me."

Randy, the doorman, seemed innocuous. *Definitely keeping an eye on him.* Trace closed his file and opened the next one, the building manager. "Probably more than one. What's up with work?"

She let go of a tight sigh. "The station manager is upset I didn't take the night off and now he's pressuring the show's producer to cancel the piece on Westmeyer and run the Hopland show instead."

"The president got to him."

"Well, dammit. You think so? God, I detest that man." She shook her head. "But I'm not giving in. I refuse to be intimidated, and besides, the Hopland story isn't ready and I won't air anything until I've fully done my homework on it."

Except apparently when it came to him.

Trace kept that thought to himself.

Lindsey's file was next. Beatrice had red-flagged her college attendance with a note in the margin. Trace didn't like coincidences. "Did you know Lindsey attended Vassar at the same time Parker did?"

"No."

"She majored in Russian Studies. What did your sister study? Something about brains, wasn't it?"

Savanna nodded. "Cognitive Science with a double major in Behavioral Science."

Trace glanced at her. "Doubtful the two of them ran in the same circles."

"You think Lindsey is in on this?" Savanna chuckled. "I can't see her being a spy for the president. She's extremely organized and efficient, but doesn't strike me as someone you would trust with government secrets."

"Why would someone with a degree in Russian Studies work at a cable news station?"

"She's the niece of Executive Producer, Mariah Olsen.

Mariah took pity on her when she couldn't find a job. I'm sure there aren't many that require a Russian Studies degree."

"Except maybe at the CIA."

Savanna's face blanched. "Oh, crap. I hadn't thought of that. Do you think she's in on this with Linc Norman?"

He scanned the rest of the notes. "There's nothing else here that suggests she's anything but what she says she is. No travel to foreign countries, no other jobs except for some waitressing in college. She has two cats, no car, and hasn't dated since a long-term relationship with her high school sweetheart ended six months ago."

"She was seeing someone? I didn't even know she had cats, much less a boyfriend." Savanna glanced out the window, still fingering the phone as if she regretted being curt with the gal a moment before. "I haven't been very nice to her. I should make her brownies or something. She likes chocolate. That I *do* know."

Trace smiled down at the papers in his hand. Savanna was this big superstar who didn't even realize her fame. She tipped the doorman twice the going rate and fixed meals for near complete strangers who showed up on her doorstep two hours late. "I'm surprised you haven't already. Why is it you don't like her?"

"I do like her. Well, sort of. I *try* to like her. She's just so…"

"Over the top?"

"In this business, that's status quo. I'm not sure what it is exactly. Just a feeling. We don't click, you know?"

He nodded. "The 80/20 rule."

"The what rule?"

"Eighty percent of the people you meet you click with. They like you, you like them. The other twenty percent, you don't click with. No matter what you do to change or do things their way, they will never like you and vice versa."

"Now you sound like Parker. She's always got some scientific reason for why people don't get along. Why criminals do what they do and the best ways to prevent that behavior."

Sounded like he and Parker had a few things in common. Except his job was to stop the criminals *after* they'd done the crime. "Has Lindsey ever done anything to make you suspicious?"

Savanna thought for a moment. "No."

Trace moved onto the next file. "Let me know if you think of anything."

She was still staring out the window, her countenance clouded. "I can't really trust anyone, can I?"

You can trust me. But he didn't say it out loud.

Because, really, the truth was, he was the biggest liar of them all.

Six blocks from the studio, Parker pulled the limo over.

The drivers of the cars tailing her were good, but she'd spotted them. They probably didn't expect the limo driver to be acutely aware of every car in the three block radius.

But she was.

"I told her she couldn't do the Westmeyer segment," Savanna's assistant said into her phone. "She insisted she is, so be prepared."

Westmeyer. The name made Parker sick to her stomach. She had to stop her sister from stepping her toes into that murky sludge of quicksand. Parker knew all too well there was no coming back from it.

The assistant's head came up and she looked around. "Driver? This isn't the studio." She returned to her phone. "I know, I know. She's stubborn, but maybe if the big guns all talk..." A pause ensued. "Fire her? You can't fire her. The network's ratings—"

Parker kept the black chauffeur's cap low on her forehead. They would fire her sister without blinking an eye. They—the ones behind all of this—would do worse than that. If only the man with Savanna hadn't screwed up Parker's plans to talk to her.

"She's coming by a different car," Lindsey said to the person on the other end of the phone conversation. "Her bodyguard didn't want to take chances on a repeat from earlier. You'll have to intercept her once she's in the lot."

Parker grabbed her gun from under the seat and flicked off the safety.

The assistant hung up and leaned forward. "Driver, what are you doing?"

Parker had seen the news about Savanna's accident. The wolves were closing in. "The man with Ms. Bunkett. What was his name?"

"Her bodyguard? Total stud, right? He doesn't have a name." Lindsey started tapping her phone's screen. "You're going to make me late. We need to go."

Parker wanted to rub her tired eyes. Or maybe bang her head on the steering wheel.

Savanna was about to get hit with a hailstone, especially if she did the Westmeyer story, but the bodyguard...he might not be who he seemed. "The man has to have a name."

"What?"

"I said, the man has to have a name. What is it?"

"Why do you care?"

"Just answer the question. What is his name and what security firm does he work for?"

"I don't think that's any of your business and if you don't put this car in gear and get me to the studio in the next five minutes, I'm going to call your boss and report you."

Parker turned in the seat, leveling her small, black handgun at the assistant's face. "His name. Please."

The girl went rigid, the cell phone in her hand dropping into her lap. "Coldplay."

"What?"

"He goes by Coldplay. Savanna isn't allowed to know his real name or ask him any personal stuff."

Coldplay. "So he works for the Rock Stars?"

The gal nodded. "Are you going to shoot me?"

Parker hit the unlock button on the door and motioned with her gun. "Get out."

"But..."

"Get. Out."

"It's freezing out there!"

God. She didn't want to shoot this pain in the ass but... Parker gave the assistant a dead serious look and put both hands back on the gun. "Are you right-handed?"

The woman swallowed and nodded.

"You like walking?"

"I don't have a car so I bike when the weather is decent. Better for the environment, too."

Kill me now. "Well, I'm going to count to three. If you're not out of this car, I will shoot you in your right shoulder. If you don't get out then, I'll shoot you in your left knee. Your right hand will be useless and you won't be able to walk or bike for a long time. One...two..."

The woman bailed, fumbling with her phone on the way out.

Parker didn't even wait for her to shut the door. She peeled away and headed south. Trace Hunter had disappeared and Savanna's safety was at risk. Staying in hiding was no longer an option. Parker had to do something.

Two options and only two. Do the job Linc Norman had commanded her to do or expose the nation's leader for the scumbag he was.

She couldn't kill her fellow scientists, regardless of what the president threatened to do to her and her family. But no one would believe her about Project 24 unless she had proof. Proof that the program had gone too far, created more problems than it had solved. All but one file had been destroyed; the soldiers selected for the experiment were all dead.

Except Hunter.

Parker drove on, the White House an imposing figure off to her left as orange rays of the setting sun made it look like it was glowing from some internal fire.

The fires of hell. If Parker wanted Savanna and her parents to live, she had to kill the three scientists who had been on her team. None of them knew all the details about Project 24—they thought it was just another experiment with soldiers to see if they could train their cognitive responses the way the armed forces trained their physical responses. Each scientist had handled one section of the experiment, but put them all together and they knew enough to be dangerous. A dangerous group Linc Norman didn't want falling into the wrong hands.

The experiment, funded by Westmeyer, Inc., hadn't worked except for Navy SEAL Trace Hunter. His reflexes had been off the charts and he hadn't experienced negative side effects. His ability to out think the enemy was staggering. He'd been her brightest star, her best pupil, and yet, she'd never met him face to face. Like any good scientist, she'd stayed objective, only reading about his outcomes from the comfort of her desk.

She'd given the okay to turn him loose. He was going to secretly make history by eliminating threats to America with the speed and efficiency of a one-man army.

The experiment was initially deemed a success as Hunter took out more than thirty threats in the span of six months. Each looked like an accident, a suicide, a natural death.

And then he'd refused a direct order. That's when Parker learned that the other participants, the ones who'd experienced negative outcomes, had all been terminated. On orders of the president himself.

She wasn't supposed to know. No one was.

Parker didn't know what order Lt. Hunter had refused to carry out, but something in Hunter's psychological makeup made him defy the president, defy the elusive and ominous Command & Control. He didn't go AWOL, just came back from the mission and met with Norman behind closed doors. Whatever happened in there, the president emerged and ordered Hunter's incarceration. The next thing Parker knew, Norman had her hand Savanna the file on Hunter exposing him as a traitor, and Parker was being told to quietly eliminate the scientists on her team.

Or else.

Like Hunter, she'd been trained to kill, but unlike him, she'd never expected to have to do it. She was an analyst, a scientist. Yes, she'd done undercover ops, extracting sensitive information from specific targets, but only from men and women like herself—scientists developing programs for their countries to increase the value of soldiers in the field. Every major country in the world was working on similar experiments, but none had the pharmaceutical drug cocktails Westmeyer did.

At first, Parker had resisted using the drugs, but her outcomes were dismal. She knew the experiment would work, but time was of the essence if she was going to prove that every man and woman in the armed services had value. Not just as a warm body but as an incredible resource of brainpower. If Parker could develop a program that enhanced their mental prowess, their decision making and combat readiness by rewiring the neural pathways, she could decrease the number of casualties, decrease the number of soldiers returning with PTSD.

So she'd used the drugs to speed up the results.

She knew better. The whole thing backfired and now she had nothing. Her life's best work had failed, her sister and parents were in danger. She'd voted for Linc Norman and not because he'd offered her a place by his side in the war on terror. He'd been the next great president, she was sure of it.

And then something had changed in the man's psychological profile. The power, or the pressure, or something else had reared its ugly head and turned him into a monster. Secretly,

Parker wondered if Linc had been helping himself to some of Westmeyer's drugs.

In a not-so-nice neighborhood, Parker ditched the limo and the cap, found a corner drug store where she bought a prepaid phone and a new hat. It was fully dark now and she stole an old, rusty Cutlass from behind a bar and drove to the nearest library.

The library's bank of computers was near the front desk and she didn't have a library card. The evening clerk was a young college kid busy putting books away and didn't even notice her slip into a seat.

The password was easy to guess and she was on the Internet in seconds. Less than a minute later, she stepped back outside and dialed the number for Rock Star Security.

Chapter Twelve

"Lindsey?" Savanna pulled up short. The girl was in her chair at the stylist booth. "What are you doing?"

Gone were the headphones normally around her neck. Gone were the skinny jeans and cheesy T-shirt. "I, um…" she sputtered, running a hand down the green power suit she was wearing. Her face was made-up, the stylist in mid-tease with a lock of Lindsey's hair. Both women stared at Savanna, frozen.

Lindsey tried for a smile. It fell flat. "You're here."

One of the runners, a kid younger than Lindsey who was showing the evening's script to her, backed away and took off for parts unknown.

"Of course I'm here," Savanna said. "Coldplay wanted increased security tonight, so I got held up at the gate getting everyone badges, but it's sixty minutes until show time. I need to get ready. Why are you in my chair?"

"Well, you and your bodyguard took off with that other man and then you didn't show up by the time I got here." She glanced at the stylist as if looking for backup. "Which believe me, was no easy task since that stupid limo driver kicked me out. She held a gun to my face! Can you believe it?"

Coldplay was suddenly next to Savanna. "A gun?"

Lindsey nodded, all cat eyes and too much lipstick. "I reported her. She was a psycho. I'm so glad you weren't in the limo, Savanna!"

A gun. The limo driver had held a gun on Lindsey? *Holy shit.*

"She? It was a woman? What did she look like?" Coldplay asked. "Did she say what she wanted?"

"Duh, she looked like a limo driver, black coat, white shirt, a hat. The usual. She wanted to know what your name was and then ordered me out of the car. The limo service is investigating."

Savanna shot Coldplay a look. His face gave away nothing, but his body—oh, boy. Rigid as steel, the menace radiating off him enough to make Savanna want to take a step back. What was up with that? Was the limo driver after her or Coldplay?

"Long-lost girlfriend?" Savanna asked him.

Coldplay's Adam's apple lifted and fell. He didn't look at her. The Rock Star bodyguard with them, a beefy guy who went by the name Poison, tapped his back. "I'm on it," he said, pulling out his phone and fading into the background while typing.

Lindsey shifted in the chair, directing her focus back to Savanna. Several people had gathered on the fringes. "When I arrived and you weren't here, Savanna, someone had to fill in, and…well…"

Savanna felt a spark of anger flare to life during the ensuing silence. "Well, what?" she forced herself to say.

The hair stylist started teasing again as if pretending she couldn't hear the conversation. Lindsey's voice went whisper-quiet even though there was no way the gathering crowd couldn't hear her. "Mariah killed the Westmeyer investigation and asked me to take your place tonight to do the Hopland segment."

"She did *what?*"

Lindsey sat up straighter. "*I* wrote the script. *I* talked to Dr. Hopland today like you were supposed to, and now, I'm the one who's going to interview her on tonight's show along with her counterpart, Dr. Tegeler, who claims post-traumatic growth is not a result of stress or trauma, but a result of personality traits. You've had a rough day and Mariah wants you to take some time off. I'm filling in."

Savanna took a step forward, anger morphing into a strange kind of fear. Cable news was a cutthroat business, and although she'd built her show into an award-winning program, she could lose her show to this woman in an instant. Lose control of her own show to the network.

All the work she'd done over the past five years came down to this single moment.

A warm hand fell on her arm, holding her back and snapping her out of the gripping fear. Coldplay gave her a knowing look and a squeeze.

She got his message. This wasn't Lindsey's doing. The president had gotten to the network's owners. If he couldn't stop Savanna with the threat of bodily harm, he was going to take away her platform.

She didn't shrug off Coldplay's hand even though she desperately wanted to. "It's my show," she ground out, the same feeling of helplessness she'd experienced at fourteen when she'd had to quit the Olympics, slamming into her full force. "Mariah can't kill the Westmeyer investigation."

"I don't know why you're so adamant about that stupid drug company being a cover for something else," Lindsey said. "Besides, people are tired of hearing about drug company scandals. They want their pills, end of story, and the fact that Westmeyer Industries is funding the president's election coffers is hardly news."

This was why Lindsey would never make a good investigative reporter. She didn't have the nose for a story or the deep motivation to hunt for one. Savanna took a breath and forced her voice to soften. "Lindsey, you're great behind the camera and I appreciate all the work you've done on Hopland, but you don't have experience in front of the camera or with reporting."

"Wrong." Lindsey's face morphed into something else. Something mature and confident. "I anchored a campus news show in college. An award-winning news show. Now, if you'll excuse me, I need to get ready. You really should go talk to Mariah."

For half a second, Savanna entertained the idea of physically hauling Lindsey out of the chair. She checked herself; the woman had done nothing wrong. She was ambitious and Savanna couldn't fault her for that, but the sting of betrayal soured on her tongue. Had this been Lindsey's plan all along? To get in good with Savanna and end up in front of the camera?

Good play, Lindsey, but this isn't over. Savanna raised her chin, shrugged off Coldplay's hand, and went to find the show's chief executive.

Coldplay fell into step beside her as she forced the crowd that had gathered to part and let her pass through.

"You should consider a temporary retreat," he said, once they were clear.

Savanna's heels clicked on the tile floor as she hustled out of the dressing area and entered the hallway leading to the executive offices. God, she'd spent so much time here, she didn't know what she'd do if she lost it all. This was her life, her everything, and she'd killed herself time and time again to make sure she was giving the American public a good show. A *real* show. If she lost this now...

A hard lump formed in her throat. *I will not lose my own show.*

In the hall, several people passed by her and Coldplay, some lifting their brows at the sight of her—or maybe him; he was an imposing figure—and then their gazes darting away just as quickly.

They know. All of them. Word about Lindsey's new assignment had spread fast.

"You're kidding, right?" she muttered to Coldplay as they passed a key grip. "Lindsey doing *my* show? What are they thinking?"

He waited for a janitor to pass by with a mop and bucket, then lowered his voice to match hers. "They aren't going to let you do the story about Westmeyer if the president got to them. You could lose your job. Maybe it's best to throw in the towel tonight and still have a job tomorrow."

He didn't understand. She couldn't explain. Not without revealing the deep, dark secret she'd kept hidden away all these years. The reason she'd gone into investigative reporting in the first place. The reason she needed to bring the truth to America every week.

But maybe she could at least convey *why* this was so important to her.

Stopping to face him, she rubbed the back of her neck where the knot was still tight. The hallway was relatively empty now, except for the janitor who was scrubbing at a stain on the floor. "This show is my voice to the American public. They trust me. If I back down every time someone threatens me, if I only do foo-foo reporting and overdramatize stories that have no real impact, I become nothing more than a talking head. I no longer have value as a journalist. I lose my voice, and in turn, the American people lose *theirs.* So while it's true that I might get fired, I'd rather be fired than give up my integrity. Do you understand that?"

He closed his eyes for a second as if debating with himself. "Yeah, I get it."

She started marching for the end of the hall again. He followed. Lights shone behind the frosted glass door of the chief executive's reception area. As Savanna burst in, Mariah's receptionist glanced up, eyes widening. "Savanna. I didn't expect to see you tonight."

"Hi Chrissy. I need to talk to Mariah. ASAP."

"I'm sorry, she's in a meeting."

Sure she was. "How convenient. Give her a message for me, will you? I'm doing the show tonight, and although I'm happy to report the Hopland segment, I will be revisiting the Westmeyer investigation next week."

Turning on her heel, Savanna marched back out the door to where Coldplay waited in the hall.

His voice was low as he spoke. "While I appreciate your gumption, and I'm all for standing up for your job, I think we're going to have to leave the show to Lindsey anyway."

"Why is that?"

He moved so fast she barely had time to react. Grabbing her, he whirled her around to pin her against the wall as something smacked into the green paint above their heads and plaster rained down.

The news never slept and neither did the studio. Eight o'clock in the evening and there were dozens of people filing around, chasing leads, prepping for the next on-air segment, positioning cameras, lights, and microphones.

So when Trace had cataloged the janitor as he and Savanna made their way to the executive office suite, he hadn't thought it out of the norm for the guy to be present in the hall. When a business was open 24/7, cleaning people didn't have the luxury of working without employees being in their way.

The man was dressed in a gray-blue jumpsuit with a name badge hanging from his neck. The thing that had pinged Trace's brain to take another look as he stood just outside the door to the executive office waiting for Savanna to do her thing was the way the guy moved the mop in his hands.

Mopping, vacuuming, shoveling…it all had to do with

weight distribution. Much like throwing a punch or handling a rifle on the move. The upper body had to move while the lower body stayed grounded.

The janitor, who was really an assassin, had probably never used a mop in his life. He hadn't even bothered to wring it out before going to work on the stained floor, dumping a large puddle of water on the tiles, which he then tried to mop up.

As the first cluster of bullets embedded themselves in the wall above his and Savanna's heads, Trace had already covered her and was in the process of shoving her back into the office suite. "Take cover," he commanded as he pushed her inside and touched the comm unit in his ear to notify his fellow SFI members he was engaging the enemy. "Shots fired. Northwest section of office building, top floor."

Someone radioed back that they were on their way, but Trace's brain was focused on the immediate threat. *Eliminate.*

In one fluid motion, he slammed the office door shut to protect Savanna and the receptionist, did a roll, and avoided the next spray of bullets whizzing by his head by a slim margin.

It was no small-caliber gun the man was using, but also not anything as big as an M4. Just a handgun he'd had hidden in the baggy pocket of the jumpsuit.

Trace felt the weight of his own gun under his arm but he didn't need it. With lightning speed, he advanced on the man, picking up a plant in a Grecian urn and tossing it at him. The man jumped back and stooped into a crouch to fire off another round as the urn exploded near his feet.

The water on the tiles had turned the floor under the man's feet slick. He lost his balance for a split second, needing to right himself before he could once again aim for Trace's head.

Trace already had a nearby table in his hands, the brochures it had held falling like rain onto the floor. The cherry wood was solid and heavy but wouldn't deflect a 40-caliber round. What it did do was provide another distraction as Trace heaved it at the man.

The assassin had no choice but to get out of the way. Once again, the water was his undoing. His work shoes squeaked as they skidded out from under him when he tried to jump sideways. He slammed against the opposite wall, firing random shots, the table missing him by inches.

End it. Trace grabbed a framed picture of the network's owner off the wall just as the door at the end of the hall opened.

The assassin glanced over to see who was joining them, ready to shoot, and Trace let the picture fly, Frisbee-style.

The sharp edge of the metal frame met the man's neck, laying it open. It crashed to the floor, shattering glass. Blood gushed from the assassin's carotid artery and he fired one last random shot into the ceiling as he grabbed for his neck and fell to his knees. Still holding the gun, his mouth worked but nothing came out as he toppled over and twitched twice before he was gone.

Emit Petit stepped through the open door, kicking away the dying man's gun and standing over him for a second, looking at the blood and broken glass. He raised his gaze to Trace. "You killed him with a picture frame?"

Trace shrugged, adrenaline fueling his limbs with a warm, pleasant hum. "Guns are so yesterday."

One of his fellow Rock Stars, now called Megadeth, sidled up to Emit and stared at the damage. "Nice," he said to Trace with a crooked grin on his face. "You're gonna have to teach me that trick."

"Coldplay?" a shaky voice said from behind him and Trace turned to find a white-faced Savanna standing in the doorway. Peeking over her shoulder was the receptionist.

Emit stepped over the body, careful to avoid the blood and the lingering water on the tiles. "When you give your statement, it was self-defense and you were protecting our client. For now, I'll clean this up and take care of the red tape." He tossed the keys to his Escalade to Trace. "Take Savanna to HQ. Poison's outside. He'll go with you and we'll regroup shortly."

"Oh, God," Savanna said, her focus on the dead man. "He tried to kill me. To kill you." Her wide eyes rose to meet Trace's. "For *real* this time."

The receptionist slapped a hand over her mouth and disappeared back inside the office. Trace heard the sounds of her vomiting as he reached for Savanna and positioned his body to block her view. There was only one way out and it involved getting her across the blood, water, and dead assassin, but she didn't need to burn the image into her brain.

He'd seen so much of this type of thing, he was immune to it. Someone like Savanna wasn't. "Ms. Bunkett is unavailable for tonight's show," he called to the receptionist. "She'll be in touch when she's ready to resume her duties."

Several people appeared in the doorway at the other end of the hall, Megadeth blocked their entrance. Petit was already dialing the authorities.

Trace took Savanna's hand and brought her in close. "Time to go. Stay next to me and do exactly what I say."

She nodded weakly. Her fingers were ice cold, her teeth chattering. She'd been through too much in one day.

And the day wasn't over.

CHAPTER THIRTEEN

The room was warm, a fire going in the fireplace, but Savanna couldn't stop shaking.

Beatrice draped a soft blanket over her shoulders. It radiated a comforting heat as if it had been warmed in a dryer or lying on a radiator. "It's the shock," she said. A second later, she handed Savanna a cup of tea. "Drink this. It will take the edge off."

Snow fell lightly outside; the lights of DC spread out below. Coldplay had assured her the windows were bulletproof and no one could see inside, but Savanna turned away from the view and sipped her tea anyway, a strange exposed feeling sending another ripple through her taut nerves.

Beatrice's office was different at night. The gas log fireplace burned in one corner and soft light pooled on her desk from her desk lamp. A set of antique floor lamps gave the rest of the room a warm glow.

Even with the blanket and tea, Savanna couldn't warm up. "I've never been shot at," she said, still feeling out of sorts.

"Welcome to the club." Beatrice sat at her desk and started typing on her computer keyboard. "Unnerving, isn't it?"

"Someone tried to kill you?"

"More than once. Hopefully, never again. I don't like it."

She was so deadpan, Savanna almost laughed. "I don't care for it either."

Beatrice glanced over and the two shared a smile.

The door opened and Coldplay burst in, Emit Petit on his

heels with a folder in his hand. "Cops cleared us," Emit said. "The bullets lodged in the walls and ceiling helped, along with the receptionist's testimony." He slapped the folder down on Beatrice's desk. "Guy's name was Russo. Lenny Russo. He's been employed by the janitorial service and working at the station for the past six weeks. Background check dies out three years back."

Coldplay stopped in front of Savanna and her insides warmed instantly.

"How are you doing?" he said, touching her shoulder.

The shaking subsided. "Better." And she was. The sight of him calmed her nerves in a way the blanket and tea never would. She'd spoken to the detective who'd taken her statement after the traffic accident. Probably the same officer Coldplay and Emit had just finished with.

Beatrice tapped the mouse pad, never taking her eyes from the screen. "So Russo was a plant to keep eyes on Savanna."

Savanna wrapped the fingers of both hands around her teacup. "Was he the person who hit us today in the car?"

Coldplay put a hand on her lower back and guided her toward one of the chairs across from Beatrice. "Probability is high."

"But you said the hit and run was just a warning. If he'd wanted me dead, he would have finished it then and there." She sat, careful not to dislodge the blanket or spill her tea. "I don't think tonight was a warning."

"His orders may have changed," Beatrice said. "Once he found out you were at the station and insisting on airing the Westmeyer investigation, he was told to stop you at all costs."

"How did he find out?" The cup in her hands shook, tiny shockwaves rippling the surface. "No one expected me to show up tonight. I could see it on their faces."

"Your altercation with Lindsey when you arrived wasn't exactly private," Coldplay mentioned. "And you had the studio send the limo like usual to pick you up. Even though you were late, the original expectation was that you *were* doing the show."

Savanna rubbed a hand over her face. "The female limo driver who pulled the gun on Lindsey. Was she in on it too?"

"Maybe it was her job to take you out," Beatrice said. "When that failed, Russo was activated."

"I still can't believe the president is trying to kill me to stop this Westmeyer investigation."

"Maybe it's more than that," Coldplay said.

Everyone looked at him, and he dropped his gaze to the floor.

A tense silence filled the air. Parker had done the same thing to Savanna many times during their childhood when she'd had a secret. She'd toss out a one-liner, then leave Savanna hanging. Whether it was for dramatic effect or her sister was simply having an inner debate over whether to spill the beans, Savanna was never sure. Every time, it made her insides freeze up a little. Her heart beat quicker.

"You think it has to do with Parker?" Savanna asked Coldplay.

His gaze finally rose to meet hers. "If the president gave her an assignment and she refused to carry it out, he may be threatening you in an attempt to get her to follow orders. I'm sure he knows you're her one and only weakness."

Savanna rubbed her neck. The tendons were tight as stone after the accident and then being thrown around at the studio. If that was true, she and her sister were both in trouble.

But I have help. She doesn't.

"Do you have any other theories about why the president is threatening Ms. Jeffries?" Beatrice asked Coldplay.

His jaw clenched and he shot Beatrice a look that could melt steel. Something passed between them—an internal struggle of wills.

Was there another theory Coldplay didn't want to offer? "That's the most likely one," he said.

Most likely? "I'd like to hear all of your theories," Savanna countered.

Beatrice stared down Coldplay for a moment, then switched her attention to Savanna. "I'd like to hear more about your Westmeyer investigation. Why is the president adamant to stop you from talking about it?"

She didn't like being shut down, but she was too wrung out to push for Coldplay to explain what other theories he may have had. She'd work on him later. Maybe he would open up when they had less of an audience.

There wasn't much to tell about Westmeyer. She gave Beatrice and Emit the basic facts she'd already shared with Coldplay. Westmeyer's founder and CEO was being investigated. Behind the scenes, she believed they were supplying experimental drugs to the Department of Defense for use on soldiers. She had the uncanny feeling Beatrice already knew everything she was saying.

Coldplay was staring at the floor again, his jaw working overtime. Beatrice removed a file from a pile on her desk. "If that's true, there are people involved who can verify it. Those in charge who've okayed it and selected soldiers to be tested. The scientists running the experiment. The soldiers themselves."

Savanna took another sip of tea. Mint. Her favorite. It had cooled but still tasted good, and talking about work gave her a bit of clarity again. "Finding those people and getting them to come forward is nearly impossible. That's why I was running with the illegal campaign contribution story while I continued to dig on the drug trials."

"You're an expert at what you do," Beatrice said. "I'm sure you can find the sources you need, but if you'd like help, please say so. I have...other resources...that might be helpful as well. In the meantime, we need to realign your security measures."

She slid the file across the desk. "I have three safe houses open at the moment. Take your pick."

"Safe houses? I can't go back to my apartment?"

"While we increased security, the threat has escalated," Coldplay said. "We have to change tactics, keep you away from places you would normally go."

Beatrice flipped open the file and laid out three pieces of paper, each with a picture of the house and the pertinent details. "La Escada is a horse ranch in Virginia. Berkley is a modern estate here in DC, and our premium safe house is on a private island near St. Lucia."

Holy shit. Savanna had just taken another sip of her tea and nearly spit it out. "You guys don't mess around, do you?"

Emit leaned on the edge of the desk, arms folded over his chest. "We service the rich and famous, Ms. Jeffries. They expect a certain level of...amenities."

"Do you have a preference?" Beatrice asked.

Beachfront in the Virgin Islands or horses in the rolling hills of Virginia. She glanced at Coldplay and let her eyes wander for a moment from his head—*cowboy hat?*—to places lower—*or Speedo?*

Damn, that was a difficult choice.

His eyes turned to her and she hurriedly glanced away from his lower regions.

"All of them are top of the line for security," he said

smoothly, as if he hadn't just caught her ogling his crotch. "The island is hidden and hard to approach without being noticed, but difficult to leave if attacked. The cabin at the ranch is also hidden and there's only one road leading in and out—except that an assassin would use the surrounding woods to go unnoticed upon approach."

She cleared her throat. "So you're recommending the Berkley estate?"

"The location is advantageous to keep others out, yet gives us multiple exits. There are safe rooms and I can set up extra layers of security outside."

A knock on the door interrupted them. The bodyguard called Poison stuck his head in, addressing his boss. "Found the limo."

Emit motioned him to enter. "Where was it?"

"Driver ditched it on the other side of town." He wore a jean jacket, motorcycle boots, and black gloves. Striding across the room, he removed what looked like a picture from his inside jacket pocket, and tossed it on the desk. "This was stuck in the dash. Checked it for fingerprints and came up with zilch."

The men all frowned and Beatrice glanced at Savanna. "Recognize this?"

Savanna leaned in and cocked her head to get a better look. "Oh, my God," she said as realization hit. "That's my favorite Gucci bag."

"Walk-in closet, third row, east side," Coldplay murmured.

"You memorized what shelf my bags are on?"

He ignored the question. "The limo driver had a picture from inside your..." His head snapped up. "Who else has had access to your bedroom closet?"

"No one." How embarrassingly true. Brady had never stayed at her place. The only person who ever saw her closet was... "Parker." A chill swept through her. A new thought dawned. "Could the limo driver have been my sister?"

Coldplay seemed to be on the same mind track. "Why would she leave you a picture of a purse?"

"I...I don't know. Unless it's to let me know she's still alive and here in the area." She put a hand over her heart. It was beating much too fast, but for the first time in weeks, she had hope. "I need to go back to my place. She may be trying to contact me."

"No," the other three—Coldplay, Beatrice, and Emit—all said in unison.

"The killer may be baiting you," Emit added. "Coldplay, Poison, and I will go."

"She doesn't know you guys. If she's in trouble, she's not going to talk to you." Savanna stood and threw off the cashmere blanket. "I'm going to my apartment."

Emit started to argue and Coldplay held up a hand to stop him. "She needs to do this. I'll keep her safe."

A warm sense of accomplishment spread through her veins. Coldplay understood her, knew her need to find Parker wasn't something she could be talked out of.

Emit's lips pressed into a thin line for a few seconds as he seemed to be sizing her up. Then he gave a tight nod. "I strongly disagree with this approach, but you're the client, Ms. Jeffries. If Coldplay feels he can protect you, I'll allow you to visit, but visit only. Two hours, not a minute more. You will not stay there overnight, nor will you be allowed to stay even two hours if any of the three of us" —he pointed between him and the other two men— "believe there is anything out of place. Your life comes first. Your sister comes second. If you don't like those terms, I'll refund your money and you can find a different protection agency."

Hardball. She liked him and his dedication to doing his job, even if the client was being foolhardy. But seriously, who else was she going to turn to? He knew he had her in a bind. "No need to strong-arm me, Mr. Petit. I agree to your terms."

Beatrice picked up the photo and fingered it. "I'm going, too."

Another round of "no's" rang out, Savanna chiming in this time.

Unfazed, Beatrice looked up at her. "When was the last time you used this bag? Is it possible there's something hidden in it? Something Parker wanted you to find?"

"I use it all the time. I would have seen anything unusual."

"Hmm." Beatrice spoke to Coldplay. "When you get there, check the linings and all the hardware on the bag like grommets and buckles. Could be something hidden in them."

"Roger that," he said.

Emit headed for the door, Poison following. "I'll bring the car around. Meet you downstairs."

As they walked out, Connor, the receptionist stuck his head in. Like the news studio, everyone here seemed to work around the clock. "Ms. Jeffries' coat is cleaned and pressed. It's at my desk when she's ready."

"Perfect timing." Beatrice rose and motioned at Savanna. "Connor will help you with the coat. I need to speak with Coldplay alone for a minute."

Savanna was getting tired of being left out of these conversations, but it made sense that Coldplay's boss occasionally needed to discuss topics with him that were none of Savanna's business.

Excited at the prospect of seeing Parker, she hoped the meeting would be quick. "Of course. I'll meet you outside," she said to Coldplay.

He nodded, looking for the world like he'd rather follow her than discuss anything with Beatrice.

⌐───────••───────⌐

Thirty minutes later

"There," Trace said to Emit, pointing at the service door in the alley behind Savanna's apartment building.

"I thought you talked to the manager about increasing security back here," Savanna said. "How will we get in?"

Emit had dropped Poison off at a building across the street where he would set up surveillance on the roof. Callan Reese had joined the party and was watching the front of the building from his own vehicle. Trace didn't want to go in the front door and alert the staff of their presence, so the service door was the best option. "The manager agreed to up the security, but he hasn't done anything yet. We'll go in here and take the stairs to the penthouse."

Emit wheeled the Escalade up to the service door where a single light bulb cast a pale circle on the ground. "I'll keep an eye on things back here."

They all had comm units, even Savanna. Beatrice had Connor insert a tracking device in Savanna's coat after it was cleaned. She'd told Trace of the precaution during their meeting. Between the tracking devices in her earrings, bra, coat, and phone, they had a good chance of finding her in the event she was kidnapped.

Beatrice told Trace she didn't believe the janitor had been sent to kill Savanna, only to create a near miss in order to keep the heat on her. Killing her over the Westmeyer investigation, when all she had was intel on the illegal campaign funding that would go public in a few days anyway when the Justice Department announced their formal investigation, seemed too reckless for the president to employ. Linc Norman was cocky, clever, and shrewd, but he wasn't reckless, according to Beatrice.

Trace knew better, but his arguing would bring up how he knew, and he wasn't ready to share that little gem with anyone.

He touched the comm unit in his ear. "How's it looking, Rory?"

"Penthouse is clear," came the man's reply from HQ where he was watching the apartment on giant security screens. "No one has been in or out since the two of you left. I backtracked the past week since we installed the upgrade, but no sign of Parker or anyone else entering the penthouse. I knew I hadn't missed anyone, but I wanted to double check. The building's previous security cameras never caught anyone either, but it was inefficient, so Parker could have been sneaking into the penthouse and was never caught on tape."

"Roger that."

Beatrice had told Trace about a female caller who'd asked for Coldplay earlier that evening. The woman had said she was interested in hiring him and wanted to know if he was available. When Beatrice didn't confirm his employment status and started asking questions, the woman had hung up.

It could have been anyone here at the apartment building or at the studio who knew his bodyguard name, but Beatrice believed it had been Parker. Trace thought she was probably correct. Rory traced all incoming calls but all he could tell them was that it had been made from a disposable phone a few blocks from where the limo had been found.

If Parker *had* been driving the limo, she'd been trying to make contact. He'd missed her once again.

Why hadn't she left a message with Beatrice? Why plant the photo of Savanna's purse in the limo? Why not pick up the phone and call her sister?

She was taking chances while covering her backside extremely well at the same time.

Linc Norman may have met his match.

Even though Trace hadn't met Parker, he liked her more

and more. Something about her determination reminded him of Savanna. "Wait for my signal," he said to his charge.

Savanna's hands were clasped in her lap and she was nervously rubbing her thumbs back and forth. "Be careful."

Careful wasn't in his nature. Cautious, watchful, vigilant? Yes. Careful, no.

He'd already been scanning the area, but as he emerged from the SUV, he did it again, logging details from the snow-covered concrete pad to the dumpsters fifty feet away. There were no tracks in the alley except from the Escalade's tires; no footprints anywhere near the door. Traffic noises from the street filtered down the narrow lane, and a church bell rang in the distance, signaling the ten o'clock hour. A few lights glowed from behind curtains in the nearby buildings but no one was looking out. Rooflines were clear.

A piece of brick, lying in the alley and mostly covered by snow, helped him take care of dousing the single light, the sound of breaking glass muffled by the falling snow as he plunged the service door area into darkness.

All it took to unlock the door was his Rock Star credit card, courtesy of Beatrice, and a flick of his wrist. The door automatically locked from the inside when closed, so he used the broken brick again, jamming the door open.

The snow was coming down good now, the wind sharp and cold on his skin. He didn't mind—it helped with their cover. Back at the car, he pulled Savanna close to his body, hustling her into the building and toward the first flight of stairs. He stopped for a second and listened, making sure they were alone.

She brushed snow from her hair, her cheeks pink from the frosty air. Her eyes tracked his every move, the blue orbs lit with excitement.

He understood her anticipation at seeing her sister. He just hoped this wasn't going to backfire on him.

Because Parker obviously knew who he was. If she showed up and told Savanna, he was dead in the water.

Should have told her myself.

He still had time, but first, they needed to get to her penthouse and find that purse.

He automatically held out a hand. "Come on."

She slipped her hand inside his and together they started up the stairs at a quick pace.

As per normal, the stairs were empty. Savanna, for all her

workouts, was winded by the fourth floor. She laughed softly, the sound warming his chest as she sprinted beside him, grabbing onto the railing with her free hand and trying to keep up with his longer legs.

Her security card got them onto the penthouse floor, and a minute later, Savanna was inside her apartment, calling her sister's name.

The place was dark and Trace flipped on the lights, going from room to room to make sure there were no visitors, regardless of Rory's assurances. He reset the security system, and assured no one was there, marched Savanna to her walk-in closet.

The purse was on the third shelf, east side, exactly like it had been a few hours earlier. It had a conglomerate of studs and spikes, zippers and hardware. She grabbed it and one hand dived in, unzipping zippers and searching the pockets. A second later, she looked up, empty-handed. "Nothing."

Trace took it to the kitchen and grabbed a knife from the butcher block. He raised the blade to start slicing when she stayed his hand in midair.

"This is a two-thousand dollar Gucci. Do we really have to cut it open?"

"In order to check the lining we do."

"Maybe Parker didn't hide anything. Maybe she just wanted me to meet her here and she isn't here yet."

"Why the picture of the purse then? Why not a note that said 'meet me at your place?' Or a general picture of the apartment?"

"Parker would never destroy a work of art like this, so if she didn't cut it open to hide something, we don't need to cut it open to find it, right? Beatrice said to check the studs and stuff."

"That still requires I damage the purse."

She bit her bottom lip and snatched the ugly purple thing away from him. "My bag. I'll do it."

The clang of metal tripped something in his brain. "Wait," he said, reaching out to finger the double metal hearts hanging on a tassel attached to the strap. "What are these?"

"Adornments, most of the handbag designers have a little leather tag or a metal one with the designer's name and logo on them."

"No, hooked in the tassel loop. Is that a cuff link?"

"A cuff link?" Savanna turned the tassel over, eyeing the flat gold-plated metal with a scrolling monogram. "That's weird. I don't recognize those initials."

"Not your boyfriend's?"

A slight sigh left her lips. "Ex-boyfriend's, you mean? No. His initials were BG."

Trace suspected she didn't have a boyfriend, yet was annoyingly relieved when she confirmed it.

Her cheeks hollowed as she sucked them in while seeming deep in thought. "I don't know anyone with those initials off the top of my head. Maybe it was someone I did a story on and Parker's trying to point me in that direction."

"Or maybe it's not about the initials." Trace removed the cuff link from the tassel loop and held it up to the light. Turning it over to the smooth side, he saw the slim line he was looking for dissecting the gold rectangle about a third of the way down. He gave a gentle tug and the top half disengaged, revealing a flat metal end. "Bingo."

Savanna leaned in. "Is that what I think it is?"

"Where's your laptop?"

Setting down the purse, she went to her desk, grabbed the laptop and brought it back to the breakfast bar.

The cuff link's USB fit snugly and sent the laptop whirring in an attempt to open it. No dice. The thumb drive was encrypted. Heavily. "This may take a while," Trace said.

Savanna opened the fridge. "I'll break out some wine."

"Not here. We need to go to the safe house."

Holding the bottle, Savanna paused. "Fine. I'll bring the wine with us. Just let me get a change of clothes and my—"

"*Incoming,*" Rory said in Trace's ear. "*Doorman coming up in the elevator.*"

Savanna, of course, heard the same warning. "Randy? What does he want?"

Trace unplugged the USB. Even after the day she'd had, Savanna still wasn't thinking like a hunted person. He knew he should have locked down the elevator and stair door, but he'd wanted to make it easy for Parker if she tried to make contact. "We're not sticking around to find out." He touched his comm and said to the crew, "Exiting south side via fire escape."

"*Copy that,*" came the replies from Reese and Petit. Petit added, "*Car's running and in place.*"

"It's only Randy," Savanna said, looking at him with an incredulous air. "You said he wasn't dangerous."

"Elevator is there. Doors are opening," Rory said.

"We have to go, Savanna. Now."

"But I need clothes. Underwear. My toothbrush."

Her doorbell rang and Trace placed a finger to his lips. He moved in close, looking down at her, and whispered, "There are clothes and hygiene products at the safe house."

"Miss Jeffries?" Randy knocked on the door. "Are you okay? Cori just told me there was a shooting at the studio. She said some other gal was on air doing your show."

Savanna frowned, her fingers turning white as she squeezed the wine bottle. Trace moved her toward the patio doors.

"Miss Jeffries?" Randy called again. "Are you in there?"

Why did the doorman think Savanna was home? He'd seen her and Trace leave earlier for the studio and hadn't seen them return.

Or had he?

At the glass doors, Trace stuck the USB in his pocket and tried to take the wine bottle from Savanna. She held tight, hugging it to her and giving him a look that suggested taking it from her would cost him something.

He'd seen the way she was staring at his crotch at the office. The open appraisal had made his dick instantly hard and he'd had to force himself back to the task at hand.

For some insane reason in this moment of subterfuge, he wanted to kiss that look off her face instead of getting her out the door and down the snow-covered metal steps.

The lure of an undercover op. It always heated his blood, made him hyperaware of everything, including a sexy woman a few inches from him.

Randy knocked again and rang the doorbell. Trace heard the distinct sound of a lock picker scratching against metal.

At this moment, what he and his overcharged libido wanted didn't matter. Keeping Savanna safe was his first job.

Unlocking the patio doors softly, he let her keep her bottle as he snatched up the laptop and hustled her out into the night.

Chapter Fourteen

Savanna hadn't even sniffed the wine but her head spun like she'd drank the entire bottle as the black Escalade sped through the night, a bullet train taking her to safety.

At least she hoped safety was still an option.

She clutched the wine bottle like a security blanket, knowing it was stupid and pointless, but needing to hold onto something. Since she didn't even have a change of underwear or her toothbrush, and she couldn't exactly grab Coldplay in a tight clench, the wine bottle would have to do.

Streetlights flashed by, the snow appearing crystalized under their glow. Coldplay sat beside her, speaking to a man named Rory on the car phone. Rory relayed instructions concerning the USB drive inserted into her laptop's side slot once more.

"The car has Wi-Fi," Rory said, giving Coldplay the password to link to it. "I'll send you the decryption software once you're hooked up. Takes a minute or two to download, then you can sit back and relax while it does its thing."

"Thanks, man." Coldplay's face was lit from the laptop's glowing screen, his brows knit as his fingers typed furiously. "I've never seen this level of encryption."

"I can see what you're seeing," Rory replied. "It looks like a cocktail of NSA, DOD, and maybe some Chinese hacker shit thrown in."

Coldplay's fingers stopped and he sat back. "Software's in. How long will it take to decrypt?"

Rory made a *hmm* noise on his end. "Couple hours minimum, up to a day, max."

"But the software *will* crack the decryption, right?"

"No guarantees, but between Bea and me, we've never found a code we couldn't crack. Our software on the black market would be worth billions."

Head still spinning, Savanna sank farther into the seat, closing her eyes. First, the accident, then the shooting. She'd peeked out and saw...

She wasn't sure what she'd seen. It had all happened so fast. One minute Coldplay was dodging bullets and the next he was whipping a framed photo at the shooter.

Bile inched up her throat and she massaged the area. The same area the picture frame had slit open on the man.

The blood. There had been so much blood.

Hugging the wine bottle closer, she swallowed the acidic burn. Her mind replayed the scene over and over. How had Coldplay moved so fast, been so accurate?

Like a freaking super soldier.

She hadn't had much time to think about it, let it all sink in, until now. The hollow hiss of the gun firing—Coldplay had told her the assassin had used a suppressor—and the solid *thunk* when the bullets tore into the wall still echoed in her head. Coldplay had known what was going to happen before it happened.

How?

Coldplay had admitted to being in the Navy, a trained soldier. It had to be that. But what if...?

An idea took hold in her head, but it was too preposterous. Too coincidental.

You're reaching for a story where there is none. It had to be the adrenaline. The whole freaking surrealism of the moment.

No matter what, she would not become some conspiracy theorist or drama whore. Her speculations would have to wait.

Stick to the facts, she told herself.

Fact one, I'm alive.

And, as far as she knew, Parker was too. Plus, she had the USB Parker had planted on the Gucci.

Savanna didn't know what information the tiny drive held, but whatever it was, it had to be something that would help her solve the mystery of what was keeping her sister on the run.

A warm hand touched hers, jarring her back to the present. "You okay?" Coldplay asked.

She'd left her gloves behind and was clinging to a chilled wine bottle. Her fingers were popsicles. The feel of Coldplay's fingers, warm and rough, made her want to trade the wine for him.

"I'm fine," she said automatically, and then caught herself. "Well, not really." She tried to laugh it off, shook her head. "I'm…"

"It's all right to be scared," he said.

"Overwhelmed was the word I was looking for."

"Ah." He withdrew gloves from inside his coat pocket and handed them to her. "Completely understandable."

How was he so unfazed by all of this? He'd killed a man earlier, yet seemed more concerned about her frozen fingers. Of course, that was his job—to protect her—but apparently being shot at and having to kill someone in order to do so, didn't bother him.

Slipping her hands into his gloves, she staved off a shiver. The gloves were too big for her, but lined with something soft and they seemed to have picked up body heat from being inside his coat.

Every one of her muscles ached. Every nerve was fried. For a second, she wished she had one monstrous-sized glove to climb inside.

But she wasn't a hider. Not since her gymnastics days. The truth had to be faced, secrets exposed. When they weren't, someone always got hurt. She'd learned that the hard way.

"So Randy was in on it?" she asked, trying to wrap her mind around all the shit.

The flickering light of the laptop glinted in her bodyguard's eyes. "He wasn't able to bypass the security system."

"That doesn't answer my question."

"Since he wasn't able to break in or engage us, I don't know his motive or have proof he's working for the president."

"Make an educated guess." Her voice came out stern, unapologetic. "You didn't hustle me out of the apartment and down the fire escape because you thought Randy was harmless."

"He may have been. I don't take chances."

"Yet, you took a chance on me, on this assignment, knowing I was being stalked by the president. Risky business."

His mouth opened, and then closed again. He looked at the laptop, focusing on the screen as the decryption software continued to work.

"How many are there? People after me, I mean," Savanna asked, her voice softening. "Is there anyone I can trust?"

Again, the slightest hesitation. His attention stayed glued on the screen. "We don't know how deep this goes. At the moment, everyone is suspect."

She knew it was coming, his confirmation. It still sucked the air from her lungs. It wasn't every day your world was turned upside down, but she'd lived through other experiences that had seemed insurmountable at the time. Experiences that had gutted her and left her gasping for air like a fish out of water. She'd made it through those and she would, by God, make it through this one too.

Setting the wine bottle on the floor, she nodded, mostly to herself. "Okay, then. What can I do to help?"

Coldplay finally looked at her, the glint in his eyes showing surprise.

"What?" she said.

The corner of his mouth quirked, the tension in his body lessening slightly. He stared at the screen once more, but not with the same intensity. "Nothing."

"Look, I'm not used to being in this type of situation—being dependent on someone else for my very life. Not being in control…I haven't felt like this since…well, that doesn't matter. I don't like this situation, and it's difficult for me to wrap my head around the fact that the president of the United States is trying to kill me, but I'm getting there. I will help in any way possible to bring this situation to a safe close for both of us, but the one thing I will *not* do is sit back and let you take all the risk. Once we figure out what's on that USB, I will help you and your team come up with a plan and a solution to getting my sister back and keeping all of my body parts intact and functioning."

She could have sworn he was pressing his lips together to keep from smiling. "That would be my plan as well."

"Don't humor me. I'm serious."

His gaze slid to meet hers and this time he smiled for real. "I'm not humoring you. I plan to use your investigative skills, intelligence, and knowledge to keep us both safe and bring a successful conclusion to this mission."

Mission. Why did the use of that term make her flinch?

An uncomfortable realization took hold in the pit of her stomach right along side the one about Linc Norman being out for her blood. She'd half-hoped she had become more than an assignment to the man seated next to her.

He'd certainly become more than a bodyguard to her, and she didn't even know him.

Swallowing past her bruised ego and the illogical thoughts about Coldplay, she nodded. "What other theories do you have?"

"On what?"

"Back at the office, Beatrice suggested you had other theories on why the president is threatening me. I want to hear them."

From the front seat, Emit said, "ETA five minutes."

Coldplay closed the laptop's lid. "After we get you settled in the safe house, we can talk more."

"Not can, will. We *will* talk more."

He didn't respond, his attention focused on the road ahead of them. His reluctance was as palpable as the dry, heated air swirling around her from the vents.

Savanna knew when to push for answers. She also knew when to back off and let her quarry think they were off the hook. She and Coldplay would have plenty of time to talk once they were at the safe house, but there was one thing she needed to clear up right now.

"Let's get something straight," she said. "You work for me, and if you're withholding information, or you have theories you aren't telling me because you're worried about my reaction, I *will* fire you. This is business between you and me, but it's my life you're screwing with. I have a right to know everything when it comes to threats against me."

The tension returned in Coldplay's body. His jaw muscle jumped. "Yes, ma'am."

That went well. He'd saved her life twice today and here she was pissing him off.

"I'm sorry to sound like a bitch, it's just…" She searched for the right words, couldn't find them. Her throat constricted as she tried to explain, the old fear cutting off her voice like it had done all those years ago. "Like I said earlier, I'm not used to being dependent on anyone. I'm not used to being scared or running from my problems, and right now, you're right. I *am* scared. I may have received a few threats over the years, but no one has actually tried to kill me."

He closed his eyes briefly, then without looking at her, reached over and squeezed her hand. "We'll get through this."

The way he made it sound like they were partners, the way his squeeze went straight to her heart, loosened the stricture around her throat ever so slightly. As long as she was admitting to the truth... "You're the only one I can trust and I don't even know your real name."

Those eyes, now shadowed, slanted down. "One of these days, I'll tell you."

That promise, spoken in the dark, warmed her heart in a way she hadn't felt in a very long time. "I'm holding you to it."

He chuckled. "I know you are."

And then they were turning into the drive of the safe house and Savanna lied to herself, telling the scared little girl inside of her that everything would be all right.

"The house is secure," Trace announced as he entered the sprawling gourmet kitchen.

The snow was coming down hard. The weather forecaster on the small TV in the corner hutch claimed they were in for another brutal winter storm.

Savanna was hunched over, hunting through one of the kitchen drawers. She'd kicked off her shoes and was barefoot, her hair still wet from the snow, and her skin too pale for his liking. "I can't find the damn bottle opener."

Two wine glasses sat on the marble countertop next to the bottle she'd snagged at her apartment. As she searched the drawer, she tossed out various utensils onto the growing pile beside the glasses. "Garlic press, cheese grater, apple slicer, meat thermometer, kabob sticks..."

Her head fell back and she growled softly in the back of her throat. "People, you're killing me. Where's the damn corkscrew?"

That growl did strange things to him, just like her closeness and fighting attitude had in the car. She didn't like admitting to being scared, but she had, and yet, her fear hadn't stopped her from also demanding he keep her in the loop and accept her help.

He suspected her bravado wasn't a false front. There was no pretense, no whining, no cowardice hiding behind it.

Setting the laptop on the island, he opened the lid and placed his phone next to it. The house's security system was top of the line and linked to his phone so he could keep an eye on all the exterior cameras and monitor the invisible perimeter lasers from anywhere inside. Still, he'd checked all three floors of the house, inspected each window lock, and personally made sure every exit was secure. The place was locked up tight, every surveillance camera working properly.

The decryption software chugged along on the laptop and he couldn't tell if it was making progress or not, but Rory seemed confident, and Trace had no other option than to trust that the guy knew his stuff.

He sidled up beside Savanna and searched a different drawer. Next to a set of steak knives, he saw what he wanted. "Got it."

She tried to take the metal opener from him, but he dodged her grasp and grabbed the wine bottle. A moment later, he had the cork out and was pouring her a glass of pale, gold wine.

"Sit," he told her, steering her to a fancy chair on the other side of the island. "Before you drop."

"I'm fine." She took the glass he handed her and sank into the chair. "Aren't you going to have some?"

"I don't drink," he admitted. *And you're not fine.*

Her brows went up and she sipped her wine. "Ever?"

"Ever."

"Why not?"

He scanned the yard outside the window. A foot of snow had already fallen.

He checked the lock and pulled the shade. Petit and Reese were keeping an eye on the long lane from the road to the house, along with Poison, who was positioned at the back of the property. Reinforcements were on the way to relieve Petit and Reese. "It slows my reflexes."

"Your reflexes are off the charts. Superhuman, if you ask me. You're not one of the Avengers are you?"

He leaned his back against the counter and purposely kept his focus on the laptop, crossing his feet at the ankles nonchalantly. "Not superhuman. Years and years of training."

"Hmm." She swirled the pale liquid in her glass. "So you never underwent any experimental drug testing through the DOD or anything? You did say you were in the Navy, correct?"

The investigative reporter was back. He couldn't let his surprise show so he zeroed in on one of the security monitors, leaning forward to type something nonsensical on the laptop's keyboard. He needed to turn the spotlight back on her and do it in a big way. "Back in the car, you were talking about control and said something about 'I haven't felt like this since...' What was that about? Since when?"

In his peripheral vision, he saw her body stiffen. She seemed to brace herself. "It's nothing. And you're avoiding my question. Don't you know that just makes me more of a bulldog?"

He glanced over the top of the laptop screen and saw her rolling the stem of the wine glass between her finger and thumb. Yep, he'd hit a nerve. "Want to talk about it?"

"My being a bulldog once I smell fresh meat?" Her joke fell flat.

"About the last time you felt out of control," he countered.

Her blue eyes met his, fierce and challenging. "No, and that was a horrible segue, by the way. You do that a lot—turning the conversation around so we're not talking about you."

Shrugging, he went to work putting the pile of utensils back in the drawers. "Nothing to talk about."

"Liar."

He chuckled, closing the drawer and turning back to her. "How's your wrist?"

Her brows scrunched. "My wrist?"

Keep the pressure on. "The one you injured. At the Olympics."

Her gaze turned wary. "Why are you asking about that?"

"Seemed like it was fine when you were doing Flying Crow pose and handstands in the gym today. Does the injury ever flare up? Cause you issues?"

"Why would you care about that? How do you even know about that? Did Beatrice tell you?"

"Is that the last time you felt scared and out of control? At the Olympics?"

She played with her wine glass, twirling it between her fingers and taking a big gulp, staring at him over the rim of the class. *Buying time.*

Finally, her eyes narrowed. "Let's get back to you. What rank did you reach in the Navy?"

He wagged his finger at her. "We can't talk about me, or you'll breach your contract, remember?"

"Ah, right. The *mission.* And here I thought we were past that." Her lips smirked. "I thought we were friends."

That smirk made him want to be so much more than friends. Her spirit, courage, and astuteness were as sexy to him as her full lips and big blue eyes. He wanted to strip off her body-hugging top and those damn yoga pants and make another grown erupt from those smirking lips.

That image led to more, his mind conjuring all kinds of pornographic scenes of her with her legs spread and chest heaving as he put his mouth to work on her.

Dangerous territory. But there was no way he was backing down. "You came home with four gold medals and had the chance at a couple more that year. You claimed a wrist injury, but there were no medical reports. No follow-up physical therapy. And you never competed again." He leaned his elbows on the island's salt-and-pepper colored countertop, putting his face directly across from hers. "Did you really hurt your wrist? Or did you pull out for another reason?"

Her throat contracted as she swallowed once, twice. Her voice sounded hollow when she finally spoke. "What other reason would there be?"

"Some people speculated you did it to improve the chances of one of your teammates to take the gold on vault."

"Illogical," she said, standing up and moving away from him in order to grab the wine bottle. "But I see you—or Beatrice—did your homework on me, at least what you could dig up from the internet. Unfortunately, that was a ridiculous theory back then and it still is."

She returned with the bottle in hand and refilled her glass, keeping her eyes diverted. "Nora was my best friend. We supported each other and cheered each other on, just like we did all the other girls on the team, but we were competitors first and foremost. We both went out and did our very best at every meet and the Olympics was it. Everything we'd trained for, suffered for, strived for. We represented our country, our families, our coaches, who'd stuck by us through everything.

"I hurt my wrist, and although there were no official reports"—she made air quotes around the word *official*—"I was seen by my personal doctor. My coach and my mother agreed with his diagnosis. If I continued to participate I could end up with a permanent injury. So, on their advice, I pulled the plug."

He could see it in her eyes. It was the company line, the one she'd practiced and spouted over and over again until she had convinced herself, as well as everyone else, that it was the truth.

He didn't believe her.

All professional athletes performed with injuries. They

wrapped joints, took OTC pain relievers, and soaked their sore bodies afterwards in ice baths. They received massage therapy, physical therapy, and when forced to back off on playing and practicing, they still did as much as they could, working through the pain.

She'd just admitted it—she'd been at the pinnacle of her gymnastics career. The Olympics! It wasn't her first injury, nor should it have been her last. In fact, included in the notes Beatrice had provided, Savanna had injured her left ankle on a balance beam dismount during a world competition earlier that year and had still gone on to compete on the floor exercise where she'd placed second. It was later revealed that she'd broken two bones in her foot and sprained her ankle, yet she had done nothing more than wrap her ankle and compete anyway.

It didn't surprise him. She was tough and determined, in some ways reminding him of himself. When the chips were down, Savanna got tougher. She didn't give up. She didn't run away.

Something devastating had happened to her at the Olympics and it wasn't a sprained wrist. She'd dropped out of gymnastics that very night and never returned.

"Do you regret it?" he asked softly. "Quitting at the top of your career?"

She was still standing, her gaze on the golden liquid in her glass but seeming a million miles away. The stress lines around her eyes fell away, her mouth softened. "Every. Day."

His comm unit crackled with Petit's voice. "Changing of the guard, Coldplay. Your new teammates will be Stone Sour and Shinedown. Reese is heading back to the apartment to keep an eye on things there, Beatrice is running a more in-depth background check on that doorman, Rory is scanning every camera in the DC area looking for Parker, and I'm going to put eyes on POTUS. See what our guy is up to."

Trace straightened and touched his comm. "Roger that. Watch your six."

"We've kept the showdown at the studio as quiet as we could, but there's still some talk and speculation out there," Emit informed him. "You might want to keep our client away from the news and social media for the time being."

Savanna had removed her earbud as soon as they'd reached the house and he was glad. "Will do."

"Beatrice created a statement for you about the incident and faxed it to Sergeant Franklin. You should have a copy in your email. Read through it and commit it to memory so if he calls to confirm it or ask questions, you know your official story."

There was a slight pause as someone in the background spoke to Emit and he answered. Then he came back to Trace. "You need anything tonight, holler."

Beatrice had covered his ass with the cops again. He owed her a smoothie. "Roger that, and...thanks. For everything."

Petit signed out. Stone Sour and Shinedown checked in with Poison. The three guards would stay outside in their vehicles doing perimeter checks on the hour and keeping an eye on things even with the storm.

All systems were go. Now if he could get his client to go to bed.

I thought we were friends.

After she'd made it clear to him that he was in her employ, it seemed odd she would make that statement. Then again, he'd refused to answer her question about his other theories, and he planned to keep her away from that topic as long as possible. Preferably forever.

"Sorry for the interruption," he said, seeing her watching him with a mixture of annoyance and trepidation.

"Is everything okay?"

"Routine check-in." He scanned his phone and the pictures from the security feed. "Everything is secure. The master suite is on the third floor. The bathroom has a jetted tub. You should check it out."

A quirk of her eyebrow told him his segue once again was horrible. "Trying to get rid of me?"

"It's been a rough day," he said, once again shooting for nonchalance. "I thought you might want to relax. If you're not ready for bed, there's a movie theatre and game room downstairs, and a library on the second floor with a nice fireplace."

He was more of a movie guy, but she looked like someone who read a lot. Books and a fireplace...yep, he could see her curled up in a chair with her wine and a juicy crime novel, although he'd much rather see her naked in that jetted spa.

"Oh, no, you're not getting off that easy. You took a shot at guessing my past. Now it's my turn at guessing yours."

Oh, shit. So much for enticing her into a soak in the tub or diving into a novel for a few hours. "My past is off limits."

She shrugged and smiled into her glass. "You don't have to confirm or deny anything, but I have a few theories about you."

He almost wanted to hear them, too.

"You're former Special Ops," she said, her gaze roaming over his features. "If you're Navy, you must have been a SEAL. That would explain the training and your ability to outthink what's going to happen before it does. Your reflexes, your intuition, your split-second decision making. Am I close?"

Trace kept his face neutral. She was too clever for her own good. God help him, it turned him on.

Her eyes dropped to her glass. "It would also explain why you don't like me."

His gut tightened. "What makes you think I don't like you?"

"That first day you showed up at my apartment, you made it pretty clear you weren't happy about guarding me. I realized it had to be in conjunction with my show, the one I did a couple years ago on that Navy SEAL who turned traitor. Did you know him? Trace Hunter?"

Trace held perfectly still, blood pounding in his ears. This was the moment he should divulge the truth. Tell her everything.

A part of him wanted to. Wanted more than anything to come clean, but doing so would jeopardize everything he'd built with Savanna so far. She would freak out, and rightly so, ending any chance he had to prove to her he wasn't a traitor and get her help to stop Linc Norman.

More than that, he simply wanted to spend more time with her.

She was still waiting for an answer.

Trace swallowed the truth. "Lieutenant Hunter and I ran in different circles."

"Do you think he was guilty? Of treason?"

The uncertainty in her voice threw him. "Isn't that what you proved on your show?"

"My show." She chuckled without humor. "I always do my own investigations. Except that one time. And now, I don't know. I have doubts about the legitimacy of the information I was given. It's driving me nuts."

He had to get her moving or he'd spill his guts and ruin everything. "You're tired and you need some rest. You should go upstairs."

She ignored him. "I think I've grown on you since that first day, but I'm still 'the mission', aren't I? This is only a job for you. What I can't figure out is why you, or anyone really, would be willing to take on the president."

Here, he could be honest. "I have my reasons."

Her phone rang from the pocket of her coat hanging on the chair. "Crap," she said, digging it out. "It's my mother."

She took a big swig of wine, then pushed the talk button, hopping off the chair and pacing away. "Hi Mom. What's up?"

As Savanna headed for another room, Trace overheard her mother ranting about the fact she'd seen the news and why hadn't Savanna called her.

That was close. He corked the wine bottle and stuck it in the fridge. *Too close.*

As soon as he found Parker, he was going to sit Savanna down and come clean. He had to, whether it ended his stint as her bodyguard or not. If she had doubts about the information she'd blasted to the world on her show, then maybe she'd listen to him and not turn him in to the Feds. Even though he had no proof that he *wasn't* a traitor, he did have something else. Information that would damn the president and bring him down.

CHAPTER FIFTEEN

Before Doris Jeffries was done with her tongue-lashing, Savanna had found the living room and turned on the flat screen over the fireplace.

She flipped to the news channel and sank slowly down to sit on the couch as she watched Courtney Collins, the nightly anchor, tell the viewers about Savanna's erratic behavior and sudden disappearance after shots were fired at the studio early that day.

Erratic behavior?

The couch cushions were soft and deep, and Savanna sunk down into them even as her body went rigid when she spotted the source Courtney had gotten her information from as the camera panned out.

"Here with us tonight is Ms. Bunkett's close personal friend and fellow *The Bunk Stops Here* producer, Lindsey Fey. Lindsey, thank you so much for joining us tonight."

Producer? Friend?

"Mom, I have to call you back." Savanna disconnected, her mother still talking. In ten seconds, her mom would call back, so Savanna turned off the phone and tossed it on the couch beside her.

As Courtney interviewed Lindsey, Savanna sank further into the couch's cushy pillows, wishing she could disappear. With a serious face, Lindsey told Courtney, and the camera, about Savanna's refusal to do a show after the staff and crew had put hours of work and research into it. How Savanna had become paranoid about stalkers and hired a bodyguard. How she'd become fixated on a conspiracy theory that had no proof or facts of any kind to back it up.

And then Lindsey told the ultimate lie. "Savanna Bunkett has not performed her own research on any of the topics she's brought to the American people in months. I've had to step in and do everything."

Lindsey stared straight into the camera, still wearing her big hair and perfect makeup from hosting Savanna's show. "We're all concerned about Savanna's health and wellbeing, but her disappearance today is only one more incident in her recent unprofessional conduct. The show's producers want the American public to know that the bunk truly does stop here. They will not tolerate unprincipled, unscrupulous, or dishonest reporting, nor will they support any reporter who acts in an unbecoming way."

"What about the accident earlier today?" Courtney asked, her face showing the world how she, too, took Savanna's misdeeds seriously. "Is it possible Ms. Bunkett was indeed targeted by a stalker?"

Lindsey gave Courtney a patient smile. "The police ruled the accident a hit-and-run, nothing more. This is DC. People run red lights every day and there are dozens of hit-and-runs in the metro area every month. She was a victim of the odds, not a stalker or crazy fan like she wishes everyone to believe."

Savanna was so stunned, she barely noticed Coldplay setting her wine glass on the coffee table in front of her.

"You really want to watch this?" he said.

She was like a gawker at a traffic accident. "I can't believe she's doing this to me."

He folded his arms across his large chest and nodded. "Been there."

"What?" she said, looking up at him.

"Nothing." He handed her the glass. "You're going to need this if you're going to watch."

Boy, did she. She sipped and the glass froze halfway back down when Courtney went to a live feed from Georgetown and a home office Savanna hadn't seen the inside of in months.

"Senator Brady Garrison joins us. Thank you, Senator, for taking time to speak with us."

Brady's smile crinkled the corners of his eyes, just like it always did, and he carelessly brushed his blond bangs out of the way. "Courtney, great to see you. It's no problem at all. The storm's keeping me at home tonight anyway."

Gosh darn and gee whiz. As if he'd be on Capitol Hill at eleven o'clock working if it weren't for this darned storm.

Savanna considered throwing her glass at the TV screen. "What are you up to?" she murmured under her breath at the oversized face of her ex.

"Who's he?" Coldplay asked, still standing formidably beside the couch.

"Brady Garrison the second. Senator." On screen, Courtney and Lindsey were giggling over something Brady has said. Even though she no longer loved him, Savanna definitely wanted to throw her glass at the two women. She forced the next words out. "My ex-boyfriend."

Coldplay seemed to stiffen. Without shifting his stance, he cut his eyes to her. "Right. I saw his name in your files. What does he have to do with them crucifying you and making you look like a fraud to the public?"

Brady's smile disappeared as he began telling Courtney and Lindsey about Savanna's fickle, temperamental mood swings and mercurial personality. He suggested she had untreated mental issues.

Bastard.

"I'm a woman," Savanna said, her voice flat in her own ears. "The surest way to undermine me is to have a man tell the world I'm emotional and bitchy. If you're male, they discredit you by showing you're a failure in your career. If you're female, it's all about your weight, your mood swings, and your hair."

"What?"

"It's like a tabloid. The famous women—actresses and TV personalities—are always being left by their men, not the other way around. No matter what the man did, it's the woman's fault. Either his wife or current girlfriend is too much of a bitch and drove him away, or the other woman is too sexy and he couldn't help himself. This is the world we live in."

She pointed at the screen where Brady continued to capitalize on lying about their past relationship. "Viewers eat this up. They don't care about real news if there's a fictitious or erroneous story that's juicier."

"Linc Norman pulled out all the stops on this one."

"You think he's behind this?"

"Did anyone mention the shooting at the studio today?"

She shook her head.

"Those bullets were directed at you, and although my team suppressed the hell out of the fact that it happened, the story got out. Petit wanted me to keep you away from the news and the internet so you wouldn't see it. But this is worse. They're running with a complete fabrication and editing out anything that suggests you're in danger." He faced her fully now. "That smacks of Norman."

He was right, like always. Savanna turned off the TV. She couldn't stand the sight of Brady, Courtney, or Lindsey a minute longer. "Lindsey got what she wanted after all."

Coldplay took a seat beside her, digging her phone out from under his butt when he sat on it. He tossed it on the coffee table. "We'll get this straightened out."

She shrugged, every bit of energy draining away as she set her glass on the table. "The damage is done. Even if I prove they falsified information and I was telling the truth, the damage they've done tonight will haunt me forever."

Flopping back in the pillows, she covered her eyes with her hands. "I'll never work in broadcasting again, so…yeah. There's that. Life threatened and career up in flames."

"I shouldn't have let you watch."

"Bullshit." She sat up, a hollow feeling in the pit of her stomach. "I appreciate Emit wanting to protect me, but I appreciate you letting me face the truth even more. I would have to eventually, anyway."

His eyes were that uncanny dark blue, staring at her like he was trying to dig into her mind, her soul. "The news is your world. Shielding you from negative publicity would be pointless."

"Exactly." Her mind was churning. Being made a public spectacle was embarrassing and eviscerating on so many levels. The Three Stooges—Courtney, Lindsey, and Brady—had managed to discredit and invalidate everything she'd worked for in five minutes flat. Every story she'd ever done was now suspect.

And if they dug hard enough, they could prove they were right. At least on one story. A headliner. *You didn't do your research on that one.*

The thought chilled her. "You did the right thing," she told Coldplay. "I hate secrets. Their accusations aren't truthful"—*for the most part*—"and I'll prove that once I'm able to confront the president and stop him. How's the decryption coming?"

"Still working. Your sister did a number on that USB. She obviously didn't want the information to fall into the wrong hands."

His steady gaze did funny things to her. What went on behind those blue eyes? She still wanted to throw the wine glass at the TV and she felt sick that her career was in danger, but there was something else. A warmth spreading in her stomach not due to the alcohol.

She wasn't in this alone. She was safe. She still had a chance at finding Parker and stopping this whole crazy charade.

Maybe it was the wine this time, but her head was spinning slightly. The quiet of the house and the intensity of Coldplay's stare made her feel lightheaded and exhilarated. Like she'd jumped off a cliff but he was her parachute.

Her fingers fiddled with a lint ball on the upholstery between them. "Do you think that USB will help us?"

"To find Parker or to blackmail Norman into leaving us—I mean you—alone?"

"Either. Both."

"God, I hope so."

"Me too." She rubbed the top of her thighs, anxious and worried at the same time, but not about her predicament or Parker. "I take it I'm not your first."

He sat back. "First what?"

"First bodyguard mission. You're so calm about all of this. So...professional. How many people have you brought here?"

For the first time since she'd met him, he seemed flustered. "I, um..."

Kiss him. "I get it. That would break the rules. Never mind."

He smiled. "I've never brought anyone else here."

Oh, that smile. Talk about eviscerating her.

That lightheaded, exhilarated feeling spread through her limbs. "So I am your first."

"Yeeesss..."

"But?"

A frown creased his forehead.

"I sensed a *but* coming," she said.

"No buts. You're my first bodyguard mission. Not sure I should tell you that since that probably makes you want someone else now."

"Why would I want someone else?"

"Because I have no experience with this."

For so many years, she'd had to be strong, unflinching, and perfect in the public eye. She hadn't needed anyone, and when she did, it was Parker. The two of them, inseparable, but now she realized, they'd each had their own secrets.

She didn't have Parker tonight. She had Coldplay. "You've saved my life twice. I'd say you're pretty damn good for someone with no experience."

And there it was again. That smile that made her pulse speed up. It made her ache. Ache to be held, to be touched. He didn't give it freely and a part of her understood that. She'd smiled for the camera daily for years, never feeling true happiness. Feeling locked inside a prison she'd created.

Since the age of fourteen, she'd suppressed those emotions. Her gymnastics career had been exhausting, the daily grind and injuries taking its toll, but it had made her feel alive. Whole.

And then it had been stripped away. Her world had crumbled. The people she'd depended on and looked to for guidance had pulled her safety net out from under her. She wasn't sure she could feel that deeply ever again.

Had Coldplay experienced something similar? Was that why he was so contained, so aloof?

"How do you remain so calm?" she asked. "If you've never done this before...and after the couple of days we've had...how do you seem so unfazed by all of this?"

He started to speak, stopped. Sighed. "Power and control come from external things. Your show, your fame—they're all tied to external objects and feedback from other people." He touched the center of his chest with a fist. "For me, power and control come from in here."

"External factors don't affect you?"

"They affect who I am, but not what I am."

"That sounds very Zen."

A grin quirked the side of his mouth. "It's like in yoga. You focus on your breathing and what you're feeling internally to perform a challenging pose. If you're distracted by the person next to you, or by street noise, you can't push through and hold the pose correctly. If you're focused on the right things—those inside you—you tune out the unimportant and tune in to your core power and strength."

He was powerful and definitely in control. All the potential she'd believed the future held now seemed out of reach. She was hiding in a safe house, afraid to go out in public, and no longer able to barter on her looks or her fame.

Yet, sitting there with Coldplay, she felt almost relieved. Happy. She had the potential now to do something really important—reveal the truth about the man in the Oval Office.

No more secrets. She wasn't keeping her mouth shut anymore.

"I'm about to do something prohibited by my contract," she said, not giving a damn.

He gave her a questioning look, but he was trained to make educated guesses. Outthink his enemy. He was wary, like always, but almost...anticipating. "And what is that?"

Before she could change her mind, she leaned forward. "We'll blame it on the wine."

Tilting her head, she gently touched his lips with hers. Surprisingly, he didn't back away.

His lips were warm and firm and she felt him suck in his breath. Closing her eyes, she kissed him again, lingering, sliding her lips to the corner of his mouth and sneaking her tongue out to taste him.

He moaned.

It was so faint, she almost didn't hear it. But he didn't touch her, didn't draw her close and deepen the kiss. He simply sat there.

Alrighty then.

Savanna sat back, then shot to her feet and looked down at his broad shoulders and his delicious mouth. His eyes didn't rise to meet hers and she felt ridiculously embarrassed.

She wanted more but he didn't. He probably got this all the time—women throwing themselves at him—even if she was his first protection case.

"I'm going to go to bed now." She put her head down. The hollowness was back and it wasn't just in her stomach now. It invaded her chest too. "Wake me if the decryption software works and you're able to read that USB."

Her feet felt like concrete blocks as she dragged herself out of the living room and to the stairs to find a bedroom.

⌐——•——⌐

He was a drowning man.

Savanna's kiss—her boldness—had nearly done him in.

He was a SEAL for God's sake. An assassin. A man in control of his body and his emotions.

And yet this woman...this willow-thin, in-your-face, beautiful woman was killing him.

The pain in her face, the incredulity of her situation, had made him want to comfort and protect her. Those huge blue eyes had drawn him in, her toughness trying to cover her vulnerability.

She'd been devastated that her own news station had turned against her, pissed that Lindsey had stolen her show, hurt that her ex-boyfriend—what a loser—had turned her into a psychotic bitch on national television.

Everything they'd said about her was a lie to create doubt about her stability and competence.

He knew the feeling.

Guilt slammed him.

Why do I feel guilty? She ruined my life and now she's getting a taste of her own damn medicine.

But he knew her now. Knew she hadn't made up stories about him and ruined his life on purpose. She'd been lied to, had put her trust in the wrong people.

He'd known she was going to kiss him. Hell, he'd *wanted* her to kiss him. And then she had and his world had spun down to that one moment, the soft brush of her lips against his.

For the first time in a long time, he'd felt need. True, honest, raw need. Suffusing. Saturating. Flooding his system with desire.

Drowning him.

He couldn't let her—or anyone—get under his skin like this. It was pretty fucking sad that after all of his training, all the shit he'd lived through, that a single kiss could upend his carefully controlled existence.

He was better than this. Emotions, feelings, a thing of his past. There was no room for them in his present or future. Detachment was his mantra, and...

Shit.

Glancing down, he realized he was still sitting rigid on the couch. Savanna's kiss had paralyzed him. All but one important part anyway. The bulge in his pants was freaking huge.

Yep, even though she'd fled the room minutes ago, embarrassed, her sweet backside beckoning to him as she walked out, his dick continued to remain hard as steel. It strained against his zipper, nearly painful in its diligence to escape.

Follow her.

Scrubbing his face with his hands, he shook off the longing, the need. While he'd entertained a few fantasies inside Witcher of fucking Ms. Savanna Bunkett *over*, he'd never actually thought about fucking her.

Now, all his mind wanted to do was think about that big ol' bed on the third floor and her spread wide on top of it, naked and waiting for him.

Pathetic. A woman hadn't touched him in so long, hadn't kissed him, he'd turned into a horny pushover the minute one did.

Trace pushed himself off the couch, adjusting his pants and his painful erection. Grabbing Savanna's wine glass, he downed the remaining liquid in the bottom, wishing it was something stronger, because it was going to be one long-ass night if he had to keep himself from taking the stairs to that master suite two at a time.

CHAPTER SIXTEEN

Compared to some of the hellholes Trace had lived in, the safe house felt like a mansion.

He found a room that would work to release his tension with tall windows that overlooked the rear garden next to the library he'd told Savanna about. His pulse was elevated and he needed to center himself.

Killing a man barely raised his blood pressure. Being in the center of combat relaxed him. He could rely on his training, trust his heightened natural abilities.

Being alone in a house with Savanna, being subjected to her probing questions and hot, supple body, however, had him crawling out of his skin.

It was no surprise she'd guessed he was a former SEAL. The part about the experimental drugs and the DOD, though, was too close for comfort.

Focus on that, he told himself. Not her kiss.

Stripping down to his underwear, he left the lights off and took a seat on the floor facing the bank of windows—the snow provided enough reflection from the night sky and the landscape lights that he could see just fine. His heightened night vision didn't hurt either.

The gardens and woods behind the house were covered in snow, the storm winding down as it approached midnight. He'd checked in with his fellow guards and all was normal.

Going through a set of stretches, he held each one until his muscles strained and his breathing increased. He listened to the sound of his breath and let the cascade of wild thoughts—and the images of a naked Savanna—flit through his mind and disappear as he took his practice deeper.

The thoughts slowed with his breathing. The images of long legs, a flat stomach, and those lips that could bring a man to his knees, didn't.

Fighting mental chaos never worked. You had to give in to it. Acknowledge it. Make peace with it.

But making peace with the fantasies running through his head would mean getting rid of the massive hard-on between his legs. And the only way he wanted to do that was by going upstairs and waking the sexy woman sleeping there.

Once his body was tired and sweating from the extreme poses he forced it into, he'd achieved a reasonable amount of headspace again. His fantasies were still there, along with the hard-on, but he could feel his pulse slowing, his breath coming easier.

Two hours. It took two hours of holding poses to feel the release he needed from the mental chaos. Never had it taken so long.

That's what Savanna did to him—threw his internal rhythms off, made him crazy.

Meditation came next, his mind happy to continue the struggle to make peace with his Savanna fantasies. Even if they were now "friends" in her book, there was no good end to this situation. Once she found out who he was, that he'd deceived her, it wouldn't matter that he'd also saved her life. She would hate him.

Like always, that thought dampened the fire in his gut, and clearing his mind came easier as he folded his primed body into a restorative sit and stared out at the snow-covered garden.

He set the timer on his watch, and a few minutes later, his body slipped into the deep space of mediation between nothingness and sleep. He welcomed it, his body needing the recharge.

Sometime later, his nose woke him before the alarm, as he picked up a scent that never failed to make his mouth water.

Bacon.

A quick check of his watch showed he'd slept for two hours. It was now four in the morning.

Tapping his comm, he checked in with his team as he dressed. "Perimeter check?"

"Frosty as ever," came the reply from Poison. "My piss freezes before it hits the ground every time I take a leak."

A snort sounded from Henley, a new arrival, followed by a horrible rendition of some Disney song, telling Poison to let it go. "Other than the frozen landscape, all's secure, mate."

"Copy that."

The laptop was still working on decrypting the USB. Sounds from downstairs made him stop for a second and listen. The occasional muffled bang of a pan, the clink of silverware—how long had it been since he'd heard those normal, homey sounds?

Trace made his way downstairs cautiously. No one could have gotten through the security team or the surveillance system, so that only left one person who could be cooking bacon.

Savanna.

At four in the morning?

A tiny amount of light spilled from the kitchen. Not enough to be from the bright overhead lights, but...

Trace turned the corner and saw Savanna standing at the stove, the bacon scent now mixed with other smells that reminded him of his childhood home, his grandmother.

Pancakes.

She was working by candlelight, humming what sounded a lot like the Happy Birthday tune under her breath. For a moment, he was transported back to a tiny kitchen, his grandmother tinkering with eggs and biscuits.

Stepping into the room, he watched Savanna for a long moment, soaking her up. She'd bundled up in sweatpants and a long-sleeve T-shirt, both of which looked too big on her, yet worked with the smells she was generating of home and casual family breakfasts.

"Are the lights not working?" he said and she jumped, flipping a pancake on the floor.

Gripping the spatula to her chest, she laughed out a nervous breath. "You shouldn't sneak up on people like that!"

"Sorry." He closed the distance to the stove and picked up the fallen pancake, tossing it in the sink. "Couldn't sleep?"

She turned her face away, and in the candlelight, he saw wetness on her cheeks. "I kept seeing that man every time I closed my eyes. All that blood." She shuddered. "I needed to do something."

"So you decided to make breakfast by candlelight?"

"The night is so quiet and so beautiful out there." She pointed the spatula at the window. "I don't get that kind of view at my apartment. The bright lights in here seemed too harsh and turned the windows black so I couldn't see outside."

Quiet and beautiful wasn't exactly how he'd describe the snowy landscape. *Cold. Brutal. Lonely.* How many times had he sat in harsh elements watching his targets at four in the morning? It was the perfect time to take them off guard. He fought the urge to close the shade. The windows were one-ways, bulletproof. He still wanted to close off the world.

She looked at him and smiled. Her face looked vulnerable, delicate. "I like candlelight. It's…gentle."

He liked the candlelight too. Watching the soft light flicker over her face, he could forget the tears on her cheeks and imagine the two of them were a normal couple. That she wasn't scared and that he was something more than her bodyguard.

But they weren't a normal couple. Hell, they weren't a couple period. Two days ago, he'd wanted nothing to do with her, and even though now he wanted to sweep her up in his arms and kiss away her tears, that was never going to happen.

The shadows of his life were as cold and dark as the landscape outside. Inhospitable and unforgiving.

Exactly why he couldn't tell Savanna who he was yet. Maybe never. Even if he wasn't a traitor to his country, he was an assassin. It had become clear to him while he was meditating. He couldn't shut off that past, couldn't deny its existence no matter how much he wanted to. She would never understand or accept that, and why should she?

He was on his own.

Shaking off the past memories and the coldness they brought with them, he motioned to a bag on the counter. "Are those chocolate chips?"

"The pantry is stocked with everything imaginable. I found three kinds of syrup too." She flipped a pancake. "Parker would be in heaven. Every year since I was eight, I always made chocolate chip pancakes for her birthday…"

Her voice trailed off and she swiped at her cheeks. "Anyway, I had a craving for pancakes. And bacon." She glanced out the window again. "I hope she's safe in this storm."

It was her sister's birthday. He'd seen it in the file, but it hadn't registered until now. "Parker is smart, resourceful, and intuitive, like you. I'm sure she's fine."

"I don't feel smart or resourceful at the moment."

"For what it's worth, you're doing an amazing job handling all of this." He touched her arm. "And we *are* friends, by the way. This isn't just a mission for me."

Her eyes tracked his hand on her arm, lifted to meet his head-on. "You mean that?"

"I do," he told her, although he wasn't sure what kind of friends they could ever be.

Relationships. Always complicated, and then when you added in his profession, his past, he didn't stand a chance at anything resembling normal or long-term.

Savanna deserved better than that.

She handed him a plate. "Help yourself."

He loaded it with bacon and pancakes, grabbed a cup of coffee from the still-brewing pot. She did the same and they settled in at the breakfast bar to eat.

"To Parker," he said, raising his coffee in toast.

Savanna did the same and tapped her cup against his. "Happy Birthday, sis, wherever you are."

The first bite was warm and delicious, an explosion of vanilla and sugar on his tongue. He hadn't had chocolate chip pancakes since... He couldn't remember when.

"Syrup?" she asked, handing him a squat bottle.

The previous evening's kiss was still there between them. She was doing a good job pretending it wasn't. "Don't need it. These are perfect the way they are."

A small smile lifted her lips and she went back to her food, crunching on a piece of bacon. They sat in silence for several minutes, eating and enjoying the quiet. Trace almost felt sorry for Poison and Henley, missing out on this incredible breakfast with a beautiful woman while freezing their asses off outside.

"You were correct, yesterday," Savanna said, cupping her hands around her coffee cup and staring at the dark liquid inside. "My wrist wasn't the reason I quit the Olympics."

His hunch had been right, yet, he sensed her hesitation to divulge her secret, so he simply nodded and kept eating. "You don't have to tell me."

"I do." She nodded, as if giving herself a mental pep talk. "Unless you don't want to hear it. It's...ugly...and you might think less of me after I tell you what happened."

Damn. There was strength in her voice, but the rawness in her eyes sucked him in. *What happened to her all those years ago?*

The idea that her secret could be worse than his was ludicrous. The fact that she thought anything she'd done could make him think less of her, even more so. "Done plenty of shit myself that I'm not proud of."

"In service to your country, though, right? That's sort of what I did, or at least that's how my mother and my coach spun it so I'd keep my mouth shut." Inhaling, she shook her head. "I kept my mouth shut about something I shouldn't have in order to keep the US Olympics Women's Team from being touched by scandal. Real heroic, huh?"

The sarcasm in her voice didn't quite cover the pain underneath. The sound of that pain crawled under his skin, a warning. He wasn't going to like what he heard. "What type of scandal?"

Her throat worked and her eyes shifted away. "Nora's coach...he..."

Goose flesh rose on Trace's skin. His gut tightened. "He what?"

"See, we had a team of coaches, and he was one of them. He was a touchy-feely sort of guy, always had his hands on us, giving us instructions and correcting postures. I didn't think much of it until a couple of weeks before the Olympics. We were already in Sydney, adjusting to the time difference and getting used to the stadium. One night after a late practice, he caught me in the locker room. Said he wanted to go over a few ideas he had on how to make my floor routine standout."

Trace tightened the hold he had on his fork. He knew where this was going.

"Coach Watson's touch didn't scare me at first. I was fourteen. I'd never even had a boyfriend, and he was a coach. A well-respected and sought-after coach. I just thought the way he brushed a hand against my bottom or my breasts was an accident that night. Later, after I'd won a couple of those medals, he caught me alone again and said he wanted to congratulate me...he had a treat for me."

Her voice had grown lower, softer. She drew in a shaky breath. "You can imagine the rest. He didn't rape me, just molested me."

Just molested. As if that was somehow okay.

Trace couldn't help it. He dropped his fork and laid his hand on her back. "What did you do?"

She stared, unseeing, into her coffee. "My whole world

shifted after that. The experience was horrible, but it was what happened afterward that compounded it."

"What happened?"

She took a deep sigh. "I've never told anyone this."

He rubbed the base of her neck with tiny circles meant to comfort. "Like I said, you don't have to tell me."

"I went to my mother, scared and looking for help, and she told me to keep it quiet. She accused me of misunderstanding or misinterpreting what had happened, and I was dumb enough to wonder at first if she were right."

Another deep breath. The coffee cup trembled. "I was naive, but I wasn't stupid. I insisted on telling Nora and her mom, because I was afraid he was doing it to Nora too. But coming out and accusing Nora's coach of sexual molestation could ruin his career and mine, my mother said. Not to mention Nora's career and the rest of the girls at the Olympics. It would taint everyone's medals, ruin everyone's careers. I would create a scandal that would go down in the history books. Was that how I wanted to be remembered?"

A tear slipped from the corner of her eye and Trace reached out and wiped it from her cheek. He wanted to pull her into his arms and hold her. "Jesus. You were just a kid."

"I was, but I did it. I kept quiet, and I tried to go on, do my routines and put it behind me, but every time I saw him watching me from the sidelines, I'd freeze up. I couldn't concentrate. I couldn't focus."

"So you made up the wrist injury and pulled out."

"Yes."

"Why would I think less of you because of that? You did what you were told to do. Your mother's the one I think less of. She should have her ass kicked for making you keep such a horrible secret. Did you have counseling, anything?"

Savanna shook her head. "I wasn't allowed to tell anyone. Then six months later, Nora came up pregnant. Her family claimed some teenage boy was the father. Nora had gone on this wild rampage after the Olympics, drinking and getting into trouble, so the story made sense. But I knew the truth. At least I think I do. It was Coach Watson's baby. He stayed around in the gymnastics world for a couple more years but that was it. He disappeared. Nora's parents made her give up the baby and she committed suicide a year after the child was born."

The cup was shaking so badly now, he feared she'd spill the

hot liquid on herself. He carefully removed it from her fingers and set it down. Then he grabbed her thighs and turned her to face him. "None of that was your fault. You know that, right? The coach was a dick, and what happened to Nora is tragic, but not your fault."

In the candlelit room, her blue eyes were the shade of the sky outside. "It *was* my fault. If I'd told someone, even my dad, maybe I could have prevented Nora from being abused and ending up pregnant. Maybe I could have prevented her suicide. If I'd just said *something*."

A familiar urge burned low in Trace's gut. The urge to kill. "Where do you think Watson went?"

"When I landed my news show, I tried to find him." She shrugged. "He must have changed his name and started over. I found no trace of him anywhere."

"Did you ever tell Parker?"

Savanna's face darkened as she caught his drift. "You think she...? No. She doesn't know what happened. I never told anyone, except my mother." Her gaze dropped to his hands on her thighs, slowly came back up to meet his. "And now you."

Pulling her into his arms would be a bad idea. He wanted to comfort her but wrapping his arms around her would lead to something else. And he couldn't go there, especially after what she'd told him. Taking advantage of her in such an emotional state broke his personal rule.

She bit her bottom lip. "About last night..."

The left turn took him by surprise. "You don't have to apologize. And your segue sucks."

Her lips twitched. "I wasn't going to apologize, because I'm not sorry I kissed you. I just wanted to say that I know it made you uncomfortable—you don't like breaking the rules and you're not into me. I get it. I wanted to assure you it won't happen again."

"I'm not apologizing either," he said.

She looked taken aback. "For what? You didn't do anything."

"For this."

He pulled her off the barstool and slid her body between the V of his legs, one hand going behind her neck as he brought his lips down on hers.

CHAPTER SEVENTEEN

Savanna fell into Coldplay's body, a freefall into hot, needy desire.

More like a magnet snapping against steel.

Her missing sister's birthday, the horrible past with the coach…all of it evaporated in the heat of his hands, his lips.

He tasted like chocolate chips and strong coffee. His kiss teased, probed, teased again—a game that left her panting, her nipples tightening under the soft cotton of her borrowed sweatshirt.

She wanted more.

Parting her lips, she flicked out her tongue, catching his as she wrapped her arms around his neck. One of his hands, the one buried in her hair, massaged the back of her neck, then traveled down her spine, his tongue going deep enough, he nearly bent her backwards. The other hand rested at the top of her butt, securing her firmly in place.

Fire. She was playing with two-hundred pounds of steel and fire.

Instead of feeling panic, she felt safe, hungry for more than pancakes.

Moaning, she pressed herself closer, her nipples begging for the feel of his hard body, her pelvis burying itself deeper between his legs. He obliged, spreading his solid, muscled thighs wider, guiding her in with his hands.

He broke the kiss, looked into her eyes. "I shouldn't be doing this, but I can't resist you."

"Not many men can," she teased, brushing her lips against his.

He kissed her back. "You're so beautiful, so smart, and so damn wrong for me."

Savanna stiffened. "Why am I wrong?"

"You don't know who I am, Savanna. You don't know the things I've done."

True. She didn't. But she didn't want to care at this moment. She owed him her life. She'd seen the gentleness in him as well as the trained killer.

She found both sexy as hell.

Did that make her sick or stupid? Did it matter if she didn't know his name or his background? Hell, she'd thought she known everything about Brady before she'd slept with him. He was the ultimate boyfriend on paper—good pedigree, great education, dreams for their future together that matched hers. They were White House bound, he'd told her. She was going to be his First Lady.

But he'd been keeping secrets. Damning secrets. He'd lied to her and ruined everything. She hadn't really known him any better than a stranger off the street.

Coldplay was an enigma. She knew so little about him and his past. Didn't care at this moment about his upbringing, his education, his future plans. She trusted him enough to confess her deepest, darkest secret. He hadn't run away. In fact, he'd comforted her and acted as if he wanted to hunt down that coach and strangle him.

She laid her hand over his heart, watching the unsettled look in his eyes. He was fighting with himself, trying to protect her again, only in a different manner. "Maybe you're not right for me either, but you are a good person, and that's all I need to know."

His chest muscles bunched under her hand. "With my...profession...I can't promise you anything. A future. You deserve better."

"I'm not looking for a commitment. I just want to be held, caressed, appreciated for a little while." *I want to forget my life.* "I could die today, tomorrow. I don't want to die with regrets." She stroked a lock of his hair from his forehead and whispered. "I want you. If you want me, too, then let's call it even. We might be bad for each other as partners in a relationship, but I bet we'll rock this house to its foundation with a bout of casual sex. What's wrong about that?"

He growled deep in his throat and kissed her hard. His hand skimmed her ribcage, the underside of her breast. She urged him on, running her hands over his shoulders, his back, his chest. He grazed her nipple with a thumb and she arched into him.

Lost in throes of sensation, it took her a moment to register the buzzing noise in the background.

And then she was airborne, corded arms of steel wrapping her up and taking her to the floor in a sudden rush that made her gasp.

Coldplay, kneeling in front of her, pinned her up against the side of the kitchen island, his face a mask in the candlelit darkness. "That's the security alarm for the infrared perimeter outside. Something's been breached. Stay here and stay silent. I'll be back for you."

Her heart stuttered in her chest, her voice mute as he disappeared from view, becoming one with the shadows.

Savanna hugged her knees to her chest as icy fingers of fear wrapped around her lungs, crept into her throat. The distant alarm buzzed in time with her pulse, the rest of the house completely quiet.

Seconds stretched into minutes. How had an intruder made it past the men stationed outside? Was he—or she—now stalking through the house? She strained her eyes, staring into the shadows, praying Coldplay was all right.

She was no stranger to fear, but it had been a long time since she'd felt such a visceral surge of it. Uncurling herself, she kept her attention on her surroundings while reaching up and over her head to feel for the silverware on the island counter.

Her fingers touched cool metal, and one by one, she pulled down a fork, a knife, another fork. Keeping one fork by her side, she clenched the other two utensils in her hands and went into a crouched position, ready to lunge forward.

A fork and a knife. A trained assassin would laugh at her, but hell if she was going to sit on the floor, paralyzed by fear, and do nothing if someone came after her.

A hard shudder went through her. *I'm not a victim. Never again.*

The alarm ceased. An eerie silence descended. Savanna held her breath, listening.

Without warning, a form emerged in the doorway and she startled, falling backward and hitting the island.

"All clear," Coldplay said, coming forward and reaching a hand down to help her up.

Her heart played hopscotch in her chest. Her breath exhaled on a hard whoosh. "There's no breach?" she managed to say as he took the knife from her hand and helped her stand.

"There is, but… Well, let me show you."

He removed the fork from her hand, and made no comment about her choice of weapons. Then he threaded his fingers through her stiff ones and led her to the stairs.

The adrenaline in her veins continued to pump. There had been a breach. Someone had gotten through. Had he killed them like he had the assassin posing as a janitor?

His hand warmed hers—touching him was like touching a furnace. He generated enough heat to melt the polar caps. Her eyes adjusted to the dark, so she didn't need to hang onto the stair railing, and she really didn't need his guidance, but she clung to his hand anyway as they ascended to the second floor. The house continued to echo with near-silence, the only sound her soft footsteps on the carpet. Coldplay's were completely mute.

How does he do that?

Following him down a hallway on the second floor, she felt herself relax. She didn't want to need anyone, but she did. She needed Coldplay.

I don't just need him. I want him.

Her body's response gave testament to that fact. Watching him, feeling his hand wrapped protectively around hers, following him into a part of the house she hadn't explored yet, felt thrilling. Sexy. She wanted to pick up where they'd left off, like an adrenaline junkie ready for her next freefall.

What is wrong with me? I was crouching on the kitchen floor arming myself with stainless steel utensils five seconds ago and here I am ready to jump his bones.

The feeling refused to leave, though, as he opened the French doors at the end of the hall and gently guided her by the elbow through them.

The room was huge and open, floor-to-ceiling windows facing the west garden. The furniture had been pushed aside, a folded towel placed on the floor to look out the windows. Coldplay's boots and sat nearby, along with her laptop, still working at decrypting the USB.

The only light came from the partial moon, streaming in through the windows. It reflected on the expanse of snow outside, turning it a pale pewter grey.

"The windows are coated so no one can see in," Coldplay told her as he drew her to the windows. "But we can see out."

Peaceful. Mesmerizing. The quiet garden was bathed in soft moonlight, the trees and statues throwing short shadows over the ground. Coldplay pointed at the far south side of the garden. "Your friends who breached the infrared."

Three deer grazed under a willow tree. A doe and two identical young ones. Twins.

As if the doe felt Savanna's gaze, she lifted her head, looking toward the house. One of the young moved closer to her.

The way it should be. A mother should protect her child, not throw her under the bus.

Shaking it off, she refused to think about the past in this special moment. The mesmerizing sensation continued to fall over her like a warm blanket. The quiet, mixed with Coldplay's presence and the beauty of the early morning...

Tears welled in her eyes for a completely different reason than they had earlier.

She was happy.

Crazy, apparently, too.

Who would be happy in her shoes?

She was in deep shit and she knew it, but for this one moment, she felt safer and happier than she had since the night all those years ago at the Olympics.

"I never got to enjoy winter like most kids," she said softly. "Building snowmen, having snowball fights, going sledding...I missed all of that."

"Why?" Coldplay asked.

"I was up early to head to the gym every day, then school, then home and back to the gym until evening. Holidays were full of practice and traveling to meets. I didn't have time, or the energy, for frivolous things like playing in the snow. By the time I quit gymnastics, I considered myself too old. Truth was, I didn't really know how."

The mother deer returned to grazing. The twins ventured a little farther from her, leaving small, dark tracks behind.

"Come on," Coldplay said, grabbing her hand again and drawing her toward the door.

"Where are we going?" She hoped to his bed.

"You'll see."

They went downstairs to a mudroom at the back of the house that led out into the garden they'd been viewing.

Coldplay flipped on the light. The mudroom held an assortment of boots, coats, snow pants, and ski equipment.

He eyed the assortment and started handing things to her. "Put these on."

"Why?" She accepted a pair of boots. "Where are we going?"

"Outside."

No shit. "Why?" she repeated.

He tugged on a pair of snow pants and sat on the bench to put on boots. "To play in the snow."

A grin teased her lips. "Is it safe?"

"I'll make sure it is."

She believed him and sat on the bench next to him to put on the boots. "These are too big for me."

He rifled through a basket of brand new socks. "Stuff these in the ends," he said.

A few minutes later, they were outside in the still, cold air. Coldplay had notified the guards watching the grounds that they'd be outside and not to panic if they heard noise and yelling.

The doe stared from twenty yards away as Savanna and Coldplay stood immobile and watched her and her babies. She seemed more curious than frightened.

Coldplay exhaled a long sigh, his breath clouding white above his head as he dropped it back and looked up at the stars. His gloved hand found her gloved hand and he squeezed her fingers through the thick fabric. "This is when you know you're really alive. In nature, alone."

She followed his gaze, living in the moment, the continuing feeling of happiness pervading her body. The crystal clear air heightened her senses. The stars twinkled.

"You're not alone anymore," she told him. "I don't know who or what you were before you took this assignment, but who you are now is the only thing that counts."

Coldplay released her hand. She heard the swish of his nylon coat and the snow pants as he shifted away.

The doe broke into a run, her babies running after her. "Coldplay, I just meant…"

The next thing she knew, Savanna was eating snow. A snowball hit her in the chest, ice crystals flying into her face and making her gasp. A second one hit her in the stomach.

He stood a few feet away, grinning from ear to ear and kneading a third snowball in his hands. "You might want to take cover," he said. "I'm a damn good shot."

This man. Laughter bubbled in her chest and she reached down to scoop up her own handful of snow. "Yeah, well, since I haven't done this before, I get a handicap, right? Like you just stand there and let me hit you?"

He twirled round and flipped the snowball at her over his head, taking off in the direction of the willow tree. "Nope!"

Even not looking at her and her dodging to the left, he managed to hit her in the shoulder. *Damn.* She fired her snowball at his back and barely managed to hit his lower leg.

He laughed and ducked to the right behind a statue. "That's the best you got, Jeffries?"

Scooping up another handful of snow, she ran after him.

CHAPTER EIGHTEEN

Thin strips of peach and pink broke the eastern horizon as Trace lay on the ground, out of breath and laughing. His army of snowmen had taken a beating from Savanna's in the last snowball fight, but he'd bested her in snow angels, making three perfect ones to her one.

"Who taught you to throw like that?" he asked her, staring up at the waning night sky as it gave way to sunrise.

"Parker. It took a minute for it to come back to me, but it did. Who taught you how not to disturb the snow when getting out of your snow angels?"

No one had taught him. The balance and ability to not disturb his environment was part of his training. He sat up, wishing the night never had to end. He'd debated about bringing her outside like this, but the estate was secluded, his team was the elite of the elite, and he knew his heightened perception would register danger even before they did. "You're soaking wet."

Savanna was grinning from ear to ear, wet strands of her hair, the result of a few snowballs to the face, stuck to her chin and neck. "This was the best night, *er*, morning ever."

A warm sensation low in his gut agreed. Rising to his feet, he stretched out a hand. "Let me help so you don't mess this one up."

She giggled and the sound made the warmth spread to his chest. "Can I lay here and watch the sunrise a little longer?"

Nothing would have made him happier. "You're shivering. We need to get you warmed up."

She huffed out a cloud of breath and sat up gingerly, putting up her hood. "All right."

He jumped out of his snow angel, then lifted her from hers, making her laugh again. Placing her on her feet, he turned her around so she could see their angels, side by side.

"I haven't had this much fun in years," she murmured.

Me either. "We can still watch the sunrise."

She looked up at him, the hood of her coat too big and hanging half over her face. "We can?"

At that moment, he would have done anything for her. "Absolutely. Follow me."

One last look at their backyard handiwork and she gave him a nod. "We should make snow forts later and have another snowball fight."

Later. Yeah, he hoped there was a later.

The south side of the house contained a covered in-ground swimming pool and sunroom. The walls and ceiling were five-inch glass that had been mixed with a high-tech polymer making them bulletproof. Like all the windows in the house, they were coated with a special film. People inside could see out; those outside could not see in.

He led Savanna through the side door to the sunroom. "Stay here. I'll be right back."

After stripping off his coat and snow pants in the mudroom, he found hot cocoa mix in the kitchen pantry. His grandmother had always made him a cup when he'd come in from playing in the snow. She always had marshmallows, the big ones, and he would cover the top of the warm cocoa with them, making her laugh.

His half-eaten pancakes still sat on the island counter. He cleaned up the plates, checked the security feeds, and grabbed the laptop while the water heated. All was quiet.

Back in the sunroom, Savanna had removed her outer clothes and sat on a wicker love seat watching the horizon. She'd pulled the seat and a coffee table over for the best view, propping her feet on the table. Trace handed her a steaming mug of cocoa and a towel, set the laptop on the table, then took the seat next to her.

She scooted closer to him, resting her thigh against his, her shoulder brushing his bicep. "I've said this a lot in the past couple of days, but thank you."

"For what? Kicking your ass at snow angels?"

She punched him softly. "For this break from real life. For giving me something I never had as a kid."

They sipped their drinks in silence as the November sun stole the shadows from the trees and bathed their snow soldiers with a golden light.

I should be thanking her.

As a SEAL, he'd always felt connected to the land, had had to know the terrain. This was different. In the quiet of a winter night, he felt something inside him expand. Something that had been crushed and smothered for too long.

She'd given him a piece of his soul back.

Birds began to chatter. The trees stood blanketed in snow. She shivered against him.

"You're still cold." He wrapped an arm around her. "We should get you in the shower."

Taking the mug from his hand and setting both cocoas on the table, she climbed into his lap. The towel fell to the floor. "I have a better idea."

She was solid and warm, her cheeks crimson from the hours in the cold air. With no makeup and her damp hair raked back from her face, she was the most beautiful woman he'd ever seen. Dark blue eyes watched him with expectant awareness.

Setting his hands on her hips, he knew this wasn't real, lasting. Her interest in him wasn't actually about him. She'd been scared shitless and he'd been the one to step in and protect her. In a world of threats, he represented safety. He was a lifeline, nothing more.

Fine with him. He could be a lifeline, her protector for now. Later, well... She wouldn't need him anymore and he'd have this one moment in time to remember when he was back in Witcher or wherever the hell he ended up.

Because, really, no one, not even Beatrice, Emit, or Cal could keep him safe from the president.

He'd have to do that all on his own.

"You're thinking too much," Savanna said, teasing his lips with hers. "You've given me the perfect morning. Let me give you something."

She traced a delicate finger across his jawline, down his neck to his collarbone. Her lips followed that line and Trace let his head fall back, his hands gripping her hips a little tighter.

"You don't have to do this," he said.

Her tongue ran over his skin. "I *want* to do this."

She lifted the edge of his shirt, those teasing fingers of hers making him suck in his breath as she touched his abs, his ribs. His cock throbbed, his mouth went dry. He needed to touch her, to get inside her. To kiss her mindless and then fuck her the same way.

The two halves of her sexy ass fit perfectly in his hands. He pulled her close, bringing her mouth back up to his. Her lips were soft and giving as he slipped his tongue inside.

Grasping the nape of her neck, he held her immobile while he explored. She sucked his tongue hard and he nearly came right there imagining how it would feel to have her mouth on him doing the same thing.

Opening her legs wider, she moved against his erection, her own tongue meeting his in a sensuous dance. She rocked against him, building a rhythm, and even though they both were fully clothed, it made fire break out in his veins.

His control broke. He wanted Savanna more than any woman he'd ever been with. He wanted to shred her clothes and take her right there on the floor in the morning light. Fuck her until she screamed his name and thanked him all over again.

She tugged at his shirt, stretching it up over his chest. He sat straighter and lifted his arms, letting her pull it off. His own hands went to her shirt, thumbed her breasts through the thin cotton. Her breath caught and she gripped his bare shoulders, digging in her nails. The bedroom was two floors up. They'd never make it in time.

She drew back, looking down at his chest.

The tattoos. The scars. Her fingers traced the scar that ran down the center of his chest, her big eyes coming up to meet his. "What happened to you?"

Too much. He could never explain it all, didn't want to rehash it in his own mind. "I've been broken a few times, Savanna. Physically, emotionally, mentally. I've survived, and come back stronger than ever. You don't need to worry about me."

Her smile held irony. "Post-traumatic growth. I should have you on my show." *If I still had a show.* The unsaid words hung between them. Her eyes filled with sadness.

Unable to stand it, Trace kissed her, long and deep. Kissed the sadness away. The truth that was eating at him inside.

Her hands went around his neck, did a sensual slide into his hair. He pressed her closer, feeling her taut nipples tease his bare chest. Oblivious to anything other than getting her naked, he started to flip her on her back onto the love seat when his comm crackled to life.

"Shift change, Coldplay," Poison said. "Creed and Crossfade coming in and we...are...out of here."

Savanna straightened, her body going stiff as she broke the kiss and looked at him.

Shit. The team's timing couldn't have been worse. Reluctantly, he tapped the comm. "Roger that."

She slid off his lap, got busy with her cocoa mug. In his ear, his new team checked in and asked for instructions.

He kept his directions simple, his gaze zeroing in on the laptop as he muted his comm.

Nothing new there. He needed to check in with Rory, see if the man would send him any video he could of the areas surrounding the accident and the spot Parker had ditched the limo.

He also needed to do something with Savanna.

Except the only thing he wanted to do was resume where they'd left off.

Her body language was stiff, her eyes locked on the snowy landscape. "I'm going to grab that shower," she said, rising and not meeting his eyes.

Taking her mug of hot chocolate, she started to flee, and he mentally let go of a stream of curses. So in tune with her, he sensed her pause behind him. "You're welcome to join me. In the shower, that is."

Her presence, that amazing energy of hers, waited for a moment and then dissipated.

Gone. An open invitation to get naked with her hanging in the air.

There was nothing he'd like better than to take her up on that offer. But he had work to do. As a SEAL, he'd always held himself to the highest of standards. That mentality had bled over into every area of his life. Even in Witcher, he'd kept himself physically and mentally at the top of his game. His survival depended on it.

Now Savanna's did too.

He had to keep his head. Both of them. He could not—would not—screw this up.

Savanna's libido was a ticking bomb about to explode. Twice in one morning she'd gotten her hormones raging and both times been rudely interrupted.

As she undressed in the master suite, it was hard to ignore the fact her body felt like it had a cyclone swirling inside. So much had happened in the past two days, it was as if she'd been sucked up by a force of nature and could no longer find solid ground.

Coldplay had been her rock, her touchstone. After the past few hours, however, even his presence was messing with her. He made her feel young and happy again, yet, he continued to hold himself back. While he might find her attractive and he'd agreed they were friends, he wasn't committed to crossing the line of no return. She'd told him a casual hookup was all she wanted just to get him in bed. It wasn't true—she wanted more, much more—but even that hadn't been enough to get him into bed.

As the shower ran, the water heating up, she considered traipsing back downstairs with nothing on and draping herself in front of that damn laptop. That would get his attention.

Hurt feelings had no place in this scenario, yet a small emptiness filled her chest at having him dismiss her so easily. For a little bit, she'd seen the man underneath the armor. They'd had a break from reality for a few hours. He'd made her forget it was Parker's birthday, and made her remember what it was like to laugh and have fun.

She hadn't done that in a long time.

She hadn't jumped a man's bones in a long time either. And it was as much her fault as his that she'd jumped off him and acted all uncomfortable when they'd gotten caught making out.

A grin tugged at the corners of her mouth. Poor Coldplay. She had to quit attacking him.

Of course, *he'd* kissed her over pancakes.

Not that she'd minded.

She touched her slightly swollen lips. The flush in her cheeks matched their color. Man, the guy could kiss. The way his lips had worked hers over, the way his tongue had swept her mouth, teasing her until she'd thought she'd die…

A shiver snaked down her spine and heated the spot between her legs. He was hot and cold, but when he was hot…

Well, when he was hot, he was the best damn kisser she'd ever encountered.

Imagine what he'd be like in bed.

Her nipples pebbled at the nagging thought. The pulse at the base of her throat tapped faster. Stripping off her clothes, she stepped into the shower and started scrubbing. Damn him for not ignoring his job and taking her right there on the sunroom couch.

The memory of his hands on her sent her already aroused body into overdrive. Her skin felt too sensitive under the spray of water, her thoughts conjuring plenty of fantasies.

And then the guilt hit.

Here she was in a beautiful house with a sexy man, building snowmen and drinking hot cocoa like she was on vacation. Meanwhile, her sister was who-knows-where, fighting for her life on her birthday. Would it be her last?

No. I won't let it. I will find Parker and put an end to this awful situation.

The shampoo was a designer brand; not hers but nice. The body scrub was fruity and made her smell like a pina colada. She wondered if Coldplay liked coconut.

Damn it. She had to stop this—fantasizing about him. That only led to thoughts about the future and they had no future. Her life was complicated, and from what little he'd said, his was even more so.

Hell, her life wasn't just complicated, it was beyond fucked up.

The time out in the snow with him, the moments in the sunroom watching the sunrise, had all rebooted her brain. Whatever Parker had left on that USB was big. Something she wanted Savanna to take to the news outlets, otherwise, why leave it with her? If Parker was an agent—and she seemed to be a damn fine one—she could've given plenty of people in the government that info to blackmail Linc Norman. But she'd left it in Savanna's apartment and led her to it.

What was it? What was on that USB that Parker had encrypted so thoroughly?

Savanna dried off and wrapped a plush ivory towel around her body. Could she trust Coldplay and the Rock Star team with that level of top-secret information? She sure hoped so, because whatever it was, Savanna planned to use it to her advantage.

She found a comb in one of the drawers and started pulling it through her hair. She had no choice anyway. She couldn't decrypt anything. Parker knew that.

And Savanna certainly didn't know how to protect herself from assassins.

But Coldplay did.

The comb snagged on a knot. She hadn't felt this type of connection to anyone before. Not male, anyway. All these years, she'd been holding herself back, afraid to get too close to any man, even Brady. She might share her body, but always held back the rest. Her mind, her true emotions. Afraid of what a man could do to her heart as well as her body.

She was a grown adult, not the fourteen-year-old girl she'd been, but that girl still existed inside her. That fear was still tucked deep down inside her very core.

Coldplay had listened to her story and not judged her. She'd never told anyone else what had happened, the guilt she carried over Nora's death.

It wasn't just his physical presence. It was his emotional presence that reassured her. She'd seen it in his eyes; he'd wanted to kill Coach Watson for hurting her. And wasn't that ironic? At first, she'd been sure he didn't have emotions.

A wave of relief swept over her, so intense, it bent her at the waist and she had to cover her mouth to hold in her whimper. He hadn't judged her for not telling someone what had happened. He hadn't defended her mother or changed the subject because it was an uncomfortable one.

Moisture seeped out under her eyelashes and Savanna wiped it away, straightened, and went back to work on the knot in her hair. She'd told her awful secret and he hadn't ran. He'd done the opposite.

The burden was gone. She felt freer, lighter. She wouldn't let Parker down. Whatever was on that USB needed to be told to the world, Savanna was sure of it.

No more secrets. No more keeping her mouth shut. She might have lost her platform, but she hadn't lost her voice.

In fact, I may have just found it.

CHAPTER NINETEEN

Twenty-four hours later, Savanna was on a rug on the second floor where Coldplay had brought her to show her the deer, stretching her stiff muscles and wishing she could rewind to the previous day. DC had received another four inches of snow, the snowmen army she and Coldplay had built was now half-buried in the backyard.

Her nerves were half-buried too. She and Coldplay had moved around each other, ate together, worked out in the downstairs gym, and he'd even sat in the library reading books and playing chess with her, but very little meaningful conversation had flowed between them. No more scorching hot kisses, either.

Savanna had dozens of questions she wanted to ask him, but he was cool, aloof, focused. He would sneak off and make phone calls, and spend hours on the house's computer searching the internet. Was he searching for Parker or something else?

The USB wasn't giving up its secrets. Coldplay had discussed trying something else with Rory, but the computer expert insisted that his program would decrypt the USB if given enough time.

The sun was bright, reflecting off the snow, and Savanna shifted the rug to a slice of sunlight. The warmth on her face felt good.

Her workout seemed off today, her body lacking its normal grace. The bulletproof glass protected her, but nothing—not even Coldplay—could keep the harsh reality of what was waiting for her at bay for long.

She was slogging through her sixth sun salutation when the back of her neck prickled in warning. Gazing down into the back yard and garden, she searched for any sign of human life.

It wasn't in the garden. It was behind her. Coldplay was in the doorway watching her, the laptop in one hand.

"Don't stop," he said, his crystal blue eyes boring into her. "I love to watch you move."

"Is everything okay? Did something happen? The USB?"

A few days of beard growth covered his jaws and neck. His eyes were tired. He wasn't sleeping, she could see that, but he'd never truly seemed tired until right now. "Nothing happened. You're safe. I'm tired of staring at security video and this laptop."

He paced toward her. Glided, really.

Like a panther on the hunt.

Savanna almost took a step back. Nothing *had* happened, perhaps, but it was about to from the look in his eyes.

She swallowed the sudden nervousness in her throat. "Want to stretch with me?"

He sunk into a nearby chair, his gaze roaming over her yoga pants and sports bra as he set the laptop, open, on the floor. "I want to watch you stretch."

The look in his eyes did strange things to her. Heat shot straight to the spot between her legs. What was going on here? Had he changed his mind? Was he simply bored?

Whatever. She was intrigued. The heavy weight of his gaze followed her as she continued her sun salutations, each movement taking on new importance. The flow became easier even though she felt unnaturally self-conscious about everything from her stomach and her foot placement to her backside. The light brush of her ponytail across her shoulders tickled her skin. She found her breath seemed stuck inside her ribs.

Coldplay noticed too. "Breathe," he reminded her and she caught his eye as she inhaled deeply.

What she saw there nearly took that oh-so-mindful breath away.

Hunger. Pure, raw, seductive. He wanted her and he was going to have her.

Libido fully engaged again, she decided to drag it out, make him suffer the way he had made her suffer the last two days. She flowed back and forward, extending her legs and using her body to communicate to him that she wanted him as much as he wanted her.

The flow of poses was like a dance, and the old routine once more became easy, graceful. She was so involved in the concentrated movements, she didn't realize he'd moved behind her. His hands touched her hips, causing her to jump, and then he ran them lightly up her sides to the underside of her breasts.

She leaned back into him, wanting him so much she ached again.

He nuzzled her ear, her neck. "I need to tell you something," he murmured. "About me."

A thrill went through her. Was he finally going to answer some of her questions about who he was? "I'm listening."

He cupped her breasts, gently, running a thumb over each nipple and making her suck in a breath. "In a minute. First, I want to enjoy this."

One hand slipped down to her pelvis, the heat of his fingers leaving a trail as he cupped her through the stretchy material between her legs. Pressing into his big hand, she arched her butt back and felt his erection, full and demanding.

Oh, yeah. This was definitely happening. After two days of torture, she was finally going to get what she wanted.

His teeth nibbled at her exposed shoulder, teasing the strap of her bra off and baring the top of her right breast. He brushed his fingers over the sensitive skin, his hot breath lingering on her shoulder as he slipped his hand inside the fabric and lifted her breast out of the bra cup.

The other hand, still between her legs, kneaded and built a rhythm. She moaned low and deep as he pinched her exposed nipple and murmured in her ear. "I want you so bad."

Oh, God, she wanted him too. "Then take me. Screw the contract and whatever you're hiding from me. I need this. Need you."

His erection pressed into her harder. "This is wrong. You're going to hate me."

Reaching up, she touched his face. Her breath came in fast gasps. "I could never hate you."

His low growl made goose bumps break out over her skin. "I've never wanted anyone the way I want you."

She placed her hands over his, forcing him to grip her breast and her pelvis harder. "I want you too." *Now, now, now.* "Please." Dust motes danced in the air around them. In her ear, Coldplay's breathing was as ragged as hers. Outside, the snow sparkled in the bright sunlight and Savanna tilted her head to the side, allowing his lips more access to her sensitive skin.

"I need more," he said, his voice vibrating against her skin. "I need my mouth on your breasts, between your legs."

Scorching need tingled from her head to her toes. Brady had never talked during sex. An earlier lover had, but used explicit language that sometimes was more turnoff than turn-on. She liked how Coldplay told her exactly what he wanted—*needed*—without degrading terms that made her feel like a porn star.

She'd never seen Coldplay's hands shake, but his fingers did as they worked her sports bra off. She didn't help him, enjoying the concentration on his face as he worked the one-piece bra over her breasts and up and off her arms. Cool air made her already puckered nipples tighten more.

The bra hit the floor and Coldplay stood, not touching her, only looking. His gaze was so intense, she nearly covered herself. Instead, she reached out and removed his T-shirt, going up on her toes to get it over his head, letting her heavy breasts brush against his ribs. He helped, chucking the shirt on the floor next to her bra.

It was her turn to stare. The tattoos. The scars. She'd seen them already, but in the sunlight, they hit her all over again. Whatever this man had been through, whatever he'd done in his life, his history was there on his skin.

Reaching out, she traced the outline of an angel holding a clock. The hands were nearing midnight. She was about to ask what it meant when Coldplay stayed her hand, brought her fingertips to his lips and kissed them.

She dropped her hand to his waistband and unbuttoned his jeans. The ridge inside them was huge and she licked her lips with anticipation. Unzipped, his erection popped free—no underwear to hold it back—and her eyes widened at the length. She took him in her hand, his hips jutting at the contact and another growl parting his lips as he closed his eyes briefly. Using her other hand, she pushed his jeans down to bare his muscled legs.

He grabbed her hand once again and pulled it away. "You

look at me that way, touch me like that, and this will be over before I get my hands on you."

His thighs were thick and powerful looking. He stood there, proud and defiant, letting her look but not touch.

Not fair.

Seeming to read her mind, he stepped out of his jeans. Then he knelt in front of her, his fingers tracing the edge of her yoga pants. His touch lingered on her hipbones before peeling the material inch by slow inch down her legs. His lips followed the progress, kissing each hip, then thigh, making her nearly swoon with desire.

A moment later, she stood in nothing but her panties, his face at their level. He slipped a finger under the satin and she shuddered at the decadent touch as he teased her with expert care.

He kissed her through the material of her panties, holding her in place as he parted his lips and tongued her through the satin.

Her knees gave out and he guided her to the floor. She parted her legs, accepting him as he hovered above her, his mouth now finding her breast, his hands ripping the panties off. She heard material tear but didn't care.

And then her breast was feeling cool air again. He reached over and pulled a foil packet from his jean pocket, opened it, and rolled it on.

Her mouth watered watching him work the thin sheath up the length and breadth of him.

She shifted again, spreading her legs wider, looking forward to finally being filled, satisfied.

"Savanna?"

Tearing her gaze away from his erection, she met his eyes. Saw the worry there. The concern.

Reaching out, she grabbed him and wrapped her legs around his hips. Guiding, guiding...

He came down, fast and hard, ramming himself into her as she arched to meet him.

Sweet Jesus. Cradling him, she felt him holding his breath, his massive shoulders pinning her to the floor as he held her in place, not letting her move. Dragging out the moment, he buried himself deep inside her.

She felt the fat length of him pulse. Just a little flick, creating a friction she'd never felt before.

He did it again. Sensation exploded between her legs. She arched her hips and whimpered, her nails digging into his back. "Please," she ground out, rocking under him.

He chuckled in her ear and started to move, matching her rhythm.

The chuckle completely unraveled her. Not the fact he was naked and glorious and taking her close to the edge. No, it was the fact that she could make him laugh, even in the midst of sex.

Savanna let herself go. Let herself *be* like the yoga instructors were always teaching. No thinking, only feeling. Total focused mindfulness enveloped her as Coldplay kissed and caressed and stroked into her over and over again. She was spinning and spinning and it felt so damn good. For a few minutes, her bodyguard could indeed keep the real world at bay.

"You're perfect," he said, his lips against her neck.

She came, breaking apart, not from his words, but from the sheer power he exuded. The sheer conviction in *what* he was doing. Her legs tightened around him and she lifted her hips, digging her heels into his buttocks and pulling him deeper.

His hands locked on to her hips and held them up, giving her what she wanted as he sunk in to the hilt. As she spun out, coming completely undone, she felt him tighten in response.

"Savanna," he cried out as he crashed into her. She felt him pulse again, this time with his own release.

She drifted, feeling his heart pounding against hers. Heard his breath coming in gasps, just like hers. He wrapped his arms around her, supporting himself on his elbows so he didn't crush her, and rested a cheek against her temple. He kissed her there, softly, as his breathing came back into balance.

Delicious. There was no other word for it. She could stay this way forever.

Far off, she heard music. A soft pairing of notes that drifted with her, repeating over and over.

"*Coldplay?*" A voice vibrated on the edge of her consciousness and suddenly the strong arms wrapped around her released her.

"*Coldplay?*" the voice said again. It sounded small and tinny. *"Are you seeing what I'm seeing?"*

He was up and gone before she could open her eyes. She blinked and followed his quick movement across the floor to the abandoned laptop, condom gone and jeans halfway up his legs.

He zipped and buttoned in one swift movement, then grabbed the laptop and scanned the screen.

His eyes closed for a split second and his shoulders dipped. "Goddamn," he murmured. "I should have known."

***

"Told you my software could crack the decryption," Rory said, his video box in the upper right hand section of the screen. He eyed Trace's naked chest. Ignored it. "Are you seeing this?"

He was seeing it all right. *The bastard better not have been spying on us.* Of course, the way the computer had been turned, he wouldn't have seen anything, only heard what was going on.

Trace ran a hand over his face. "I see it."

Savanna, lids half closed as she popped her head up, snatched her bra off the floor. "What is it?"

"The software decrypted the USB," Trace told her, wishing he could be happy about it.

She pulled on her sport bra, then her pants, her panties no longer viable, and raked her hands through her hair as she hustled over to look at the screen.

This was *not* how he'd planned things to work out. He'd wanted to hold her, jump in a shower with her, maybe take her to bed again. When he'd had his fill of her—was that even possible?—he'd planned to tell her the truth. Who he really was.

He'd stewed about it for days. Decided he had to come clean.

God, it had felt so good. Being with her. Touching her. Letting her touch him. Too damn long since he'd been touched in that way. With care, with respect. Just the thought of her spreading her legs for him, guiding him inside her, made him hard all over again.

"It looks like gibberish," Savanna said, bringing him back to the present.

It was. Gibberish that hid a specific database of intel. He'd seen a similar file before.

Savanna leaned over his shoulder, studying it more carefully. She smelled like shampoo and sex. "Why would Parker leave me this?"

He shifted slightly, hoping to hide his blatant erection with the laptop. Parker had an agenda. An agenda he was definitely a part of.

"The files are in code," he told Savanna. *And I'm the only one who can figure that code out.*

"A complicated alphanumeric code," Rory said, his mug still sharing screen time with the decrypted file's contents. "Without the legend, I have no hope of decoding it."

Savanna's hand rested on Trace's shoulder. The memory of her tracing his tattoo flooded his mind, doing nothing to help him quench his need to take her again. "Do you think Parker hid the legend in the handbag with the USB?" she asked. "Did we miss it? Should we go back to my apartment and look for it?"

"I'll send Cal and Emit to check on that," Rory said. "Meanwhile, I'll run it through all of my known coding databases to see if it's close to anything. If it is, I may be able to figure it out, even without the legend."

Trace fought the smell of sex, the shockwaves her touch sent down to his dick. He needed to think, to clear his head of the last few minutes and get back into bodyguard mode. No emotion, no wasted effort of any kind.

"What should we do?" Savanna asked, and he realized she was asking him, not Rory.

Rory scratched his beard and answered anyway. "Sit tight. I'll get back to you as soon as I have a lead."

His video feed went black.

"I know nothing about codes," she said. "Do you?"

He knew about codes. Had used quite a few in his time. "A little."

"Why do you think she used one on these files? They're top-secret, aren't they? That's why she encrypted them."

Top-secret? Hell, they were worse than that. "That would be my guess." He dragged the laptop closer, his focus laser-beamed in on the lines of letters and numbers. "It's a database," he said. "One with twenty-four entries."

"Whatever it is, I think Parker left it for me to decode and take to the media. It's something big, probably something on the president. What do you think?"

"I don't know yet."

"But you have an idea, don't you? I can tell by the way you're avoiding my questions."

He tried not to sound indignant. "I'm answering your questions."

"In an evasive way. You won't even look at me."

He sighed and closed the laptop in case Rory was listening or decided to pop back in. Shifting it aside, he revealed a partial truth. His blatant erection.

"I'm hard because I want you again, but it seemed inappropriate to bring that up in the middle of our breakthrough with the decryption. So I was hiding it and avoiding your eyes because I was trying, and failing, to concentrate on work instead of the images in my head of you naked."

"Oh." She had the decency to blush. But then she laughed and whipped off her sport bra. "Seems like we have some time on our hands while Rory's working on decoding Parker's files. We might as well make good use of it."

His good sense went out the window. Carrying the laptop with him, he chased Savanna up the stairs to the bedroom.

Chapter Twenty

They ravished each other, showered, slept, ravished each other again. The master suite became their playground. One end held a king-size bed that they put to good use. The other held a sitting area with fireplace and TV. They found interesting ways to try every piece of furniture, every wall, the floor.

Coldplay brought her grapes and cheese and crackers in the afternoon. In between bites of cheese, Savanna took bites of him.

Then he fed her grapes while he bent her over a chaise and fucked her blind.

The suite was growing dark when she woke on that chaise sometime later, covered with a flannel blanket. She scanned the shadows of the room for Coldplay's presence but didn't find it. Her phone buzzed softly on the nightstand.

Caller ID showed it was her mother. Savanna hit the Ignore button and went to the bathroom.

She washed and dressed, taming her hair that was unruly from hours of lovemaking. Back on the chaise, she turned on the TV and found her news channel.

Top of the hour news was about President Norman and his trip to Jamaica. No wonder he'd left her alone for the past couple of days. He was visiting there to assess the cleanup and recovery after a hurricane had done tremendous damage in the fall. Video showed him walking through debris with top Jamaican officials and handing out bottled water.

A man of the people.

But what have you done to my sister?

Her phone buzzed again and Savanna checked it. She couldn't help it. What if Parker called?

She was staring at the screen when Coldplay walked in, the laptop under his arm.

"Is it your mother again?" he asked, seeing the expression on her face.

"She stopped leaving messages, but she won't quit calling me."

He touched her shoulder, kissed her temple. "Maybe you should answer. She's probably worried."

Let her worry.

But the old guilt made her thumb the accept button. "I'm fine, Mom," she said without preamble. "But unless you've heard from Parker, I can't talk to you."

"Where are you?" Dory Jeffries practically yelled. "Why haven't you returned my calls? Why is that woman on the news filling in for you? Are you sick?"

"No, my health and wellbeing are in danger, much like they were when I was fourteen, but this time, someone is going further than molestation. He's gotten me fired and is trying to kill me."

"Kill you? Oh, Savanna. You were always so dramatic. The misunderstanding with Coach Watson happened fifteen years ago. Get over it."

Savanna's hand tightened on her phone. "Get *over* it? He molested me. That was no *misunderstanding*. And I know he was molesting Nora too. It was his baby she was pregnant with. If I had said something all those years ago, Nora might still be alive."

Silence met her ears. Coldplay kept a hand on her, massaging gentle circles into her shoulders, the base of her neck.

"I'm hanging up now," Savanna told her mother. "I don't wish to speak to you again unless you hear from Parker. She's in danger, too, and when this is all over, if I'm still standing, I'm telling everyone what happened to me all those years ago. I'm not going to be silent about it anymore, so you better prepare yourself. The Daughters of the American Revolution may have a few questions for you."

Disconnecting, she tossed the phone on the bed. It felt good to stand up for herself. Good to confront her mother, even if it was over the phone and not face-to-face. Good to take control of whatever future she had left.

The shakes started in her thighs, her hands. She folded her arms across her chest, trying to stop them from spreading. From letting herself shatter all over the floor.

But then the tears came.

So much anger. So much fear. Coach Watson had gutted her. Cost her a future in gymnastics and caused a good friend to commit suicide. She couldn't hold it in any longer.

Coldplay sat on the bed and pulled her onto his lap, wrapping her in his arms and stroking her hair. "Shh," he whispered. "You're going to be okay."

As long as he was with her, she believed it.

Ugly sobs tore from her throat and her tears soaked his shirt as she clung to him, never wanting to let go of his solid presence.

He held her and rocked her, murmured reassurances. Finally, the tears tapered off, but she clung to him anyway.

Beside them on the bed, the laptop dinged with an incoming message. Coldplay ignored it, continuing to hold her.

"You should get that," she said, sliding off his lap, even though it killed her to leave the security of his arms. He was a good man to let her snot all over him, but she really should wash her face and get him a clean shirt. "It's probably important."

His hand trailed down her arm and gently squeezed hers as she backed away. In the bathroom, she avoided looking at her red, puffy eyes and blew her nose. She heard Rory's voice on the computer. "Found something."

Forgetting her disheveled appearance, Savanna raced back into the bedroom. Coldplay sat on the chaise, a muscle in his jaw jumping. "What?"

Rory's image filled the screen. "I've been searching videos of the area around the place where the limo was ditched like you asked. ATMs, gas stations, traffic cams. Some took longer to hack into, but I think I found her."

Savanna's heart jackhammered against her breastbone. "Parker?"

Coldplay made room for her on the chaise. She gripped his hand.

"She left us another message," Rory said. "This was recorded at the ShopIt convenience store two blocks from where she dumped the limo."

A black and white image replaced Rory. There was no sound, only video. A woman in a chauffeur's outfit entered the store, scanned the aisles, and grabbed a bag of peanut M&Ms. At the counter, she had to glance up to look at the clerk behind the counter.

Parker.

The two exchanged conversation and Parker smiled. She paid for her candy and said something else. The clerk searched behind the counter and handed her a piece of paper and a pen.

She wrote something on the paper, then looked right at the camera. Raising the slip of paper, she faced it toward the lens.

Blocky handwriting spelled out *PAT. 13.*

She crumpled the paper in her hand, stuck it in her pocket and nodded at the clerk who looked confused. She walked out with her M&Ms.

The video rewound to Parker's face, the screen split, and Rory appeared next to Parker. "This video was taken about three hours after she ditched the limo."

"Pat 13," Savanna said, relieved Parker was alive and communicating with them. Why didn't she just call her? "Who is Pat?"

"Not Pat," Rory said. "P-A-T-period. It's an abbreviation."

An abbreviation for what? A location?

"Patent? Paternity? Pattensburg?" Savanna reeled off possibilities as adrenaline hit her. Her mind knew it was illogical, but her body wanted to run back to the city and start looking for her sister. "Pattern?"

Coldplay stared at Parker's frozen face on the screen. His voice was low, controlled. "Patient," he said. "It stands for Patient 13."

"Patient?" The house's furnace kicked on and Savanna felt a chill creep under her skin even as the dry heat fell from the vent overhead. She frowned. "How do you know?"

"I know..." He sat immobile, his face hard as stone. Gravel in his voice this time. "Because I was patient 13."

Chapter Twenty-one

"The alphanumeric code is my full name plus the number combination in the thirteenth entry of the form," Trace told Rory.

Then he closed the laptop screen, severing the connection.

Savanna had taken a step back. "Patient 13. What does that mean? Patient of what?"

Trace had faced every obstacle, every heartbreak in his life with head-on determination and bravery. He'd gone into battle, taken lives, and fought for his own on many occasion. He never backed down, never gave up.

Seeing the confusion and wariness in Savanna's eyes, the tension in her body, he wanted to back down now. He'd known this moment was coming and it was time to face the truth. He had to come clean.

He was a fraud.

Everything he'd done up to that moment didn't matter if he couldn't convince her he wasn't.

Hard to do when he didn't believe it himself.

He set the computer on the floor, interlaced his fingers together to give his hands something to do. He tried to maintain eye contact, couldn't.

"Project 24 was a joint Department of Defense and National Intelligence research program that included twenty-four test subjects," he said. "We were given various drug cocktails to increase our natural abilities, then put through endurance trials and intense training modules to figure out which cocktails worked. The drugs increased our physical skills as well as our cognitive ones."

"Holy crap." Savanna stared holes through him. "Super soldiers?"

"The details—from our names to our outcomes—were highly classified. There were three people who knew about it, and a couple of the nation's leading scientists, with exceptionally high clearance, who handled the program."

The light of understanding came on in her eyes. "Parker was one of them?"

It was the only explanation to why Parker had been trying to contact him. Why she'd come to Witcher.

Savanna's fingers twitched. She tugged on the hem of her T-shirt. Her eyes darkened and she took another step away from him. "That's why she had this file. That means...you know my sister."

Hurt, confusion, the seeds of betrayal—Trace wanted to reach for her, wanted to draw her near.

He shook his head. "We never met the scientists behind the scenes. I only ever saw one doctor who was assigned to me, and I didn't know his name or anything about him. As far as I know, the doctors didn't know our names or personal details, either. They knew us only by our patient numbers. They didn't have a clue what exactly they were giving us in the drugs, they were simply there to monitor our health. The training instructors were the same. They knew they were part of a top-secret project, but they didn't know the details or who was in charge. Hell, I didn't even know the other test subjects. Never saw them. Everyone was isolated. So, no, I don't know Parker, never met her, but she apparently knows me. She knows I was Patient 13, which means she had to have been involved with Project 24."

"The president knows about this program?"

"I was his best soldier, Savanna. It was his program, and I served at the pleasure of the president, but the things I did..."

Two steps and she was at his side, her amazingly beautiful body sliding in next to him. Her hand, feather light, touched his, as she scanned his face, brows drawn down. "You did what you were commanded to do."

"That's just it." He couldn't hold her gaze. The willingness to exonerate, to absolve him of guilt was too much. "I wasn't forced into the program. I volunteered. I thought it would be an amazing opportunity to help my country. To make a difference in a world constantly on the brink of disaster. I didn't realize I was selling my soul to the devil."

"My God, what you must have been through. What you've survived. Your skills…that's why you're so fast, why it seems like you can outthink everyone. You can, can't you?"

He wanted to rewind the past twenty-four hours. To take her back to bed and make love to her again. She was no longer edging away from him, in fact, just the opposite. Regardless, he was afraid to move. Afraid he'd grab her and never turn her loose.

Afraid the wrong move, the wrong word, might send her running away again. "To some degree, yes, I can predict what others are going to do. I have hyperawareness, quicker than normal reflexes, and the ability to see multiple outcomes at once in my head. I tend to know what's going to happen in a fight, for example, right before it does so I can counter an attack or outmaneuver an opponent."

She was silent for a long moment. Her stare made him uneasy. "You're the perfect bodyguard."

He was the ideal killer, which was exactly what the president had wanted. "I'm a monster. A freak. I can never take back what I've done."

Her hand cupped his cheek and brought his chin up, forcing him to meet her eyes. "I know it's bad; I get that, even though you haven't told me any details and probably can't. But you're not a bad person. You wouldn't be here helping me, keeping me safe, if you were."

Laying a hand over hers, he held it tight for a second, then removed it from his face. If only he could tell her the rest and not lose her in the process. "The theory I didn't tell you at the Rock Star headquarters? Linc Norman is most likely after me as well as you. Just like Parker, whom I'm pretty damn sure was part of this project, I could blow everything out of the water, ruin him. You were already on track to uncover part of it, but without someone like me, someone like your sister, you would have never gotten the entire story."

Her brows furrowed again. Another piece of the puzzle snapped into place. "Westmeyer. I was right. They supplied the drugs, didn't they?"

"That would be my guess. Project 24 only lasted nine

months before it was aborted. Something tells me Linc Norman and Westmeyer have a new project up and running."

"Why was Project 24 aborted?"

"Because everyone died but me."

Her face fell. "My God. How? From the drugs?"

He wanted to keep her at arm's length, tell her he wasn't worth her sympathy or kindness. Instead, he found his arms going around her, his nose burying in her hair.

One last time. He wanted to hold her one last time.

Her arms went around his neck and she hugged him back. For the first time in his life, he wanted to stop running, to stop fighting. He wanted her.

"What happened to the others?" she asked softly. "You have to tell me."

His arms didn't want to let go, but finally he kissed her temple and did. Bitter acid burned up his chest, into his throat. No matter how she made him feel, it would never wipe away the stain on his soul.

He cleared his throat, seeking the control he'd lost at some point outside in the snow. If he was going to tell her the truth and survive the aftermath, he had to rely on his mind, not his heart. "From what I gathered, the drugs worked for a while but they had nasty side effects. The test subjects became unstable. One cocktail caused erratic blood pressure spikes. The scientists adjusted the formula and then some of the test subjects experienced extreme rage and mental disorders."

Savanna sat back. "You don't die from rage."

Trace gripped his knees, stared at the floor. His soul was forever tainted. If only he'd questioned the president's orders sooner. "Those with negative outcomes were...put down."

"What?" Shock widened her blue eyes. Eyes he wanted to drown in. "The soldiers were killed?"

He'd pulled the trigger not knowing who he was killing or why. He'd been a good soldier. He didn't ask questions, only did what his commander-in-chief told him to do.

"Parker would never be part of something like that," Savanna insisted, standing up and pacing. "She may have lied to me about being a spy, but she's not a mad scientist mixing up lethal doses of drugs and killing off test subjects who go Frankenstein on her."

"She didn't kill them, and I don't know how deep her

involvement is, but she *was* part of it, Savanna. At least initially, I'm guessing."

"You can't know that. Maybe she stole this file from the president and that's why he's after her. She has to stay in hiding so that's why she gave it to me. I can expose Project 24, and that's exactly what I'm going to do."

She headed for the bed.

"What are you going to do?" Trace asked.

"Call someone." She snatched up her phone from the sheets where she'd tossed it earlier after she'd cried in his arms. Her body language was completely different now. The confident investigative reporter was on the scent of the biggest story in history. "I still have a few friends in the news world."

Trace was by her side, snatching the phone from her hand before she could hit the keypad. "That's not an option."

Her face hardened. "Give me my phone."

He held it out of her reach. "You're talking about the president of the United States, Savanna. We don't have proof yet. Wait until Rory and I get those data files from Parker decoded. Until we have that, it's your word against the president's."

"But I have you. That's better than a file or any other kind of proof. I have *you*. A walking, talking man that they experimented on and then forced into doing the president's bidding without any oversight. All we have to do is get this in front of the American people. I can interview you. You can tell everyone what happened, what's happening now—that the president is trying to stop us by killing us."

She was so desperate, it tugged at his heartstrings. More than anything, he wanted to give her what she wanted. "There's no way I can go on national TV and out the president."

"Why not? You may have broken a few laws, but it was under his direction. You were following orders."

Until the last one. "There's something else you need to know. Something about one of the other Project 24 test subjects."

Savanna stopped trying to get the phone away from him. "What?"

He started to tell her about Patient 6 when her phone rang in his hand.

Private number on the caller ID. He showed it to her.

Her eyes went wide. He saw her throat constrict and those saucer eyes came up to his. "It's him," she said. "Linc Norman."

The design of telescopic sights since World War II had improved to such an extent that shooters could cover long distances with optical precision akin to superhuman eyesight. Seeing through reflective glass windows meant to conceal the inhabitants from the outside world, however, took a special scope.

Parker lay in the snow in a ghillie suit 400 yards east of the safe house on a wooded hill overlooking the property. A slender stream cut along the base of the hill, frozen in the winter temperatures and covered by several inches of snow. To her right were woods, security cameras and infrared sensors. To her left, more of the same. She'd counted four security guards making rounds of the property, scanning the hills with military grade binoculars. She'd made sure to cover herself with pine boughs and snow.

Trijicon had earned the respect of soldiers in the Middle East. Now, a Trijicon scope with enhanced night vision and optics designed by some engineer in the CIA allowed Parker to see through reflective glass.

Hollywood had it wrong about so many things. IR imaging. Heat reflection. X-ray vision. Seeing through walls and glass to detect bodies wasn't as easy and straightforward as they made it seem.

Adjusting the light transmitter on her scope, she could make out heat signatures of two human forms in the master bedroom on the top floor of the safe house. Her scope was the stuff Hollywood made up, only hers actually existed.

The safe house had been a bitch to find, even with ON16 trying to assist her hunt. He'd been the one to confirm her suspicion that Coldplay was indeed Lt. Hunter, and while Parker had put tracking devices on Savanna's phone, laptop, the USB, one by one, Trace Hunter and the Rock Star Security group had disabled them.

The phone's tracking device had been first to die. Next had been the laptop, but that had been in the vehicle winging south of DC, narrowing things down to a five-kilometer area. The

USB had taken its time giving up its secrets and, although Hunter and his team had managed to clean it while their software program broke her multiple levels of decryption, each level had held a code that sent out a notifier to her when the software began working on it. The notifiers weren't the same as GPS, but one by one, she'd honed in on the location, using common sense to look up recent real estate purchases and pinpoint the best candidates for safe houses.

She was used to having access to everything—well, almost everything—at the touch of her fingers. Spending multiple days tracking down Savanna had nearly made her lose her good mood.

There were half-hidden snowmen in the back yard, evidence of a snowball fight or two. What had Savanna been doing with her bodyguard?

Having a good time from what Parker could see through the windows. The only two people ever in the house were Hunter and her sister. Which meant the two bodies spending lots of time in the bedroom together had to be them.

Good for you, Savanna. It's about time you had some fun.

But had she and Hunter figured out the encryption?

Parker shivered inside her suit. She needed caffeine and food. Some sleep. To get out of this blasted, damn snow.

The last of the decoding notifiers had gone off two hours ago and she'd set up camp here to watch the house. Between Savanna and Hunter, they would figure out the data she'd left them and get it to the public. Once the story was out, President Norman would fall from grace. Impeachment was the least of his worries. He was going to prison for a very long time.

She'd be free. No more running. No more hiding. She was the last of the Project 24 group, with the exception of Hunter. If only one of them survived and told the truth, it would be enough.

How long would it take them to find the message she'd left? How long before they figured out the legend for the code? No code or decryption was foolproof, but she'd had to make sure that if the information fell into the wrong hands, she'd have time to switch to Plan B.

Plan B—killing the president—was definitely her second choice.

If she survived, she wanted out, not to end up in prison. She had future hopes and dreams. New projects she wanted to work on. Not like the government programs she'd been instrumental in establishing, but back to the private sector where she could study the brain from the comfort of her lab. Keep the real world at a safe distance. Project 24 should have been her crowning achievement. Instead, she'd be lucky if she didn't end up in prison alongside Linc Norman.

The snap of a twig behind her and off to her left made her freeze. She held her breath. Who was on the hill with her? A deer? They'd been roaming the hills, the property, following the stream for most of the night. Had one of the guards seen through her careful camouflage?

She was a master at blending into urban settings. Going unnoticed by people and getting the information she needed. Lying in snow-covered woods and spying on someone with a stolen scope she'd used once during a training exercise in college was not her forte.

No getting caught. Not at this point. Although she *had* given serious consideration to marching down to the safe house and demanding entrance. The security guards would have stopped her before she'd gotten close to the back door, but they wouldn't shoot to kill unless she presented an imminent danger.

She was definitely a danger to Savanna. There was no going down for a warm, Hallmark family moment. Not yet. There was one more thing Parker had to do.

A minute passed with no further noise. She let her breath ease out slowly, keeping her eye off the scope and watching the nearby surroundings instead. Nothing she could see or sense to the left. Nothing to the right except more trees and an owl sitting on a skeleton limb, watching the rolling hill for a two a.m. snack.

Too many days on the run. There was too much stress and adrenaline built up in her body. The flip side was gnawing exhaustion.

Another minute passed. The owl continued his watch. Parker resumed hers as well. She had four hours before the guard changeover at sunrise. Four hours to finish what she'd started and make sure the blowback didn't hurt Savanna.

Running the plan through her head, she shifted the scope slightly to see the army of snowmen in the garden. Would she live long enough to have kids? To ever play in the snow with them?

She was pondering that thought when she heard another twig snap.

Chapter Twenty-two

The phone stopped ringing, the president hanging up before the call went to voicemail.

"Give me my phone," Savanna said.

Coldplay had done a total reversal from the man telling her about the drug trials a moment ago. He'd gone quiet, restrained. Totally controlled once more.

"You can't talk to him."

The phone began ringing again. "I have to take it," she said.

"No matter how hard you try not to, you could end up giving away our location without even realizing it."

"What if it's about Parker? I can't ignore Linc Norman, no matter how much I want to."

He let out a tight sigh and handed her the phone.

Her fingers shook and she nearly dropped it. He steadied her hand and the phone, closing her fingers over the hard plastic.

With a grateful nod, she hit the answer button, closed her eyes, and prayed for the right words.

There was no script for this. No teleprompter. It was just her and the most powerful man in the world about to go head to head.

She dispensed with pleasantries and got right to the point, turning her back on Coldplay and walking toward the fireplace. She needed to focus, had to get this right. "What do you want?"

Norman's laugh was soft, patronizing. "Van, long time no see. Did you really think you could hide from me?"

Before Savanna could say anything else, the phone was snatched from her hand.

Whirling around, she found Coldplay tapping the speaker button. He nodded at her to answer the president's question.

Deep breath. You can do this.

She didn't need a script or a teleprompter. She had Coldplay. His faith in her showed in his eyes.

"I have the file," she said to the president, pushing her nerves aside. It was time to be ballsy. "All I have to do is expose that file and you're done."

"And what file would that be?" She heard the clink of ice in a glass. Norman made slurping noises. She could just see him tipped back in his chair, downing a couple fingers of scotch. "Oh, let me guess...some made up bullshit your sister concocted to make me look like the boogie man? Good luck with that. You don't even have a platform anymore, Van. The whole nation is shaking its head over what a fraud you are while my approval ratings rose once again after my pilgrimage to *Meh-he-co.*"

Was he drunk or just high on his own ego? She snatched the phone from Coldplay's hand. "You were in Jamaica, you idiot, not Mexico. And I still have plenty of friends and colleagues in the business. Any one of them would be thrilled to have the scoop on your devious, undercover activities."

"I'm sure I have no idea what you're talking about." She heard the clunk of ice cubes again. "I saw that video of your accident. I didn't recognize Hunter at first without all that hair. God, he looked like a crazy man back in the day, didn't he? I suppose between him and Parker, they've filled your head with all kinds of self-righteous glory, haven't they? Made me into the big, bad wolf knocking on your door."

Savanna frowned and stared at the phone as if the answer might be spelled out on the screen. "Hunter? What are you talking about?"

"He escaped Witcher last week. Been looking all over for him. I figured he was coming for me, but I guess he was after you all along."

"What?"

She looked at Coldplay and shrugged. His face was totally devoid of emotion. Was he remembering all the people Linc Norman had commanded him to kill?

She wanted to throw her arms around him and wipe those memories away. "You're drunk and confused," she said into the phone, "but mark my words, Mr. President. What you did to the man protecting me, and all those other soldiers, is going to be your downfall."

"Are you really that clueless, Van?" the president enunciated every word as if she were slow or hard of hearing. "Lieutenant Trace Hunter. Remember him?"

She dropped her eyes to the phone screen again. "Of course, but—"

"Trace Hunter is your *bodyguard*."

Savanna felt like she'd been hit. Confusion stumped her for a moment, and then the realization slammed into her full throttle.

She stumbled back.

Trace Hunter.

Her gaze snapped to Coldplay's, a sharp hiss of fear rushing through her body and making her dizzy. Oh God...

The look she saw there. The cold remoteness.

"Good old fashioned *revenge*," Norman said, still exaggerating his words. "You pissed off the most dangerous assassin to ever set foot in Washington and now he's going to kill you. Hot damn. Guess I won't have to then. He wants that file, too, I'm sure. The details of that are...messy. Maybe you can cut a deal. Ask him to spare your life." His laughter this time was pure enjoyment. "Good luck with that, Van."

The line went dead.

Savanna felt as cold as the frozen ground outside where her snowmen soldiers were all but buried.

"Savanna," Coldplay said. He took a careful step toward her. "I can explain."

Her feet felt like fifty-pound blocks but adrenaline pounded in her veins. Her body wanted to flee, but her feet were rooted to the floor.

She scooted backward, skirting him, and holding out a hand. As if she could divert him or stop him if he attacked. *What a joke, Savanna. You couldn't hold off a mouse.*

Still, instincts were instincts. "Stay away from me."

He flinched as if she'd struck him. "You know I would never hurt you."

"*Do* I know that?" Her brain felt like it was on fire, trying to figure out why she couldn't place him with 100% confidence. But Norman was right—*if* this was Trace Hunter standing in front of her, his features were different than the single photo she'd ran on her show all those months ago.

But *something* in her psyche had tripped her memory when he'd shown up at her door, hadn't it?

Dumb Savanna. Why hadn't she followed through? Dug deeper?

I was a little busy staying alive. "Are you Trace Hunter?" she asked, her voice tight with stress.

He held his hands up, palms out as if trying to placate a scared, injured animal. "Savanna, this is not what it seems. Linc Norman is wrong—"

She cut him off, raising her voice. "*Are you Trace Hunter?*"

And boy, didn't she sound exactly like a scared, injured animal. *Get control.*

She'd slept with this man, thought she knew who he was because he was doing his job of protecting her.

If he wanted me dead, why would he keep me alive?

The president's words rang in her ears. *He wants that file, too...*

Coldplay lowered his hands, stood motionless. "Yes. I'm Trace Hunter, the man you crucified in public on your show because of intel your sister received from the president and told you to run."

Fear wrapped its fingers around her heart. Anger did as well. "Why are you here? For Parker's file?"

"I didn't even know that file existed until we found the USB. I'm here to protect you, Savanna, and help you find your sister."

Right. Again, she heard Linc Norman's words. *You pissed off the most dangerous assassin to ever set foot in Washington and now he's going to kill you.*

The idea was ridiculous, but that didn't stop her from taking another step closer to the door.

Even if all Hunter wanted was Parker's file, he could have already taken the USB and bugged out. He had brought her here, pretended he cared about her. Had taken her to bed like a lover and encouraged her to stand up to her mother and stop hiding in the shadows of the past.

He was definitely there for something more than a file on Project 24.

Revenge. The word circled her brain. "Wow. The president's correct on all counts. I *am* clueless. And gullible, apparently. You seduced me so I'd fall in love with you. You're not here to kill me, just rip my heart out. Nice."

"Love?" He seemed shocked by the idea.

She started for the bathroom, and Trace started to follow. "Don't," she said, holding up a hand once more. She'd had it, and damn it, she was not going to cry in front of him. No matter what. She might throw something, but never would she cry. "Get out of my sight."

His face morphed into something she couldn't name. "The intel in the file Parker gave you on me wasn't true, I swear. I've done a lot of shit in my life that I'm not proud of, but I would never betray my country. I would never hurt you."

"And yet, you hid your identity from me this whole time."

Just saying it out loud ripped her heart a little more.

"I needed to prove to you that I'm not the scumbag you exposed on your TV show eighteen months ago. You would have never given me the chance if I'd told you who I was upfront."

He was right, but that didn't make his betrayal forgivable. "When were you going to tell me?"

He closed his eyes for a second, opened them, but didn't look at her. "I tried to tell you multiple times. Things between us got out of hand. I..."

"Out of hand? So you thought it better to lie to me by omission? Figured you'd get me in bed first, then lay the big reveal on me, and I'd be so wowed by your sexual prowess I wouldn't care? Well, good job burying your lead, Lt. Hunter. You totally suckered me."

She couldn't stand to look at him anymore. Fleeing to the bathroom, heart fluttering like a manic bird, she closed the door behind her, flipped the lock, and beat a fist against the wall.

Dammit. What was she going to do now?

Trace stood outside the bathroom door, quiet as a cat, listening, his guts shriveled to a tight lump in his stomach. The look on Savanna's face had crushed him. That fear—how could she believe, after everything they'd been through, that he would hurt her?

Fucking Linc Norman.

No point blaming him. It was his own damn fault. And he *had* hurt her. He'd totally screwed her over in more ways than one.

Love. She'd said he seduced her so she'd fall in love with

him. Seemed like she'd been doing the seducing and he'd fallen for her. It wasn't love, though. It was…

Infatuation?

Passion?

Admiration?

Shit, he didn't know at this point. He'd never loved anyone outside of his grandmother.

Savanna's fear had been followed by the realization he'd deceived her and that kind of pain, in Trace's experience, was worse than any kind of physical hurt.

In all the ways he'd fucked up in his life, this was the worst. She'd trusted him. Relied on him.

Behind the door of the bathroom, he heard little noises. Noises like muffled crying.

Ah, shit. He'd made her cry. "Savanna."

No response.

He tapped on the door. "Savanna, I never meant for that" — whatever *that* had been—"to happen. The sex. The…seduction."

"That makes me feel tons better," she yelled through the door. "Thanks. Now go away. I want a new bodyguard. Wait…"

The door creaked open two inches. Savanna's face was puffy and red. Yep, definitely crying.

"Did Beatrice know about this? She did, didn't she? She said something to me that first day about me persecuting innocent people. Jesus! How could I be so stupid?"

The door slammed shut again and he laid a hand on the frame. "Beatrice is the one who convinced me to take your case. She knew Norman was after me, but not why. She thought you and I could help each other."

A sarcastic laugh exploded on the other side. "Help each other? Yeah, we sure did that. I'm still alive but we're no closer to finding my sister, and you… Well, I'm not sure what you got out of this other than toying with me. Although, I'll admit, I did the seducing. God! The first time I ever go after a guy, and it's one who's dicking with me!"

Love. He wasn't lovable, even when he wasn't trying to kill people. Far from it. He was a messed up piece of shit that didn't deserve one look from Savanna, much less her love.

Trace laid his forehead on the door. *Think, Hunter. How do I fix this?*

He heard those tiny sounds again and it gutted him. She was crying into a towel.

Water came on. She knew the towel wasn't enough to hide her crying. *So damn tough.*

He wanted to kick in the door. Wanted to grab her and hold her until she realized he wasn't going anywhere. Wasn't leaving her alone, no matter how much she hated him, because he would protect her come hell or high water.

"I'm sorry, Savanna," he said through the door, hoping it carried over the water noise. "I'm so, so sorry."

"Me, too," she yelled back, trying to sound angry. "Now get me a new bodyguard."

"I will, but I need to tell you the rest of my story. In case something happens to me. I need you to know."

No response, so he waited. And waited.

The water shut off. There were no more crying noises.

He put his back to the door and slid down to sit on his butt. Leaning his head back, he closed his eyes. It shouldn't take Rory much longer to decode the Parker data. Then they'd have to decide what they were doing with it.

God, he was tired. More tired than he'd been in his whole life. He couldn't force himself on Savanna. Couldn't make her listen if she didn't want to.

He could get her a new bodyguard. He wouldn't leave her completely, but he'd stay in the shadows.

"I'll go call Beatrice," he said. "I'll get you the best damn bodyguard she's got."

To his surprise, the door opened once more, but again, only by a few inches. "What's the rest of your story?"

He couldn't see her; only triangulate her position from the sound of her voice. She was sitting on the inside of the door, opposite of him. How long had she been there? Why hadn't he heard her? Felt her?

His emotions were overriding his skills.

Dangerous territory.

"I'm listening," she said. Her voice was flat. "You have two minutes."

Taking a breath, he searched for where to start. "I was sent after a woman, to take her out. Her file said she was a hacker selling defense intel to the Chinese. I had a whole folder of offenses to verify her traitorous activities. When I got to my setup point, I saw something that stopped me. Made me question an assignment for the first time ever."

"What?"

"She was pregnant."

Silence.

"I got closer, watched her for a while," he went on. "She was living mostly off the grid. No computer, no cell phone, not even a TV. The facts I had in her file didn't ring true. She seemed to be avoiding electronics, but why? I went back to my spot where my rifle was set up, tried to put it out of my mind. Tried to do my job. I looked down my scope and put my finger on the trigger, and…"

"You didn't kill her."

Smart. Intuitive. "No, I didn't. I couldn't."

"Who was she?"

"I broke into her house and interrogated her. Turned out, she'd been in the program with me. She was one of us."

"A super soldier?"

"She wasn't crazy, didn't have any adverse side effects."

"Why did Norman want her dead then? Because she got pregnant? Was he worried the baby would have side effects from the drugs?"

"The only side effect would have been because of the father, not the mother."

"Who was the father?"

Trace let her chew on it a minute, and sure enough, that smart, intuitive brain of hers figured it out. "No. Are you saying? Linc Norman…?"

"That's what she claimed. She had graduated from the program, like me, and went to work for a top-secret agency under Norman called Command & Control. Her thing was languages and cyber security. Next thing she knew, she was summoned to some cabin in Vermont. The president was there with a couple of Secret Service agents, but that was it. He offered her champagne, talked about all the good she was doing in the world, all the enemies of State she was going to eliminate. Her first target was a Chinese hacker. Norman gave her the details and the next thing she knew, it was morning and she woke up alone and naked in the master bedroom."

"He'd drugged her?"

"I was skeptical. Figured she double-crossed the U.S. and hooked up with the hacker." He ran a hand over his face. "But she had proof. She'd taken both of the champagne glasses and had them tested. Hers showed evidence of GHB."

"The date rape drug."

"The president's champagne glass had his DNA. The tests results for the baby came back ninety-three percent positive."

"She took the results to Norman and he put out a hit on her."

"No, she was too smart to go to him. He'd drugged her and raped her. She had no illusions about him becoming a standup guy once he found out she was pregnant with his kid. She couldn't hide it long from Command & Control, and decided she couldn't go through with an abortion. So she ran and tried to stay off the grid."

"But he figured out what happened and sent you after her to eliminate her and the child."

"I let her go. She went on the run again. I went back to Command & Control with my first and only failed mission. Got called on the carpet by the president himself. I told him I knew the real story and I wouldn't keep blindly following his orders."

He heard her sigh. Resignation. "So he branded you a traitor and made up a bogus file on you for Parker to give to me."

"He sent a couple of other assassins after me, none of whom got the job done. I took them out. His only other hope was to incarcerate me."

"And the woman? Is she still in hiding?"

"She was in an accident while I was in Witcher." If he'd been free, he might have protected her. Wishful thinking, since he hadn't known where she was going, but the guilt still ate at him. He could have done something to help her if he hadn't been incarcerated. "Both her and the baby died."

Tense silence. "It wasn't an accident, was it?"

"The brakes failed on her car, probably because someone fiddled with the brake fluid line."

A few beats passed. "How did you get out of prison?"

"I was in Witcher for eighteen months, most of the time in solitary. Every time I came out, someone tried to kill me. A chance came along for me to escape, and I took it. Figured it was another ploy for the president to send an assassin after me, but I couldn't go on in that place. Happened to be Emit Petit, not the president, who was after me. In exchange for busting me out, he wanted me to work for him. I didn't have a lot of options. Seemed like a better deal than going back to Witcher or ending up dead."

"And then I came along."

"Yeah."

The night closed in around him. His ears picked up the

sound of a clock somewhere downstairs, the second hand ticking softly. He waited, not saying anything, not moving, only hoping Savanna was going to open the door all the way and give him a second chance.

She closed it a moment later and flipped the lock.

CHAPTER TWENTY-THREE

Savanna switched off the voice-recording app on her phone, washed her face and pulled her hair up in a ponytail. The story Coldplay—*Trace*—had told her rewound and played over and over in her mind.

He'd warned her she wasn't going to like him once she found out about his past. He was right. She didn't like him too much at the moment.

But it wasn't over his past.

He'd been used. Followed orders and then gotten the shaft when he refused to kill a pregnant woman. A woman who was having the president's child.

The soap opera storyline alone would annihilate the president. He would be impeached, thrown in jail.

But she had no proof other than Trace's confession on tape.

Which would put him in hot water too. He'd taken out the other patients in Program 24, following his commander-in-chief's orders, but he'd still murdered American citizens on American soil. If there were no proof of those orders—and she was sure Command & Control didn't keep a log lying around—his word wasn't enough.

On top of that, he'd escaped a maximum-security prison. His supposed crimes were bogus, but again, she had no proof. He was a federal fugitive.

What she did have was Parker's file. A file she hoped would show a secret drug testing program that created super soldiers. Did it also track what had happened to them? If something in that coded mess of gobbledygook actually pointed a finger at the president, that he was running some type of off the books black ops group doing his bidding, uncensored, she was in business.

All she needed was five minutes on air.

And the decoded file.

Opening the bathroom door, she found the bedroom suite empty. Her heart fell. A tiny part of her had hoped Coldplay—*Trace, dammit*—was sitting out there waiting for her.

The laptop was on the floor where he'd left it. His clothes were gone.

He's gone.

A hollowness filled her chest cavity. *What did you expect, Savanna? You told him to go. You asked—no, demanded—a new bodyguard.*

Her legs trembled ever so slightly as she stared at the bed where hours before he'd made love to her.

Sex. We had sex. There was no love involved.

Her heart didn't believe it.

In just a few short days, she'd come to rely on him and his solid, steady presence. His sudden absence left a void she knew she couldn't fill.

She'd always been independent, strong. Still was. She hadn't needed anyone since she was fourteen. The walls she'd built around her heart were tall and fortified.

Lt. Trace Hunter had bored right through every one of them.

A dinging came from the computer. Savanna made her way to the chaise and picked it up.

"I've decoded the information," Rory told her a moment later.

"Good. Send it to me."

Rory fiddled with some keys and the file appeared in her upper right screen. Then he fidgeted, seemed like he wanted to say something else.

"What is it, Rory?"

"About Coldplay. This information could—"

"You don't need to explain. He already did."

"Yeah, he probably told you all the crap, some of which is in this file from your sister. Did he tell you about all the heroic shit he did as a SEAL before Project 24? The people he saved? The men he rescued from behind enemy lines? Did he tell you about Palestine? Bahrain? Mumbai?"

She wanted to ask him to tell her about Trace's heroics. She had a sudden need to know. But what difference did it make now?

He was gone and there was no way she could fix the mess they were in, regardless of what he hadn't told her.

Rory took her silence for what it was. "I didn't think so. You might keep in mind the fact that he was a hero, Ms. Jeffries. In my book, he still is. I was a SEAL once too. Did some wet work for the CIA after that. Everything I did weighed on my conscious, but I did it for the good of the country. To keep people like you safe so you could enjoy your freedom of speech and go to bed every night in a country free of war."

Her throat was tight. "I appreciate your service."

"Words. Those are just fucking words. If you want to prove you appreciate what men like me, and Reece, and Lt. Hunter have done for the American public, then do something to clear Hunter's name."

He was about to leave their video chat, but Savanna wasn't done with him yet. "Let your boss know I'm coming to see her."

"It's three in the morning."

"I assume she knows I requested a new bodyguard and there are several things I want to discuss with her. I'll be there in twenty minutes."

Savanna closed out the video chat window. Her hands weren't shaking, but she clasped them tight in her lap anyway, staring at the blue file folder in the upper right corner of the screen

Closing the laptop, she went downstairs. She couldn't help but peek into the second floor den where she and Trace had done yoga together. Where he'd taken her on the rug.

He wasn't there. She knew he wouldn't be, and yet a trickle of hope had made her look.

Maybe he's in the kitchen.

She chastised herself even as her feet picked up their speed going down the stairs.

In the kitchen on the first floor, her heart sunk a little more. No surprise Trace wasn't there. Another man with a lean face, an athletic build, and a goatee leaned against the counter with a plastic coffee cup in hand. "Hello, love. Coldplay said you were an early riser."

His deep-set green eyes mocked her. His British accent turned his hello into *el-lo.*

"Where is Coldplay?"

"You requested a new bodyguard." He boosted himself away from the counter and set his cup on the island. "Name's Henley. I'm at your disposal."

Didn't answer my question. Maybe Beatrice would. Savanna slipped her boots on and grabbed her coat from the mudroom. "Henley. That's not a rock band I'm familiar with."

He grinned, saying nothing.

Okay then.

"Get the car, Henley. We're going for a ride."

"Where to, love?"

The 'love' moniker was going to get on her nerves. Fast. "Rock Star Headquarters."

Henley didn't seem surprised. He spoke into his watch, alerting the crew outside. Three black SUVs pulled up at the covered side entrance a few minutes later, and for a moment, Savanna wondered if Trace were in one of them. The dark windows didn't allow her to see in. She didn't honestly believe he would leave her, *really* leave her.

But then again, she didn't know him. All she knew was what he'd wanted her to see. A fake. A fraud.

That was what gutted her the most. Not the facts about his past; the fact that he'd deliberately misled her. Lied to her. That she'd confessed her deepest, darkest secret to him and he'd still felt compelled to keep his identity and his intentions from her.

As the SUVs slipped quickly through the night, Savanna sat in the backseat of one and opened the laptop. The blue file was still waiting for her.

She clicked it open and started reading.

ROCK STAR SECURITY HEADQUARTERS

"You lied to me and put me in danger."

Savanna sat across from Beatrice in her office, the coffee Connor had brought her untouched. The heavenly smell clouded the air but Savanna's stomach churned. From Trace's admission and his subsequent disappearance. From the file's contents that made her angry and sad all at the same time.

Beatrice seemed unconcerned. For such an early morning, the pregnant woman appeared completely polished. As if she'd been expecting a call. Her vivid purple pantsuit made her blond hair and green eyes pop. "I withheld Coldplay's identity as I do with all the security specialists on my team. You were advised that would be the case. You signed the contract."

"He wasn't a stranger whose identity you were protecting. You knew our past...interaction."

"How did I put you in danger?"

"I ruined his life and helped put him in prison. You didn't think revenge might be on his list?"

"Revenge is spurred by emotions. His personality tests all suggest he has no desire for revenge because he's a High Logic. He doesn't run on emotion. He seeks justice. Need I remind you he saved your life multiple times in the past week?"

Beatrice had an answer for everything. Every little thing. It was infuriating, yet Savanna admired her. Once upon a time, on her show, she'd been the same way. Always in control.

Now she was anything but. The past week had broken her down. "You broke him out of prison. Why?"

A beat went by. *Hesitation?* "I received a rather cryptic message suggesting Coldplay was innocent of the charges brought against him. The message stated you needed him to find your sister. I dug into his past, uncovered a few things that made me suspect the message was accurate. The group he formerly worked for is familiar to me. I understand what they're capable of."

"Message? What message?"

"It came to me from ON16. I now believe it was from your sister."

"You think Parker is ON16?"

"No. I know who ON16 is. In this case, he was simply a third party relaying information. At the time, I didn't know who the sender was, and as you've probably figured out by now, I don't like not knowing things. As our interactions with you proceeded, I figured out it was Parker. She sent you to ON16. She made an attempt to reach out to Coldplay while he was in Witcher, probably to confirm her suspicions about his innocence or to seek his help. When that failed, she had no choice but to stay underground and keep sending us bread crumbs to uncover the president's plan."

"So who *is* ON16?"

"Sorry, I'm not at liberty to divulge that information."

Savanna sat for a moment. The coffee had cooled, much like her anger at confronting Beatrice. "Where is Trace?"

"If you're unhappy with Henley, I can find someone else."

She was unhappy with Henley, all right, but there was no one else who could fill Trace's spot. It wasn't Henley's fault, it was hers. Sweat broke out along her hairline. Her stomach continued to churn.

Damn Trace Hunter for causing her so much turmoil. For keeping her emotions bouncing all over the place. She wanted to hate him for his lies, for his deception, but she couldn't.

Rising, she tucked her laptop under her arm. "I should fire the lot of you."

"Your emotional side demands that, yet your logical side has you here in my office looking for answers. Rock Star Security isn't simply bodyguards. We're problem solvers. We're fixers. There's no one else in Washington DC who can help you with your problem and provide a successful outcome. You know that."

"You're awfully smug."

"The truth, stated openly, often appears as overconfidence or conceit. I assure you, in this case, it is neither."

"I need to use the restroom."

"Of course." Beatrice rose and walked her to the door. Henley waited outside, those green eyes watching her like a cat before glancing at Beatrice. The slight nod from his boss seemed to tell him to stand down. He slouched once more against the wall, waiting.

Beatrice pointed at Savanna's laptop. "We should talk about Parker's file and what you plan to do with it."

"I haven't decided yet," Savanna said, marching past both of them.

It was a lie. She knew exactly what she was going to do with the information.

The restroom was down the hall and around the corner. She didn't need Connor to show her the way but knew Rory or someone was probably watching her on a hidden camera.

Ducking into the ladies room, she prayed they didn't have cameras in there.

She'd left her coat on to talk to Beatrice. As she shrugged it off and hung it up in order to use the toilet, her phone rang from inside the pocket.

Private caller. Savanna swallowed hard. What did Linc Norman want now? Should she ignore it? Her thumb hesitated over the green button. There was no one there for support this time. She was on her own.

She hit the button. "What?"

"I have your sister in custody," Norman said. "I think it's time we make a deal."

For the first time, she was right. The call was about Parker.

Savanna didn't know whether to be relieved or pissed. Maybe a bit of both. Parker had figured out the truth about Project 24 and had recommended shutting down the program. She noted the president's refusal in her files, had started adding more personal notes to each of the participants.

Patient 13—Trace Hunter—had been her favorite; his outcomes had been exactly what she'd been shooting for. She'd wanted to redefine the program's parameters, stop the drugs and try a fresh approach with cognitive intensive learning techniques.

But the president rejected her ideas, and soon, Parker discovered her star patient was being ordered to kill off the other participants who didn't work out. She must have confronted Norman, threatened him, and that's why she was now on the run.

Had been on the run, if Norman was to be believed. "What kind of deal?" Savanna asked.

"You give me the file. I'll give you your sister."

Right. And she was born yesterday. "I want proof of life."

He chuckled, sounding slightly inebriated. "She's deep in the bowels of Langley, being interrogated. Every minute you waste, she's in pain, Van. She's not up for talking right now."

Savanna's already queasy stomach revolted, sending hot, bitter acid up her throat. Was he bluffing? Could she take the chance that he wasn't? "This discussion is over until I hear from her."

She hung up, bending at the waist and praying for forgiveness. *I'm so sorry, Parker.*

But she had to know if the president was bluffing.

And there was no way she was giving him the file.

He wouldn't risk that she'd blab the information down the road. He wouldn't risk that she hadn't made backup copies. He would scrub her apartment, destroy any and all computers. He would go after her parents, wipe out her bank accounts, whatever it took to make sure he'd covered his ass.

Including killing her.

Parker, too, if she was still alive.

Hell, he'd come after Rock Star Security and wipe them out too. Desperate men did desperate things.

She'd pay good money to see Beatrice take on Linc Norman.

The thought almost made her smile.

Unfortunately, she couldn't put a group of innocent men and women in the line of fire. No matter how good, how canny, how intelligent Beatrice and her cohorts were, they couldn't take on the president of the United States and win.

The image of Trace aiming his weapon at a pregnant woman flashed into her mind.

She'd be doing a similar thing if she took Beatrice and RSS down with her.

So like Trace, she had to refuse the order.

Straightening, she dampened a paper towel with cool water and wiped her forehead and the back of her neck. Her reflection in the mirror showed strain, sleeplessness, fear that she couldn't save her sister.

I can't save anyone.

She needed Trace. He would know what to do.

He's not here. You have to do this on your own.

Her eyes fell to her laptop. She had to get the information in the blue folder out into the world.

Picking up her cell, she dialed a number she hadn't used in a long, long time.

The man on the other end answered before the third ring. "The goddamn zombie apocalypse better be happening if you're calling this early in the morning."

"Your alarm is set for fifteen minutes from now, Zeb. Consider this an early wakeup call."

"You coming back to work for me? If not, hang up," he growled. "I'm busy."

"I need ten minutes of air time."

"Local high school football reruns are scheduled until five. We don't go on air until then."

"I need you to meet me at the station. It'll take me fifteen or twenty minutes to get there. The football replays will have to be interrupted."

She heard him shift in his bed, sit up, the smell of a scoop getting to him. "You got something big or are you getting an old newsman excited for nothing?"

"This is going to make your coverage of Ollie North's trial look like child's play."

"Don't dis a man's crowning glory, girlie."

"You'll meet me at the station?"

"Couldn't sleep anyway," he grumbled. "You gonna need hair and makeup and all that fancy cable network crap? This is public access. I don't have staff."

"All I need is a single camera and a computer hookup."

"Boss man will have my hide for this."

Zeb *was* the boss. "Do you need some cheese with that whine?"

It was a line he'd used on her many times when they were both at the public television station and she was a new reporter, digging up stories and hitting brick walls.

"What do I get out of this, missy?"

"Your ratings are going to go through the roof."

"Throw in a box of cigars and it's a deal."

He loved a scoop more than cigars, but in typical Zeb fashion, he was determined to be a curmudgeon. "Deal." *If I'm still alive and not in jail.*

Her phone buzzed, display showing she had a call coming in. Shit, was it the president again?

"See you in fifteen," Zeb said over the squeak of mattress springs.

Savanna clicked off and accepted the incoming call. "Hello?"

"Savanna?" It was Parker's voice. "Gosh, I've missed you."

Savanna's knees went weak. "Parker! Where are you?"

But it wasn't Parker who answered her. "Satisfied?" Linc Norman cut in. "Your sister is alive. If you want her to stay that way, you'll pony up that file, Van."

Damn it. Her arms and legs buzzed with adrenaline. Her chest felt like static electricity was zapping her heart. "Don't hurt her. I'll bring you the file."

"Good." He rattled off an address in the low rent district, not far from the public television station. "I'll meet you there in an hour. Don't do anything stupid."

She couldn't keep the snark out of her voice. "Isn't this where you tell me not to contact the police and to come alone?"

"Nah." Linc Norman chuckled. "Bring your bodyguard. Hunter and I have plenty of catching up to do."

The line went dead.

Savanna removed the studs from her ears and the GPS

tracker from her bra. She laid the gold bracelet on the sink.

Pocketing her phone, she donned her coat and grabbed the laptop. She'd removed the tracking device inside the phone on the way over, sliding it into her pocket. Now, she took it out and tossed it in the sink.

Unlocking and opening the restroom window, she crawled out into the cold, dark night.

CHAPTER TWENTY-FOUR

"Where the hell are you going?" Trace mumbled to himself as he watched Savanna struggle through the side window and plop unceremoniously into the snow. She got up, dusted herself off, looked both ways, and headed east.

He was sitting in the rear Escalade, motor idling. Someone, probably Rory, had patched him into the conversation in Beatrice's office. Savanna had been mad and trying not to cut loose. He couldn't blame her. Between Parker, Linc Norman, and Rock Star Security, she'd been manipulated in almost every way possible.

"She took a call from that private number," Rory said in his comm unit. "Then she placed a call to Zebulon Riceman, owner and operator of a small-time public access television station. He's also top dog at the local PBS station. Decides on programming and hosts his own travel segment."

She was going public.

"Riceman gave Savanna her start back in the day," Rory added.

The building sensors had alerted those inside that there had been a breach. Henley stuck his head out of the open restroom window and, although Trace couldn't hear him, he knew he was swearing a blue streak.

"Your girl has the left the building," Rory said.

She was chugging through the heavy snow at a fast clip. Trace put the Escalade in gear. "I have eyes on her."

"Do you want us to follow?"

"Let me see what I can do first."

Beatrice's voice came over the comm. "You think it's wise for you to engage her in her current emotional state?"

Wise? Hell, no. Necessary? Yes.

Only the running lights were on as he wheeled out into the street. Her bright coat bobbed in the distance. "Did you listen in on the conversation with either man?"

"We do not normally eavesdrop in the restrooms," Beatrice said. "However, in this case, it seemed logical to keep a close eye— or in this case, ear—on her."

"And?"

"She made a deal with the president. She asked for proof of life, and at one point, it seemed as though she were speaking to her sister."

So Norman had finally caught up with Parker Jeffries. No wonder Savanna was sneaking off to meet him.

Brave or stupid? Maybe both. "Track her and send me the coordinates of Zeb's public access station. I'll be in contact when I have more information."

"Roger that," Rory said. "Just so you know, she's disposed of most of her trackers. The one in her coat is still active, though."

Thank God for that. Trace didn't plan to lose her, but better safe than sorry.

Savanna was only a few feet off the road as he approached, the snow too deep for her. Luckily, in this area of DC, at this time of night, traffic was light to nonexistent.

When she heard the sound of the engine, she jerked her head to look over her shoulder. He flashed the lights, then killed them again.

She kept walking, chin up, eyes ahead.

Stubborn woman.

He hit a button to lower the passenger window and slowed so he was keeping pace with her. Did she really plan to walk all the way to the station? The coordinates that had just hit his GPS said it was twelve blocks. Piece of cake for him, even with the snow and ice. For her, it might be more of a challenge.

"Need a ride?" he called out.

She shot him a death glare, then went back to a half-walk, half-run. The laptop was clutched to her chest. "Not from you."

There wasn't much conviction in her voice. "I promise not to interfere with whatever you're doing, even if it *is* stupid."

That got him another death glare. She had to slow her pace

to talk. "I'm doing my job and trying to save my sister at the same time."

Her job was over. She'd been fired.

Her conviction told him she still saw herself as an investigative reporter who needed to right a wrong. Reveal the truth and blow the whistle on Norman.

"All I want to do is protect you, Savanna. I...care for you."

"Care for me?" She lost her footing for a second, nearly tossing the laptop into the snow bank, before she righted herself. "Bullshit. I was a means to an end for you. You wanted to out President Norman about Project 24 and save your ass. You played me."

He continued to creep forward to keep up with her. The outside temperature was in the twenties and her teeth were chattering. He gave her another two blocks. Three tops.

Turning the heat up a notch inside the car, he tried to think of a way to get through to her. "Let me at least get Henley to drive you. You're going to have frostbite before you get to the station."

She stopped dead. Unprepared, he had to slam on the brakes and back up half a foot to see her. She faced him. "How do you know where I'm going?"

He hesitated to tell her. Didn't have to. Her quick brain figured it out.

"Oh, my God, you were eavesdropping on me in the restroom."

"Not me specifically, but...yeah. For your own good. Besides, there's a tracker in your coat. Guess Beatrice forgot to mention that."

"Is nothing sacred to you people?" She started marching again. "And don't *ever* tell me you did something for *my* own good."

"Savanna, no one is going to stop you from going to the TV station and broadcasting the information in that file. Let us drive you. If you don't want me, fine. Henley will do it. Hell, at this point, Beatrice would do it."

"She probably would, just to get me off her ass."

True. "You're still under our watch. Something happens to you, Henley will get fired. You don't want that on your conscious, do you?"

"That's low, Trace. Even for you."

Her words hurt, but he'd hit a nerve with her too. She

stopped walking again and lowered her chin. He braked beside her, hoping she'd feel a warm blast of air from the cab and decide to get in.

"What time is it?" she asked.

He told her.

"Dammit, I'm not going to get there in time." She dropped her head back, blew out a plume of frosty breath. Grabbing the handle, she wrenched the door open. "Fine. You can drive me, but that's all. Got it?"

He tried not to smile. Tried not to let her see the relief on his face as she climbed in.

"I suppose you already know where I'm going," she said.

He popped on the SUVs lights, shot off down the road. "Some broadcasting station?"

Savanna warmed her hands in front of the air vents. "You're not going to like what I'm about to do."

"Didn't figure I would."

They drove the rest of the way in silence. The station's parking lot was deserted. A plow truck had recently scraped off the worst of the snow, allowing black asphalt stripes to show through in places.

Savanna pointed north. "Go around to the back."

"Is someone meeting you here or are you breaking in?"

"My friend is here."

Trace didn't see any other vehicles. "The minute you go on air, you'll be giving away your location. Let me call in the team. We don't have to come inside, but at least let us keep an eye out from out here."

"No." She hopped out of the SUV. "You have to leave now."

"Leave?"

"You can't be here when this goes down, so I'm officially relieving you and Rock Star Security of duty." Her face was bland, neutral, but her eyes wouldn't hold his. "Get lost."

"Savanna—"

Now she met his gaze straight on. "When I go live in a few minutes, your fugitive status will become known to the world. You can't clear your name from inside a prison cell or if you're dead. I'm giving this to you. I care about you, too, even after you deceived me. Please don't throw that back in my face. Take my gift and get out of here."

With one last, long look, she closed the door and made her way to the back door. The door opened from the inside, a man who must have been waiting and seen the SUV pull up, giving Trace a steely look. He spoke to Savanna as she passed by him. Then he nodded at Trace and closed the door.

Trace banged his hand on the steering wheel. *I care about you, too, even after you deceived me.*

Maybe there was still hope for them after this was all said and done.

But only if he kept her alive.

Going back to Witcher was a small price to pay in return.

He touched his comm unit, gave Rory instructions, and cut the SUV's lights. Then he settled in to watch and wait.

Savanna touched her hair, smoothing back the strands that had come loose from her ponytail. A week ago, she would have never considered going on the air with her hair in such a mess or without makeup. A week ago, she would have never considered sitting at the anchor desk in yoga pants and a T-shirt.

A week ago. Seemed more like a lifetime ago.

"Ready?" The earbud in her ear came to life with Zeb's voice from the control booth. "I've got your computer hooked up and ready to roll. Tap the desk to cue me when you want me to switch to that from your face. Sure you don't want that second camera moved in to do side takes?"

The public access station had three cameras total. The other two sat in the shadows, out of the way. "That won't be necessary." Head-on was how she had to handle this. "Remember, you're to bug out as soon as you switch the camera back to me. No hanging around. You never saw me, didn't know I was here. Got it?"

"Don't you worry about me."

She *was* worried about him, but he'd been in DC a long time and knew politics like the back of his hand. Fiddling with her phone, she called up the voice recording she had of Trace's confession and cued it to the part she wanted to air.

"Ready," she said. *Let's get this over with.*

The red light on top of the camera blinked as Zeb counted her in. "We're live in five...four...three...two..."

The camera's light went green.

"Good morning, America," Savanna said, falling into newscaster mode. She had no idea who or how many people were up at four in the morning watching public access television, but it didn't matter. Even a handful of watchers who would talk about it, upload the video to the World Wide Web, start asking questions, would do the trick. "This is Savanna Bunkett coming to you from your local public access broadcasting station, CableNet1Z.

"As creator of *The Bunk Stops Here,* I've been on a special undercover assignment that has put my life, and the lives of many others, in great danger. Because of what I have discovered, my platform at my former news station has been stripped from me, an assassin has tried to harm me twice, and this broadcast will no doubt be shut down momentarily by government forces who don't want the truth to be told.

"So be forewarned. What I'm about to tell you is beyond classified. Beyond top secret. And in the coming moments, they will try to shut me up in one way or another."

She took a deep breath. The speech she had prepared in her mind was ready to go. She sent one last mental prayer to Parker. *I hope you understand.*

And then she proceeded to tell her sister's story.

She gave the background. How she'd come across the information, where it had led. When she was ready, she tapped the desk with her finger. The green light went to a pulsing red, letting her know Zeb had switched from her camera to the computer screen, where the details about the patients and outcomes of Project 24 were listed.

Point by point, she walked the viewers through the data listed in the report. Then she got ready for the gold mine sitting at the desk with her.

The camera light once again went green. Savanna cleared her throat. "One of the survivors of Project 24 told me a harrowing tale about what he was expected to do at the order of President Linc Norman. What he discovered, and how he finally realized that the men and women he was sent after to assassinate were innocent people in the president's game of building super soldiers, will send chills up your spine."

She turned on the voice recording and let it play. Her voice, asking Trace about what had happened on that final mission was picked up by her mic. She closed her eyes and listened to him respond.

Halfway through the recording, a commotion erupted in the front of the building. A moment later, two men in dark suits rushed in, dodging the lights and other equipment, and heading right for her.

Savanna didn't run, didn't even get up. "Don't let Linc Norman get away with this," she pleaded at the camera to the American people. "He's experimented on and killed American soldiers in the name of national defense, but this has nothing to do with protecting Amer—"

The first suit reached her, snatching the phone off the desk and smashing it under his feet. She'd seen him accompany the president before. Secret Service.

The second agent shot the camera, *bam, bam, bam.* Glass exploded, bullets ricocheted off metal. The reverberation caused her to cover her head and duck.

Steel hands clamped onto her arms, hauling her from the chair, then shoving her down on her stomach and knocking her forehead against the floor. Pain exploded above her eyes, her head bouncing from the impact. Her hands were jerked behind her back and handcuffed.

Yanked to her feet, she lost her balance and nearly toppled into the destroyed camera, its parts spread all over the floor. Out of the corner of her eye, she noticed a soft green light glowing from the shadows.

Zeb was getting everything, God bless his old curmudgeony heart. The damn fool better get out of the building in time. If not, Savanna hoped Trace would save him. She knew better than to believe Trace had left like she'd instructed. She'd known what she was getting into; Zeb was an innocent bystander.

The first agent hauled her out the front door into the snow. Linc Norman stood idling beside a black limo, head tipped back, stargazing. A third man stood guard a few feet away.

Norman wore a dark wool trench coat, his blond bangs lifting in the breeze as he tipped his head down and looked her over. "See, I knew you'd do something stupid, Van, and I really hate it when my high school football replay is interrupted by mindless drama."

The agent holding her kicked her in the back of the knees, forcing her to kneel at the president's feet.

The wet snow instantly soaked through her pant legs, the freezing air biting at her skin. She scanned the front parking lot; the lights here were in working order, but still fighting with the night to illuminate the place. They reflected off the snow, throwing weird shadows over the president's face.

"Where's my sister?" Savanna demanded.

Norman laughed. "Actually, I have no idea."

"What? You said you had her."

He shrugged. "I lied. Sue me."

"But…we had a deal."

The door banged open and the second Secret Service agent shoved Zeb out into the snow. He was cuffed, too, and blood ran from his nose.

Norman shook a finger at him. "You're in deep doo-doo, Zeb, helping this traitor. I thought you'd retired."

Zeb spit on the ground.

Retired? Zeb would never retire from broadcasting.

"Leave him out of this," Savanna said. Her teeth were chattering and her head pounded. She could feel a lump coming up on her forehead. "He had nothing to do with this. I forced him to open the studio for me."

"Really? You *forced* him? What did you threaten him with, a microphone?" Norman smiled at his own joke. "Where's your bodyguard, Van?"

"He's not my bodyguard anymore. I fired him. Where's my sister?"

His smile faded. "She's still in the wind."

"You said she was at Langley. I heard her voice on the phone."

"You heard a recording."

At her look of confusion, he continued. "On her last trip abroad, I had her phone conversations recorded. I suspected she was up to something and I might need some leverage down the road. Oh, Savanna. I miss you!" he mimicked and laughed.

The saliva in Savanna's mouth went dry. A sharp stab of hate set her chest on fire. But if he didn't have Parker, that was good. "Thank God she's too smart for you, you conniving son-of-a-bitch."

"You think you're the only one who can trick people?"

"Seems like you should win a Golden Globe for tricking people. You've done a bang-up job of deceiving the American public."

He waved a hand. "A bunch of whiners and slackers. I'm building a super army and getting ready for the future. To protect them while they sit in front of their televisions eating fast food and watching *The Bachelor*."

"Without any oversight or Congressional approval. You've become a dictator."

"I don't have time to wait on Congress. I thought Parker understood that. Her program was going to be a pivotal turning point in my administration, in the future of counterterrorism. But don't worry, I *will* find her, and when I do, I'll make sure that incredible brain of hers is turned to dust."

"You're using people for your own devices, just like the female soldier in the program you drugged and raped. When you found out she was pregnant with your child, you sent the only super soldier you had left from Project 24 to kill her."

He smiled and held up his hands. "I admit, I got a little greedy, but with great power comes great responsibility. That child would have destabilized my presidency, don't you see? Should I be judged by one unfortunate accident after all the good I've done for the country?"

He'd twisted the famous quote around for his own self-serving purposes. "You call drugging and raping a woman an unfortunate accident?"

"Always hung up on details, aren't you, Van? Well, here's a detail for you. You're about to die."

He snapped his fingers at the guard holding onto Zeb. "Where's the file?"

The agent produced her laptop from inside his coat and handed it to Norman. "It's on here."

"I assume this isn't the only copy?" Norman said to her. "You're too smart for that. The good news is, no one can corroborate this information. It's sad, really. I'm going to tell everyone that you were so distraught after being fired, you had to make up some crazy story about me in an effort to get your job back. You staged everything to dupe the American public. Now, you're feeling guilty and are about to commit suicide, taking Zeb, here, with you."

He tossed the laptop through the limo's open window, cocked his chin at the man holding Zeb. "Burn the place down. We don't want any evidence."

"Yes, sir," the man said, heading into the building.

Norman held out a hand to the closest guard. "Give me your weapon."

"Sir?"

Still holding out his hand, Norman took a step closer to Savanna, towering over her with a sinister look of glee on his face. "I've waited for this moment for a long time. This kill is mine."

The Secret Service agent took a black gun from a shoulder holster inside his coat and handed it to the president. Then he stepped back.

Bloodstains and brain splatter were so hard to get out of clothes after all.

Norman's leather glove squeaked in the cold air as he tightened his grip on the stock of the gun. The sterile metal barrel bit into Savanna's forehead and she clenched her teeth to stop their chattering.

Where was Trace? Had he really left her?

Her body felt frozen, her heart doing a staccato beat in her chest. *Think, think, think!*

The president had the upper hand, but then, he'd had the upper hand all along. All she could do was hope she'd gotten enough of the information out there that someone would take up her cause. Parker was still alive and so was Trace. They could corroborate the facts.

She'd done her job.

But there was no way she was going down without a fight.

Raising her eyes, she stared up past the barrel of the gun at Linc Norman. "You're done for, Mr. President."

"Really?" He chuckled. "Because out of the two of us, Van, you're the one about to die."

And then, out of nowhere, a snowball hit the president in the back of the head.

Snow flew around his hair and he gasped, recoiling and whirling around. The agent who had no gun grabbed him and began to hustle him into the limo, but Norman shoved him away.

An explosion sounded from inside the building, making everyone flinch. Flames shot out from a busted window.

The agent next to Zeb drew his weapon and moved it in an arc, scanning the parking lot as he walked forward, ready to cover the president.

"Hunter," Norman called. "Is that you? Show yourself, you coward."

One second, there were only shadows at the edge of the parking lot, the next, Trace emerged. "I can't let you shoot her."

Norman laughed. "About time you showed up."

Trace approached, walking casually, no weapon in sight. He

didn't look at her and, for a split second, Savanna's thoughts went to a dark place. Was Trace Hunter in cahoots with the president?

Nonono.

Suddenly hyperventilating, sensation disappeared in her fingers and toes.

"Let her go," Trace said. He stopped a few feet from the president and held open his arms. "You can have me. Take your best shot. I'm the one you wanted all along. It's personal between us, isn't it?"

She couldn't see Norman's face, but she saw him raise the gun. "I like this arrangement."

Trace finally looked at her, his eyes saying it all. Sadness. Regret. Love.

He was willing to sacrifice himself for her.

Savanna's stomach fell.

"First, you let her go," Trace said, returning his attention to the president.

"What? You don't trust me?" Norman scratched at the back of his head where the snowball had struck. Snowflakes fluttered down. "Ah, Hunter, you know I can't do that."

She didn't hear any cock of the gun. Didn't sense any change in Norman's body. But she couldn't let him kill Trace. In an instance, she was up and moving, charging the man she hated most in the world.

A cry of anger left her mouth as she launched herself at his back. At the same time, Trace yelled her name, his voice lost in her own shout, his eyes wide as he ran toward her.

Startled by her cry, Norman turned. Savanna hit him full force, the impact forcing the breath from her lungs. She heard the crack of the gun, felt the tear of flesh.

She knocked him down, unable to stop herself from falling on top of him.

The gun went off again, the sound an explosion in her ears.

Above her, there was shouting, more gunshots. They seemed distant. She no longer felt cold.

She was lifted from Norman, who was spewing words at her that she couldn't quite make out. White-hot pain drilled her body. The world spun.

Her eyes had to be playing tricks on her. From the corner of one eye, she noticed Zeb had taken down a Secret Service agent. Another lay on the ground in an unmoving heap.

Trace.

Solid arms held her. Over the ringing in her ears, she heard him saying her name over and over. He laid her on the ground behind the president's car. A fireball went up; the building belching smoke and heat like a furnace on steroids. *Maybe that's why I'm not cold.*

"Trace?" she said, but couldn't hear her own voice.

Her eyelids were heavy. Too heavy. She saw boots, shadows, the president jumping up from the ground. The bastard was still alive.

Blood covered his wool coat, his hand. The hand still holding a gun...raising it...pointing at someone just out of her sight.

"No!" she screamed at the top of her lungs. "Trace!"

A boot came up. A boot she'd seen a hundred times. Connecting with Norman's hand, sending the gun flying.

The glint of the fire—*so pretty*—reflected on the metal as the gun sailed through the night air.

Two men wrestling, snow flying, ashes from the fire falling.

Her lids fell, she jerked them open.

They fell again.

Help Trace! Stay awake.

Parker's face swam into view, a dream. Her lips were moving, but Savanna heard nothing. Parker's hands were moving, filled with snow. She was packing the snow.

Wanna play? A snowball fight now?

I'm hallucinating.

Savanna blinked, trying to force the image away.

Love you, sis, but I need to help Trace.

Savanna closed her eyes. Forced them open again. Parker's face was gone.

She tried to roll over, tried to reach out and grab something, anything, to leverage herself upright. *Move, dammit.*

Her body was numb, nothing would obey her commands. Not her hands, not her feet, not her eyelids.

The stars look so close, she thought.

And then she couldn't breathe.

Chapter Twenty-Five

The president's goons were accounted for, their bodies strewn across the parking lot where snow was turning to water as the building burned.

The old man, the station owner, watched the fire with a stoic face. He'd tried to run to Savanna, to help her, but Norman had stopped him.

In the distance, sirens sounded. In his ear, Trace heard Rory briefing him on the coming deluge of police and fire fighters headed his way.

Trace stood motionless, facing down Linc Norman. The usual calm he felt in battle had deserted him. His mind whirled with takedown scenarios, his heart threatened to beat out of his chest.

Save Savanna, save Savanna, save Savanna.

Norman had fired off three bullets by Trace's count and recovered the gun in their scrimmage. If the magazine in the gun had been full, that meant he had twelve left.

Twelve bullets he'd be happy to put in Trace.

At least one of the three fired was now lodged inside Savanna. From behind the back of the limo where he'd moved her, blood now mixed with the snow.

Too much blood.

From the bloom of red on the front of her shirt, he knew she'd been gut shot. She would hemorrhage out if he didn't get to her soon.

Twelve bullets. He'd take all twelve of them if it meant she would live.

Norman's hand shook as he kept the gun raised and trained on Trace. *Scared. Cornered.*

Cornered animals were the most dangerous.

The sirens drew louder.

Trace raised his hands. "Just let me stop Savanna's bleeding. We can leave before the police get here and you can kill me somewhere else and dump my body."

Norman looked like he was actually considering the idea. His gaze darted to the old man, back to Trace, then he grinned. "No one is stopping Van from bleeding out. She's done. You and Zeb here are—"

Trace lunged, not waiting for him to finish. Norman was solid, twenty pounds north of his ideal weight. Hitting him was like hitting a bear.

A fist to his jaw knocked him sideways but didn't take him down. The gun fired harmlessly into the air.

Disarm him.

Trace grabbed the arm with the gun, forcing it away as he knocked his elbow into Norman's chin. The guy's head snapped to the side and Trace brought Norman's gun hand down on his knee, knocking the gun free once again.

Norman tried to throw him off, losing his balance in the process and slipping on the melting snow. He grabbed Trace, pulling him sideways. Trace kicked out and caught him in the knee.

He wasn't going to kill the president. He wasn't.

From the corner of his eye, he saw Zeb rush by, kicking the gun out of Norman's reach and ducking behind the limo next to Savanna. His face popped around the bumper. "We're losing her!"

"Clotting agent," Trace shouted. "The Beast should have a bag of it."

Zeb dove into the front of the car while Norman regained his stance. "You son of a bitch."

Norman charged, unsteady on his feet but fueled by anger and adrenaline. Trace went to sweep his legs, but the guy anticipated the move and dodged away from Trace's kick, rotating his body toward the gun. As he dropped to his knees, sliding on the slick snow and reaching for the gun, something clicked in Trace's head.

Linc Norman wasn't a fighter, had never been in the military or even had basic defense training. How was he still standing?

He's enhanced.

The president had taken his own cocktail of the drugs to make a super soldier.

He still hadn't undergone training. Not the type of training Trace had endured.

Can't let him get that gun.

Trace dove; the two came together in a flurry of snow and bodies, Trace's momentum sending both of them crashing into the side of the limo. Norman had the gun, but barely by the stock. Trace spun him around, trying to knock his arm on the windshield, but Norman stomped on the top of his foot.

And then a shot rang out and the stab of pain like a red-hot branding iron went through Trace's upper right shoulder, the impact slamming him and Norman into the hood of the vehicle.

Norman went slack, dropping the handgun as blood gushed from a wound in his chest. Trace pushed off of him, searing pain in his back, shoulder, and chest making him gulp smoky air into his lungs.

The bullet, wherever it had come from, had gone straight through Trace and into the president.

Shit.

Trace flipped the man over and took him to the ground, pinning the president's hands behind his back. He glanced around, trying to locate the shooter and saw a petite figure in white camo jogging from the side of the burning building toward him. Beneath the hood of the jacket, a familiar looking face peeked out. Slung across her back, she carried a rifle.

"Parker?"

"Lt. Hunter, nice to finally make your acquaintance." She dropped a zip tie on top of Norman as she jogged past. "Don't mean to rude, but I need to check on my sister."

Blood oozed from his wound, the pain akin to the cold bore of an ice pick. "I need some of that Quik Clot," he called to Zeb as he tied the president's hands. "How's Savanna?"

Zeb appeared out of the shadows behind the car, tossing two packs at him. "She's in need of a hospital, and by the looks of things, so are you."

Norman was muttering as his blood poured into the slushy snow underneath him. Trace rolled him over, undid his coat, and ripped open a pack of the clotting agent with his teeth. He dumped the stuff on the president's wound, his right hand beginning to lose feeling.

"What are you doing?" Zeb asked, falling to his knees beside Trace. "That was for you, not this asshole."

Trace opened the second pack and layered it on top of the first. The bullet had lost energy after passing through him and was now lodged somewhere over the president's heart. "Can't let him die. He's the only one who can exonerate me."

Zeb disappeared for a moment as Trace's head swam. He'd been hurt plenty of times in the field, but the blood loss on top of the adrenaline was playing havoc with him.

He got to his feet, staggered, and was lucky Zeb had returned and was there to catch him. The flash of red and blue could be seen in the distance. "Whoa there, son," Zeb said, trying to get Trace to sit. "Let's get some clotting agent in you now."

"Got...to...take care of...Savanna."

"Her sister's got it covered."

"She shot me."

"She did at that. Never had a clear shot at Norman and she was afraid you would kill him. So she shot him through you." Zeb jerked Trace's coat open and eyed the holes the bullet had opened. His fingers made quick work of opening another pack of clotting agent. "She thinks you and her sister have half a chance at a future together and she didn't want you tied up forever with legal matters over killing the president of the United States."

Trace's fresh wounds burned from the powder as Zeb packed them with it. "Who...who do you work for?" he ground out.

"Ah, figured that out, did you?" Zeb chuckled. "It was a long time ago and I don't like to give away trade secrets, but let's say you never really retire from certain agencies."

CIA? NSA? Could have been any of them. "You're ON16, aren't you?"

Zeb finished packing the wound in Trace's back. "I have no idea what you're talking about."

The tone of his voice suggested differently.

Trace headed toward the back of the limo, his footsteps faltering. "I need...to see...Savanna."

Zeb caught his arm and helped him to where Savanna lay. Parker had unslung her weapon and a backpack. She had the first aid kit Zeb had retrieved from the Beast and was working on her sister, whom she'd wrapped in her coat.

"Two bullets," Parker said, her voice shaking as she started an IV. "One to her stomach and one to her arm. She's lost a lot of blood, but if we get her to a surgeon, she'll be okay."

Trace heard it in her shaky voice. She didn't believe her own words.

Stripping off his shirt, he laid it over Savanna's stomach and pressed gently. *Too much blood.* The clotting agent had stemmed the flow, but there was no telling how messed up her internal organs were.

Not much time.

Her skin was too pale, her lips blue even in the orange glow of the fire. He wanted more than anything to see her open her eyes one more time. Wanted to tell her he loved her.

Love. Funny word for him. He hadn't believed he was capable of such an emotion. Hadn't believed he deserved any such kindness from someone else.

But now he wanted it. He could taste it on his tongue, feel it in the erratic beat of his heart even as the pain in his shoulder and chest blocked his senses. He needed to thank her—for her kindness, for loving him even if it was for only a little while. The drugs that had been pumped into this body made him faster, stronger, smarter than other men, but the only thing that made him human was Savanna.

The fire engines rolled up, police on their heels. Behind all of them came five Rock Star Security SUVs. As chaos reigned around him, he took one of Savanna's cold, lifeless hands and brought it to his lips. "Don't you die on me, Savanna. Don't you dare die."

Chapter Twenty-six

The antiseptic smell of the hospital filled Trace's nostrils. His still-wet boots squeaked on the linoleum as he paced outside the waiting room.

Savanna was in the OR, fighting for her life. He'd received treatment for his bullet wound, and had been forced to spend the past few hours repeating answers to the questions shoved at him by the police and the Feds, and still, Savanna wasn't out of surgery.

The president was at a different, unnamed location, receiving emergency medical care as well. If he lived and Savanna died...

Trace punched the wall, drawing looks from a couple of passing nurses.

The only thing that had saved his ass from the Feds was Zeb. The old guy had not only aired Savanna's news report live, but when Norman's men had stormed the building and dragged her outside, Zeb had switched the live feed to the parking lot's security cameras. They had picked up everything until the building had exploded.

Parker had taped the rest with a camera mounted on her rifle from a few hundred feet away on a nearby rooftop. The audio tended to cut out here and there, but a picture really was worth a thousand words.

Trace hadn't seen Parker since he'd been brought to the hospital. He'd been about to rush in the moment Norman showed up at the studio, but Parker had called his cell phone and told him to stand down. She had a plan and needed

Norman's confession. Trace had refused, but Parker had insisted she wouldn't let Savanna die. She had her covered.

He'd spotted her on the roofline across from the studio, so he'd sat on his hands until he couldn't stand it any longer. He'd known she would shoot Norman to save Savanna, but had felt it was his job, not hers, to take down the president.

Somehow, she'd gotten the best of him anyway.

Beatrice had handpicked the people Trace had told his side of the story to. Sergeant Franklin had been one of them. Franklin and the Feds had seen the video of Savanna's report and the follow-up video taken by Parker. They'd seen the president holding a gun to Savanna's head, ordering his men to set the studio on fire, and his fight with Trace. They'd forced Trace to walk them through the incident over and over, forced him to go over the details multiple times, but he was still a free man. He wasn't sure who or what to owe that to, but he suspected Beatrice and her lawyers had some connections high on the federal food chain.

Parker wasn't so lucky. They had a lot more questions for her. Beatrice had assured him Parker would be free by morning. Trace wanted to believe her—Beatrice had performed a few miracles already—but he didn't. Parker had shot the president of the United States, even if it had been through Trace. Linc Norman was in deep shit, but attempted assassination was still a serious charge.

A TV droned in the corner of the waiting room, running the story about Savanna and the president. Every station had some form of the video and Savanna's face playing in an endless loop. The only reason a bunch of news vans weren't parked outside the hospital was because the Feds had put a lid on Savanna's whereabouts.

Congress had called an emergency meeting behind closed doors. It was rumored the attorney general and vice president had also been behind closed doors for hours. Speculation ran rampant on all the news channels, including Savanna's former station.

Beatrice, Cal, and Emit were at the hospital with Trace, bringing him bad coffee and offering silent reassurance. He couldn't stop pacing. The painkillers the doctor had given him earlier had worn off and he welcomed the biting sting in his shoulder. Physical pain was easier to deal with than emotional.

Emit seemed to know every doctor who passed through and

had managed to squeeze out a couple of updates on Savanna. The arm wound had been superficial, but the bullet she'd taken in the lower stomach had done some damage. The surgeons didn't know to what extent yet, but it appeared to have nicked an intestine.

Cal stood at the window watching the parking lot below, and Beatrice read from a book on physics and DNA sequencing, every once in a while rubbing her pregnant stomach. A pink fruit smoothie sat next to her.

Blood had dried on Trace's shirt and coat. On his hands. Beatrice had brought him a clean shirt, but even after he'd washed his hands repeatedly, he couldn't get all the stains off his fingers, from under his nails.

This is my fault.

If he'd questioned Linc Norman sooner, if he'd exposed his corruption, if he'd kept Savanna from going to that public access station…the loop ran endlessly in his brain, keeping up with the news stories on the TV. *If, if, if.*

He'd been able to outthink the enemy for years now, and yet, he hadn't guessed that the president might have helped himself to the enhancement drugs. Hadn't guessed that Savanna might charge the man in order to save him.

He dropped into a chair and put his head in his hands. If she didn't pull through, if she didn't want to see him again, he might as well let the Feds handcuff him and put him back in Witcher.

Which could still happen. He didn't know what Beatrice and her lawyer had slipped in the packet she'd given to Sergeant Franklin, who'd passed it onto the Federal agents during Trace's interrogation, but he knew this whole situation could backfire on him at any moment.

Zebulon Riceman entered the waiting room. His face was drawn, lips tight. "Any word?"

Trace shook his head. "Not since the last time you asked ten minutes ago."

"Don't get snippy with me, boy. I saved your goddamn, measly life back there."

He knew how to pack a wound, that was for sure. "Thank you."

Zeb nodded. "That's more like it." His countenance shifted. "She'll be all right. She's a fighter."

Was he trying to convince Trace or himself?

Trace picked at his nails, raked his hands through his hair, jumped up from the chair. "I need some air."

Out in the hallway, Zeb caught up to him. The two walked down the hall in strained silence. Zeb wanted to tell him something, but Trace wasn't sure he wanted to hear it.

In an alcove off the hallway, Trace stopped at a bank of vending machines. "What does ON 16 stand for?" he asked the aging man.

"Well, you're too young to remember the Iran-Contra scandal back in the eighties, but look it up. You could learn a thing or two."

"Oliver North." Trace pretended to scan the contents of the vending machine in front of him. "Did you help him sell the weapons to Iran or were you on the other side diverting funds to the Contra rebels in Nicaragua?"

"Neither." Zeb stuck a dollar bill in the pop machine, followed it with a second. "I may have played a part in outing him, though. You didn't hear that from me, by the way, and if you ever tell Savanna who I really am, I'll kill you."

"And the number 16?"

Trace could see Zeb's reflection in the glass. His face morphed into something akin to happiness. "Sixteen days in Paris with the most beautiful woman in the world. First and only time I ever fell in love. Nearly killed me."

The tension in Trace's body wouldn't relent, but for a moment, he could focus on Zeb. "What happened?"

"She was a double agent. I knew it, but it didn't matter. I loved her, tried to get her to run off with me. Change our identities, live on some remote island, have a few kids. The whole happily-ever-after thing. She turned me down and when she couldn't get the information she wanted out of me for her superiors, she poisoned me."

Jesus. "Love sucks."

Zeb waved him off. "She didn't give me enough to kill me and she knew it. But it definitely put a damper on my love life after that. I never got over her."

A short gal with long, dark hair and a couple of dollar bills in hand interrupted them. They parted so she could snag a bag of pretzels. After she left, Trace asked the question that had been bugging him. "Linc Norman knew you. Did you ever work for him?"

"Look, kid. I know all about Command & Control, but I

never got mixed up with that group. I may have run in the same circles as some National Intelligence officers and rubbed elbows with a few presidents, but I steered clear of Norman. He was too much of a pretty boy. I didn't trust him."

"That's how you knew Parker."

"Parker's work garnered attention she didn't want, but you don't say no to the president, right? She needed some input from someone who'd been in a tight squeeze before. Norman didn't tell her at first what he was using you for; she figured it out the hard way. Then he told her she had to take out her fellow scientists to keep the project under the radar. She wouldn't do it. So he used her family as leverage to try to blackmail her. She still refused. One thing about those Jeffries girls, they don't take kindly to threats.

"When things fell apart, Parker needed a way out. There was only one I could find if she wanted to keep Savanna and her parents alive."

"Me."

Zeb touched the tip of his nose with a finger. "You got it."

"You broke me out of Witcher."

"Nah, that was all Beatrice and Emit. I just gave 'em some ideas on what to do with you after you came around. You needed a public platform to redeem yourself. Parker needed one to out the president. Savanna could do both, but she needed protection. You were the answer."

"I may end up back in Witcher before this is all over."

"Your original arrest and conviction will all be reviewed, and trust me, the case will be thrown out."

Friends in high places. Or maybe enemies who didn't want you to take them down like you had Oliver North. "I have the feeling I owe you for more than packing my wound with Quick Clot."

"That you do, boy, and don't forget it. But I'll tell you what. You take care of my favorite two Jeffries girls and I'll go easy on you."

"I lied to Savanna. Didn't tell her who I was. She's pretty pissed at me."

"Then get down and grovel. That girl couldn't hold a grudge if you paid her to. She'll forgive you in time. And from the way you look right now, I'd say she's your number 16, so don't blow it. Let her know you love her and do whatever you have to in order to make her happy. Life's short."

Zeb walked to the doorway, where he stopped and turned back to Trace. "One more thing," he said. "Take a page from Ollie's playbook. When you get called in front of Congress and the nation, which you will, take responsibility for the shit you did, but don't take personal responsibility for carrying out direct orders. You were a decorated SEAL who deserves to have his medals returned and his status reinstated. You haven't, in your ten years of uniformed service to the United States of America and your commander-in-chief, ever violated an order, have you?"

"Just one, sir."

"And that's the one that landed your ass in Witcher."

Trace nodded.

"You refused to kill someone at the president's direct request, if I heard that taped interview of Savanna's correctly."

Did it matter? He didn't want his medals back or his status reinstated. Not following that order hadn't kept the woman or her baby alive. They'd been killed anyway.

Cal Reese suddenly appeared, peeking his head around the opening. "Surgeon is out and wants to talk to you."

Trace bolted, blowing past Zeb and Cal and hightailing it back to the waiting area. The surgeon had changed into fresh scrubs, but his lips were tacked down in a frown, his eyes shuttered.

Trace pulled up short.

She's not going to make it.

"Hospital policy is that I speak to the next of kin. In this case, I've learned the patient's sister is being detained and questioned by police and her parents have not been reached."

She's already dead. Trace staggered back, his legs colliding with a chair. Good thing it was there. He collapsed into it.

The doctor folded his arms over his chest. "I'm told you and Ms. Jeffries are...involved, so while this breaks protocol, I'm going to give you an update on her status. I've..." He cleared his throat. "I've seen the news footage."

Trace covered his eyes with a hand. *She's gone. Oh, God, she's gone.*

"The wound in her arm should heal without issue. The stomach injury will take some time. The bullet passed through and damaged several areas in her small intestine. We sutured the wounds and are giving her high doses of antibiotics to tackle infection.

"We had to give her a blood transfusion, but because of the clotting powder and her sister's quick actions with the IV fluids, her shock was mild. She appears to have a mild concussion, so we'll need to watch her closely for the next twenty-four to forty-eight hours. She suffered mild frostbite on her toes and fingers. There should be no lasting nerve damage, however."

Frostbite? Concussion? Wait. Trace dropped his hand. "She's alive?"

The doctor cocked his head. "She's in serious condition, and it could be touch and go for the next few days, depending on if she has any infection or problems with the concussion, but she is alive, Lt. Hunter."

Relief and hope mixed in his system. He bolted out of the chair. "Can I see her?"

The doctor looked uncomfortable. "Again, that's usually reserved for family."

Beatrice stepped forward and squeezed Trace's arm. "But in this case, you'll make an exception, right Dr. Azram?"

The man hesitated briefly, then nodded. "Follow me."

Zeb, in the hallway, had heard the news and slapped Trace on the back as he passed by. "Tell her hi from me when she comes around."

Trace stayed on the doctor's heels through a set of double doors, around a nurses' station, and down another long corridor. The sun was up and blasting through the window at the end of the hall. Each room was marked ICU with a number. Savanna had been placed in room 4.

Monitors beeped. A nurse was fiddling with a tube running into the pale skin on Savanna's left arm. Her hair had been scraped back from her face, her lips no longer blue but as pale as the rest of her skin. Her eyes fluttered under her closed lids. Her chest barely made the sheet rise and fall on each intake of breath.

She's alive.

Trace's knees felt weak.

"We're all good here," the nurse said. She looked at Trace. "Can I get you some coffee? You look like you've had a hard night."

He almost laughed from the overload of stress. "I'm good."

She nodded. "We're monitoring everything, but if you sense any distress in her, you press the call button, okay?"

Her shoes whispered as she left. The doctor simply nodded and followed her out.

Trace dragged a chair next to the side of the bed but then just stood, watching the slow rise and fall of her chest. He had to touch her, and so he did, laying his fingers softly against her cool cheek, running them down her neck, tracing the veins on the back of her hands.

"I'm sorry I withheld the truth from you, Savanna. It was wrong and I deserve a harsh kick in the ass. But that means you're going to have to get out of this hospital bed and give it to me, okay?"

Convinced she was indeed alive, he sat in the chair and kept an eye on the sheet, willing her heart to keep beating. "Breathe," he softly reminded her. "Just breathe."

Six hours later

Savanna floated up through hazy dreams of her sister and a shadowy figure, a man that she wanted to talk to but he stayed just out of her reach, annoying her. A buoyant sensation filled her limbs, her left arm itching. It felt as though she were levitating right off the bed. If she could just get the lump on her arm off so she could scratch that itch, she'd feel spectacular.

Beep, beep, beep. An alarm sounded from somewhere far off, making the dreams disappear. A man's voice shouted and there were other sounds, too. The rasp of a door opening. The rhythmic warble of another alarm.

Someone was futzing with her arm. She tried to jerk it away.

"Hold still, Savanna. You've pulled out your IV."

Coldplay. His voice made her open her eyes. Or at least try to. Her eyelids were so heavy, she could barely crack her eyes open.

"Hey there," he said, bending over her.

He was so beautiful, light from the window illuminating one side of his face. His jaw sported a few days' worth of beard and his eyes were bloodshot. He smiled and Savanna saw relief in his face.

She opened her mouth to respond, but a jerky burst of memories from the night before flooded her brain. Even through the drugs in her system, she felt a flash of anger, rage, fear.

Her tongue stuck to the top of her mouth, her lips were parched. "Trace," she finally forced out, voice raspy.

A nurse hustled to the other side of the bed. "Good to see you're awake, Savanna, but you need to leave your IV in, sweetie."

As the nurse went to work fixing the damage Savanna had done, Trace peppered her with questions. "How do you feel? Are you in pain? They can up your pain meds. Do you remember what happened? Do you want some ice chips? Water?"

The poke of the fresh IV stung, her left shoulder ached, and her stomach felt like it was swaddled so tight, she couldn't move. Looking at Trace's smiling face, however, none of that mattered. "I'm good," she croaked.

"I, uh..." He closed his eyes and sucked in a breath, holding it, for a second and a feeling of dread filled her. What had happened?

"Is it Parker?" she half whispered, her throat closing up. "Is she okay?"

He flipped his eyes open. "Parker's fine. She's meeting with some lawyers and telling the attorney general her story. Everything, Savanna. Between what you did and the evidence we have on Linc Norman, he's going to be impeached. The AG will probably bring criminal charges against him as well."

The nurse secured the IV with a fat piece of tape. "Just once I'd like to vote for someone who wasn't a criminal," she said. "Now, relax. You've got your heart monitor going crazy."

She left the room and Trace took Savanna's hand in his. "Slow, deep breaths," he reminded her, wrapping his hand around hers. Heat enveloped her cool fingers and the familiar feel of his calluses sent a shiver through her.

His shirt was lumpy on the right side over what looked like padding. "What happened to you?"

He squeezed her hand and relayed the story in a measly five sentences, leaving out some juicy bits, she was sure.

"We're both still alive," she said, feeling sleepy again. "We survived."

"What you did was brave and very, very stupid." He sank into the chair next to the bed without releasing her hand. "Norman was mixing his own drug cocktails based on Parker's experiments. He could have killed you even without the gun."

"He was going to shoot you." She closed her eyes against a

sudden welling of tears. "I knew he was. I couldn't let him do that."

He brought her knuckles to his lips. "I was supposed to be guarding your body, not the other way around."

The floating feeling was back, playing with her senses. Time seemed to ebb and flow. Her eyelids dipped, snapped back open. "What were you going to say a minute ago? When the nurse was still here."

It had been important. That she was sure of.

Tipping his chin down, he rested his forehead on her knuckles. "I need to tell you something."

"I'm listening."

"Sixteen days," she heard him whisper. His breath was warm on her fingers.

What was he talking about?

He raised his head and he met her gaze head-on. "I want more than sixteen days."

The drugs and sleepiness were messing with her understanding. "What?"

"I want more than sixteen days with you."

How long had she been out? They'd only been together a week. "What are you talking about?"

"I...uh..." His mouth moved, but words stopped coming out. He cleared his throat. "I thought I nearly lost you, and I... I'd like us to start over. But first I have to know, can you forgive me for misleading you?"

Starting over. Today was a new beginning for them. He was so sincere, so determined, a smile hovered at the corners of her mouth. She wished she could sit up and hug him.

The most strength she could conjure was to pat his face. "I might if you promise never to lie to me. Oh, and one other thing."

"What's that?"

"Come on my show and be interviewed. For real this time."

"You don't have a show anymore, Savanna. Remember?"

"I will," she countered. "I have the scoop of the century. I'm going to have plenty of job offers."

He grinned and put her hand back under the covers. "I promise never to lie, and we'll negotiate the terms of my surrender with the interview when you're feeling better. For now, I better go let your parents know you're awake. They got here a couple hours ago and are very worried about you. They went down to the cafeteria for a bite to eat. Do you think you're up to seeing them?"

Hell no. Her eyes were too heavy to hold open and she wasn't sure she wanted to see her mother just yet anyway. "You should let them know I was awake and making plans for the future, but I'm going back to sleep now."

He tapped her hand through the covers and leaned forward to kiss her forehead. "I'll tell them."

"Thank you," she said, closing her eyes. Precious, perfect sleep waited for her. "By the way?"

"Yeah?"

"I…want more than sixteen days too," she said around a yawn. "Whatever that means."

Snuggling down in the sheets, she kept an image of Trace's smile in her mind as she let the sweet, peaceful darkness consume her.

CHAPTER TWENTY-SEVEN

ONE MONTH LATER

Savanna's stomach revolted at the lunch she'd packed herself. Ever since leaving the hospital, she'd had to eat small meals and stay away from carbonated beverages. The doctors had declared her healed, but soda and jalapeños were no longer part of her diet.

A knock sounded on the door and Charity, her new assistant popped her head in. "They're ready for you in make-up, Ms. Bunkett."

"Thank you, Charity. If you're going to the corner deli for lunch today, would you pick up one of those strawberry-banana fruit smoothies for me?"

The girl had gotten her hair cut, her dark curls framing her lovely face and making her look her age instead of like a high school student. She had a soft southern accent and the organizing efficiency of Martha Stewart. "Like the one you had yesterday?"

Savanna nodded. "Solid food just isn't working for me again today."

"Sure, no problem. I'll be back before you go on air." She started to shut the door. "Oh, and Mr. Riceman wants a moment with you after the show to discuss the breaking news out of Oregon and that guy the FBI arrested for child porn. Says there's a story there for you."

Savanna nodded and Charity hustled off. Zeb was Savanna's

new boss after she had threatened to sue her old network for the rights to her show. They'd tried to get her to come back, now that she was America's sweetheart again, but she'd told them to shove it. The lawyers had worked things out and she'd moved *The Bunk Stops Here* to her new network. She'd cut a deal with the executives of CNBC and Crime Investigations to bring Zeb with her, putting *The Bunk Stops Here* back on a national platform and getting back to work.

Lindsey had been left without a show but Savanna had heard she'd come up with a new cold case investigation show, and so far, it had decent ratings. Beatrice could not tie her to Norman and they'd all concluded that Lindsey was after Savanna's job, but nothing more. Savanna wished her well and hoped they never crossed paths again.

The same was not true of Randy, the doorman. Rory had done some digging and was sure Randy was really a former, old-school CIA operative named Langston Covington. He'd done a few operations for various secret groups, including Command & Control at one point. He'd probably been assigned by Linc Norman to keep an eye on Savanna in hopes Parker would pay her a visit.

Parker *had* been visiting when Savanna was away but she was too good to get caught, even by someone like Covington.

Savanna had been offered multiple career deals, just like she'd predicted to Trace in the hospital. All she'd wanted was to be back on the air, under her own terms, debunking conspiracies and blowing the whistle on corrupt government officials, big businesses, and anything else that fell under her radar.

Every news outlet in the country, and a few outside of it, had asked her for an interview, to tell her story about what had happened with the president. She'd declined. Soon she'd have to go in front of Congress and give testimony. That would be the only interview she would ever do on the subject.

Several publishers had asked her to write a memoir. She'd considered it for half a second, then said no. If Parker or Trace wanted to write a book about what had happened, she'd give them her blessing, but she didn't want to keep reliving the events of the past few months.

She suspected they didn't either.

"Hey sis." Parker blew into Savanna's room in a royal blue trench coat with some wicked looking heels. She was smiling and looking like the weight of the world had been lifted off her shoulders. "Can I borrow that new Michael Kors bag again tonight? Henley asked me on a second date."

Savanna accepted a hug, then shook her head at her sister. "No way. He took you to that German bar last time for a hotdog and soccer and you spilled beer on it."

"I cleaned it off."

"Took me two days to get the smell of that place out of the leather. Yuck."

"We're going to the Smithsonian with Beatrice and Cal to see *Einstein and the History of the Brain* exhibit." She leaned a hip on Savanna's table and picked at the uneaten lunch, snagging a couple of almonds. "There will be no beer involved."

"Sure there won't."

It was good to have Parker back. They'd been nearly inseparable since Savanna had left the hospital. Parker had helped her move into a new, more secure building, and they'd spent quite a few nights telling each other the secrets they'd both been keeping.

This thing with Henley, though…

"You really like him?" Savanna asked, watching Parker stack a slice of cheese on a cracker. "He's not your type."

"That's an understatement." Parker chuckled but the blush on her face said it all. Normally, she gravitated to brainy types like herself. Geeks. Not bad boys with shady backgrounds and even shadier restaurant preferences. "I guess I'm up for a little 'not my type', you know? He's so funny, and he can change his accent on a dime. No lie, he can do Southern Texan, Upper East Side New York, and everything in between. Irish, Scottish, British, East Indian. Aussie. He wants kids someday."

Kids? Holy cow.

But there was that look in her sister's eyes. The one that said Parker was happy.

And maybe in love.

Damn. That made two of them, only Savanna's shady bad boy had left her high and dry.

It's not like we were dating.

He'd said he wanted to start over. They sure had. He'd stuck around for a week after she'd left the hospital, taking her to physical therapy, and making sure she had everything she needed at her new place. Driving her to and from meetings with federal officials to give her statement and to meetings with the heads of various networks who wanted her to join their news teams. It had been a whirlwind of fun. Then, poof. He'd disappeared without so much as a 'see ya later.'

"You can have the Kors bag," Savanna said, heading for the door. Work was the only thing that kept her mind off the emptiness she felt every time she thought of Trace's absence. "I have to get to makeup. Talk later, I promise."

"Have you heard from him?"

Savanna stayed her hand on the doorknob. Parker didn't need to say his name for Savanna to know who she was asking about. "Yes and no."

"What does that mean?"

Beatrice had told Savanna that Trace had been called to San Diego by the Navy for some meetings, but he wasn't responding to her texts, and her calls went straight to voicemail. "Well, I haven't heard from him directly since he left two weeks ago. However, the breaking news today about the guy in Oregon the Feds arrested?"

Parker's eyes lit up. She still thought like an undercover operative even if she no longer was one. "You think Trace is behind that?"

Parker had told her most of what she could about her life undercover, and Savanna had told her sister about the coach who'd molested her. There were no more secrets between them. "The man is going by an alias, Parker, but it's *him*. Coach Watson."

Parker came off the desk. "No. Are you shitting me?"

Savanna shook her head. "Trace went after him. For me, I'm assuming."

"That guy." Parker smiled. "I really like him."

Me too. "He is not a good communicator."

"Really? He went after a man who hurt you as a kid. Knowing Trace, he probably wanted to kill the guy but that wouldn't have given you justice. Having the asshole arrested and embarrassed on national TV? Oh, yeah, *much* more satisfying. His alias will be stripped away and the truth of what happened all those years ago will come out, Savanna." Her sister winked. "Seems like that's a pretty strong message from a guy who loves you. You now have the opportunity to reveal everything that bottom-feeding piece of scum did to you and Nora, and make sure he never hurts another girl again. *That's* justice, little sister."

Maybe she was right. But love? Did Trace love her or was

he acting out of a sense of duty and honor? Or, God help her, friendship? "Why can't he text me and just say he's okay?"

"That would leave a trail to Watson, and one thing he's a master at, is not leaving a trail. He's doing it anonymously and that's the only way for him."

She hadn't thought of that. "At first I thought he ran because they might throw him back in jail, but his name's been cleared. Beatrice said the Navy wants him back. They want to put him in charge of his own SEAL team. Have him teach them and take them into the field. She claims that's why he left, but why wouldn't he tell me?"

"Maybe he didn't want you worrying about it. Of course, the Navy wants him back. He's the ultimate fighting machine. Do you think he'll do it? Go back to being a SEAL?"

Savanna shrugged. "Like I said, he doesn't tell me anything. If he goes back to the Navy, it could take a year or more before his platoon is ready to go." Rory had filled her in on how things worked with the Teams. "And that would mean he'd be in San Diego and I'd be here."

Parker closed the distance between them and squeezed her arm. "He'll be back soon and you guys can talk. You haven't told him how you feel about him. He's making decisions without knowing the truth. You said no more secrets, but you're keeping a very big one from him."

Her stomach clenched sending a new way of nausea through her. Maybe Parker was right. Not telling Trace she loved him, wondering if he loved her, was keeping her nerves on edge and affecting her mending stomach.

"If he would return a call or text me, I could at least get a feel for what he wants. Does he want a relationship? Does he not? I can't say anything until I know. If he wants to go back to the SEALs and he ends up not doing that because of me, I couldn't stand that. It would ruin things. I won't be the reason he doesn't go back to serving his country, Parker."

"You read the file I brought you? The real one?"

Savanna nodded. She was using some of the basic information from it for her show in an hour. "That's what I'm talking about. He's a bona fide hero. The quiet, unsung hero. Maybe that's what he still wants to be."

"Or maybe he wants to start a new life with you. I'm telling you, that man loves you. I saw it the night you were shot. He'll be back, I promise. I know how his brain works. And as soon as he is, you two need to talk and then we all have to go out and celebrate our new jobs."

Parker had walked away from National Intelligence and taken a position with a private company, working on a new brain study on memory function. After being cleared of any wrong doing by the attorney general and turning state's evidence on the president, she'd presented her findings to a couple of scientists in the field and received an invitation to join an elite group doing groundbreaking work with Alzheimer's patients.

"Speaking of jobs," Savanna said. "I really do need to get to mine."

They hugged and Parker left. Savanna made her way to the hair and makeup station, wondering once more if Trace had gone back to the SEAL teams. Tonight's show was about him and the heroic work he'd done in service to his country before she'd taken it all away. There would be no photos, no information about his whereabouts or his current status—which she didn't know anyway—but she had to right the wrong she'd done to him. She had to fess up to not doing her homework and wrongfully accusing him of being a traitor nearly two years ago.

There would be no blame placed on Parker or even Linc Norman. Savanna would never *not* do her own investigations again, and the American public needed to know Trace's public humiliation and downfall was her fault, not anyone else's.

She just hoped that wherever he was, he was watching.

As a SEAL, he'd been trained to control his emotions, not let anything or anyone get to him.

Savanna Jeffries Bunkett, all one-hundred-and-twenty-pounds of her, had taken that away from him.

Nineteen months and two days after she'd destroyed his career, his reputation, and his future, she went on national television once more to clear his name and tell the world he was a hero.

Sitting on the couch in her new apartment, he turned off the TV and let the shadows engulf him. Her show had been over an hour ago, but he'd been too stunned to move afterwards.

He was neither hero nor traitor. He was a man with a damaged past and an empty future.

For the first time in his life, he didn't have direction. There were no longer bars holding him hostage, but the idea that he had no clear path in front of him, no orders to follow, no bad guys to hunt down, no one to protect or keep secure, was worse than any prison cell.

I need Savanna.

But she didn't need him. The idea haunted him, had driven him away for a while. Yet, here he was, back in DC needing to see her so badly his chest ached. She kept his demons at bay, made him feel normal.

So be it if she didn't need him the same way. He could live with that fact. She had her career, rising again, and she loved her life. It was evident in everything she did. He hoped by being close to her, in whatever capacity she would let him, some of that love of life would rub off on him.

Because even if he didn't love his life, he loved her.

"Incoming," Rory said in his ear comm. "She's in front of the building."

Trace touched the unit. "Thanks, man."

He was back working for Shadow Force International for now. No more security work—he was in the deep, dark stuff now. Petit had already talked to him about a new assignment, this one in Panama City involving a drug gang and a kidnapping.

Dangerous work. Work that would take him away from Savanna for a time. He needed to see her reaction when he told her. See if she would be upset he was leaving again so soon, or maybe filled with relief.

His sensitive ears picked up the sound of the elevator doors, heard her crossing the hallway to the penthouse.

She keyed in her security code, came through the door, then closed it, backing up against it and closing her eyes.

She looked exhausted. Drained. She had a pink colored drink in one hand, her laptop bag in the other. Still leaning against the door with her eyes closed, she kicked off one high-heeled shoe and then the other. Her toes curled and she let go of the computer bag, setting it on the floor. She made a little sound in the back of her throat. "Much better."

He couldn't stop staring at her. That sound, that look of utter relief and joy, made his heart ping around in his chest like a pinball. How many times had he made her look like that in bed? How many times had he heard that sound when he touched her in certain spots?

Opening her eyes, she pushed off the door and fumbled with the buttons on her coat.

"Nice show tonight," he said from the shadows. "You almost made me sound like a decent human being."

She startled, the coat still half on, and nearly dropped the smoothie. "You! What are you doing here?" One hand went to her chest. "You nearly gave me a heart attack. Why are you sitting in the dark?"

Flipping on the lights, she gave him a hard stare, then finished getting the coat off and came over to stand in front of the coffee table. She set the cup on the table and showed him her cell phone. "See this?"

He nodded, trying to maintain eye contact while her legs and her bare feet taunted him. There were no yoga pants today, only a tight-fitting skirt that stopped shy of her knees and showed off her sexy calves.

"This," she said in a scolding voice, "is a phone. You call people with it, you text them. Hell, you can even access crazy stuff like email, and I'm pretty sure you have one that's even fancier than mine."

He liked it when she was fired up. All that annoyance. All that irritation and frustration.

If he could get her in the bedroom, he could help take care of the frustration.

"I'm sorry I didn't stay in touch. I had my reasons."

"Was one of those reasons the breaking news today out of Oregon about Coach Watson?"

He remained silent, giving her a small smile.

She paled. "Did you find proof he was *still* molesting girls?"

"The child porn suggested it was a strong possibility."

She nodded and some of the bluster went out of her. "Thank you for that. For tracking him down and making sure he was arrested. You didn't have to do that."

"Remember back in the hospital, I told you I'd like us to start over?"

The phone joined the cup on the coffee table. Savanna stayed standing. "I remember."

"I needed to make sure we were both starting with a fresh slate."

"Zeb and I talked about it today. Watson's true identity is already public and it's been revealed that he was a former coach with the 2004 Olympic team. A few reporters have already called to see if I have a comment. Zeb is handpicking someone to do a sit down and interview me for primetime. I'm going to tell my story. My mother will never speak to me again, but I have to stop keeping this secret."

"That's why I went after him. Yes, I wanted to make sure he wasn't hurting other girls, and maybe I wanted some payback for you, too, but I also knew you needed the opportunity to tell your story so you could put the past behind you and move forward. If seeing him go to jail is enough, then so be it, but if you need more, like exposing what really happened on *The Bunk Stops Here*, you have that choice now."

Slowly, she sank into the chair across from him. It was a velvety sapphire blue that matched her eyes. "Parker was right about you."

"Oh, yeah? Why's that?"

"She said you have your own way of communicating. I can respect that."

He heard an edge in her voice. "But?"

"No buts. I just... I need to tell you something, and right now, I'm feeling pretty unsure of the best way to do that. I'm usually good with words, but not so much right now."

His stomach dropped. From her tone and the rigidness in her body, he sensed she was about to drop a bomb on him.

His gaze dropped to the cup on the table. The phone. The urgency he'd heard in some of her messages. "Aw, shit, Savanna. Are you...?"

"Am I what?"

He choked out the word. "Pregnant?"

Those pretty blue eyes went wide and she teetered on the edge of the chair, half-laughing. "God, no. Trust me, I already checked. My stomach's been a queasy mess, but it's because I've been so stressed out about *you*."

Relief flooded him. Not that he never wanted kids, but he wasn't father material. He'd made up his mind a long time ago that that type of happily ever after would never happen for him. "Then what is it?"

She clapped her hands in her lap, worrying her fingers. "I guess I was hoping that the show I did today would tell you how I feel about you."

"I'm not a hero, Savanna."

"You are to me." Her next words rushed out on a heavy breath. "I just... I don't want you to go back to the Navy. And I know that's wrong, but you'd be in San Diego, and I'd be here, and well... I would miss you."

Trace sat forward and put his elbows on his knees. "Who said I was going back to the Navy?"

"Beatrice said they called you in for a meeting to offer you a new assignment training a team of SEALs."

"They did."

"And?"

"I take it you haven't talked her today. I'm going back to Shadow Force."

"Shadow Force?"

"Shadow Force International. Rock Star Security is a cover for the real work Emit and his teams do. Yes, RSS is real and we all take turns doing the bodyguard thing, but Shadow Force is the group behind that. We perform private intelligence, security, and paramilitary missions, helping people who have nowhere else to turn. Dangerous shit that will require me to go out of the country and keep some things from you for your safety as well as our clients'."

"I suspected there was more to the bodyguard business than Beatrice was letting on."

"My days of taking orders are over, Savanna. I've always done what I was told to do, always followed orders and did the right thing, no matter what it cost me. I'm not doing that anymore. From now on, I'm doing what makes me happy."

Her gaze locked on his, scanning, searching. "And what is it that makes you happy, Lt. Hunter?"

"You."

A tiny smile touched her lips. She ran her palms over the tight material of the skirt, played with the hem, drawing his attention to her beautiful thighs. "Okay, cool, I'm just going to say it. The thing I need to tell you."

He gave her a chin cock to continue.

"I thought you knew this already, but maybe you don't, and I need to say it. Straight out."

He waited. Watched her work up her nerve.

"I love you." Her lips folded in for a second and when he didn't say anything, she murmured, "*awk*-ward," under her breath.

"Okay, then," he said.

"*Okay then?*" She stood as if someone had poked her with a hot branding iron. "*Okay* then? Wow. I guess you don't feel the same. No problem. I get it."

Coming to his feet, he reached across the table and grabbed her arm before she could run off. "I didn't say that."

"Yeah, you kinda did."

"Savanna." He went around the table, still holding onto her arm, and came to stop right in front of her so he could look down into those eyes that made him feel like he wanted to drown in them. "I'm not you. I *do* suck at communicating with words. Actions are easier for me. I've never said the words I love you to any woman before, but... I *do* love you."

He dug in his pocket for the $10 ring he'd bought at a minimart down the road and held it up. The fake diamond on top reflected the overhead light. "Now that I'm no longer a fugitive, I can get my hands on my bank accounts again, and I promise I'll buy you a real one of these if you say yes."

Now *he* was blabbering. "I know as much about engagement rings as I do love, Savanna, so I figured maybe you'd want to go with me to pick one out. Maybe that's the first thing we can pencil in on our fresh, clean slate together. A ring buying trip."

Her focus shifted from his face to the cheap substitute ring to his face again. "Are you asking me to marry you?"

"Yes...?"

Her laugh started low in her belly and radiated up. She threw her head back and let it out, and for a second, Trace worried that she was laughing at his very poor attempt at expressing himself.

If so, he deserved it. He sucked at this shit.

But in the next second, Savanna threw her arms around him and kissed him square on the lips.

Hers were soft and needy, drawing him to her like wildfire. He kissed her back, parting her lips and sliding his tongue inside as he held her close, her body molding to his.

After a moment, she drew back and wiggled her fingers at him. "Let me see that ring."

He handed it to her and watched as she slipped it on her left ring finger. It was a little loose, the big plastic diamond canting to one side.

"I love it," she said. "And I love you. Your actions speak louder than words."

"So that's a yes? You'll marry me?"

"Two more things, since I'm not keeping secrets anymore."

His insides shrank a little again. "What?"

"I want kids. Not right away, but soon. And I need you to keep an eye on Henley. He's after my sister. I'm not sure he deserves her."

Trace laughed. "Whatever you want, Savanna, although I'll probably suck at being a dad, but since you're an overachiever, you'll make a great mom, so I'll do my best and hope the kids take after you. As far as Henley, I'll kick his ass if he so much as hurts Parker's feelings."

She kissed him again, long and deep, wrapping one slender leg around his and murmuring when she came back up for air, "How about I *show* you all the ways I can say yes to your question, then, Lt. Hunter?"

Trace picked her up, enjoying her whoop of happiness, and carried her to the bedroom. He had a few things he wanted to show her too.

The End

Thank you for reading FATAL TRUTH.

Turn the page to read about the next installment in the
Shadow Force International Series.

FATAL HONOR

Miles is Charlotte's one and only weakness.
He's also her only hope...

To stop a madman and clear her name, British Intelligence officer Charlotte Carstons has no choice. She must track down former Navy SEAL Miles Duncan and ask for his help. Nine months ago, his team was gunned down in the Carpathian Mountains, killing everyone but him. While stranded in her cabin and waiting out a harsh winter, Charlotte nursed Miles back to life, losing her heart to him in the process. He now works as an operative for Shadow Force International and holds the key to completing her mission. What she doesn't count on is Miles' refusal to help her...or falling for him all over again.

Charlotte is his fantasy woman.
She's also the biggest mistake of his life...

Miles has never wanted a woman more than he wants the sexy, mysterious MI6 agent who left him without so much as a goodbye after their six-week affair. Back in the States and working as an operative for Shadow Force International, Miles provides private security and covert paramilitary services for those in need. Searching for Charlotte has turned up little, except the fact she's skilled at deception and considered a traitor by her own country. Was their fling nothing but a lie?

Together, they can save the world.
Or destroy each other...

When Charlotte shows up on his doorstep asking for help, Miles knows better than to get involved. But she's determined to go back to Romania with or without him. He fears she's walking into a deadly trap with a Romanian crime lord and a cover-up with MI6. Can he keep her safe as they travel across continents...and explore the depth of their feelings for each other...in order to access the truth? Or will misplaced honor and treasonous loyalties prove fatal for them both?

About the Author

USA TODAY Bestselling Author Misty Evans has published over thirty novels and writes romantic suspense, urban fantasy, and paranormal romance. She got her start writing in 4th grade when she won second place in a school writing contest with an essay about her dad.

Misty likes her coffee black, her conspiracy stories juicy, and her wicked characters dressed in couture. When not reading or writing, she enjoys music, movies, and hanging out with her husband, twin sons, and two spoiled puppies. Get your **free Super Agent story** and sign up for her newsletter at www.readmistyevans.com. Like her author page on Facebook or follow her on Twitter. Bloggers and reviewers, if you'd like to join Misty's Rockin' Readers review group, send her a message at misty@readmistyevans.com and she'll hook you up!

Made in the USA
Middletown, DE
26 December 2022